A HIGHCLERE INN & CARRIAGE HOUSE MYSTERY

A BOX OF FROGS

JOSH HELLYER

Disclaimer: This is a work of fiction. Everything in this book, including the setting, story, locations, events, all characters, all circumstances, all motivations, and all behaviors are entirely imaginary and complete fiction. The actions, opinions and interpretations expressed are those of the fictional characters and should in no way be confused with the author's. Any resemblance to actual persons, living or dead, or actual events is purely coincidental.

While the Canadian Senate, Royal Canadian Mounted Police, Ontario Provincial Police, and the Metropolitan Police are real institutions, their processes, policies, and functions have been fictionalized for narrative purposes and should in no way be confused with their real-life functionality and governance.

Copyright © 2024 by Josh Hellyer
All rights reserved.

Connect with the author:
X: @joshhellyer
Instagram: @joshphellyer
Threads: @joshhellyer
Website: www.joshhellyer.com

No part of this book may be used or reproduced by any means, graphic, electronic, or mechanical, including photocopying, recording, taping or by any information storage retrieval system without the written permission of the publisher except in the case of brief quotations embodied in critical articles and reviews.

ISBN: 978-1-998847-05-1 (pb-b) / 978-1-998847-04-4 (eb)

MapleCrest Press
2967 Dundas St. W. Toronto, ON M6P 1Z2
info@maplecrestpress.com

Land Acknowledgement: The author wishes to acknowledge that this book was written at and largely takes place on traditional Indigenous territories across Canada. He wishes to express gratitude to Mother Earth for the resources used in the creation of this book, and honor all the First Nations, Métis and Inuit people who have been living on the land since time immemorial.

All references to and about the Indigenous community of Canada, including the creation of Indigenous characters, have been done in consultation with a Traditional Knowledge Keeper.

Printed in The United States of America

For E.J.V.H

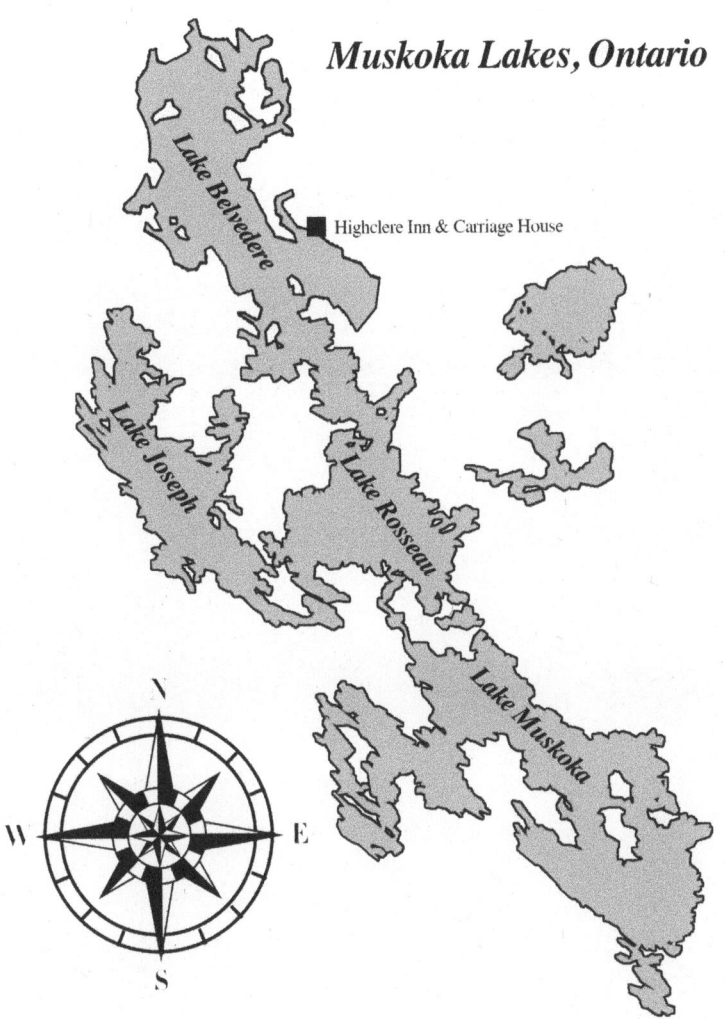

Cast of Characters

The Family

Miles "The Tank" Valentine – Former Canadian Senator, widower of Lady Jean Fernsby-Valentine, and second husband to Aida Clifton-Valentine.

Lady Jean Fernsby-Valentine – First wife of Miles "The Tank" Valentine; died in 2004.

Lawrence Valentine – Son of Miles and Jean Valentine; father to Mason Valentine.

Piper Valentine – Wife of Lawrence and mother to Mason Valentine.

Mason Valentine – Grandson of Miles and Jean Valentine; son of Lawrence and Piper.

Drusilla Valentine-Brisbane – Eldest daughter of Miles and Jean Valentine; twin sister to Stuart Valentine; widow of Clarence Brisbane.

Stuart Valentine – Eldest son of Miles and Jean Valentine; twin brother to Drusilla; married to Guillaume "Gil" Regan.

Guillaume "Gil" Regan – Husband of Stuart Valentine.

Jocelyn Valentine-Campbell – Youngest child of Miles and Jean Valentine; married to Ezra Campbell.

Oliver Valentine – Eldest child of Lawrence and Piper Valentine, Mason's older brother.

Cordelia "Cici" Bradshaw – Second cousin to Mason Valentine, great-niece of Jean Valentine.

Tobias Neuman – Husband to Cordelia "Cici" Bradshaw.

Diane Bradshaw – Mother of Cordelia; niece of Jean Valentine.

Aida Clifton-Valentine – Second wife of Miles Valentine; mother of Laverna Clifton-Lehrman; widow of Wentworth Clifton.

Laverna Clifton-Lehrman – Daughter of Aida; stepdaughter to Miles Valentine; married to Philip Lehrman.

Philip Lehrman – Husband to Laverna Clifton-Lehrman.

Highclere & Valentine Staff

Ahren Dawn – Long-time, semi-retired groundskeeper at Highclere.

Makayla Dawn – Granddaughter of Ahren and an employee at Highclere.

Norah Tripplehorn – Executive Assistant to Miles Valentine for fifty-five years.

Geneviève Talbot – Miles Valentine's Toronto housekeeper for over forty years.

Louise Harris – Long-time lawyer of Miles Valentine.

Marko Crouthers – Student of Cordelia "Cici" Bradshaw.

Family Friends

Lady Rosamond Farnsworth-Ford – Childhood best friend of Lady Valentine in the UK; grandmother of Joyce Redstone.

Joyce Redstone – Granddaughter of Lady Rosamond Farnsworth-Ford.

Baroness Margaret "Margot" Ambrosia – Member of the British Preservation Society; married to Stellan McManus.

Stellan McManus – Commissioner of the Metropolitan Police Services; husband to Margot.

Bianca Anders – Best friend and roommate of Laverna, Miles's private nurse during hospice.

Skye Cadieux – Friend and colleague of Mason in Toronto.

A BOX OF FROGS

William Marshall – Archivist for the Privy Council in Ottawa.

Andrea Romero – Farnsworth Marble & Designs expert in London.

Highclere Guests

Dr. Louella Stone – Therapist and oldest living guest of Highclere; friend of Miles and Jean Valentine; widow of Atticus Stone.

Roland Mast – Semi-retired lawyer; husband to Viviane Mast.

Angel Conner – Eccentric Highclere guest with a pet squirrel named Lenore.

Lenore Conner – Angel Conner's pet squirrel.

Rev. Bernard St. Joy – Long-time guest and preacher at Valentine Chapel.

Brian and Prunella Fisher – Guests who found Highclere through their cult.

Trent Callahan – Combative neighbor of Highclere Inn & Carriage House; husband to Kendall Callahan.

Prologue

Worms. Tenacious eaters or lazy nibblers?

Lady Jean Fernsby-Valentine wasn't your average death-questioning person.

No, instead of pondering the afterlife, her mind fixated on something far more pressing—how long would it take for a fancy pewter urn to decay when attacked by a pack of ravenous garden worms? Sure, it may sound ridiculous given the circumstances, but Lady Valentine was greatly admired for her commitment to the important things in life—in this case, her dark sense of humor.

After all, she had to keep cheery somehow—her doctor had been trying to reach her all day. She knew what he was going to tell her.

She could feel it.

Lady Jean Fernsby-Valentine, known as "Lady Valentine" or simply "Lady V," had therefore begun to wonder how her obituary would read. Would it say she was pragmatic? Perhaps.

Righteous? Unlikely.

An indignant woman of often great sadness? Only if she wrote it herself. And knowing her husband, Senator Miles "The Tank" Valentine, as she did, she was certain the headline would read "Obituary of the wife of Miles Valentine"—her name only appearing as a footnote.

Yes, that sounded just about right.

Standing statuesque amidst the towering trees of her summer home and family-run resort, Highclere Inn & Carriage House, Lady Valentine watched as her longtime groundskeeper, Ahren Dawn, placed loose earth over an urn containing the remains of her twelfth and final prize-winning Golden Retriever.

Lady Valentine knew it was a pragmatic decision to end her 60-year tradition of breeding her beloved purebreds. Pageant masters used to hail Lady Valentine's goldens as pageant-ready, possessing regal beauty and a graceful trot that perfectly heeled to their owner's side.

Training her flawless goldens was one of her most beloved traditions and passions. They were her greatest companions whom she knew would never betray her or her secrets. Yet, despite the joy her dogs gave her, it was time to end the line. Lady Valentine knew that a newborn puppy would outlive her, and she couldn't in good conscience trust her husband to care for it upon her death. That she knew for sure.

As the last patch of earth settled over the freshly interred blue-ribbon winner, Lady Valentine scanned the headstones of the family members and pets buried at this specially designated burial ground. For decades, Lady Valentine had joked—with morose satisfaction—that the peaceful, circular plot of land in Highclere's back forty acres, bordered by clusters of pines and balsams, would one day be her burial plot.

As a gift for her 50th birthday, her husband gave her a framed certificate that announced the legal designation of her burial plot as an official graveyard for humans and animals. With a classic eye roll, her ladyship was rumored to have said that it was the dumbest gift he'd ever given her—at the time, anyway.

Yet, as loved ones began to pass of old age and sometimes tragedy, Lady Valentine appreciated those she loved the most were buried at her favorite place, where she could visit regularly and work through her grief.

The burial plot, as it turned out, wasn't a terrible idea after all—not that she'd ever give her husband the satisfaction of knowing that.

As Ahren said, "good night," and left for home, Lady Valentine turned and walked a few paces toward an imposing, large white marble monument displaying her name and birthdate in what she felt were exceptionally tacky 12-inch-tall Comic Sans lettering. Senator Valentine had come to her in the early 1980s to announce that he felt it would be practical—his code for cheap—to have their headstones designed and installed at the burial plot before their deaths.

Lady Valentine could be superstitious at the best of times and felt unnerved by the prospect of having to look at her headstone for upwards of thirty years. She felt its very existence would rush her to a premature demise. However, after more than five decades of marriage, she knew the Senator would do whatever he wanted whether she liked it or not. It wasn't worth the fight anymore, at least not without a stiff Manhattan at the ready.

With the last of the day's sun nearly replaced by darkness and the flicker of stars, Lady Valentine removed her signature Ferragamo flats and planted her bare feet deep into the manicured grass. She instinctively started burrowing a small hole using her big toe until she could feel the cold soil against her skin. It was as close to "kicking the tires" of a final resting place as anyone could hope for.

Stepping back to look up at the cloudless night sky, Lady Valentine felt peace that the stars she'd loved looking at since childhood would soon guide her to an existence beyond this life. At least, she hoped that's how it worked. If not, she prayed the worms came with a healthy appetite.

No, Lady Jean Fernsby-Valentine didn't know what would happen after life, but she knew what was going to happen *in* life after *her* death. She had no doubt about it.

Lady Valentine turned to look once more at the names of those who'd gone before her. She bowed in silent tribute before whispering, "I'll see you all soon. But first, I have something to do."

* * *

Lady Jean Fernsby-Valentine died at home one year, nine months, one week, and four days later.

Chapter One

Obituary of the wife of Senator Miles Valentine—1922-2004

The Honorable Miles Valentine is devastated to announce his wife of sixty years, Lady Jean Emerald Fernsby-Valentine, died on June 5, 2004, after a courageous two-year battle with cancer. Lady Valentine is survived by her exceptional husband, Miles, their four children, Drusilla (Clarence), Stuart, Lawrence (Piper), and Jocelyn (Ezra), as well as her six grandchildren, Oliver, Donatella, Mason, Montgomery, Jeannie, and Judge. She is predeceased by her sisters, Ladies Fiona Fernsby-Bradshaw and Margaret Fernsby-Collins.

Born in London after the First World War to The Earl Artemis Fernsby and his wife Emerald (née Clarke), Lady Valentine was raised at her family's ancestral home of Fernsby House in Sussex, where she remained with her parents and sisters until late 1944.

The Fernsby family immigrated to Canada from the United Kingdom in 1945. Upon moving to Toronto, Lady Valentine met Miles Valentine, and they were married five months later. Lady Valentine's greatest passions were supporting her husband's political ambitions, needlework, her Christian values, and animals.

> *"I love you, Jean.*
> *I don't know how I'll survive without you!*
> *I'll have to be brave. It won't be easy for me, but I'll try."*
> — **Miles Valentine**.

A visitation will take place at Shrubb & Gunn Funeral Home in Toronto this coming Wednesday and Thursday from 2:00 p.m. to 5:00 p.m. The funeral will be at Valentine Chapel on Highclere Hill at Lake Belvedere, Muskoka, on Saturday at 1:00 p.m., followed by an interment at the Valentine burial grounds at Highclere Inn & Carriage House. All services are open to the public.

* * *

Nineteen years, two months, and one day later...
* * *

Obituary of Senator Miles Aldrich Valentine 1923-2023

The Honorable Miles Aldrich "The Tank" Valentine, former Senator and Cabinet Minister, died at his home on August 6, 2023, succumbing to injuries sustained from a fall into electric fencing during a rainstorm on May 21st. He was 100 years old.

Miles is survived by his wife of 18 years, Aida Clifton-Valentine, as well as his four children, Drusilla, Stuart (Guillaume), Lawrence (Piper), and Jocelyn (Ezra). He will be missed by his six grandchildren, Oliver (Angelica), Donatella, Mason, Montgomery (Sarah), Jeannie (Forrest), and Judge (Christopher), as well as his six great-grandchildren, Armstrong, Mika, Harrison, Sage, Liam, and Maximus. He will never be forgotten by his stepchildren, Laverna (Philip) and Julius (Meghan).

He was predeceased by his wife of 60 years, Lady Jean Fernsby-Valentine, his son-in-law, Clarence Brisbane, and sisters Florence Valentine-Jones and Murielle Valentine-Howser.

Miles Valentine was first elected to Parliament in 1947, becoming the first Liberal candidate elected at the farming-come luxury vacation district of Muskoka Lakes in Ontario. Valentine was defeated in the following election and moved to Ottawa to run via a by-election following the death of Ottawa-South's MP. He was re-elected to Parliament in 1953 and joined the cabinet as Heritage Minister. Valentine won each successive election, becoming Minister of Transport, Agriculture, and Veteran Affairs. Valentine was nicknamed "The Tank" by the press because of his aggressive governing style and unyielding belief in his abilities and vision for Canada.

He resigned from the House of Commons in 1979.

Miles settled with his wife, Jean, in Toronto during the spring of 1981, where he entered business and became a sought-after political commentator, author, and investor. A vocal and influential critic of his former political party following his Commons resignation, Valentine was appointed to the Canadian Senate in 1985 by the Conservative Government as a commendation for his financial and public support in defeating the Liberals in the prior election. Miles remained in the Senate until retiring in 2010. During the final 13 years of Miles's life, he became one of the first prominent, high-ranking politicians to become a global conspiracy theorist. Miles wrote 11 books, was a panelist on multiple political television talk shows, and was a part of the Ontario-based barbershop quartet "The Politic-sings."

While he will be remembered by the public for his political career and eccentric beliefs, those closest to Miles will remember him most as the owner of Highclere Inn & Carriage House, a rustic cottage resort at Lake Belvedere in Muskoka. Every summer for over 100 (non-consecutive) years, the Valentine family, beginning with Miles's father Hollis, have welcomed guests from around the world to their humble escape, creating warm and lifelong friendships amongst the Valentine family, staff, and the coterie of colorful guests who inhabited the property summer after summer.

This season, in celebration of Highclere's 150th anniversary, the Valentine family re-opened its doors to their long-time guests one final time in celebration of the century and a half's worth of memories and moments that have lived so brightly in the souls of so many. Sadly, Miles's accident occurred weeks before the summer kick-off, and Miles couldn't join the festivities he planned.

Per his wishes, he will rest in peace at Highclere, the place he loved the most.

Operational Note: Shrubb & Gunn Funeral Home is managing the funeral arrangements. A small private service will be held at Valentine Chapel on Highclere Hill on Labor Day Sunday, presided over by the Reverend Bernard St. Joy. The Valentine family will then proceed on foot behind Senator Valentine's casket from Highclere Hill to their family burial ground at Highclere Inn & Carriage House.

The public is welcome to meet with the family along the procession from the chapel to the gravesite. The burial is open to the public; however, because of space limitations, only 100 mourners will be permitted to the gravesite and admitted on a first-come, first-served basis.

Chapter Two

Mason Valentine couldn't stop laughing.

The entire day had basically been a delightfully kooky acid trip with notes of *Fawlty Towers*, *The Vicar of Dibley*, a sprinkle of *Schitt's Creek*, and some extra weirdness from the *Twilight Zone*.

True, Mason had some inkling that his grandfather's funeral services would be less than ordinary ("colorful" was the politically correct term for it). Still, he definitely didn't foresee the swarm of weirdos who descended upon the family's resort to honor the late Senator Miles "The Tank" Valentine. It could best be described as a circus without the clowns and cotton candy. Actually—on second glance, maybe the clowns had arrived.

Mason valiantly attempted to maintain his composure. He tried every breathing rhythm and mindfulness exercise he could think of. He played with his suit buttons, avoided eye contact, and tried to think of every awful tragedy he'd ever lived through. In the process, he'd suspected he'd done a Kegel exercise or two! Unless it wasn't possible for a man to do Kegels? He wasn't sure.

However, the surprise bellow of Julie Andrews yodeling about goat herders from the speaker system was such a shock that it caused every bird in earshot to dart out of the autumn-tinged trees in distress, defecating with remarkable accuracy on the eclectic group of guests. Hitchcock couldn't have planned it better, and Mason couldn't hold his laughter any longer. And to think, Mason worried *he* was going to be the party pooper!

In the years following the death of his first wife, Lady Jean Valentine, the Senator, who was already known for his eccentric behavior, had become the world's highest-profile conspiracy theorist. Testifying before Congress and appearing on television shows around the world, he touted his "privileged" access to information concerning the "truth" about everything from the "New World Order" to extra-terrestrials. Did the Senator have "privileged" information about life beyond the stars or a cabal of banking aficionados bilking the public for their own private enjoyment? No. Of course, he didn't. Like so many politicians, the Senator was born with a "spotlight" complex. He'd have thrown himself on

Celebrity Survivor and noshed on donkey testicles if it was sure to get him press. Being in the news aroused him to near orgasm every time.

That said, the Senator's fame—for reasons only Freud or Jung could explain—always had an unparalleled ability to attract oddballs and nutbars, which Mason assumed were the correct clinical terms to describe them. Indeed, during his life—particularly when Highclere Inn & Carriage House was operational as a resort—most of its annual guests would fall somewhere on the spectrum between delightfully eccentric to one lost marble away from a straitjacket. The Valentine family felt the cross-section of guests made the resort business amusingly quirky—though profitably futile—with most guests returning year after year and becoming eccentric extended family to the Valentines.

The conspiracy theory contingent, however…well…they were another matter altogether. As Mason scanned the sizeable crowd, he felt he'd mistakenly wandered onto the Island of Misfit Toys—or into a kinky cosplay den.

It was a rare sight to have the property brimming with activity. Highclere Inn & Carriage House had been closed for 20 years, but Senator Valentine reopened for the summer to a select contingent of loyal guests to celebrate the 150th anniversary of Highclere's building. "Select" was a rather generous word considering the actual qualifications for an invite were one, being a former guest and two, still being alive. Thanks to Father Time, the pool of invitees had whittled down to about a dozen couples and a handful of amorous ghosts. Adult diapers, Metamucil, and Poligrip had replaced the traditional bottle of wine and box of chocolates as the guest welcome gift.

However, the Senator never again returned to Highclere alive.

* * *

Earlier, the Senator's coffin, ostentatiously draped in a Canadian flag, traveled to the burial plot atop a make-shift gun carriage from the picturesque, tiny, white clapboard steepled church at the peak of Highclere Hill—where a private family service was conducted by one of Highclere's most stalwart guests, the Reverend Bernard St. Joy. In truth, it was never clear to the Valentine family, and even to the Senator himself, what exactly Bernard St. Joy was a reverend of. Their obtuseness had gone on too long, however, and it was past the point anyone could reasonably ask Bernard what his credentials were.

Further puzzlement piqued when Bernard conducted the funeral wearing a kippah and an old, black sash draped over his shoulders like a shawl that read "Bachelorette Party," with hand-drawn crosses added in silver Sharpie at each end.

Following the private service and the arrival of a windowless white van that Mason assumed was the local asylum looking for its runaways, the procession kicked off from Highclere Hill to the burial plot. The gun carriage—an extremely loose description for a wobbly old hospital gurney decked out with bicycle tires being pulled by two ponies—led the way down the uneven, dusty rural road, leaving plumes of kicked-up dirt in its wake.

Mason, the middle child of Senator and Lady Valentine's son Lawrence, was surrounded by his parents, siblings, cousins, aunts, and uncles, all walking in step, waving the kicked-up dust out of their faces. Mason became briefly energized when he realized how utterly fabulous it was that the procession was beginning to resemble a scene from *Evita*! However, he thwarted his sudden urge to raise his arms into a high V-shape and sing "Don't Cry for Me Argentina" by imagining—of all things—puppies drowning. A skosh dark, sure, but it did the trick.

The dirt raised by the horses pulling the casket dissipated as the cortege passed the old rotting gatehouse and moved onto the property's aged tarmac. With the light and dust out of their eyes and finally able to see ahead of them, the Valentine family was...befuddled. Bemused? Maybe something more akin to wanting to run away in high-pitched screams? When dozens of mourners came into view, lining the driveway, wishing to pay their own nutty last respects to the Senator.

To start, several dozen (organized by the leader of the Senator's fan club, "The Tanks") were dressed in red hoodies and on bicycles, with pictures of the Senator affixed to their handlebars. Or, in the case of a few resourceful and dedicated fans who had access to a 3D printer, small busts of Tank poked through a posy of daisies in wicker handlebar baskets. All paying tribute in a manner obviously dreamed up by stalwarts of the film *E.T: The Extra-Terrestrial*. First *Evita*, and now *E.T....*

Mason burped out an accidental guffaw as John William's *E.T.* theme song started swirling in his head.

Dead puppies...dead puppies.

The tributes became increasingly eclectic the further the procession traveled through the property. It was akin to the tunnel of horrors from *Willy Wonka*. The next group of mourners were all dressed in suits and handcuffed together with signs around their necks saying, "Jail the Cronies—New World Order Styles."

Evita, E.T, New World Order. Check, Check, Check.

Dead puppies...dead puppies.

The procession followed the slight bend in the road and continued toward the narrow, grassy, tree-arched footpath that led to the burial plot. As the family reorganized themselves into single file to pass the threshold, they encountered the last set of mourners from "The Tanks." This bunch was a hodge podge containing a mix of fans carrying signs that read "9/11 AND TANK VALENTINE—INSIDE JOBS," some dressed as Ghostbusters displaying the initials "JFK" on their left breast pockets, while others were in black painted astronaut suits. Finally, a man in a Donald Trump mask wearing a number 46 jersey stood among the crowd.

Evita, E.T., New World Order, 9/11 conspiracy, JFK truthers, plus moon landing and election deniers, ALL in the same place at the same time. Oh, what a beautiful morning—er, afternoon.

Dead puppies...dead puppies.

After what felt like traveling through different dimensions and realities, the procession entered the burial plot—a one-acre, circular piece of the Highclere grounds designated as a cemetery decades earlier. The Senator's wobbly assembled gun carriage was wheeled within feet of his vast, self-designed monument, which sat above a specially built vault where the Senator would rest in peace.

The burial plot was primarily filled with close family friends, colleagues, distant relations, and, of course, the living guests of Highclere Inn & Carriage House. Distinguished semi-retired lawyer Roland Mast and his wife Viviane, guests of Highclere for 40 years, greeted the Valentines at the front of the group. Roland and Viviane had stumbled across Highclere one evening and fell in love with the property. While the Masts were fashionable, grand people in nearly every sense, their inclination for pomp and sparkle faded whenever they drove across the threshold of Highclere. Their inclination for a very stiff drink, however, never failed to follow them to their summers away, resulting in some rather loud, though entertaining, nights watching the pink, orange, and purple hues of the sunsets melt into darkness.

Behind the Masts was Angel Conner, another long-time guest, accompanied by her pet squirrel, Lenore, who stood at attention on the end of a bedazzled leash. Angel, heavy set with wiry silver hair, a penchant for patchouli oil, and dressed in a custom caftan—embellished the night before using Highclere's flowers and leaves—would largely be considered one of the resort's most colorful...though marble-missing...guests. When Angel arrived two weeks earlier with Lenore, the family realized that the old fable of pets looking like their owners remained true of species outside of the traditional cat and dog. Angel and Lenore could've been twins! While Mason hadn't seen Angel in two decades, he'd learned in the previous days that she and her husband Robert had divorced some years earlier after Robert's therapy pet alligator named Flipper ate Angel's pet, which at the time was a rat named Maureen. Unable to go on with the marriage because of her grief, Angel filed for divorce. Sadly, Robert was killed two years later during a pilgrimage to Florida to introduce Flipper to her relatives in the Everglades. It was mating season. Flipper found her match, and Robert got in the way. Rescuers salvaged Robert's watch from the stomach of a neighboring gator.

Next to Angel Conner stood Brian and Prunella Fisher. Their devotion and love of Highclere began in the 1970s when the cult they were a part of booked a two-week retreat at the property. The cult, as it would turn out, had intended to climax their trip with the group's self-death in the bowels of the lake. The manager of Highclere at the time was a woman named Germaine LeBlanc, who, upon hearing the plans of the group 48 hours before their earthly checkout, quickly ensured she processed the credit card on file. Once payment cleared, it occurred to her she should also alert the authorities—and one assumes the asylum that increasingly holds more and more of the Valentine's nearest and dearest—who scuppered the plan before its execution. Execution is quite literal in this case.

Two days later, Brian and Prunella checked back in. Their lanky, handsome bodies were clad in hip waders and wearing bucket hats with fishing paraphernalia sewn in. The couple carried two tiny suitcases and asked for the smallest room and the nearest fishing boat. They left their cult and joined the clan of Highclere Inn & Carriage House.

Lastly, seated beside Angel Conner in a distinguished-looking wheelchair was Dr. Louella Stone, the oldest surviving Highclere guest. At 93 years old, Louella had known Senator and Lady Valentine her entire adult life. A forceful personality whose svelte aging body could no longer be relied upon to comfortably carry her, Louella remained refined while hunched with a perfect silver bob. She was a confidante for Lady Valentine and the Valentine children, and she, alongside her late husband Atticus, was one of only three families welcomed to continue holidays at Highclere every summer after the resort ceased operations. It was their favorite place in the world. Next to Louella was the polished grave of her husband, Atticus Stone, who was buried a decade earlier.

Every person braving the heat in black funeral garb on an unseasonably warm Labor Day weekend held a special place in the hearts of the Valentine family. Their lives intertwined by fate, experience, happenstance, love...and a whole lot of nuttiness.

The soloist, Senator Valentine, had specifically requested sing at his service, "conveniently" discovered she suffered from "seasonal allergies" during rehearsal the day before. The funeral directors had no choice but to use records and a speaker system to honor the Senator's musical wishes.

As Mason removed his extra-large, square sunglasses to dab the sweat now beading down his forehead, his thoughts went back to "The Tanks" at the gate, the *Evita* procession, Bernard's "Bachelorette Party," sash, rat-eating alligators, leashed squirrels, and the amusing online conspiracy theories about the Senator's death. He smiled again.

Dead puppies...dead puppies.

Suddenly, a squeal pierced the thick, humid air from the speaker system. Julie Andrews yodeled about goat herders, and every bird in the adjacent trees—which of late hadn't been many—flew off in terror, shitting a storm on the manicured guests and meticulously curated service. This was a level of absurdity too far, and Mason burst out in laughter and couldn't stop.

* * *

As the funeral directors distributed wet wipes, the gentle lilt of the opening bars of "Edelweiss" enveloped the circular burial ground. This was the *Sound of Music* song they were looking for.

Mason stifled his girlish cackle with his hands and tried to regain his composure when he looked across the burial ground to see a well-dressed woman, whom he guessed to be in her fifties, staring at him with a warm smile. Wearing three strands of pearls, a black cocktail dress, and carrying a stunning gold-plated box, she looked familiar…but he couldn't place her.

Who was she?

The pallbearers removed and folded the Canadian flag that draped the coffin of Senator Valentine before transferring the casket onto a hydraulic lift to begin its sacred descent into the vault below. Despite the absurdity around them, the family felt the somber ritual. The Valentines were visibly moved, their faces pronounced by grief. At the Senator's request, his semi-retired groundskeeper, Ahren, had the honor of controlling the casket's descent into the vault; he'd then return the excavated earth mounded next to the Senator's monument onto the casket until it became one with the soil below.

As the earth consumed the polished wood, a tearful Laverna Clifton-Lehrman, Senator Valentine's stepdaughter, walked to the monument bearing the face of the man she had just buried and removed a red velvet cover to reveal the etched date of a few short weeks earlier. The date Senator Miles "The Tank" Valentine had died.

Chapter Three

Following the burial, the funeral directors thanked "The Tanks" for paying their respects and advised them it was time to go. While the bikes, Ghostbusters, and conspiracy theorists tootled off the property, family and close friends were invited back to the old inn for tea, coffee, cake, and, with Roland Mast behind the bar, undoubtedly something stronger alongside light karaoke.

Mason remained at the burial plot to thank a handful of well-wishers and to give his chafing nether regions a break before trekking to the inn. The way too small men's Spanx he powdered himself into had conspired with the heat to create an awkward pool of sweat in his underwear. A super sexy adult diaper rash was the last thing Mason needed.

The joys of getting older, thought Mason as he noticed how the sun had moved and elongated his shadow across the lawn. He could see in his silhouette that he was no longer the 20-year-old boy his mind's eye believed him to be. His six-foot frame had begun to melt from fit and firm to soft and bloated. His dirty blond hair, formerly thick and full of life, had started to shed from years' worth of stress, challenges, loves lost, loves won, work successes, failures, an unanticipated illness, and the rocky conclusion to a ten-year relationship he felt would last a lifetime.

With the burial plot empty, Mason stood alone, facing the marble monuments dedicated to his grandparents, and bowed his head. For him, death was now a marker of time gone by—history confirmed and written. Fate discovered, analyzed, and fulfilled. Whether that fate was good or bad, it was now finite. That was that.

A sudden chill pulsed through him; goosebumps appeared on his arms. The wind had picked up, and he felt that the predicted cold front had found him—the heat was about to break.

When he opened his eyes, he was startled to see the silhouette of someone else projected onto the marble monstrosity in front of him—a figure whose wavy red locks were blowing wildly in the rising wind.

* * *

"Christ Cordelia! If I had a bottle of my well-aged, fermented asparagus pee, I'd have spritzed it at you like pepper spray before bolting to the trees," Mason spat out at his cousin while bending over, clutching his chest and gasping exaggerated breaths for comedic purposes.

"Your obsession with how pee smells after eating asparagus has to stop. I can't take it," said Cordelia, smiling. "Please tell me you don't actually bottle it?" she asked, honestly uncertain of the answer.

"What can I say, cuz? It's my favorite Eau de Toilette," he joked while pretending to spray cologne on his neck.

"It's Highclere, right? It has to be ground zero for breeding the crazy. What other explanation is there for how strange and quirky we've all turned out and the type of guests we've attracted over the years?" she laughed.

"We're like Sunnydale sitting on a Hellmouth, except Highclere is built on a vortex of straitjackets and padded cells," snarked Mason.

"Where's Sunnydale?" Cordelia asked.

Mason became slack-jawed before replying irritably, "It's where *Buffy the Vampire Slayer* lives!" he practically shouted at his cousin's expressionless face. "Your education has failed you, cousin." He smiled before adding, "I was about to head to the inn. Care to walk with me?" he asked, gesturing for her to link her arm through his.

"I'd be delighted," she replied.

Cordelia Bradshaw, known as "Cici," was Mason's second cousin through Lady Valentine's side of the family and an internationally recognized investigative journalist turned university professor. Cici and Mason's grandmothers were sisters, and Lady Valentine was the person who heard Cordelia say "Cici" rather than "Cordi" as a child and took credit for coining the defining nickname that had lasted nearly half a century.

For ten summers, Cici managed the resort, and, in many respects, she had become as much a part of the fabric of Highclere Inn & Carriage House as the immediate Valentine family. Despite 12 years separating them in age, she and Mason shared a deep bond, the echoes of their laughter forever etched into Highclere's storied summer adventures.

They walked beneath the canopied throughway of the burial plot, emerging into the lowering sunlight and feeling the rising breeze on their faces—drying Mason's Spanx-induced sweat—thank God!

"So, speaking of crazy—that was pretty bat-shit!" Cici said with a big laugh. "We all knew today was going to be strange, but I did not expect it to become a convention of..." she paused, not sure how to say it politely.

"...a convention of those who have a tenuous grasp on what we like to call reality?" Mason piped in with great gusto and a wide smile. He hadn't been able to be funny all day and needed to burn his pent-up energy and amusing observations.

"I was going to say 'of alternate reality,' but same difference. Did you see the group with tin hats? Why tin hats?" she asked.

"I thought they were noodle strainers, to be honest. Either way, I think it's to stop us from using our evil space lasers to read their minds. That said, I'd rather read the mind of Angel Conner's pet squirrel. At least it would have something interesting to say."

"I don't understand why the heavyset, blue-haired lady sitting by the gatehouse was carrying a framed picture of Charlton Heston's colostomy bag. Is that a thing?"

"Lord—beats me!" Mason admitted though he was now equally curious. "I thought the chap with the naked Marilyn Monroe doll riding the bronzed shotgun that allegedly killed JFK did have a charming quality to it."

"No one ever believes me when I tell stories about the characters of Highclere Inn & Carriage House and those who do think we're all crazier than a box of frogs."

"Hey, hey, hey. You stole that line from my gran!" replied Mason.

"I did, yes." Cici nodded. "It's a phrase that fits us like a glove."

"Oh—*Bee Tea Double You*, how fab..."

"Oh, hold it right there," Cici interrupted in a playful tone. "Why can't you just say 'by the way' like a normal person? Why spell it out?"

"Flare, my darling cousin! If you're going to say something, do it with style," Mason smiled with a finger snap so diva-like, even he thought it came across as too camp. "Anyways, as I was saying, how fabulous was it accidentally finding ourselves in a scene from *Evita* during the procession?" he asked, his mouth wide with goofy excitement as they merged onto the pebbled, uneven walking path.

"Oh my God! So *THAT's* what you were excited about on the walk from the chapel! I thought you must've seen Matt Bomer running naked through the woods because you looked so joyful," Cici laughed, her tight, pale skin creasing around her lips.

Mason came to an abrupt halt before releasing himself from his cousin. Closing his eyes, he held out his hand for Cici to stop.

"Never, EVER joke about Bomer's bottom. That's a gay sin," he said, shaking his head in disapproval.

"My apologies." She curtsied.

The cousins continued to walk toward the main inn—a poop-brown colored building with a bizarre Noah's Ark architectural vibe. It was the central hub and oldest building on the property.

"You're feeling ok about everything?" Cici asked as the faint sound of a door slam echoed in the distance.

"I am. He was a complicated man with many contradictions and a complicated relationship with his family. But he lived a unique and interesting life. I mean, he left this world as unpredictably as he lived in it—who else could manage to be zapped by an electric fence in the middle of a blackout?" Mason laughed. "We weren't always best friends but ended on good terms. I have no regrets."

Another loud bang was heard coming from the inn. Cici and Mason looked at each other after hearing the noise meander through the burgeoning autumn leaves.

"Someone needs to put padding inside the doors up here," Mason noted with another eye roll.

"Forgive my tackiness, but have you seen the will?" Cici asked with mild hesitation.

"No," he replied. "All we know is that Aida and her daughter Laverna are the executors. They've seen the will, but we haven't yet."

"That's a bit controversial, don't you think?" she asked, puzzled. "If they've seen the will, and there isn't anything dodgy in there, why not send it to the family?"

Mason nodded his agreement.

"True..." he said, gathering his thoughts. "Though I don't think there will be anything shocking in it."

"Does everyone think he'll leave his entire estate to Aida?"

"They do and believe it's the right thing. She was his wife, after all," said Mason, who paused at the sight of a hummingbird zipping in front of them. "That said, we don't know how much money he had left. While he was the luckiest businessman alive and made trucks of cash through his investments, he also bankrupted himself before Gran died. Once she passed, he lived off her limited family fortune—the balance of which Aida will now inherit. Of course, Tank was spending like a drunken sailor over the last few years, so my guess is, there isn't too much left."

"I worry that won't go over too well with the Cliftons," replied Cici, grimacing at her reference to the family's initial concern that Aida married Tank—just four months after Lady V's death—for the *"cha-ching, cha-ching,"* rather than *"bow chicka wow wow."*

"Well, maybe we were wrong about their motive. The Cliftons took great care of him as he was dying. In fact, they took great care of him in life, too. So, debt settled in my mind," finished Mason as a stout, older bald man in a bespoke royal blue suit approached, holding out his hand.

"Hello Mason, I'm sorry for your loss," said a stony-faced Trent Callahan, Highclere's long-time and often combative neighbor.

Trent's uncanny resemblance to the Monopoly man—sans top hat—always gave Mason the urge to throw dice at him just to see if he'd say, "Go back three spaces."

"Thank you, Mr. Callahan," replied Mason with a smile, shaking Trent's hand. "And I'm sure you remember my cousin, Cordelia Bradshaw," he said, turning to Cici, who smiled and also shook Trent's hand.

"Oh yes, I remember Ms. Bradshaw very well. You didn't make an effective resort manager, but I've followed your journalism career ever since."

Trent spoke without a smile or, from what Mason could tell, any movement of his forehead or facial muscles. *Botox?* Mason thought.

"Oh, Mr. Callahan," Cici began, dripping with charm. "I can assure you I was an effective manager. I believe it was the Muskoka Lakes Association's expectations that were at issue. For whatever reason, I just couldn't seem to get them—or you—to understand that children's laughter is joyful and not a nuisance," Cici sneered, taking her hand back. "Are you still chair of the group?" she asked with forced politeness.

"I am," confirmed the diminutive older man before turning back to Mason. "If you could please pass along my condolences to your father as well, I'd appreciate it. I have to be getting back to Toronto," Trent nodded before waddling up the drive and past the old gatehouse.

"Ballsy of him to show up," noted Cici.

"I suspect he's sniffing around to see if we're selling now that Tank is dead," suggested Mason. "His mission to push us out of Highclere over the years has been unrelenting. The only part of the waterfront he doesn't own is our 49 acres," he added as the sound of another door slam barreled toward them.

"Oh, for F's sake! Can't we silence that bloody door somehow?" Mason exclaimed with exaggerated annoyance.

As the cousins turned to face the inn, they found themselves staring into the intense eyes of the familiar, though comfortable stranger Mason noticed earlier.

With his sunglasses still perched on his nose, Mason returned the mystery woman's gaze before launching into a ludicrously noticeable side-mouthed whisper to Cici, which—unbeknownst to him—made him look like a stroke victim.

"Does she look familiar to you?" Mason asked his cousin.

"Very," Cici replied while trying to remember. "I think she might have stayed at the inn back in the day. Maybe when I was a kid or in the early years of being the manager? She can't be much older than me. Do you know who she is?"

"No idea," he whispered sideways, "but she's walking this way...act natural."

Mason put his hands in his pockets and pretended to say something interesting while Cici—thanks to her prize-winning journalism training—was the epitome of calm in every situation.

Mason had been a "z-list" talking head on television for a brief period in his twenties. He was now an author and community leader who had become accustomed to being the family member strangers felt most comfortable talking to. His outrageous sensibilities and camp manner drew people to him—which always surprised Mason since he found himself to be annoying as all heck.

The leggy brunette approached the cousins with an undeniable radiance and confidence. Her once black umbrella had acquired rather unfortunate spots and now resembled a Dalmatian, courtesy of Julie Andrews' shitting birds.

"Hello, Mason," she said in a posh British accent. "I must apologize if I've been rather rudely staring this afternoon. I assure you, it was not my intention to be gauche." She laughed a dainty, self-aware titter. "Joyce Redstone," she introduced herself, "I read one of your books on my flight over. Tremendous fun—tickled my wits and wisdom!"

Mason extended a warm smile to Joyce. "Pleasure to meet you!" he beamed. "Your flight over? Based on your accent, I'm guessing you're from the UK. I hope you didn't fly all the way here for such a simple ceremony."

"Oh—don't be daft. Mr. Valentine's intergalactic fans were worth the price of admission. I'm sorry for your loss." She turned to Cici. "Terribly sorry, I'm Joyce."

"Lovely to meet you," Cici said, "I'm Cordelia Bradshaw. Mason's cousin."

"Bradshaw? You must be related through Aunt Jean's side then. Lady Bradshaw...Fiona?" Joyce deduced in a stream of consciousness.

"Yes!" said Cici wowed. "You clearly know the family history! I am Fiona Bradshaw's granddaughter. So...Lady Valentine's great-niece. In more ways than one." She winked.

"Aunt Jean?" questioned Mason, removing his thick, black sunglasses. "I hate to ask, but are you related to us?" He grimaced. "I'm so sorry if I should know this. You look so familiar, and I'm struggling to place you."

"No, no! Don't worry, you aren't losing your marbles..."

"To be fair," Mason interrupted, "on this property, we already have a deficit of marbles, to begin with," he teased as he watched Angel Conner chase after her squirrel Lenore, who seemed to be mounting something resembling a run to freedom.

"...we aren't family. Well, not biologically, anyway. I'm the granddaughter of Lady Rosamond Farnsworth-Ford..."

A light went off in Mason's head, "Oh—Lady Rosamond Farnsworth! She was my grandmother's best friend from childhood! We haven't spoken about her since my grandmother died—I knew you looked familiar."

"Have you been to the inn before?" asked Cici. "You look quite familiar to me, too."

"No, this is my first time..."

Cici looked surprised. Mason knew she rarely forgot a face. She must have met Joyce Redstone before. If it wasn't at Highclere—then where?

"I've heard so much about this place over the years. I'm so thrilled that I'm finally able to see the setting of so many of Aunt Jean's charming stories. My grandmother died just over eight years ago. She and my mother were in a small commuter plane flying from Boston to Martha's Vineyard when an engine combusted, and the plane crashed into a beach house. Granny was 94, so she had a good long life. Mum was only 70 and should've had a few more years ahead of her. Anyway, 'accept the things we cannot change,' as they say."

Cici tilted her head. Joyce's recitation of the story was peculiar. It was too clinical, too fact-based, and without emotion.

"I'm very sorry for your loss," said Mason.

"Well, I must confess I am here on a mission," Joyce announced rather business-like, followed by another slam and raised voices from the inn. "I was under strict instructions to bring this to you upon the death of Mr. Valentine."

Joyce Redstone raised the perfectly polished gold box she'd been carrying at the burial, its shape resembling a treasure chest with melted liquid pearl used to accent the edges and tiny cut emeralds fused along the flat top.

Mason, confused, took the box from Joyce. He held it to eye level and noticed the impeccable craftsmanship. There were no lines or hinges visible. The box appeared to have been birthed in perfect, completed form; it showed no indication that it was hand-crafted.

"What is it?" Cici asked Joyce, breaking Mason's concentration.

"I'm not sure," she confessed. "It's been in the family vault for over 20 years. All I know is that in my grandmother's will, there was instruction for her estate to deliver this box '*with haste to the family of Jean Valentine upon the death of Senator Miles Valentine*,'" she read from a piece of paper she took from her purse.

"This is from my grandmother's will. It outlines the instructions." Joyce handed Mason the paper. "Incidentally," she added, "it notes that if she died before Senator Valentine, then my mother was to be responsible for its delivery. In my mother's will, she provisioned that if she died before Senator Valentine, then I was responsible for its carriage to your family. It's all noted in those pages."

All three looked at the box in silence.

"I didn't open it," said Joyce, eager to know what was inside.

"I should probably wait to open it with my family, but let's take a look."

The gently lowering sun reflected ferociously upon the gold box. Mason, Cordelia, and Joyce stepped back into the shadow of the trees to avoid the glare and better see what was inside. Mason wasn't sure which side was the front. The opening so seamlessly blended into the top of the box that it wasn't obvious how to flip it open.

After moving his fingers around the pearled edges, he found two inconspicuous indents on the sides. He pressed his thumbs into the indents and heard the faint sound of something unlatching inside the box, followed by another door slam from the inn and muffled words that sounded like, *"Which trucks' wheels are on the bus?"*

Mason ignored it. However, Joyce and Cici's eyes darted to the inn in surprise. They quickly forgot the unfolding drama as Mason pulled the lid back.

Upon seeing the contents of the box, all three tilted their head in comical unison.

"What the hell are they?" Mason asked to the thumping of more doors slamming and voices rising behind him.

Chapter Four

"That's it? That's all you have to say to us?" yelled Senator Valentine's eldest child, Drusilla, to his stepdaughter, Laverna Clifton-Lehrman.

Having removed the contents of the mysterious gold box to examine them, Mason quickly placed them back once he noticed the storm brewing ten yards away. He turned to Joyce Redstone.

"I can't thank you enough for bringing this all the way here. I'll be in London later this week and would have been very happy to come and collect it from you—"

"What about my mother's things? What about her wedding rings, for God's sake? Her family jewels and art?" shouted Drusilla in the background.

"—However," Mason continued quickly, "if you'd be so kind as to give your coordinates to Cici, I'll touch base once we have a better opportunity to look at the box's contents. I'm afraid I'm about to be needed to referee a brawl, and not the fun kind with mud and speedos."

Out of the corner of Mason's eye, he could see his father, Lawrence, and Drusilla's twin brother, Stuart, exit the inn to follow the women toward the entrance of the carriage house. Originally horse and buggy stalls, the carriage house was repurposed in the 1980s as the garage and entrance to Senator Valentine's newly constructed quarters on the lake-facing side of the building.

Mason then saw his brother Oliver follow the group as well.

"Really lovely meeting you! Chat soon!" shouted Mason to Joyce in an accidental prepubescent squeal while taking several long steps toward the action.

"Excuse me!" said Mason as he joined the group. "What the hell is going on here?"

"They won't return my mother's things!" shrieked Drusilla in her light, other-worldly accent.

"As I just said, we would if Uncle Miles's will contained instructions to do so, but it doesn't. So, I don't know what you're all talking about or expecting. If it's not in the will, there's nothing I can do," Laverna retorted, her tone dripping with moral superiority as if addressing a group of toddlers.

"I don't understand," Mason said, puzzled. "Why would you not give us my grandmother's things? They don't mean anything to you."

"Because..." said Laverna, pausing to savor the moment and smooth invisible wrinkles on her black pantsuit. "His letter clearly states that he doesn't want you to have anything that belonged to him. Therefore, I. Can't. Help. You!" she forced out, loosening her shoulders and raising her chin. Her nose—pointing to the navy hue of the sky—revealed a distractingly large, crusted booger glistening in the late sun.

"What letter?" asked Mason, stepping backward to avoid being the accidental target of Laverna's nasal projectile.

No response.

"This is crazy!" Lawrence Valentine howled in frustration. "You're really going to be this cruel? You knew what that letter said. You'd read it! Yet you still felt it was appropriate to bring it to my father's burial? To stand there as his moronic lawyer read it out loud to a grieving family in our home?"

Laverna opened her purse to search for her keys, her lips curling into a tight, almost maniacal grimace. Two of the three carriage house garage doors rose at that precise moment. In the front passenger seat of a white sedan sat Senator Valentine's widow, Aida, with Laverna's best friend—who was also Tank's private nurse—Bianca Anders, seated in the back. The engine of a white panel van also roared to life at the far end of the carriage house. It inched forward, driven by Aida's son.

Those tall enough, like Mason and his even taller brother, Oliver, saw that the van was filled with Aida's belongings.

"As we've lost our right to be here now that Uncle Miles is dead, we thought we'd save you the trouble of kicking us out by packing up and leaving ourselves," Laverna recited to the Valentine family, her tone dripping with coyness as she took several steps toward her mother's car. "We do reap what we sow, don't we?" she spat, moving to the driver's side of the vehicle.

"How do we know what you're telling us is true?" Lawrence asked calmly.

"How do you mean?" replied Laverna, turning back to face him.

"How do we know Dad wrote that letter? How do we know we can trust you with what you say is in the will? You're not acting in good faith, which precipitates questions about your motive and secrecy...wouldn't you agree?"

"Is that a threat, Lawrence?" Laverna asked in annoying cliche, her poise beginning to fade as she threw her purse into the car, knocking her mother's glasses off.

"I heard no threat," pointed out Oliver. "What I did hear is the son of your mother's late husband—who was only her husband for 18 years, I wish to remind you—question the executor of his father's will, only to be met with evasive answers. Naturally, that leads anyone with a functioning brain to wonder what you're hiding. If you're not hiding anything, then show us the will."

"No," replied Laverna. Red flushed her cheeks, her eyes squinting with anger and resentment. "If anything involves any of you, you'll be notified by our lawyer. Otherwise, here is the letter."

She held out an envelope and handed it to Oliver, who walked over to take it.

"You can see it's in Miles's handwriting," she said breathlessly as she slid into the driver's seat, slammed the door, started the car, and sped out of the carriage house. Julius, Aida's son, followed in the panel van. They drove up the driveway, past Angel Conner—who was climbing a tree looking for Lenore—leaving Highclere Inn & Carriage House for the last time.

* * *

Mason joined the rest of Miles Valentine's children and grandchildren as they walked back to the inn. They gathered in the lounge, where they found an assortment of other family members and friends.

While the outside and most interiors of the inn were dilapidated with chipped paint, warped wood, and flooring from the 60s, the Highclere lounge was one of the few rooms of the building that had barely been touched since it was first built. Its floor-to-ceiling windows overlooked the inn's sandy beach and the four small islands that housed the larger cottages belonging to the Valentine family.

An enormous stone fireplace was the room's centerpiece, surrounded by comfortable wing chairs, loungers, and an extensive library. Gentle piano music streamed through two small speakers that had been added to the bookshelves years earlier, and a small bar—currently being manned by Roland Mast—jutted out from the far wall, with every type of alcohol, beer, and beverage one could imagine. The pièce de résistance was a remarkable, gilded painting hanging over the fireplace, which had been gifted to the inn by Lord and Lady Carnarvon, the owners of Highclere's name's sake castle in the United Kingdom.

"Anyone dead out there?" Roland Mast asked jokingly with a wide, toothy grin. "Viviane and I decided to stay put and protect the alcohol from gunfire. I've made Manhattans and cued up the song 'War Pig,' on the karaoke machine! Felt apropos," he explained with boyish joy.

His shock of white hair was windswept from the rising breeze outside. He placed the Manhattans on a tray and passed them around.

The room was otherwise silent. The Valentine family looked out the windows with glassy-eyed confusion. Lawrence's wife, Piper, walked into the room from the screened porch to perch on the side of her husband's chair. The only sound was the rattling trees outside and Roland Mast humming "Gonna Fly Now," the theme song from the *Rocky* movies.

Cordelia hesitated as she reached the wide French doors that opened into the lounge. Mason noticed she paused, looked at her cell phone, and then muttered something that looked an awful lot like "shit" and "fuck" before dragging a chair from an old dining table into the lounge to join the discussion. She held the gold box safe on her lap.

"So, what the fuck was that all about?" Mason asked with little care for his language. "I missed the start of the blow-up. What happened?"

"Here," said Oliver as he handed his brother the letter from their grandfather. "Laverna and Tank's lawyer Louise Harris—"

"A real flake if I do say so myself," interjected Roland back at the bar, smile still wide as he jiggled his martini in a pewter shaker while swiveling his hips.

"—said they had reviewed the will, and since none of us are named beneficiaries, there wouldn't be a reading of it. Instead, they pulled out that letter and read it out loud."

The room fell silent, a cue Mason knew to mean "open the fricking envelope." He did so and read what was written on the paper.

My dear family,
If you are reading this letter, it means that the Lord has called me home. My work on Earth is complete, and my next task, helping the Creator ensure Heaven is a place of unstifled joy, has begun.

Mason snorted at Tank's pomposity.

I've asked Louise, Aida, and Laverna to read this letter to you instead of a will reading. It's important to me that I make my thought process very clear. When I married Aida Clifton four months after your mother died, I was distressed at the selfish and over-blown reaction you all had to my decision. After all, I lived my life the way we all should, in a way that brings me genuine happiness. Aida has brought me more joy than I could ever have asked of anyone. She made me whole. She saved my life and taught me what real love is.

"Gran is going to beat the crap out of you in the afterlife for that comment," Mason muttered to himself.

At the time, your incendiary concern Aida was marrying me for "comfort"—which was both offensive and utterly baseless (especially since she had been friends with our family for years)—was second only to your concern about the future of Highclere Inn & Carriage House. Although I planned to (rightly) leave a significant portion of it to Aida and her family, you all wrestled the place from me in the most extraordinary act of extortion I've ever experienced. My father, Hollis, had left Highclere to me, and it was his express wish that I do with it as I pleased—just as he had! However, my children thought they knew better than my father and me.

Over the years, I have thought long and hard about that bitter time. While we—as a family—have found moments of grace and enjoyment together, I can't help but think how much happier my life would have been if my children acted more like the Clifton children rather than the spoiled, disrespectful group I'm bewildered to have raised. The frigid, combative, and rude welcome you gave Aida when she married me is an embarrassment I cannot forgive. The Lord would have me mention that you have been unfairly antagonistic toward me your entire lives'.

As I've sat down with Louise to re-write my will, I have considered your lifetime of behavior toward me, and since you have indicated that all you ever wanted was Highclere—that is all you will get. Any other item, heirloom, or piece of memorabilia that was promised to you by your mother, me, or in earlier wills has been revoked. At Aida's discretion and pleasure, my grandchildren will be allowed twenty minutes to select a single memento from our home. These collectibles will not be of any significant value.

I'm sorry that you all felt putting your own self-interests ahead of mine was more important. My children and my family (other than my great-grands) have been extremely disappointing to me. It is my heartfelt wish that you start to emulate and take inspiration from the pristine behavior displayed to me by the Clifton children. They understand what is important in life and have never made me feel otherwise.

I look forward to seeing you again someday, should you arrive here.

Cheers,

Dad, Grandpa, Tank, etc.

January 2, 2018

"'*I look forward to seeing you again someday…***should*** *you arrive here?*' Does he think we won't join him in Heaven if it exists?" Mason asked with palpable disdain. "What an egotistical fuck nut," he spat out, producing too much saliva and causing the ink on the page to bleed.

Mason laid the pages of the letter on the floor and took out his phone to snap pictures so he'd have a copy.

"It was unnecessarily vicious, completely one-sided, and couched in his eternal love of God, so we can't argue with it," added Mason's Aunt Drusilla (or Aunt Drew as her nieces and nephews called her). "His and Mrs. Clifton's self-justification irritates me to levels I'm unable to articulate."

The family sat silently as Roland passed around large glasses of white wine while humming "Battle Hymn of the Republic."

"We can sue them," offered Roland. "I'll do it on the house. Take the bastards to court and drain the resources Tank the Twit left them!" He nodded amusingly while looking around the room, his bleach-white smile reflecting the ancient coloring of the walls, hoping someone would agree to his proposal.

"Does anyone else feel hoodwinked?" asked Oliver in a quiet though commanding voice. "Tank refers to our '*incendiary concern Aida was marrying*' him for money," he paraphrased. "Yet, if Aida and her family had indeed grown to love us and considered us family after all these years, as we believed they had and we did them, they wouldn't have let that letter be read. They wouldn't be cruel and disingenuous about family items, heirlooms, and Gran's belongings being diverted to them instead of the family.

"If this wasn't about money, if this wasn't about items or things, and was about a loving, combined family…then they'd have sat us down, asked for help itemizing what's in the house, who owned what, and what sensible heirlooms and pieces should be kept by Fernsby and Valentine descendants. But they didn't. They had their opportunity to strike. It's pretty clear to me this evening that it was all a game…their pretend affection toward us was a means to their end, and we desperately didn't want to believe that was true."

To say Oliver wasn't the most emotional member of the family would be like saying Elton John lacked flamboyance. To see Ollie affected by Tank, his wife, and her family's duplicity was yet another surprise on a day of unexpected twists.

"I suppose this was their revenge for our less than warm welcome to Aida at the start of their marriage," suggested Drusilla's twin brother, Stuart.

"On the revenge scale, this was pretty tepid," said his husband Guillaume "Gil," Regan. "As long as it ends here."

"I once had a cousin who got revenge on a neighbor by inserting an eight-inch World War One-era artillery shell into the neighbor's rectum while he slept. They had to close the whole hospital to pull the sucker out in case it blew!" Roland laughed hysterically before sighing, "Oh, the good old days."

Mason signaled his disbelief at Roland's story through dramatic squinted eyes before remembering the gold box Joyce Redstone had delivered earlier in the evening.

"Settle yourselves. There is still one more twist to share!" said Mason as he lifted the gold box from Cici's lap, who then stood to join the conversation.

He once more ran his fingers around the pearled edges of the box to find the subtle indents that unlocked the flat, jeweled top. Once he found them, he pushed inwards until he heard the clasp unlatch. Mason opened the box and took a further look inside before turning it around to show his family.

They all stared in silence.

"What are they?" asked Ollie.

"I think they're ornaments," said Mason as he pulled out a beautiful polished gold sphere that resembled a closed pocket watch, complete with an opulent hook on one end. As far as Mason could tell, there wasn't an opening.

Mason passed the sphere to his father, who put on his reading glasses and stepped closer to a lamp, tilting the shade for more light.

"Wow," Lawrence said with surprise. "This is stunning. It's quite heavy—I assume it's solid. Mason, did you notice that one side appears to have the Fernsby family crest engraved on it?" he asked.

"I did, or at least we thought that's what it was. I haven't seen anything Fernsby in a very long time but Cici and I both recognized the etching. Do the lines on the reverse side mean anything to you?"

Lawrence flipped the gold sphere and examined the expertly etched collection of shapes on the reverse side. Thick, deep lines, circles, squares, and triangles were layered on top of each other.

"The shapes and their positions in connection with each other seem deliberate, but I can't think of what it might be."

"Are there more?" asked Piper.

Mason removed the other three items from the box. All were the same shape, though slightly larger than the first sphere. However, these were silver—cheap silver from the look of them. Rather than engraved symbols and images, they had various painted lines and circles. A transparent plastic film encased each silver trinket, and none had a decorative hook like the gold one. He handed one to his mother, the second to his brother, and the third to his Uncle Stuart.

"These are in the same vein as the first, but I suspect they were made separately from the gold one. They're silver and painted. No real craft to them. Even the paint looks cheap."

"And this Joyce Redstone came all the way from the UK just to give these to you?" asked Piper.

"To give them to *us*," clarified Mason. "They are clearly important if Gran put this much effort into ensuring they'd get to us."

"What did you think of Joyce?" Ollie asked Cici.

"She was lovely, kind, and easy to talk to. But there is something odd about this. To spend $6,000 dollars on a flight from the UK to Canada to pass along a box of surprise trinkets to people you've never met is peculiar. What's even more peculiar is the lack of accompanying instructions or an explanation of why Auntie V entrusted this mission to Joyce's grandmother and her descendants. Why go to the effort and not send along an explanation? Also, why didn't she give them directly to you when she died?"

"Maybe she knew old Tank would marry 'Granny No-bucks,'" snorted Roland, spilling a bit of his martini over the lip of the glass.

"You might have a point, Rolly," replied Cici, examining the ornament in Stuart's hand.

Viviane Mast rolled her eyes at her husband, mouthed "I'm so sorry" to the Valentines, and grabbed her husband's hand to guide him out the door and to his bed. Most of the group followed suit, leaving only Mason, Lawrence, Piper, Oliver, Cici, Stuart, and Gil to think silently about possibilities.

"If only Granny V had that kind of foresight," said Mason as he placed the mysterious spheres back into their beautiful box.

Chapter Five

Baroness Margaret "Margot" Ambrosia finished her meeting with the British Preservation Society just after twelve noon. The meeting, which always took place over tea at the St. Ermin's Hotel in the heart of London, England, was called to review the progress of the properties selected for preservation.

The group, made up of peers, philanthropists, and architects, diligently synthesized the work ahead of them, from minor building adjustments to the complete demolition of late 21st-century interiors to restore the storied classic buildings to their original glory.

As the meeting ended, Lady Ambrosia bid farewell to her colleagues while closing her red leather-bound, monogrammed folio. After then securing the lock on her luxury handbag, she glanced up and noticed a member of the wait staff staring at her feet. Intrigued by what could be so captivating, Margot looked down and realized she was wearing two completely different shoes. This was not unusual for Margot Ambrosia; brilliant, beautiful, and sophisticated as she was, her eclectic, oft-ill-fitting garments rarely complimented her intellectual, political, and community achievements. Her luxurious, though dilapidated fashion, at the very least, gave people something to laugh about—and she liked to believe she was in on the joke—though she had to admit it was a challenge to gaslight herself on an "Eeyore" day.

She placed her well-worn, royal blue blazer over her pink blouse and walked down the hotel's historic and grand staircase. Painted white with intricate detail, Margot always sensed she was starring in a revival of *Hello, Dolly!* as she descended the stairs and exited the building.

Lifting her wrist to see the time, Margot panicked when she realized that she'd be late for lunch with her husband—the head of the Metropolitan Police Force—if she didn't get a move on. Not having checked her messages for two hours, and with one child home sick, she pulled her phone out of her bag while double-stepping toward St. James's Park.

Weaving her way through gawking tourists, she approached Bird Cage Walk, pressed the walk button, and illuminated her mobile to see if she'd missed anything important. Her panic, already elevated, doubled when she saw her husband had called six times in two hours—never a good sign. She checked her voicemail—he hadn't left a message. *It couldn't have been that important*, she thought—she hoped. Deciding it wiser to be safe than sorry, she dialed him back, hoping he was still at his desk.

"Metropolitan Police, Stellan McManus's office. This is Victoria. How may I help you?" asked the perky, youthful voice on the other end of the line.

"Why hello, Victoria. I do hope all is well. This is Margaret Ambrosia. Is there any chance my husband is still in his office? He was trying to reach me…"

"I'm so sorry, Ma'am. Unfortunately, he left some time ago to travel to a crime scene. He did, however, ask me to tell you to call his mobile as soon as possible if I should hear from you."

"So, lunch is off then?" asked Margot.

"It is, Ma'am, but that's not what he needs to speak with you about."

"Right," Margot said, her voice trembling. "I'd best hop off and give him a ring," she added before ending the call with her patented polite send-off, "As always, thank you so much for your help, Victoria. Best wishes as always."

She hung up before her husband's assistant could return the pleasantry. Still standing on the edge of Bird Cage Walk, she scrolled through her missed calls and pressed her husband's number. Stellan McManus answered on the first ring.

"I'm so sorry to cancel lunch," said Stellan without first saying "hello."

"No bother," she replied. "Victoria said you needed to speak to me on something of an urgent matter."

"I do," said Stellan, dropping his voice to a whisper. Please don't repeat the following information I'm giving you, except to the one person I need you to call."

Margot listened attentively to her husband, nodding along as he spoke of matters he typically would never share with her. The instant the conversation concluded, she flagged down an iconic London black cab without considering her surroundings and hit the face of a nearby tourist.

Apologizing on impulse for her mistake, Lady Ambrosia jumped in and instructed the driver to take her home so that she could fulfill Stellan McManus's request with haste.

Chapter Six

"5:17 am..." Makayla Dawn mumbled to herself while trying to keep the light of her phone from revealing her presence. She was alone again—but knew it wouldn't last much longer.

"Come on...I'm running out of darkness," she whispered, looking up at the cloudless night sky. The moon's brightness was dimming as morning inched its approach.

Wrapped in a dark blue puffer coat, camo yoga pants, riding boots, and the toque knit by her late grandmother, Makayla left her house shortly after 2:00 am, determined to implement the plan she devised days earlier. However, as she arrived at Highclere Inn & Carriage House, she was surprised to see others also using the cover of darkness to hide secretive deeds.

Makayla watched as two people carried what looked like large "T" shaped objects from the carriage house. She thought she had counted 12 objects throughout the night—but wasn't sure. With every hour, she grew more concerned that her plan may be foiled thanks to her unexpected conspirators' equally unsavory activity.

She pulled out her spiral notebook to check the approximate time of sunrise, "Sunrise = 6:39 AM," she'd written in thick black ink.

That left her an hour. She dog-eared the page, closed her notes, and returned the book to her bag.

Suddenly, a decisive crunching noise jumped into Makayla's ears. Her heart raced. The direction of the crunch couldn't be easily identified.

It stopped.

Breathing heavily, Makayla remained still until she heard a loud crack from behind her. She crouched lower and balled herself up by putting her head to her knees and didn't move.

Letting what felt like the longest minute of her life pass and hearing no further noise, Makayla slowly unrolled and turned to see if anyone or anything was behind her. All clear. She heaved a sigh of relief, wiping her terrified tears and runny nose on her coat sleeve. She was all good, but it was all one hell of a rush!

She moved her gaze to the property entrance, scanning the rustling trees, hoping to prepare her nerves for another loud crack when she saw the two faceless people with their handheld flashlights approach the property for the seventh time. Having been blinded by the beams of their powerful lights all night, Makayla hoped to use the rising sun to sneak a glance at their faces. In a single hop, she leaped from behind her protective tree and landed on her knees next to the old gatehouse. Her landing made an audible squish noise at the exact moment the pair of flashlights switched off.

Oh no. Did they hear me? Wondered Makayla.

They were ten paces away from her, she guessed.

Now five...

Three...

Two...and just then, right as the dark figures were in line with the old gatehouse, one stopped and flicked their flashlight back on.

Makayla couldn't breathe.

Was she caught? Only a few dilapidated, worn pieces of brown painted wood separated Makayla and her unexpected company.

She closed her eyes and kept hold of her breath.

She heard nothing.

The flashlight turned off again, and the figures continued to move toward the carriage house. Makayla knew she needed another hiding spot. As the two faceless people walked past her, she collected her things and moved on her tiptoes behind a large, moss-dressed boulder about five yards from the carriage house. She still couldn't see faces; flashlights were off, and the outside lights of the carriage house weren't illuminated either. But even without their features visible, she determined the hushed voices were those of a man and a woman. She just wasn't sure if it had been the same duo all night or a rotation.

As the figures once again entered the carriage house through the west side door, Makayla looked down at her phone to see that it was 5:57 am. The night's darkness was lifting.

She remained behind the green boulder, which was now dripping sweat and emitting steam. The sun had added violet clouds and orange light beams to the sky, yet the mysterious duo she'd been watching all night hadn't yet left.

Suddenly, a light on the second floor of the inn turned on. Then, the closed cream curtains of the inn's lounge switched from dark to soaked in light just as the individuals in the Senator's quarters reappeared, exiting through the same west side door. Running with speed and silence, their bodies almost appeared to hover above the ground. Rather than running back up the drive, they ran through the tree-lined border between Highclere and the neighboring property owned by the Callahans before diverting themselves out of view and into the dark forest.

The maple tree above Makayla shook the morning dew off its leaves, dripping water onto her toque. She was confident that the strangers had left—this was her shot.

Having inherited many of her grandfather Ahren's responsibilities over the previous years, she was in a unique position to know every trinket, piece of art, cataloged book, accent table, lamp, flower bulb location, dusty corner, and blind spot at Highclere Inn & Carriage House. Her eye for detail seared the contents of every building and every room into her brain. A gift she was now putting to the test.

Noting it was 6:03 am, Makayla unzipped her loot bag to remove plastic gloves, a faded green gilded note card, and a steak knife. She then crouched speedily toward the carriage house door before disappearing inside.

* * *

Cordelia Bradshaw would've loved nothing more than a full night of blissful sleep, dreaming naughty dreams of her husband and waking on the last day of summer rested and ready to take on the new school year. But alas—no such luck.

Sat alone in the lounge of the original inn, Cici scrolled through online chat rooms while scribbling notes onto a piece of paper. The appearance of Joyce Redstone with the gold box and spheres, Aida and Laverna's refusal to reveal her Uncle Tank's will, and the troubling text message she received after the burial had kept her awake.

While perhaps each event was unremarkable individually, Cordelia knew from experience that stories rarely ended at face value. Her instincts warned her that there were more curiosities to come. From where, why, and the connection of it all? She didn't know.

Taking a sip of coffee, Cici opened a fan page and chat room operated by someone called the "Leader of The Tanks" when she heard the old floorboards creaking beneath someone's feet in the adjacent room.

"Good morning," whispered Drusilla Brisbane, Tank's eldest child and Stuart's twin sister. Drusilla's creamy blond, shoulder-length hair had already been brushed to perfection, the strands emanating a subtle whiff of Chanel No5.

"You're up early," Cici replied, looking at the silver mantle clock, which showed that it was 6:45 am.

"Troublesome sleep," Drusilla admitted while opening the curtains to peer outside.

"Are you at all interested in going to the carriage house for an early morning snoop?" she asked, turning to Cici, a mischievous smile playing on her lips as she dangled the key from her finger.

Chapter Seven

Mason's phone vibrated somewhere near his torso as he rolled over to see his clock flashing 7:35 am. He must have finally fallen asleep—and heavily—after spending most of the night watching shadows of leaves dance on his ceiling in the vivid moonlight.

Mason rummaged around for his phone, which had become caught in the sheets. Once he fished it out, he noticed two missed calls from a +44 number—a prefix he knew well to be the United Kingdom, though he didn't recognize the number. Deciding not to worry about it, Mason clicked the screen off and made a mental note to google the digits later in the day.

He then noticed a text message from Cordelia on his home screen:

Mason! Urgent! If you're awake, come to the inn!! -C

"What could be urgent at this hour?" he wondered. After quickly getting dressed, Mason ran down the stairs, unlocked the door to his cottage, Athabasca Cottage, and sprinted toward the old inn. He slowed his pace after he slipped on the morning film of water layering the bridges. Painted white, the four footbridges connected the small islands housing the Valentines' family cottages to the mainland. Once he regained his footing, he looked up at the inn and saw Cici's profile in the window of a familiar room.

Mason jumped over the bottom step of the bridge, his boots landing on the sand of the beach, and marched his way up the sweating grass.

Letting himself into the inn, Mason meandered through the laundry room, past the outdated industrial kitchen, and toward an old-fashioned door with a frosted glass windowpane—the word "private" painted on it. It looked like the entrance to a private detective's office, yet it was where he and Cordelia had spent more hours together than they'd ever be able to count—the inn's old office.

Mason opened the door with boisterous energy and, in a comedically deep howl, said to Cici, "How the hell is there drama already?" he tapped wildly at his naked wrist while continuing, "It's just after 8:00 am. Usually, it's noon by the time someone calls me to say the condom broke and they're in need of the morning-after pill."

During the years Cordelia was manager of Highclere, Mason routinely stepped into the office and sat in the old brown corduroy chair next to the rickety manager's desk so the cousins could gossip about the resort's goings on. No one knew the corduroy chair's age or where it came from. Mason long assumed it was covered in the semen of many past staff members and had likely been home to several families of promiscuous mice over the decades. Still, it was a treasured item that held wonderful memories.

"Which, by the way, did you know in some Caribbean islands the morning-after pill is called 'After D'? No joke!" he added as he kicked off his boots and took position on the ripped, beat-up chair, which looked worse than he remembered. The fabric surface, now so worn, didn't appear to be corduroy anymore.

Sitting with the windows behind him, Mason looked at his expressionless cousin.

"Cici?" he asked, noticing confusion on her face.

"So," began Cici, taking a sip of her coffee, "Drusilla and I went to the carriage house this morning for a bit of a snoop—"

"Good!" interrupted Mason, who felt creatures moving within the seat cushion beneath his ass, "I was thinking someone should go through the place and make sure Aida didn't have sticky fingers while going out the door." Mason smiled. "By the way, I'm totally sitting on a family of mice," he noted before standing up and placing a pillow between the seat cushion and his bottom, "perhaps we should gift this chair to Richard Gere," he joked.

Cordelia's expression remained unmoved, which was unusual compared to the cousins' typical witty banter.

"From what we can tell," continued Cici, taking another sip of coffee and turning to face Mason, "many things are missing. Drusilla hasn't been inside the carriage house since Auntie V died, but there are several dusty shelves with patches of clear wood, meaning whatever was there departed in the last day or two. But it's not what was missing that bothered us," she added while Mason's eyes widened, "it's what we found."

Chapter Eight

"*Do you think your treachery will be ignored? Do you think people who do what you did deserve to have it all? We don't. We're reclaiming what's rightfully ours. Piece by piece. Sleep with your eyes open. Lock your doors. Board your windows. Nothing will stop us. Watch it. We're coming for all of you.*"

Mason read the letter aloud to Cici. The message had been written on 5 x 10 stationery with the Fernsby family crest emblazoned in green wax at the top. The paper, while faded, was in good condition. A heavy steak knife had violently tacked the note to a wall in the carriage house, slicing the gilding of the Fernsby coat of arms.

"Jesus! You found this tacked to the wall?" he asked.

"'Tacked' makes it sound like it was politely dangling beneath a rainbow-colored pushpin. This, my dear cousin, was violently knifed into the door. Whoever left it deliberately slashed through the Fernsby crest at the top," she replied. "Feels pretty pointed to me."

"You know," he said, looking out the window, "it's strange. We haven't seen the Fernsby crest for decades, and then it appears twice within eighteen hours—first on the gold sphere and now this," Mason noted. "Why would Aida leave this?"

Cici sighed and sat back while puffing out her cheeks, thinking.

"Should we call the police?" Mason asked.

"No," Cici replied after a quick inhale.

"No?" Mason repeated, surprised. "Why not?"

Cici leaned forward, folding her arms onto the desk.

"Mace, something weird is going on," she said.

"Oh God, are you about to board the conspiracy train to Nut Land—which, last I checked, is just beyond the border of Cuckoo Circle and March Hare Lane?" Mason joked.

"Ha, ha. Just hear me out," she said with a smile. "Yesterday, after the convention of the Kingdom of Crackpots, a woman who we've allegedly never met, despite her familiarity to us both—tells us that under strict instructions left by your late grandmother, she flew 3,000 miles to deliver a box containing one gold sphere and three silver spheres with no indication of their purpose. Then, Aida hightails it out of Highclere—having already planned to leave dramatically—doing so, I assume, because she knew that the family would not be happy at the will being withheld. When you think about it, there's really only one reason not to share a will."

"Because they're hiding something in it," Mason nodded.

"Exactly," she continued, "We don't know what the spheres mean, and we don't know what Aida and Laverna are hiding in the will. Those are two big, funky question marks in my mind. Add in this morning's *'what the fuck is happening'* discovery via the threatening note, and it's clear something hinky is going on. What that is, I don't know. How or if any of this is connected, I don't know.

Mason felt his stomach flip. Cordelia's instinct for sussing out enigmas with nefarious undertones was nearly flawless. She'd won almost every top investigative journalism prize because of it.

Cici slid open her phone and scrolled.

"Yesterday afternoon, an old colleague named Kate Sampson texted me. It says, *'Hi Cord—sorry for the loss of your uncle. We've been following the online chatter spearheaded by the Leader of the Tanks re: Senator Valentine's death being an orchestrated assassination. They claim to have intimate knowledge, and I've been assigned to investigate. Let me know if we can talk about it—Kate.'*"

Mason rolled his eyes.

"Oh lord...you have indeed jumped on the conspiracy train. Don't worry! There's a stop at Level-headed Hill. You can get off there before reaching your destination!" Mason said hurriedly, just as his phone vibrated.

He glanced down to see the +44 number calling again. He hit decline and focused his attention back on Cordelia.

"Cici, I don't think there's anything worth investigating here," said Mason, fear warbling his voice ever so gently.

"Mace—listen, Uncle Tank slipped and fell headfirst during a blackout, causing him to be electrocuted by a garden fence. *Why* was he going into the fenced-off garden? Because that's where the generator lives, which he needed to turn on. *Why*? Because the power was out. However, before he even fired up the genny, he fell into the fence and got zapped with voltage uncommon in commercial fencing. Tell me, where did the fence's power surge come from without hydro or the genny on?" Cici posed.

Mason shrugged.

"I don't know Cici. The police investigated and said there was no foul play. They speculated that hydro had been restored briefly and surged through the fence because of faulty wiring. The conclusion is that the assassination theory is a figment of the imaginations of the colorful wackos who visited us yesterday."

Cici kept pushing, "Ok, even if we remove Uncle Tank's fall from the mix of suspicious happenings at least the spheres, will, and threatening note need to be looked into—agreed?"

Mason released an elephant-sized sigh as his phone vibrated. Looking at the screen, it once more was the intrusive +44 phone number—and he once again sent it to voicemail before turning back to Cordelia.

"Ok. I agree. Especially since the Cliftons projected a sense of having won, which is strange considering we assumed Tank was leaving them everything, and we were always ok with it."

"Exactly!" Cici agreed, "and Auntie V wouldn't have sent Joyce without, at the very least, a note explaining the spheres. One of which has the Fernsby family crest etched into it—the same family emblem adorning the threat left in the carriage house."

Mason had to admit that while he knew Cici was right, and she was inviting him to help her dig into the mysterious occurrences surrounding his family, he was scared. He was no longer at the age when confidence and adventure came in abundance. Having made more mistakes than he'd care to remember—because of reckless abandon and sometimes selfishness—his personality had shifted to sensible and safe. Of course, maybe he'd been playing it so safe he wasn't living at all.

After a few moments of comfortable silence, Mason slapped his hand down on the old desk and said to Cordelia with boisterous enthusiasm, "Alright. Let's do this *THANG*! Watch out bitches! Here comes your worst nightmare—the galactic team-up of the fabulous Mason M. Valentine 'lover, not fighter' and Cordelia J. Bradshaw 'investigator and ass-kicker.'"

He stood up.

"No evil doer will stop us. We will circumvent injustice. We will find the truth," he roared while pointing to the ceiling, "and we will come out of it alive!" he all but shouted. "Please, God," he tagged on in a whisper. "Come on, Cici, to the bat poles!" he added with an enthusiastic jump before hearing a loud *thunk* on the floor.

Mason and Cici followed the noise's direction and saw a book splayed out on the office's worn wood floorboards.

"That's not the Bible, is it?" Mason asked with a wince.

Cici bent down and picked it up.

"Yes, it is," she laughed, wiping off the dust.

"Not a sign, you don't think. Right?"

"Of course not. It was the timber of your booming voice," Cici assured him.

"What chapter had it opened to when you picked it up?"

"Leviticus."

"Phew," Mason smiled. "I skirted that warning from the ol' B-I-B-L-E some time ago." He laughed as his phone echoed a ping, signaling a new WhatsApp message.

Mason snatched his phone from the desk and read the text, which he was delighted to see was from his friend Baroness Margaret "Margot" Ambrosia.

Dearest Mason, I apologize sincerely for disturbing you and being a pest. It is I who has been calling you. I'm using an encrypted mobile, which I suspect is why you didn't recognize the number. I typically would never pester you during a time of grief, as you know. Yet, Stellan asked me to relay a message of great urgency to you. Unfortunately, time is of the essence. Should you be able to ring me back as soon as possible, I'd ever so appreciate it. Love, MA x

"Shit," sighed Mason. "Can you give me a minute to return a call, and then we'll divvy up what needs to be done?" he asked.

"You bet," she replied.

Mason, holding his phone in his left hand, opened the office door, causing a cross breeze to rip through the tired timbers of the aged building, blowing a flimsy box of Monopoly cards onto the floor. As Mason went to step into the main inn, he stopped to read the Monopoly card that had landed at his feet.

"Cordelia, this card says, 'Don't pass go,'" he called back to his cousin. "Not a sign, right?" he asked, shaking his head.

"Of course not," reassured Cici with a skeptical wince.

* * *

"Cici!?" Mason shouted as he walked toward the office following his twenty-minute call with Lady Ambrosia.

"Yea?" she hollered, still at the desk.

Mason entered breathless and sat down on the corduroy chair with an awkward smile.

"So. In your experience, and please be honest, how many seemingly random events related by the thinnest of connections go from coincidence to suspicious?"

"Why?" she asked, curious.

"Well...I just became privy to a new development concerning the Fernsby family, and this one includes a dead body."

Cici's eyebrows rose to her hairline, the faintest of a wrinkle appearing.

What the hell was going on?

Chapter Nine

"Hear 'ye, hear 'ye, let it be known to all within range of my voice that I do declare *Ted Lasso's* Hannah Waddingham to be an absolute international treasure. That is all," announced Mason in a loud broadcaster voice as he marched into the reception area of his office in Toronto, having driven back from Highclere the night before. "Oh, also, someone is going to have to cut me out of my Spanx before I get on my flight to the UK tonight—thanks!" He laughed as he pranced into his office and sat at his desk before bending over to unbuckle his suede Chelsea boots.

"You know I love you, but you're officially being extra today. If you don't want to become irreversibly encased in a human-sized elastic, then don't wear them!" retorted Skye Cadieux, Mason's long-time friend, colleague, and advisor.

"I've been in the same pair for two days...and if I'm being honest...the same undies too...I think they've fused to my body. The chafing, Skye! The chafing! Ugh!"

"Well, that's your problem. What does Hannah Waddingham have to do with your Spanx?" she asked.

"Nothing, I just think she's fabulous, and I wanted to say so," Mason said with a smile.

Skye had only just moved to Toronto from Peguis First Nation in Manitoba when she met Mason at a traditional ceremony held by a local Indigenous community organization. They became fast friends. When Mason's media career started to have a detrimental effect on his mental health, he devoted himself to creating an organization that could provide free support to those suffering from the most challenging forms of mental illness and addiction.

It was important for Mason to offer support options rooted in traditions from across the cultural spectrum—so it was a no-brainer to ask Skye to join the operation. Skye's spirit name translated to "Guardian of Sky Medicine." Her bright, bouncy personality was one of the sparkliest Mason had ever encountered. Skye's purple-hued hair, normally in a braid over her right shoulder, was her trademark, which she always accented with vibrant contrasting lipstick and manicured eyebrows. She shone from the inside out, and at first glance, no one would ever guess she was old enough to be a grandmother.

"It was a beautiful service," Skye said, sitting across from Mason, who had finished adjusting his boot buckle behind his plexiglass desk. The desk, a purchase he thought would look lovely and be a symbol of transparency and welcome, had become a major pain in his ass. It was constantly patterned with his fingerprints, or worse—a thick film of ass sweat if he'd absentmindedly sat on top of the desk during a quick meeting, which was something he often did. Therefore, he had to learn to surreptitiously wipe the sweat by wiggling his bottom before standing up—a move referred to as the "Mason Maneuver" in the office.

"A lovely service?" Mason quizzed with a smile. "Were you at the same funeral I was?"

Skye responded with one of her warm, full-hearted laughs.

"I didn't want to be the chump sitting here saying it was weird! The bird dung was epic, though. I give your family points for never being boring."

"It was a long way for you to travel for a man you only met once, so sincerely, I thank you," Mason said softly.

"*Chi Miigwech*, for allowing me to be part of your family's healing journey and be witness to your grandpa's spirit returning to Creator and his body returning to Mother Nature. We are family now, Mason—you and me. I'll always love and be there for you."

"So that's a yes to cutting me out of my Spanx?" joked Mason, and they laughed.

"How was the reception afterward? Is the family holding up alright?"

"Oh God, Skye, you better settle in...here's what happened after you left."

Mason told Skye everything that had happened with Tank's letter, the Cliftons, the threatening note, and Joyce Redstone before segueing into his call from Margot Ambrosia.

"Lastly," Mason said, taking a breath, "I received an urgent call from my friend Margot Ambrosia in London. She's married to Stellan McManus, the commissioner of the Metropolitan Police Services. Apparently, my 'ancestral home,'" Mason said using air quotes, "called Fernsby House, became a state-run asylum once my grandmother, her parents, and siblings immigrated to Canada following the Second World War."

"Yikes. So, you really do descend from a loonie bin after all!" Skye joked.

"Apparently," Mason nodded with a grimace. "Anyway, I guess it was a nasty type of institution—experimental treatments for mental illness, chemical castration for homosexuals, and the like." He shuddered. "It ruined the lives and brains of the people who were institutionalized there, and after it closed, it played host to an alarming number of suicides, including one a few days ago.

"This death, however, has been deemed suspicious for several reasons, but the main one being—and why Margot called—the dead man was wearing cufflinks. They're reversible with an image engraved on one side and a pattern of sixteen gemstones on the reverse—seven of which look like micro-cut sapphires, while the remaining nine are tiny white diamonds. The stones are identically patterned on both cufflinks."

Skye nodded, eager to understand the implication.

Mason continued, "However, it's the engraving on the reverse side of the cuffs that had Stellan think of us—because the engraving is of the Fernsby family crest," Mason paused for effect, "and he's wondering if the dead man could be a relative."

Skye shook her head in wonder.

"Well, what in Creator's name is happening with your family?" she asked, dumbfounded.

"I don't know, but there's been more action at Fernsby House of late because the British Preservation Society is prepping for its refurbishment to honor its significance as a historical building.

"So! I'm going to Fernsby House while I'm in the UK to give the MET a DNA sample. Dad is going to have the spheres and box Joyce left us looked over, and my cousin Cordelia will try to get a copy of Tank's will to see what the Clifton's are hiding."

"Does the UK really have to wait for your DNA sample? I mean, can't they contact an ex-British fling of yours to speed up the process?" Skye laughed.

Mason playfully scowled at his friend before they fell into contemplative silence, which was broken moments later by a shrill scream from reception.

* * *

Cordelia "Cici" Bradshaw had just wrapped her first lecture of the semester at the University of Toronto. The campus, brimming with young, interested, and eager students from around the world, had an infectious sense of optimism, which Cici found inspiring at the start of every year.

Her class on investigative journalism was hugely popular at the beginning of the school term—thanks to Cordelia's recognition as one of the great investigative reporters of the era—only to become a "quick drop" for many students once they realized the syllabus wasn't going to teach them how to be Lois Lane or Carl Bernstein overnight. Cici taught the methods and ethics of investigation as rigorously as she taught self-discipline and storytelling. What many of Cici's students failed to understand was the responsibility of being an investigative journalist and the human cost of the job.

Cici had dozens of stories with which to regale her pupils about stakeouts and espionage techniques, but also cautionary tales, including how her profession impacted her family life. As she aged and became wiser, Cici knew she was jeopardizing the health and happiness of everyone in her life each time she'd run off and follow a story. That burden was one she knew she couldn't continue.

The final straw proved to be her last-ever investigation. Cici had been targeted by organized crime assets overseas who cleverly misled her. They designed credible evidence, leading her to confuse the "bad guys" with the "good guys." The aftermath of which she still hadn't reconciled within herself.

It's the real-life examples that Cici used to ensure her students knew that being a journalist wouldn't be just excitement and code-breaking—it could be heartbreaking.

The beautiful post-Labor Day weather enticed Cici to walk home from campus rather than take public transit. She had crossed University Avenue to the green forested patch of Queen's Park when she received a text message on her Apple Watch.

Hi Cordelia. I'm so sorry you had to witness the kerfuffle with Uncle Miles's family at Highclere. We hoped that they'd be dignified and respectful of Uncle Miles's wishes, which they obvi aren't/weren't. It's going to be a difficult few months. There is something I was hoping to pick your brain about. Is there any chance you'd be free for coffee, lunch, or a drink in the coming weeks? Much love—Laverna.

"Unexpected," said Cici to herself as she reread the message to ensure she wasn't imagining it.

Tank's death had become a nuanced monster. She took her phone out of her purse and composed a new message.

Chapter Ten

Skye Cadieux jumped from her seat when she heard a scream echo from reception. She watched a leashed squirrel—sans owner—run through the hallway, past Mason's office door, and toward the sweat lodge. Skye turned to Mason in panic.

"Skye...don't worry. I know that squirrel."

Mason smiled with a subtle eye roll.

"Lenore! You come back here. You know you aren't supposed to run from me. And in a medical center of all places! Bad squirrel! You get back here," yelled a heavy-set woman as she hurried down the hall in a caftan made of old plush toys. Mason thought he could see the heads of Grover and The Cat in the Hat on her lapels.

Skye looked at Mason, confused.

"I know that squirrel also," Mason nodded, standing.

As the "Great Squirrel Escape of 2023" concluded, the subtle squeak of wheels could be heard approaching Mason's office. Skye and Mason walked into the hallway just as Dr. Louella Stone, graceful and classy as ever, asked her godson Stephen to stop pushing her chair as she arrived at Mason's door.

"Mrs. Stone! Welcome," greeted Mason, who was thrilled to see her.

He leaned down and kissed her on both cheeks. Angel Conner approached from behind with Lenore safe in her arms. Mason also hugged her, though he could feel Lenore gnaw at his left nipple while he did so.

"You remember my godson, Stephen, don't you?" Louella asked Mason in her husky voice.

"Of course I do! So good to see you again, Stephen," said Mason as he shook Stephen's hand before stepping back to bring Skye into the group, introducing her to Louella, Angel, and Stephen.

"I'm surprised to see you here. Mom said you left Highclere in the middle of the night because you were unwell. Please, come in," Mason said, gesturing everyone into his office.

"Steve and Angel, would you be dears and bring in the boxes? Also, Angel, please leave Lenore in the car. We needn't have more distractions," Louella instructed.

Her companions obeyed without complaint. Mason noticed the heads of Fozzie Bear, Princess Leia, the purple Teletubby, and Big Bird amongst the collage of children's toys decorating Angel's latest design.

Skye pushed Louella's wheelchair beside Mason's desk and sat beside her. Mason sat on his desk, regretting it immediately. He was sweating more than usual, thanks to his Spanx. Happily, he had bought Windex.

"Yes, we left in the night, but I lied. It wasn't because I was unwell. Well, maybe a little indigestion. The food had enough garlic to scare off a werewolf—"

"Vampire," Skye corrected.

"Right...whatever. Anyhow, the events following the service, I think we can all agree, were unfortunate. I've known Miles and Jean Valentine since I was 19. They were my best friends, and their deaths have reminded me that my time is running out," Louella said, her voice catching. "And I don't want any regrets, which is why I'm here."

Stephen entered, placed two white banker's boxes on the floor, and left without speaking.

"When Jean died, my heart broke for Miles," Louella continued. "I never doubted that they were the loves of each other's lives. While they had their problems, which I helped to counsel both as a friend and therapist, I assumed Miles would die soon after Jean. Neither Atticus nor I could fathom how Miles would survive without her. She made him...softer. Easier to be around. Kept him in line.

"Several weeks after Jean's death, Atticus and I had dinner with Miles at Highclere, and we were both struck by how at ease Miles was with losing his wife. There wasn't an evident sadness. Just a sense of 'that's done. What happens next?' It worried me, but I didn't say anything," Louella said.

Angel entered the office and placed two brown banker's boxes next to the white ones. She turned and skipped out, but not before the felt head of Bart Simpson fell from her backside.

Louella continued, "When Miles married Aida Clifton just four months after Jean's death, I couldn't understand the rush but attributed it to post-traumatic stress. The woman who was by his side for sixty years had died—that is a trauma few people can navigate easily. When my Atticus died, I didn't want to go on. My heart has never healed—and never will." Louella paused to clear her throat. "Several months after Miles and Aida's wedding, I became concerned at how easily Miles had replaced Jean with Aida. I saw how he pushed his biological children and family aside for the Cliftons. The rough edges of his personality sharpened. It's hard for me to admit this..." Louella paused again.

Mason and Skye looked at each other, wide-eyed, then back to Mrs. Stone.

"...Louella?" Mason asked.

"Mason, if you don't want to hear this, I won't continue. I don't want to upset you, but..."

Mason hopped off his desk and kneeled next to Louella's wheelchair. "Mrs. Stone, there aren't many people I respect more than you. Go ahead," he said.

Louella smiled weakly, a tear streaming down her face. "Thank you, Mason. Maybe this is harder for me than for you."

Mason got back on the desk, wiping his ass sweat away with his pants in the process.

Louella continued, "I had long observed that Miles innately lacked empathy. From a clinical standpoint, his attachment to Jean and his family seemed imperceptible, even before he remarried. He was called 'The Tank' for a reason. He valued his thoughts, ideas, and opinions above anyone else's. Jean loved him but couldn't stand him half the time. While he always exhibited signs of what, in the profession, we would call classic narcissism, I chose not to believe it. I often forgave or dreamed up context to his actions to let him off the hook when I shouldn't have. Narcissists are magnets to chaos. Their sense of order comes from their sense of superiority. His narcissism is why he believed marrying Aida so quickly was a good idea.

"Narcissists are highly insecure, often envious people, but do know right from wrong. However, right and wrong are less important than what glorifies or denigrates them. When Jean died, Miles felt denigrated by not having a wife. Even though he was in his eighties, he quickly remarried to show the world how desirable he was. Exuding a sense of desirability made him feel superior to others, which is a narcissist's goal—and was his goal. Thanks to Miles having known Aida for decades, he knew she could fill the void while offering her security in return."

Louella took a breath.

"Mason, you must be wondering why I'm telling you this and why I left Highclere in the middle of the night to get those four boxes to you."

"A little," Mason smiled.

"Do you remember when Miles and Aida's basement flooded last year?"

Mason nodded.

"After the water was drained, Miles asked if he could store boxes and larger items at my house while his basement was being repaired. I live alone in that big old brick monstrosity, so I said yes. Laverna and her roommate...what's her name again? Miles's nurse?"

"Bianca," answered Mason.

"Yes, that's her name. Sweet girl. Anyway, they came around and dropped off the items. The boxes were labeled and organized—work files, Highclere paperwork, family photos, correspondences, and Clifton items—that sort of thing.

"It was only a few weeks later when Aida called me about Miles's fall. I was in shock. Yet, out of habit, I put on my therapist hat to console Aida as I assumed she must've been in utter despair. The instinct of grief can make you do and behave in ways that aren't sensible. We give space and leniency during periods of grief. Remember, Aida had just told me my oldest friend had a horrific accident, an accident that would most certainly end his life. Yet, her very next sentence was to tell me that Laverna would ring around the next day to pick up the items stored at my house. Her voice...it was cold as ice."

"But their basement hasn't been redone," Mason pointed out.

"Exactly," confirmed Louella. "I told her I didn't mind holding onto everything. I advised her that she was rushing through things to feel a sense of control. Aida repeated firmly that Laverna would collect the items the next day."

"Did Laverna pick up the items?" asked Skye.

"She did, but only after I returned from a two-week hospital stay."

Mason's eyes widened. "Oh gosh, Louella. Are you better now?"

Louella half-smiled. "Of course, I'm not better, Mason! I'm a thousand years old. I just said I was in hospital."

"Why?"

"Because I wanted to know what the Clifton women were desperate to get back before Miles was even dead!"

Chapter Eleven

Mason and Skye lifted the four boxes Stephen and Angel had carried in and placed them on Mason's desk. Mason ripped the clear packing tape off the first box, removed the cardboard lid, and threw it onto the ground.

"Angel was kind enough to help me rummage through the contents of each box. Stephen also took pictures, so we had our own inventory and could put items back where they belonged," Louella shared as they removed objects from the box.

"Should we be wearing gloves while we do this?" Skye asked.

"Nah," answered Louella. "I've told them that Laverna and Bianca picked up all the boxes, and if they're missing a few, they must have miscounted."

"Any idea what they were so keen to get back?" asked Mason, grinning while looking at sepia-toned glossy images of Highclere during its early construction 150 years earlier.

"Nothing specific. As far as we could tell, there wasn't anything of real value or importance. Highclere documents, old political dossiers, campaign memorabilia, and letters from Miles's parents. Old family pictures, letters, date books, those sorts of things," Louella said. "Oh, and the original layout of the burial plot. Mason, as you'll remember, Miles had Laverna redesign it ten or so years ago to make way for his grander monument and casket."

Mason nodded while holding a small silver-framed picture with cracked glass.

"Do you know where this was taken?" Mason asked, handing the frame to Skye, who placed it within Louella's vision.

The photo appeared to be from the early 1940s. Tank was in full military uniform next to Lady Valentine, with American flags and war propaganda around them. They posed in front of a cluster of palm trees, Lady Valentine, out of character, overtly exhibiting a ring with glee that Mason didn't recognize.

Louella studied it, "Florida is my guess...around 1943 or 1944? I didn't meet Miles and Jean until 1948 when Atticus and I first stayed at Highclere."

Skye passed the frame back to Mason, careful not to dislodge the glass shards perilously held in place by the decaying rabbet.

"This can't be earlier than 1945," he noted. "My grandparents only met in 1945."

"That's not your grandmother, Mason," Louella replied.

Mason moved closer to the large, half-frosted window behind him. Louella was right—it wasn't Lady Jean Fernsby.

"Who is it?" he asked, turning the frame over to check if anything was written on the mounting board.

"It's the fiancé he ditched for Jean. I can't remember her name."

Mason ripped the paper off the back of the frame, still searching for identifiers. Once he peeled back the soft brown covering, he blew away the sawdust that coated the back of the picture. Written in barely visible pencil, Mason read the inscription aloud, "'*Miles and Caroline—Miami 1944.*'"

Mason looked up from the frame, his steel-blue eyes wide and dazed.

"So, you're saying Gramps Valentine was engaged to this Caroline lady?" Skye asked.

"He was. Jean told me that Miles and Caroline had a wedding date chosen, invitations out, the whole nine yards. Miles was stationed in America at the time as a mechanic. He traveled back to Canada for the holidays in 1944, where he met Jean just after midnight at a New Year's Eve celebration in Toronto."

"He broke off with Caroline *for* Gran?" asked Mason.

"After spending two days with Jean he sent a telegram to Caroline, who was at that moment on a train to Canada to finalize their wedding plans, telling her the engagement was over. Mason, you won't be surprised to hear that Miles didn't want to lose the deposits on the wedding planned with the Monroe girl, so he kept every aspect of the wedding the same, just switched out the bride."

"My brain is exploding. Tank never mentioned this. Nor did Granny V, now that I think about it."

"Interesting behavior pattern...isn't it?" noted Louella.

"How so?"

"The merry-go-round. He swapped Caroline Monroe for Jean, and then, sixty years later, he swapped Jean for Aida Clifton. Remember what I said earlier—Miles exhibited acute signs of narcissism. Attachment for narcissists is transactional rather than emotional. Inserting a person or people into roles glibly would be fine for a narcissist as long as the assignment supported his needs and goals. He displayed attachment to the perception—the image—of the spouse, which in some ways dictated the person who filled it.

"Caroline looks lovely in that picture, but Jean had outward sparkle. Star power. Her aristocratic breeding kicked up Miles's societal position. Ms. Monroe didn't stand a chance next to the beautiful daughter of a British peer. It's why Miles could roll over Caroline with barely a thought for the repercussions of his actions. Jean fit the bill better. But Jean was emotionally complicated...whereas Aida is not. Narcissists don't like implicit emotional complications because they can't control them. Which is why children of narcissists struggle to connect with them or ever obtain their approval."

Mason had, in the past, referred to his grandfather as a narcissist, but it was a description that he used more out of frustration and amusement than an actual medical diagnosis. Louella made sense. The Senator was predisposed to steamrolling his family—especially his children. After all, Lady Valentine had been dead for less than four months by the time Tank married Aida, a widow and long-time family friend.

Disinterested in his family's feelings or opinions, Tank presented the marriage as a fait accompli. The wedding was set, and he announced he had started amending the Highclere Family Trust to ensure Aida and her heirs inherited half of the inn upon the Senator's death—a property that three generations of Valentines had owned. For Tank's family, this was one insult too far.

They demanded that the trust be amended to exclude Aida Clifton, which Tank begrudgingly agreed to. However, between Tank's lashing out for feeling strong-armed coupled with decades of mutual resentment, the relationship with his children and grandchildren reached an all-time low.

"We think there's something in the will that the Cliftons don't want us seeing," said Mason.

"Without a doubt, and what it is must have been amongst the contents sent to me, or at the very least, they believed it to be," agreed Louella.

"Where do we start when we don't know what we're looking for?" asked Mason.

"Miles wrote in a diary every day of his life for seventy-five years. Without fail, each night in the same type of lined notebook year after year. The answers you're looking for could be in them. If not, you might find an unexpected truth that could work in your favor. I made sure his diaries remained safe and put them in the fourth box."

Mason bit his bottom lip, thinking, trying to will the powers of the universe to drop into his head the clue he should be searching for.

"Mason, Miles caused chaos in life because solving a problem could bring him the adulation and affection he felt owed to him whether he deserved it or not. It was to his benefit to find a solution to the very problems he created. However, the chaos he'd leave in death would be done knowing he wouldn't be the one to solve it. If that's any indication of what he could've done, I'd suggest it's significant and messy. Don't think the worst, but expect it could come."

* * *

The vibration of her phone spurred Makayla Dawn awake. It was 3:32 pm. She'd been in bed since 9:00 pm the previous evening to catch up on the sleep she'd forfeited the night she kept watch of the carriage house. Through bleary eyes, Makayla saw two unread messages waiting for her at the top of her home screen.

M—will meet at 6 pm—usual place for handoff. Please confirm.

Mack nodded her understanding and prayed she had enough supply in stock. Her focus on Highclere had impeded her side hustle.

She flipped to the second.

Media looking into death re: theories online. Ensure the camera system is destroyed.

Chapter Twelve

Mason's eyes flicked open as a piercing alarm reverberated through his suite at the St. Ermin's Hotel in London. It was 6:30 a.m., though it felt much earlier—an unpleasant side effect of his sleep deprivation and time change.

After a quick shower and a cup of hot British tea, Mason threw on his green utility jacket, rubber ankle boots, and sunglasses. As he gave himself one last look in the mirror, he saw that the hotel's shampoo had made his hair look thinner and more stringy than usual, so he added a baseball cap to his outfit and exited his room.

He took the old, two-person elevator down to the hotel's mezzanine level to grab a few more bits of sustenance before meeting his companion for the long trip to Fernsby House.

"Good morning, Mr. Valentine," greeted Victor, the long-time doorman dressed in a charcoal overcoat and matching bowler hat on his bald head. "Lady Ambrosia has arrived, sir. She has parked on the street just west of the courtyard. She said she'll be standing on the sidewalk waiting for you."

"Thanks so much, Victor! I'll be back tonight," Mason said as he moved toward the door.

Victor removed his bowler and tipped it toward Mason as he bid him adieu.

Mason exited the hotel, only *just* avoiding being bopped in the face by the automatic door as it swung toward him. After stepping through, he marched down the white marble stairs while finishing the last of his scone.

As Mason reached the end of the courtyard, he turned to see his friend Baroness Margot Ambrosia standing on the sidewalk, looking down at her phone. Dressed in a denim overcoat with polka dot pink patches peppered throughout to cover wear and tear, her hair in a ponytail, and wearing what Mason suspected was her husband's boots, she was her usual, eccentric, fabulous self.

"Hello, hello Margot!" Mason shouted, frightening the Baroness, who was deeply attentive to the contents of her phone.

As she looked up, a broad smile brimmed from her face.

"Mason Valentine! Darling—how are you!? It's been too long," greeted Margot as Mason approached her and leaned in for the very British greeting of a double cheek kiss. "How are you holding up? I'm sure it has been an absolute nightmare since your grandfather died."

Mason gave a quick guffaw and said, "Oh, there's a lot to talk about there. I'll fill you in on the ride. I've collected some snacks from the breakfast buffet for our travels," noted Mason as he lifted the paper bag emblazoned with the hotel's logo.

"How divine, Mason! You certainly do think of everything. Please do get in the car. We have a long drive ahead of us, but thankfully, it gives us ample time to catch up. Stellan will meet us there." Margot spoke in a feminine staccato voice, often ending her sentences with an upswing in pitch that Mason found comforting and delightful.

Mason walked toward the passenger side door, only to open it and find the steering wheel. He wasn't awake yet. Different country—different side of the road.

"Are you driving?" Margot teased.

"Sorry," said Mason. "I'd been up for several days until last night. I forgot where I was."

The two Ms switched places, with Margot hopping into the leather interior of her luxury vehicle as Mason jumped into the passenger seat.

"Gina tells me we should make respectable time this morning. The drive shouldn't be more than two hours," announced Margot as she typed Fernsby House's address into her GPS system.

"Who is Gina?" asked Mason while tonguing something free from his back molar.

"Gina!?" Baroness Ambrosia squealed back in a pitch higher than her natural speaking voice.

Mason stared at his friend.

"Gina Lolabridgida! My SatNav!" announced Margot with uninhibited laughter. "I'm sorry, Mason," she added, "I forgot you wouldn't know that I've named my SatNav Gina Lolabridgida."

"I call mine Judith Light," Mason smiled as he took a pastry from his paper bag.

* * *

Margot and Mason chatted amiably as they drove out of London.

Two hours later, Baroness Ambrosia exited the motorway onto a winding side road that promised to lead them toward Fernsby House.

Margot turned right and ascended a steep green hill. The pebbled road was overgrown by weeds and grass, obvious signs of decades of decay and neglect. The trees of early September were still as lush as the first of spring. There was a sense of peace in the area. A peace, Mason suspected, was never achieved by any inhabitants of the property, both pre-and post-loonie bin designation.

As they further climbed the precarious hill, Mason saw chimneys and a layered steepled orange roof behind the trees. They slowed as they approached the front gate, patrolled by a police vehicle and two officers. The iron, ornate, and imposing gates had a ruined carving of the Fernsby family crest. In his nearly forty years, Mason had never encountered Lady Valentine's family shield as often as he had over the last four days.

"Pip, pip!" Margot chirped out the window to the police officers standing in charge. "I'm Margot Ambrosia, here to see my husband, Stellan McManus," she said with a level of cheer that could've shooed away the dark clouds overhead.

"Good morning, your ladyship. He is indeed expecting you. Please drive through and up to the forecourt," said the stout officer before collecting his radio from his belt to alert Stellan of his wife's arrival.

Margot passed through the gates, and the two Ms continued to climb up the hill. The road, torn up for repaving, was bumpy and uneven. Mason felt his jowls and stomach jump up and down—likely thanks to the half dozen scones he chowed down on—until they reached a wide, gravel forecourt shadowed by the towering, ruinous pile that had once belonged to Mason's ancestors. Police vehicles, forensic vans, and representatives of the British Preservation Society were all buzzing about as Mason and Margot exited their navy-blue chariot.

"This feels eerie," Mason mumbled as he looked up at the home in front of him. "I felt peace in the car, but now I feel unease."

"That is indeed the correct feeling, but once we're done with the place, it will be a sanctuary to the locals and a piece of British history preserved for future generations. We'll kick out any nefarious spirits before we open," Margot said as she tied a Hermes scarf upon her head. Mason didn't have the heart to tell her there was a significant hole in the silk that wouldn't stop intruding wind and rain.

"You know, no one's told me why Fernsby House is so important that it's worth preserving," Mason noted.

"Follow me," instructed Margot, and the pair walked toward a scissor lift stationed at the far end of the graveled acre. "Let's get a bird's-eye view of the place," she suggested.

Mason walked backward as he took in the building's architecture. He was surprised to see the size and detail of Fernsby House. At four floors, the house was taller than it was wide. The center of the house was a three-level semi-circular portico with Palladian and neoclassical architectural styles. On each side of the portico were two bays of windows. The main entrance was at the portico's ground floor, flanked by a double staircase leading to outdoor landings, which Mason assumed had been used for entertaining, dining alfresco, and sun during the summer months. The second and third floors of the portico contained boarded-up windows with ionic columns between them. The fourth floor of the portico was an open-air balcony with an entrance flush against the white brick of the building. Mason couldn't help but think the house looked like the architect had squished and elongated the blueprints for the White House in Washington as a basis for the design (even though Fernsby House was built in 1750, 25 years before the home of the American President).

The house sat smack in the middle of several acres of open green space.

Margot waited in the scissor lift as Mason finished his initial review of the front of the building. He turned and picked up his pace, leaping into the scissor lift seconds later.

"It's not at all what I expected," Mason confessed. "I was envisioning a short, fat house with significant wings," he added.

"The height of the house is part of the story," noted Baroness Ambrosia.

Seconds later, they rose into the overcast sky, wind pulling strands of Margot's hair through the hole of her Hermes scarf. Mason was happy he'd worn a hat as he couldn't afford to lose more hair follicles.

"Fernsby House sits on 200 acres of prime hilltop land," began Margot as they continued to elevate to the sky, at first level with the trees and then flying above them. "The first Earl Fernsby—your third great-grandfather—was schoolmates and best friends with Charles Howard, the Earl of Surrey, who would later become the 10th Duke of Norfolk."

The lift came to a stop, and Mason was mesmerized by the view. He noted a bell tower (sans bell) on top of the house, which wasn't visible from the ground.

Margot continued, "The Dukes of Norfolk have lived at Arundel Castle since 1067. They are the Earl Marshalls to the Household of the Monarch. If you look closely, you can see the Norman Keep of the castle in the distance," she pointed.

Mason followed her finger, and sure enough, though difficult to spot against the gray sky, was Arundel Castle. He took out his phone and took pictures.

"Charles Howard petitioned George III to create a hereditary Earldom for the Fernsby family and requested this piece of land to build an estate. The elevation of the land and the height of Fernsby House were chosen so the first Lord Fernsby and Charles Howard could see each other in the distance. They often communicated with torches at night using their own type of morse code. Although we've searched, we haven't found any key to recreate or decipher their code." Margot repositioned herself and pointed Mason back toward the house and the property.

"Now, this is where things become most fascinating," Margot began excitedly. "Over the decades, the home remained relatively the same. While the grounds are 200 acres, in the early days of your family living here, there was only meadow, farmland, and a rather modest home neighboring the property—which made it feel vaster than it is. As the years went by, additional homes and estates were built around Fernsby House. By the beginning of the 1900s, the view from the bell tower would match what we see today, with estates sitting on top of each other. While we are unaware of any continued generational relationship between the Fernsby and Norfolk families, your relatives were well-regarded in the area. They became one of the unofficial governing families of the community, often bringing together neighbors and workers for holiday soirées, summer dinners, and game weekends. That type of thing."

Margot took a breath and stopped to look at Mason.

"Mason, what do you know about your great-grandmother?" she queried.

"Not a great deal. Mainly her name was Emerald Fernsby, and she died in the early 1950s. Granny V and Tank didn't speak of her. Of course, Tank would've only known her for five or six years."

"Right—let's go back down then, shall we? But before we do, please look over at that concrete patch."

She gestured to a large area on the southwest side of the house.

"What am I looking at?" Mason asked. "All I see is grass and a black box on concrete."

"That darling Mason is exactly what I wanted you to see."

The lift began its descent back to the ground.

* * *

Once they returned to the gravel forecourt of Fernsby House, Margot and Mason marched toward the object Margot had pointed to from the scissor lift.

"I'm not quite sure how to say this to you, Mason," started Margot. "I don't want to tell tales out of school, but weighing it up, I think, on balance, you should know a bit of context as to what we are about to see."

"Alright," Mason replied as they walked at pace to their destination.

"Your great-grandmother, as you rightly noted, was Emerald Fernsby née Clarke, who married the eventual sixth Earl Fernsby, your great-grandfather Artemis. Artemis was a commanding officer during the Great War and had left Fernsby House for the frontline three years before the war ended. While your grandmother, Jean, wasn't born until 1922, her eldest sister had been born in 1915, some weeks after your great-grandfather had left for the war."

"That much I know," noted Mason as they slowed their walk. Mason could now see a large rectangular object, almost resembling a giant cereal box, sitting on top of a cement square the size of an above-ground swimming pool. It was, to all who saw it, a bizarre sight.

"While I don't know the inner workings of the family, the scuttlebutt amongst the locals was that Emerald Fernsby became mentally unwell after being left alone with a young daughter. Often over-imbibing in alcohol and creating such 'works of art' as this!" Margot finished her sentence just as she and Mason arrived at the alleged work of art.

Baroness Ambrosia guided Mason's attention to the monochromatic, oversized cereal box by gesturing like she was a model on the *Price is Right*.

"She created a large black rectangular box and called it art?" mused Mason skeptically. "And this is why the house is worthy of preservation?" he added, unconvinced.

"No, no, no. The black is a protective layer," Margot responded while flipping the clasps on the skinny side of the box. After freeing the fifth latch, she removed the cover and placed it on the ground.

"Mason Valentine, without further ado, I give you Emerald Fernsby's 'Door to Nowhere!' Isn't it marvelous?" she beamed, clasping her hands together.

Mason's jaw was tight. He had always suspected he was going to go crazy eventually. It was hard to deny when considering Highclere and his ancestors...but this further proved it.

"A door to nowhere..." Mason mumbled as he nodded his head with a mild smirk. He inspected the 10-foot lonesome door, free of rooms and walls but complete with glass knobs on both sides. The paint, having once been a cream color, was now weather-stripped and a mish-mash of gray, white, and brown.

"Well, that proves it, Margot! Get out the straitjacket. Take me into custody now!" joked Mason.

"Oh, Mason. The story isn't done yet!"

"Thank Creator," giggled Mason.

"When your great-grandmother first built the door, their neighbors and friends assumed it was a rather whacky piece of décor which they attributed to your family's known eccentricity and Emerald Fernsby's declining grasp upon reality."

"I'm doomed, aren't I?" Mason interrupted.

"We all are, dear Mason! I'm nearly done with the story," assured Margot. "When your great-grandfather returned from the war, he was startled by the 'Door to Nowhere.' He took it as a sign his wife was not well. They had two more children over the following years. Lord Fernsby decided to resign from his seat in the House of Lords—requesting that his title become extinct upon his death—to focus on municipal matters and stay close to his wife rather than leaving her alone. When Hitler rose to power and Britain went back to war, the Home Office requested that Lord Fernsby return to the frontline in a similar capacity as in the first war. He decided he couldn't leave his family and requested a post on home soil. He was asked to be a double agent, with the mandate of ensuring the safe travel of goods through the United Kingdom without the Germans finding out or interfering."

Mason was entranced by the story.

"You see, Fernsby House's elevation means, in a similar capacity to Arundel Castle, that not only could it be seen from far and wide, well...when the trees were smaller...but it also had an impeccable view of the River Arun. You can no longer see it from this vantage, but seventy years ago, it was clear from this view. While the Germans were watching normal transportation channels throughout the United Kingdom, they were unaware of the country's robust and interconnected canal system. The mouth of the River Arun is near Littlehampton and is accessible via the sea. This allowed British troops and government officials to clandestinely travel key supplies, munitions, and soldiers through the country. The canals weren't being watched, and several prominent citizens in the area, your great-grandfather included, ensured easy transportation. As a double agent, Lord Fernsby would know when enemy spies were in the area or flying overhead on surveillance. He'd then warn the captains of the barges—who were often women—as to their safety level. He did so by using this fabulous piece of whimsical décor!"

Margot smiled brightly as she again caressed the door as if she were Vanna White and it was a puppy.

"How?" Mason asked. "Like if the door was open, you're good, but if closed, you're in danger?"

"Ah, now this is where old-fashioned ingenuity came into play. As you can see, if you turn the doorknob to the right, the entire door swings open on its hinges, and you can walk through the frame." Margot demonstrated as she spoke, though she did struggle to push the door open. "To most, this was all the door could do, and they laughed about it. However, in the darkness of night, Lord Fernsby and his neighbor, Lord Farnsworth, repurposed the door's structure. When you turn the handle to the left..." there was a subtle click as she did so, "the outside panels become false doors and open to this."

Mason stepped forward. The panel opened to reveal a wall of sixteen glass cylinders in a four-by-four pattern, built into a black plank running the height of the door. It reminded Mason of an exaggerated stoplight.

Margot concluded, "The canal captains, Lord Fernsby, and the Home Office devised a code system to communicate a threat level. Lord Fernsby would receive his intelligence from the Germans and would then share that with the boats by illuminating a pattern of these cylinders at night. They are specially-made bulbs that are dimmable based on the weather. It has been determined that thanks to your great-grandfather, more than one thousand troops and over £290,000 worth of goods and munitions safely traveled to their destinations without being intercepted. Remember, this was during rationing, so traveling supplies to communities could mean food for a town or starvation. The refit of this 'Door to Nowhere' was genius. This is why we chose Fernsby House for preservation. We intend to ensure the door's history is fully displayed when the house is completed."

Margot smiled self-assuredly. They stood in silence for a moment while Mason absorbed all the information.

"Nothing is what it seems, is it?" said Mason.

After Margot gave a subtle look over her shoulder to see if Mason was speaking to someone else, she drew out his thoughts.

"How so, dear Mason?"

"Everything I thought I knew is turning out to be incorrect or missing significant slabs of details. After all that has happened over the past few days, I now learn that the great-grandfather I knew nothing about was a hero and that something called a 'Door to Nowhere' was a device to ensure the safety and prosperity of thousands of people. Margot, very little appears to be what it seems in my life at the moment. What are you supposed to do when everything you know turns upside down?"

"Find the truth," answered Margot definitively.

She moved closer, taking his hands into hers as the sun broke through the gray clouds.

"Mason, none of these discoveries are a coincidence. If important aspects of your past are now proving to be the opposite of what you had come to know, then you need to look hard at everything and find the truth. Most people are not as good or bad as their best and worst deeds, and no one is immune from contradictions, even when one tries to live a life of intellectual honesty and consistency. Maybe Senator Valentine was a narcissist, but does that negate the good he did for people in life? The Cliftons are proving to have been more dubious than you thought, but does that erase the good moments, memories, and laughter you had together over the years? Life and situations are complicated, but much like this 'Door to Nowhere,' maybe you must turn the handle a different way to find the truth. In my experience, the truth exists within the frame where we're looking, just not always at first glance."

Mason became a smidge glassy-eyed. The jet lag, fatigue, and ongoing family discoveries had made him emotional. Lady Ambrosia was right. The answers he, Cici, Louella, and his family were searching for all existed—he just had to read between the lines and in the margins.

Which reminded him...

"So, onto lighter subjects. Tell me about this dead body we've come to talk about?" laughed Mason. "Watch him end up being my cloned twin or a long-lost uncle with three eyes and a pet pig, which will give me even more emotional turmoil to unpack."

Margot chuckled at her dear friend, linked her arm in his, and the two strolled back to Fernsby House, leaving the fabled "Door to Nowhere" at their backs.

Chapter Thirteen

To: Cordelia 'Cici' Bradshaw
From: Mason M. Valentine
Date: September 10, 2023
Subject: Fernsby & Dead Man

Cici—I spent an interesting day with my friend Margot Ambrosia at Fernsby House. I think you'd like her, she's our type of eccentric, witty and enthusiastic.

Anyhoo, FH isn't at all what I expected. It's lanky but evidently overflowing with wonderful family secrets (I'm being facetious about the wonderful part).

Re: The dead man. SUCH A MYSTERY! He was an older gentleman who took his life in the grand foyer. As far as the MET can tell, once the man was inside Fernsby House, he walked up the stairs to the landing and gobbled hundreds of pills. He then crashed through the railing and fell in such a way that his neck severed when he hit the floor. He was dressed to impress. Hermes tie, Omega watch—the whole nine yards—including cufflinks with the Fernsby crest on one side and a pattern of sixteen micro-cut sapphires and diamonds on the other. The cufflinks appear to be WWII-era.

That alone would be strange enough; however, no one can determine how he got onto the Fernsby House property to begin with. Due to the increasing number of suicides that take place at the property each year, the police and preservation society installed CCTV cameras monitoring every inch of the perimeter and added chicken wire for additional deterrence. Yet, besides a titch of mud and a few fresh nettle cuts and bruises, the dead man had no injury to indicate he climbed a fence or dug a hole. No suicide letter has been found, and there hasn't been a missing person's report filed that matches the man's description. They've hit a complete wall with their investigation. However, because the man was wearing Fernsby cufflinks, they still wonder if he was a relative—I gave them a DNA sample to test against.

I've attached a PDF with pictures of the Fernsby cufflinks. The gemstone/diamond pattern is fascinating, but I have no idea what it means (if anything). I'm meeting with Aunt Drusilla tomorrow to snag some old interior photos of the carriage house, update her, and check in.

How are things on your end? Any news
Xx
Mason

PS—I have attached some info on a good thing our great-grandfather built and used during WWII. It's called the "Door to Nowhere" (the story starts with GG Emmy's mental illness but ends with saving lives!).

PPS—I emailed Joyce Redstone—but bounced back. The number she left also isn't in service. I am in meetings for the rest of my stay but I will attempt to check social media for her.

* * *

To: M. Valentine (Cousin)
From: C. Bradshaw
Date: September 11, 2023
Subject: Re: Fernsby & Dead Man

SUPER interesting about the "Door to Nowhere!" I'm looking forward to hearing more about it. I like the idea of our great-grandparents being secret war heroes.

I'm at a loss about the dead man until they check against your DNA. Do you think Joyce Redstone might know anything about it? She came into our lives out of thin air…maybe there is a connection?

A BOX OF FROGS

News on my end: Skye and I have started to go through the boxes Louella brought to your office, and so far, there's only been one discovery that you'll find curious—we found a manila envelope containing 37 threatening letters addressed to Uncle Tank. What's more peculiar is that the signature has been cut off the letters using scissors. Some are dated, but with the rest, there's no real way to tell how old they are. However, Skye and I agree they've been typed on a word processor and printed using an ink-jet printer.

Here's a sample:
"You've been a piggy at the trough for years. Abusing your power to imprison your enemies instead of allowing proper judicial review. You disgust me, and you will be held accountable in one way or another. I wouldn't rest too easily, sir."

Can you print and ask Drew if she knows anything about them? There is writing on the outside of the envelope that we think says "TIC," but we aren't confident we're reading it correctly.

Roland Mast called me last night (he didn't want to bug you with the time change). He has reviewed Auntie V's will and has confirmed that pieces of her jewelry collection and specific heirlooms were properly willed to her children, which Tank held in trust after she died. A letter is being sent to Aida tomorrow requesting she return the items within 72 hours. If not, the property will be reported as stolen, and the authorities will come and collect the items. Roland will keep you updated.

My contact at the courts has confirmed that Tank's will has been filed for probate. It could take some months before a public copy is available. She's going to work some magic.
Xx
Cici

* * *

To: Cordelia 'Cici' Bradshaw
From: Mason M. Valentine

Date: September 12, 2023
Subject: RE: Re: Fernsby & Dead Man

Why am I saved in your address book as "M. Valentine (cousin)"? Are you worried that early dementia will set in and you'll forget who I am? LOL. I JOKE. I LOVE YOU!

Good news re: Rolly and Granny V's possessions and the probate petition. I'll be curious to see if we can gather anything untoward just from that.

I am seeing Auntie Drew tonight. I will show her the threatening letters. Do we think they're connected to the one you found on Fernsby letterhead? I've honed in on a few people who could be related to Joyce Redstone on social media and have sent friend requests. I'd love to track down her home addy so I can swing by and chat with her. I wonder if Margot Ambrosia can get it for me.

I will update you before I fly back if I have news.
Xx
M

PS—You know what I miss? Movie scenes from the 90s when people would break into song for no reason. I was watching *The First Wives Club* last night on ITV, and when Diane Keaton, Bette Midler, and Goldie Hawn belt out "You Don't Own Me" during the finale, it delights me to no end and brings me so much joy I can't even describe it. I DEMAND Hollywood bring back random singing into all productions moving forward!!!!

PPS—I'm meeting Aunt Drew at an exhibit called "The Eye of Vulva" at the British Museum…yes…Eye. Of. The. Vulva. Shoot me now.

Chapter Fourteen

Laverna Clifton-Lehrman dreaded her daily visits to the Medfield Long Term Care & Assisted Living Center north of Toronto. For 23 years, she had been subjected to the home's putrid scent—a noxious combination of cleaner, disinfectant, and human waste that seemed intent on sapping away at Laverna's soul. Despite this overwhelming tide of odors, however, she was duty-bound by her vows to continue paying these regular visits, an obligation she found hard but unceasingly faithful in fulfilling most days.

On this day, however, Laverna was eager to embark on her trek north of the city. She'd awoken with more energy than she had in years. The bags under her eyes had cleared, and she'd taken time to go to a salon for the first time in…well, she couldn't remember the last time she went to get her hair professionally done. Over the years, she had designed an aura, an image of a woman who had been knocked down by life but kept fighting. She hated the gray but felt it blended in nicely, giving the sense of an unfussy woman, thankful for her blessings and focused on the important matters in life.

Laverna was tired of playing her self-assigned role, and now, after two decades of manipulating her persona to accumulate admirers best and attract sympathy and pity, she was free. Free to achieve the sophistication and refinement she had long envied in socialites and even the family of her late stepfather, Senator Miles "The Tank" Valentine. In Laverna's eyes, the Cliftons were just as glamorous and generous as the Valentines—they didn't have the money or resources to do it until now.

Now that her stepfather had passed, she had the upper hand in life, and she was going to make damn sure that the Valentines were put in their place once and for all.

The Labor Day confrontation was only the beginning. The high she got from that moment left her smiling for days. The best was yet to come. She could hardly wait.

As her taxi pulled up to the Medfield building, Laverna gave her new paisley pantsuit a once-over to ensure there weren't any creases or accidental stains. Taking her phone out, she turned on the camera and checked her makeup and hair.

The blond color she chose was perfect and accented her tanned skin beautifully. Her red-soled shoes were uncomfortable as hell, but she was making a point—that her life was now enriched and worthy of envy.

The thrill of her new look made her giddy. She exited her taxi and walked through the revolving doors as she'd done thousands of times before. She'd then follow the winding red line through the corridors to the elevator that would take her to the seventh floor.

"Ummm...ooh la la! '*Hello, society pages. I'm calling with a celebrity sighting in the brain injury wing of Medfield Long Term Care. Send a photographer!*'" joked Bianca Anders as Laverna exited the elevators and walked to the nurse's station.

"Why, thank you! Like the suit?" Laverna asked Bianca while doing a self-conscious twirl in front of the desk.

"'Like' would be an understatement. You look absolutely smashing!" gushed Bianca.

Laverna first met Bianca on her third visit to the Medfield care facility two decades earlier. Bianca was the attending nurse that day, and she and Laverna instantly bonded and became the best of friends. As Laverna's children got older and prepared to leave for university, she came up with the idea that Bianca should move in with her to ease the loneliness that comes with an empty nest and ease some of their mutual financial burdens. After weighing the pros and cons, Bianca agreed, and they'd been roommates for 11 years.

Bianca, an only child from Norway, had an upbeat and unpretentious personality. She proudly wore figure-hugging outfits despite her pear-shaped silhouette. Her friendliness, kindness, and easy laugh made her an invaluable part of Laverna's life and, by extension, that of Miles and Aida Valentine. Bianca was as much a member of the family as Aida's children. She loved Miles Valentine, and after he fell into the electric fencing at Highclere, she took a leave of absence to be his private nurse once he moved home for hospice care.

"How's Phil doing today?" asked Laverna as the pair arrived outside room 774.

"He seems to be having a good day. He recognized me this morning, which is the first time in a year that he's remembered a face and name for more than 24 hours. I checked his chart about 15 minutes ago. He's groggy from his new medication but awake. The *Price is Right* is on, so good luck pulling him from that. I'll leave you to it and see you at home."

Bianca walked back to the nurse's station as Laverna knocked and entered the room.

"Are you decent?" Laverna joked as she walked toward the man in an oversized leather chair.

His gaze was fixated on the television screen in front of him. Laverna walked closer and placed her hand on his.

"Phil? It's Verna. I hear you're having a good day today," she said quietly.

Barely audible over the sounds of cheers from the TV, she pulled up an old beaten-wood chair and sat next to Philip Lehrman, her husband of twenty-eight years.

"I miss Bob Barker," exclaimed Phil without turning to face his wife.

She smiled.

"I miss him too. I think he's still alive, though," she lied, knowing that Bob had died days earlier. "He's about 100 years old...maybe?" she added, unsure Phil was listening. Even if he had been, he'd forget she was there and what she said, anyway.

Laverna and Phil had only been married for five years at the time of their accident. A transport truck lost control and slammed into them on their way home from a church service. Their two children only had scrapes and bruises. The airbag deployment saved Laverna's life. Phil's, however, didn't discharge, causing his head to hit against a piece of steel that fell from the transport truck and shattered their windshield. The doctors said he was unlikely to regain his motor skills and his ability to speak. He defied the odds, in large part thanks to the care and special attention that Bianca provided him as his nurse. While he'd learned to walk and talk, his vocabulary was limited, and short-term memory was virtually non-existent.

His wife hated having him locked up in a facility. She wanted him home but knew the exorbitant cost of home care would be impossible to manage. Then, her mother married Senator Miles Valentine—a union Laverna advocated for as soon as the Senator showed an interest in remarrying after Lady Valentine died. Laverna was always fond of Senator Valentine, having known him and Jean her entire life. She had called him "Uncle Miles" for as long as she could remember, and she knew he could be a means to an end for her. Even if not immediately, his finances could get Phil out of Medfield and back home. She felt hopeful for the first time since their accident. The Senator, however, had longevity on his side, and Laverna underestimated his life expectancy. She had assumed he had seven to ten years left when he married her mother. However, the bastard wouldn't die! He had a few close calls but always fought back to life, even when the odds were against him.

Finally, the day came. Laverna knew the cranial damage and electric shock burns from the Senator's fall would be the beginning of the end. Sure enough, a little under three months later, her stepfather, whom she had grown to love, passed away. She cried. Cried more than she thought she would, but he had been good to her and was the father figure she'd gone too long without.

What she knew, but very few others did, was what was about to happen next.

The day Miles "The Tank" Valentine died, she scuttled her fake pretense once and for all and planned the Labor Day confrontation at Highclere. She'd rehearsed it for hours. Deciding when to attack, what she'd say, and how she'd further twist the knife before leaving the property. She'd then give the Valentines a bit of relief before the next strike.

"Phil. I want you to know I love you. You've been very patient, having to live here for all these years. I promised I'd bring you home as soon as I could, and it's taken longer than I had thought, but we are so close now. So, so close. There are a few more administrative pieces I need to sort out before the money starts coming in. Once I get the next check, I will move you home. I promise," she said as a knock sounded from the door.

Phil kept his gaze on the television. After several moments of silent togetherness watching a segment of disastrous Plinko be played on the *Price is Right*, Phil Lehrman turned to face his wife. Looking her up and down, he asked, "Will Bob Barker be there when I go home?"

After a second round of knocking, Laverna stood and kissed the top of Phil's head before opening the door and exiting the room. Standing outside waiting for her was Highclere's long-time neighbor and adversary, Trent Callahan.

Chapter Fifteen

TO: Mason Valentine (personal); Cordelia 'Cici' Bradshaw
CC: Drusilla Valentine-Brisbane; Stuart Valentine; Joss Valentine-Campbell
From: Lawrence Valentine
Date: September 20, 2023
Subject: Spheres

I took the spheres and box that Joyce Redstone brought from the UK to my local jeweler. Long story short, the gold sphere is 24-karat. It's solid and apparently worth a fortune. The Fernsby crest was engraved by hand, as were the geometric shapes on the reverse side which Ralph (jeweler) believes were done in the last twenty-five to thirty years. The silver ones are worthless. They are stainless steel, though solid, with no hidden compartments. The paint used for the geometric shapes is fresh and was likely done in the last 12–18 months. The configuration of shapes was run through different programs and reverse imaging to find a match online, but so far—babkas.

So…it makes sense and is plausible that Mom sent Joyce's grandmother the gold sphere to hold in trust (even if we don't know why), but the steel spheres we can reasonably determine were created in the last year or so. Therefore, Mom would've known nothing about them. The paint being recent is the dead giveaway.

Ralph also mentioned that the insert cradling the spheres is steel with a velvet overlay. When taken out and flipped upside-down, it's clear that the three circles housing the silver spheres were hammered wider to accommodate their larger size, whereas the circular indent for the gold sphere was a perfect fit.

With the flawless craftsmanship of the gold box (not a nail, screw, or glue anywhere—it is one big piece of pure gold that was melted and molded into the shape it is), the box maker wouldn't have been so sloppy as to use the correct dimensions for one sphere and not the other three.

I'll keep researching the geometric shapes and lock up the box and gold sphere for safety until Mason can collect them. Roland Mast is storming "Fort Clifton" tonight with police to retrieve Mom's things. He'll circulate a FaceTime group so we can watch.

While the business of the spheres is strange, I don't think we need to worry too much about their mystery once we have Mom's things back. That's all we really want, anyway.

-L

Chapter Sixteen

"What ho!" a perky Mason Valentine greeted his receptionist, Michelle, upon jaunting into his office. Despite his travel and the ongoing—and ever-growing—oddities surrounding his life, he had slept well and discovered he'd lost four pounds when he stepped on the scale that morning. At least he thought he lost four pounds; it was a bit difficult to read, squinting through one eye.

"Who are you calling a hoe?" shouted Skye from the doorway of her office.

"You! You, saucy wench," Mason replied.

"Excellent description of me! Maybe we should add it to my business cards?" laughed Skye.

"Well, you told me I wasn't allowed to greet people with a 'heigh-ho' anymore," smirked Mason.

"Only because you sounded like Kermit the Frog. If I wanted to work with a felt green frog with a hand up its ass, then I'd be ok with it. But this is a place of business."

"What, wait? I'm not a felt green frog with a hand up my ass!? Skye! I'm now disillusioned—how dare you!" mocked Mason.

"You'll create a new identity. You always do!"

"You're such a buzz kill," giggled Mason.

"Says the Spanx-Wonder!" retorted Skye.

"You've gotten funnier in the last week, Skye. Bravo to you," Mason said while putting his bag on the floor and performing his imitation of Nancy Pelosi's insincere clap after Trump's State of the Union.

"Indeed, bravo me!" said Skye, smiling wide.

Michelle handed Mason his mail, and Skye followed him into his office and closed the door.

"Good trip?" Skye asked.

"Weird trip, though I've happily reconfirmed that I'm gay as the day is long. After spending a little more than two hours interacting with AI-programmed talking vaginas, monologuing about gentle cleansers, and laser hair removal, my sexual orientation was once again confirmed. Also, for some reason, I never want to eat prosciutto again."

"I didn't realize that was touch and go for you," laughed Skye.

"Prosciutto?"

"No, your LGBTQ2S+ membership."

"Ah, it isn't, but I think it's always good to reconfirm these things. Like, I hate tomatoes, but one day, I might be interested in trying them!" he joked. "Anyways, it's not every day you have to give a DNA sample to help identify a dead body and then have a frustrating visit with an aunt—while surrounded by a choir of animatronic singing labia, I might add—who refuses to see the flaws in her father that drove her batty while he was alive but has forgiven now that he's dead. She did give me a bunch of interior photos of the carriage house so we can cross reference and determine what—if anything—is missing."

"Labia can sing?" asked Skye.

"Majora only. The minora only hums—underdeveloped lips."

"Ah. So, status quo for the whacky world of the Valentine family," proclaimed Skye. "Box of frogs," she winked.

"Indeed," confirmed Mason while flipping through his mail, "box of frogs all the way."

"Cici is running a bit late. She texted. I love her, by the way! After three evenings of reading Gramps Valentine's invoices, death threats, letters from his wackadoo fans, and medical records, a real bond was formed."

"I'm glad!" Mason said as he finished scanning the bills and correspondence. He then opened his computer and brought up his father's email.

"Take a look at this," said Mason, inviting Skye to read the update about the mysterious spheres.

As Skye got to the end of the email, they could both hear the click-clack of towering heels coming their way.

"Sounds like Cici is here," noted Mason as he stretched his neck to see around the frame of his internal window.

Cici strode through the door carrying a brown envelope displaying the logo of the Ministry of The Attorney General of Ontario. She greeted Mason and Skye with a perky "Hi, hi" before sitting down.

"Good trip?" she asked.

"Weird trip," responded Mason, echoing his conversation with Skye.

"Well, talking vaginas, dead bodies, and ancestral homes will do that to you," mused Cici. "Skye, you saw the email from Mason's dad?" asked Cordelia.

"I just read it," Skye said. "What are you both thinking?"

"I think someone intercepted the gold box at some point over the last twenty years and swapped out three very pricey gold spheres for cheap steel ones," said Cici.

"Well," started Mason, "I think someone intercepted the box over the last 18 months and swapped out three very pricey gold spheres for cheap steel ones."

"Cute," smiled Cici. "Did Drusilla have any ideas about the threatening letters in the TIC file?" she asked.

"No. She pointed out that threatening letters sent to Tank weren't out of the ordinary, but she suggested we connect with Tank's former executive assistant, Norah Tripplehorn. Norah might have read them and could know who sent them. After all, she worked for Tank for 55 years."

"Were you able to find Joyce Redstone?" asked Skye.

"She's vanished! I called the number she left with Cici, but it was disconnected. The email address she provided bounced back, and I went to the only address of a Joyce Redstone I could find online, and it was a condemned building. I've sent online friend requests to a few people I think could be related to her, but no acceptances as yet."

"I wouldn't accept your friendship either," laughed Skye.

"Too late!" replied Mason.

"Could Joyce Redstone have been a fake name? What was the name of her mother again?"

Mason pulled out his notes to remind himself.

"I don't have a name for her mother, only her grandmother, Lady Rosamond Farnsworth-Ford. Maybe I can pull up a family tree on Ancestry?"

Skye's head jolted, "Wait—we've seen that name recently, eh?" she thought aloud.

Cici sat up straight in her chair, her file from the courthouse still resting on her lap.

"Yes. Yes, you're right. It was in one of the boxes Mrs. Stone brought over."

"A letter?" asked Mason.

"No, it was something else..."

"We sorted the boxes. If it wasn't a letter or a diary, it would be in box one. I'll look," said Skye.

Mason's eyes shot to the envelope in his cousin's lap.

"What's that?" he asked.

"I picked it up two days ago—I think it could be the big news of the day," Cici announced, opening the envelope and throwing the contents—a multi-page stapled document, onto Mason's desk.

"And here I thought the big news of the day was going to be Roland's raid on 'Fort Clifton,' and my learning nothing can actually get lost inside a vagina which I think is most reassuring," said Mason nonchalantly as he flipped the papers over to read the heading on the first page.

"Oh, yay! I can't wait for all the wonderful facts you're going to share with us about the vagina over the coming days. What a great idea it was for Drusilla to drag you to The Eye of the Vulva exhibit," Cici said in a sarcastic, childlike tone, ending with an eye roll.

"It also self-clea..."

"Stop!" Cici shouted, "And just read the God damn papers."

Mason brought his focus back to the document in front of him—his mouth slacked open once he realized what it was.

"The petition for probate? How the hell did you get this!?"

"A friend owed me a favor."

"Any highlights to share?" asked Mason.

"Skip to the last page."

Mason did so. He stared at the page in silence, seeing dollar values associated with his late grandfather's estate and working to understand their relevance by reading the definitions provided. Skye, who was still looking through the boxes for the Farnsworth reference, stopped rummaging to see what the silence was about.

"So, his personal property, which is defined as cash and investments, is valued at just $1,207,202!" Mason exclaimed in disbelief. "That can't be right. He was spending like a drunken sailor in his final years, but knowing what he inherited from Granny V alone, I can't believe he only had $1.2 million left."

"Keep reading," encouraged Cici.

After staring at the financial figures for a few moments, Mason looked up.

"The real estate value has to be wrong as well. His only personal holding was his house, and it is not worth $14,892,920. The last time I checked houses in his area, a comparable was $5.1 million. They've inflated the value of the house by nine million dollars?" asked Mason.

"Read the next box," nodded Cici.

"Real estate, net of encumbrances $2,816,012. What does that mean?"

"It's a mortgage."

Mason pushed the papers away.

"There's no way he had a mortgage on his home. He lived there for forty years and bought it dirt cheap. It doesn't make any sense!" exclaimed Mason.

"No, it doesn't make sense, Mason. Think about it: Uncle Tank had $1.2 million in cash, which is less than we all thought. That wouldn't be enough for Aida to live on, and the $2.8 million dollar mortgage now has to be repaid because he's dead. However, the $14.8 million dollar property is noted as 'passes by survivorship' to the next of kin, who is Aida. So that $14.8 million is clear sailing to her plus the $1.2 million in cash. I suspect he took out a mortgage against his house to help his cash flow in his final years."

"If that's the case, then where did his money go? Unless he bought the $14 million dollar property using his nest egg, which depleted his cash."

"It's not Highclere, is it? The mystery holding?" wondered Cordelia, though they all knew the answer.

"No. Highclere is in a trust, the same trust it's been in since 1993."

With Miles "The Tank" Valentine, you could never be too sure.

"You guys didn't see anything in the boxes about property purchases?" asked Mason.

"I didn't," Cici answered. "Skye?"

"Nope. It could be in his diaries, though. We left those for you," she responded.

"It's going to be a needle in a haystack," advised Cici while fiddling with her wedding ring.

"I guess we can assume that it's the $14 million dollar property they're hiding in the will," Mason suggested, speaking his thoughts, "and when you add in the house, Aida walks away with just over a $20 million dollar inheritance," he marveled with a weak whistle.

"Do you think they're worried you might contest the will because his estate is worth more than you thought?" asked Skye.

"Maybe," said Mason, "but more likely, there's something sketchy about the $14 million dollar property outside its value. Something more secretive."

"Something worth killing over?" tossed Cici, referencing their conversation from Labor Day about the illogical way the Senator died.

"Short of the TIC file and the online conspiracies being spread by the 'Leader of The Tanks,' we have no real reason to assume Tank was killed," reminded Mason.

"Except the crazy ass way he died," smiled Cordelia.

"Until someone can explain to me how the night of his fall could be so perfectly engineered—including the weather—I'm not putting my head into that space. I'm willing to—but not yet."

"Found it!" Skye shouted making both Mason and Cici jump in their seats. "Oh, sorry!" Skye said, covering her mouth while chuckling. "I knew I'd seen it. Here it is! Three cashed checks were written out to Farnsworth Marble & Designs. One dated 1983, another dated 1993, and the third dated 2002. Nothing was written in the memos on either 1983 or 1993 checks, but the 2002 says '*measures $2 + 1.5 + .75 / 2 \times 6 = (12)$ & $4 \times S + B$.*'" Skye stacked the three checks in sequence and handed them to Mason before adding, "They're all signed by Lady Jean Fernsby-Valentine."

Mason checked the signature on each check for authenticity, "That's her alright," he confirmed.

"One more thing," teased Cici, leaning back in her seat. "I'm not the only person to request Uncle Tank's petition for probate in the last week," she paused for dramatic effect.

Mason looked to Skye and then back to Cici. "Who?" he asked.

Chapter Seventeen

Mason could hear the blasted clock on his desk ticking away the seconds as he sat nervously looking at his computer. He had just logged into a group FaceTime call with his father, Uncle Stuart, Aunt Joss, and Roland Mast, who was giving a live view of all he was seeing.

"You can hear me, ok?" asked Roland, practically holding the phone in his mouth.

"Yes, we can, but we don't need to see your tonsils, Rolly. Pull it out," said Stuart.

"Pull it out? Already?" came a joking voice from behind Stuart.

His husband, Guillaume "Gil" Regan, stepped into view, creepily appearing and disappearing into Stuart's digital backdrop of leopard prints and rainbows.

"Don't be crass, Gil!" shouted Joss.

"Christ—Aunt Joss, don't yell! We can hear you just fine," snapped Mason.

"You're just jealous because Gil has said the gayest thing on this call so far," replied Joss.

"Julie Andrews, Ruby Slippers, 'Somewhere Over the Rainbow,' Ru Paul, Karen Walker, AbFab, Size Queen, Astro Glide, 'Spice Up Your Life,' Grindr, colonic, and 'Turn Back Time,'" Mason rattled off in one breath. "There, I win, Aunt Joss. Gil loses. Can we now focus on what's going on?"

"I'm interested to know what colonics have to do with grinding pepper, but I'll save that for cocktail hour at Highclere," voiced Roland.

"Roland, walk us through this," asked Lawrence, choosing to ignore the previous exchange.

"Right, ok. Here I am with my boys in blue."

Roland flipped the camera around to show six police officers walking through brass gates of the waterfront community where Miles Valentine had lived for forty years. Roland's wide, bleach-white teeth were highly visible in the setting sun as he swung the camera back to himself.

"I love this shit! Very Justice League!"

"Roland!" shouted Stuart.

"Sorry. As you all know, we sent a note two days ago to Mega Rip-off and her daughter Manerva Joyride," Roland smirked at his long-standing nicknames for Aida and Laverna, "saying that pursuant to the 'Last Will and Testament' of the Honorable Lady Jean Fernsby-Valentine, 18 items including jewelry, heirlooms, and art had been held in trust by Tank Valentine after her death. Those items, however, were properly willed to specific family members in her estate documents. Therefore, the 'Rip-offs'...I mean, Cliftons...had 48 hours to collect and return the items to my office, or we'd have to report them as being stolen. Not a word was heard from them, so here we are! They are officially considered stolen property, and 'Big Louis' here has a wonderful warrant to enter the home and retrieve the property. Which we are about to do."

With that, Roland went quiet and turned the camera back to the police officers, who switched on their body cameras. Big Louis rang the bell, and seconds later, a very nervous-looking Aida Clifton-Valentine answered the door.

* * *

"How the hell did this happen?" demanded Lawrence Valentine ninety minutes later to Roland Mast. "None of it's there?"

"Not one item on the list," said an exasperated and disappointed Roland. "Everything is gone, and they claim not to know where any of it is."

"They must have gotten rid of it in the last 24 hours," said Jocelyn. "Did you send them the itemized list?"

"Of course, we sent the list, Joss! These grifters are cleverer than we thought. Move quickly as well."

"How could they have gotten everything out of the house in 24 or 48 hours?" asked Lawrence.

"What if the items no longer exist? What if Tank got rid of them years ago?" asked Stuart's husband Guillaume, his black bald head and left hand poking out of a leopard spot. "Same with the missing bits and bobs from the carriage house? He sold them?"

"I'm going to ask the neighbors for their camera footage. There are also security drones flying around here. I can make a few calls," answered Roland.

"Roland, when you ask for the security footage, request the dates around the time Tank fell," suggested Mason.

Everyone stopped talking and looked at him for more information.

"There's too much detail to go into, but the basement and some rooms on the main floor of their house flooded months before Tank fell. When renovations were about to get underway, Laverna, Bianca, and I think you too, Stuart...?" Mason asked mid-thought but didn't stop for an answer, though his uncle nodded to confirm his participation, "...moved most of the items affected by the flood, and I suspect items of value, to Louella Stone's house before the repairs."

"You think it's all at Louella's house?" asked Roland.

"Not at all. Louella came to see me after Labor Day and told me that after Tank fell, Aida and Laverna demanded all the items Louella had been storing be returned immediately. He wasn't dead yet, still in hospital. Louella tried to stall them, which she was able to, and made an inventory of the items she had in her possession. She kept four boxes from the Cliftons, which she felt should go to the family, so I have them. Cici and my colleague Skye have taken a cursory look through them, and there *are* a few things of interest, but nothing that Aida would notice was missing.

"I also have the inventory list that Louella put together, and from what I can tell, none of Granny V's belongings were moved to Louella's house. However, there was something or things that Aida and Laverna needed back ASAP, and they needed it back before Tank died. If they were moving furniture and large-scale items back into the house before he died, there is no reason to assume anyone would've thought it unusual if they were moving other items out. That's why I'd check security from those dates. I'll quickly add that although I haven't been able to confirm it, I might have an idea why they wanted the boxes back."

"Jesus Mason! You're practically Perry Mason at this point!" said Roland.

"Cici got the petition for probate for Tank's estate. He had a little over a million dollars left in cash and investments, which is much lower than any of us thought. But even more surprising, he died with a more than two-million-dollar mortgage or reverse mortgage and another estate worth over fourteen million dollars," Mason let that sink in.

"Where the hell is the fourteen-million-dollar mystery property, and why didn't we know about it?" asked Lawrence.

"Manipulative, sneaky fuck that Tank was, eh? How'd he lose his money and when?" added Roland.

Everyone waited for Stuart to chime in, but he sat silent, staring into the distance.

"Cici is going to check land registries under Tank's name, company names, and Aida's name to see what's in official files."

"Anything else?" asked Lawrence.

"Cici and I think that someone intercepted Joyce Redstone and took what we suspect were three additional solid gold spheres and replaced them with silver junk."

"I had the same thought," Lawrence agreed.

"Last thing, Cici isn't the only person to request access to Tank's petition for probate. Trent Callahan did as well. He also asked for a copy of his death certificate," Mason concluded.

"Why?" asked Joss.

"To confirm his enemy finally snuffed it?" suggested Roland with a snort.

"He came to the burial. I think he's working toward his long-time mission to push us out of Highclere and buy it," suggested Lawrence.

"Trent would know we aren't selling. Maybe he's looking for whatever the Clifton's are hiding? Of course, why would he care?" said Mason.

"Why did Callahan have a hate on for old Tank?" asked Roland.

"Don't know," admitted Lawrence before the song "Bat Out of Hell" blared through Roland's phone.

"We will figure this out. Cici and I are on it. Whatever the Cliftons are hiding, wherever this property is, whatever they were looking for at Louella's, whoever intercepted Joyce Redstone and Trent's nosing around will all be figured out. I'll send an update when I know more."

The call ended with each participant clicking out of the group. Mason turned off his screen just as his phone buzzed.

Hello darling! Apologies for the late hour of this message, though heaven knows it's later for me than you, but we've been rather busy with work at the preservation society. C'est ça as we say! Stellan asked me to let you know your DNA did NOT match with the dead man. They were, however, able to isolate a titch of DNA from the cufflinks themselves and have matched it to a family name in their database. Frustratingly, the dead man's DNA also doesn't match the sample from the cufflinks. I will keep you updated! With Love—Margot.

Curiosity piqued, Mason wrote back:

Margot—Can you tell me what name matched with the DNA? Xx

Mason stood and started pacing his office, waiting for her reply. He knew she'd have to ask Stellan, and there was no guarantee the commissioner would be awake or willing to share information about an ongoing investigation. How were all these events connected, or were they? The dead man and his Fernsby cufflinks—both with identical patterns of sixteen gemstones. The missing gold spheres. The property that no one in the family knew about. Lady Valentine's heirlooms are all missing. Aida Clifton wanting all of Tank's things returned before he died. Trent Callahan acting strangely—heck, even Uncle Stuart seemed cagey on the call. Joyce Redstone vanishing—if she ever existed at all—the menacing message on Fernsby letter...*Fernsby House*...Mason stopped.

"Oh shit."

Mason ran back to his phone. He had no response from Margot but sent a new question. He sat down, waiting, *willing* his friend to still be awake. To give him the answer that could help connect the dots. Biting his thumbnail, his right leg became restless. He sat up straight when he heard the ping on his phone. It was the answer to his second question.

£8.8 million. Waiting for S to give me all clear to share the DNA name. Hang tight xx.

Mason pulled up a currency converter, typed in eight point eight million British Pounds, and pressed enter.

"$14,362,891 Canadian dollars," Mason said out loud, alone in his office.

He threw his phone onto his desk and leaned his head back, rubbing his temples in disbelief.

"Fuck. Fuck. Fuck!" Picking up his phone again, he was about to text Cici when Margot's name slid atop his screen. He swiped up.

The DNA matched a Farnsworth. Mean anything to you? Xx

* * *

Cordelia Bradshaw sat in bed attempting to read, but her mind was running through the implications of her Uncle Tank's mortgage and pricey mystery property.

"You haven't turned the page in almost an hour," observed her husband, Tobias Neuman, who too was sitting in bed attempting to read. "What's on your mind?" he asked.

As Cici opened her mouth to share with her husband the details of the petition for probate, her phone made the distinctive chime associated with a message from her cousin Mason. She picked up the phone and covered her mouth in shock.

Granny V's "things" are all missing from Aida's house. Police and Rolly couldn't find them. Also, the dead man had Farnsworth DNA on cufflinks. However, his DNA didn't match Farnsworth either. We have got to find Joyce Redstone! She is a Farnsworth, after all!!

PS—Worst of all—I think Aida Clifton inherited Fernsby House #FFS

* * *

Stuart Valentine closed his laptop and laid his head on the cool gray surface of the machine. His mind was going a mile a minute. The walls were closing in. Should he say something? Could he mitigate the damage if he'd just told his family what had happened? Save them the energy of having to exhaust an investigation to find only a few answers. With Cici on the case, it was bound to come out. He sat back up fixing his stare out his living room window.

"You ok?" asked Guillaume, who placed his hands on his husband's shoulders. Recoiling at his husband's touch, Stuart picked up his phone and went to his bedroom without saying a word.

* * *

Makayla Dawn had finished checking each building at Highclere to ensure all the windows were closed ahead of the looming storm. Her phone vibrated in her hand as she switched off the outside light of the main inn. She looked down and read the message.

They're becoming a bit more ruthless than I had expected. Is the security drive destroyed? Please confirm.

Makayla wrote back a one-word answer.

Yes

Her phone vibrated again with a new message.

I don't believe you. You know I'll find out if you didn't.

Growing nervous and exasperated by this arrangement, Makayla tried to end the conversation. She'd done what she said she would do—months of work completed. As far as she was concerned, the deal was no longer valid. She wrote back.

I did it all without complaint. You promised me that would be all I would be asked to do. You promised. Please stop texting me.

Makayla knew she'd just poked the bear. But enough was enough. She couldn't keep up the act. She wanted it all to stop. She wanted to move past her one stupid decision in life and forge a path ahead. But her SMS tormenter wasn't having it. As she started to walk the footpath back to her home, her cell phone rang. She looked at the caller ID and considered not answering it, but she knew the calls would keep coming or worse. Angry and tired, she slid her thumb across the screen and raised the phone to her ear. Her voice was hoarse and warbly, and for a second, she thought she wasn't brave enough to say it, but she did.

"Stop fucking calling me. Stop texting me. Stop targeting me and manipulating me. Stop all the shit you've been doing. I've had enough. You got what you wanted. I agreed not to say anything, but if you keep calling, I may go back on that agreement, and I don't give two shits if I go down with you. I'm OUT!" Makayla was all but yelling by the time she hung up.

She took a deep breath to calm her nerves. She was proud that she had spoken her mind and prayed she'd been heard. Seconds later, a familiar voice broke the silence of the night air.

"Mack? Who were you talking to? Who is manipulating you?" Ahren asked.

Makayla turned and looked Ahren in the eyes. Unable to speak, and tears blinding her vision, she collapsed into his arms, with only the words, "Grandpa...I screwed up," whispered from her trembling mouth.

Chapter Eighteen

To: Louise Harris, KC
From: Laverna Clifton-Lehrman
Date: September 30, 2024
CC: Aida Valentine; Bianca Anders; Clifton Family-ALL

Louise,
Pull the trigger. But do it over Thanksgiving while they're at Highclere.
Laverna

Chapter Nineteen

"And a ONE and a TWO and—ok, Mom, press PLAY!" Mason shouted to his mother, Piper, as his four nieces and nephews stood on both sides of him.

Each had a stand with a plastic old-school broadcast microphone attached to the top. Mason grinned, and the kids giggled once the opening bars of the Spice Girls' song "Stop" blasted through the living room speakers with all its campy, 90s-trumpeting fabulousness for all to hear.

"Ok, kids, remember the choreo. Start by swaying and snapping. Here comes Ginger Spice," instructed their Uncle Mason before mouthing along with the lyrics while rocking a slightly undersized—though beautifully bedazzled—Union Jack hoodie.

"Good swaying kids. Now, step forward and back as Sporty jumps in. Remember, we're taking an inch then running a mile!" he shouted, paraphrasing the verse to prompt their moves. "Alright, grab your microphone stands, and after each line, we'll lean with it. Lean right," he instructed at Posh Spice's line. "Now to the left! Back to the right! Final left! Ok, here we go! Mics in the middle, hands at the ready to stop right now..."

Mason continued singing, shouting instructions, and miming the moves while the song played. He was proud of how well they'd remembered everything. They danced, mimed, and shook through each line of the song.

When the song ended with each kid in a classic Spice Girls pose, complete with a peace sign, Mason ejected confetti from small air poppers he'd bought online.

"AND SCENE!" yelled Mason as a round of enthusiastic applause and even a standing ovation greeted the end of their routine.

"HAPPY THANKSGIVING!" shouted the children in unison while popping more confetti, which landed everywhere in Athabasca Cottage's spacious, sun-drenched, double-floored living room.

"Happy Thanksgiving," responded their audience, comprising Mason's siblings, their spouses, his parents Lawrence and Piper, his uncles Stuart and Gil, Louella Stone, Cordelia, and Tobias, along with their children.

While Highclere Inn & Carriage House always found a time of day or year when its rustic bristle and dilapidated buildings looked beautiful regardless of their condition, it was the autumn afternoon sunlight and technicolor trees of Canadian Thanksgiving that gave the entire property a golden glow of unmitigated beauty.

* * *

Earlier in the day—and inspired by the latest episode of *Only Murders in the Building*—Mason and Cici converted the office of the original inn into a make-shift investigative headquarters. To keep their vibe from the days when Highclere was operational, they repaired the famed corduroy chair (once confident it was free of all mice and potential vermin, an exercise that was apparently so hilarious Tobias thought it should've been recorded for TikTok), so they could sit and think, pass around ideas and research in a setting that brought them joy and comfort.

While Margot Ambrosia was skeptical of Mason's theory that Aida had inherited Fernsby House, she offered to confirm the owner's details ASAP to be sure. Cici also recruited a student interested in extra credit to help search property listing databases for connections to Miles Valentine—the results had so far produced nothing.

Replete with corkboard, an old-fashioned whiteboard, and monitors, Mason and Cici tacked copies (the originals were elsewhere for safety) of the three checks made out to Farnsworth Marble & Designs, all signed by Lady Valentine, as well as the menacing note on Fernsby House letterhead found at the carriage house. Copies of the intentionally censored threatening letters from the TIC file and printed photographs of the gold box, gold and silver spheres, velvet inlay, and steel underside. The petition for probate, a list of vanished heirlooms once belonging to Lady Valentine, and a large satellite map of Fernsby House, which was now potentially Aida Clifton's new home. The cousins hoped to discern how the dead man apparated onto the property undetected. Photos of the dead man's cufflinks were also pinned to the board, each cuff engraved with the Fernsby family crest on one side and a pattern of sixteen gemstones—consisting of seven micro-cut sapphires and nine small white diamonds—on the reverse, along with a drop of almost invisible Farnsworth DNA.

After hours of searching soul-sucking social media posts, Cici found an image from Tank's funeral featuring Joyce Redstone, a Farnsworth descendant, and the vessel entrusted to complete Lady Valentine's posthumous request. Cici enhanced Joyce's face but couldn't get a crisp enough angle to run through online facial recognition databases.

Pleased with their setup, the cousins armed their new investigative headquarters and returned to Athabasca Cottage in time for cocktails and the annual song and dance performance.

* * *

As cocktails ended, the sound of a car horn could be heard in the distance.

Walking toward the door of the wraparound deck, Mason turned to look at Oliver. "Do you hear that?" he asked.

"It sounds like it's coming from the inn," Ollie replied while trying to peer through the trees toward the main inn.

Confused, Lawrence, Mason, Stuart, and Cici grabbed their coats and walked over the white footbridges to the sandy beach, where they saw a black SUV parked at the bottom of the roundabout.

A gaunt-looking man, dressed in a full suit with tie and dark overcoat, stood outside the passenger door campily waving as the Valentines came into view. He grinned broadly, accentuating his sunken, pale cheekbones. He tilted his face toward the honey-hued autumn sky, taking a theatrical, long breath of fresh air while rubbing his hands together. It was clear he wanted the Valentines to see him looking carefree and unbothered.

"Hello, hello! Happy Thanksgiving!" the man cheerily greeted the Valentines as he opened the SUV's back door and pulled out a large sign with a wood stake attached to it. "What a stunning evening! Picture perfect—and what a beautiful piece of paradise you have here," he added, his smile remaining in place, looking like Jack Nicholson's version of the Joker.

"I'm sorry, who are you?" asked Lawrence as they approached.

Mason could tell the man was enjoying the invasion and the troubled look on the family's faces.

"And you are?" the man inquired.

"I'm Lawrence Valentine. I'm one of the owners of this property," he answered.

"Delighted to meet you," he responded. "My name is Charlton Matthews of Matthews, Harris, and Fields, a law firm in Toronto. The Honorable Miles Valentine was once a client, so I'm sure you're acquainted with us."

Before Charlton received a reply from Lawrence or anyone else, he pulled a hammer out of his briefcase and pounded the wooden sign into the soil with a rehearsed blast of theatricality.

"I apologize sincerely for surprising you, but I won't be long," he added.

After four flourished hits to the top of the wood stake, he handed Lawrence a letter-sized envelope.

"You'll find the terms all quite reasonable if not generous. Per your father's explicit, and if I may add extremely kind instructions, you have until the Victoria

Day long weekend of May 2024 to vacate the premises," Charlton said while swiveling the front of the sign to face them.

"For Sale!" an enraged Mason read out.

"I'm not sure what makes you think Highclere Inn & Carriage House is for sale, but let me assure you—it is not. My father did not own the property personally. It is held in a long-standing family trust. I'd have assumed Louise Harris would've explained that before sending you on this errand. In fact, I know she'd have told you."

"It does appear as though your information is embarrassingly outdated," Charlton replied, once again smiling with white menace. It was all Mason could do not to grab the hammer and knock the man's teeth out. "You are correct. This property was held in a trust. However, it was a revocable trust, and Senator Valentine revoked it some years ago. If you turn to page three of the package I just gave you, you'll see his signature and date. Aida Clifton-Valentine now owns this property, and as she said to me personally, she has her 'memories' from Highclere to keep her warm at night and returning wouldn't be the same without her beloved husband. Therefore, she's instructed us to prepare the property for listing."

Besides being a dick, the man was a hack. He couldn't keep his story straight, conflating the decisions of Tank and Aida within successive statements.

"That is impossible," a calm Lawrence said. "He could not change the trust without our approvals, and it was not his to revoke."

"Again, Mr. Valentine, I am afraid you are incorrect. As you may recall, the original trust, signed in December 1993, maintained that upon the death of a trustee or beneficiary, their claim of ownership would be transferred to their spouse. As I understand it, when the Senator announced his intentions to remarry, you decided that Mrs. Aida Valentine and her children should not inherit and, therefore, blackmailed your father into changing the conditions of the trust to allow for the property to be passed down to legitimate issue—adopted or otherwise—of a beneficiary rather than the deceased's spouse. The amended trust was signed in 2005, I believe?" Charlton Matthews smiled, swaying back and forth on his heels, enjoying the drawn-out emotional punch he was delivering.

"That's correct," Lawrence agreed.

"Well," Charlton began, flicking imagined dust from his lapel, "the 1993 trust had a clause permitting the settler to revoke it at any time—a clause that transferred to the 2005 trust agreement. The settler revoked it in witnessed instructions in 2012."

"Miles Valentine wasn't the settler of the trust. His father Hollis Valentine was," pointed out Lawrence.

"Unfortunately, as you've just discovered, that's legally not the case," said Charlton Matthews, his smile having evaporated for the first time since his arrival. "I suppose some would consider this punishment for the ice-laced rollout you gave Mrs. Valentine when she married your father, but it's not my job to provide idle commentary."

"Funny, all you seem to be doing is providing idle commentary," Mason replied, his red cheeks beginning to burn.

"Please leave," said Lawrence with steel and ice in his veins. Charlton Matthews gave no further comment except to follow Lawrence's direction.

Charlton turned the "For Sale" sign to face the property's entrance before climbing back into his symbol of masculine overcompensation. He turned to the gathered family and once again flashed a smile across his face.

"May 24th, Valentines. Good luck getting packed."

Lawrence, Mason, Stuart, and Cici retraced their steps back to Athabasca, where Louella Stone and others could see the distress on their faces. Lawrence flipped through the documents provided to him by Aida's lawyer and could feel his jaw clench.

"What happened?" asked Louella.

"We've been sold out," replied Mason.

"By Aida?"

"By Tank."

"How so?" asked Louella.

"The real question should be, for how much," said Lawrence as Mason's phone buzzed.

Dear Mason—I have confirmed that a government holding company leased Fernsby House to the preservation society. The property wasn't and is not owned by an individual—so I'm distressed to burst your assumption, but the multimillion-dollar property you're looking for is not Fernsby. Love Margot.

"Of course, it's not," said Mason under his breath as his father handed him the papers from Charlton Matthews.

Mason glanced over the document; upon flipping to the last page, he saw the heading "VALUATION" in large bold letters, images of the property underneath, and a brief history. At the bottom of the cream page were the words "Determined Value: $14,892,920" and "List Price Recommendation (Per: Commercial Property): $17,800,000."

Found it.

* * *

With the turkey uneaten and the children put to bed, Mason and Cici went to the deck to collect the plates, glasses, and appetizers left behind. It was almost warm. The sky was without stars, and no wind was caressing the curvature of the house.

"What I don't understand is, if Uncle Tank revoked the trust in 2012, then why did his letter—dated 2018—say otherwise?" Cici whispered while stacking plates.

Mason nodded, "I dunno, Cici. He was a man of a thousand inconsistencies and wasn't exactly firing on all cylinders in his final decade."

"It's another contradiction to add to our growing list. Was there a specific reason for putting the property back into a trust in the early 1990s?" she asked.

"Drusilla and Stuart's respective health problems. Tank and Granny V were under pressure to safeguard everyone's interests in the property."

"I think I better get the handwriting of the 2018 letter checked for authenticity," Cordelia added.

"Why? What would that prove?"

"It could prove that they inherited Highclere through illegal means. If the Cliftons forged the letter, they might have also forged the revocation. We could get Highclere back."

"You honestly think Aida or Laverna have the metal to pull off this kind of fraud? Marrying for comfort is one thing. Criminal behavior is another."

"True, but their 'life after Uncle Tank' comfort level was becoming less certain the further his bank accounts fell," said Cici before adding, "It's crazy to think you added language in 2005 to ensure Aida couldn't inherit Highclere and of course, now she's gotten the whole kit and kaboodle because everyone misunderstood a line."

"You know, if Tank revoked the trust in 2012, maybe that's when he started to have financial trouble."

"Now, that's a good point! The plot thickens!" smiled Cici as she handed soiled napkins to her cousin.

"Why do you sound happy about that?" asked Mason.

"As they say, *'if there is a question, then there is an answer. If there's no answer, then the question would never exist!'*" quoted Cici.

"That's a little 'chicken or the egg,' don't you think?"

"Maybe, but one day, someone will also discover the answer to that question!" Cici laughed as Gil, Stuart's husband, tip-toed out the sliding door to join his nephew and cousin-in-law.

"Psst. Can I borrow you both for a second?" Gil whispered.

Mason and Cici looked at each other before nodding in unison.

"If you had to guess, what's the most likely outcome of all the mysteries surrounding the family? I'm only asking because Stuart has been experiencing a lot of stress lately. I'm wondering if there is any real incentive to keep investigating or will his hopes be dashed?" he wondered.

Cici looked surprised.

"I'm sorry Stuart hasn't been doing well, but I'm not sure we can predict the outcome. It could swing anywhere from getting Highclere and Auntie V's things back to being shit out of luck. My gut says we need to keep going as long as it takes to get closure and answers," she replied.

"I understand," agreed Gil. "I think you should keep digging also. I just worry about Stuart's mental health. All I ask is that you're cautious about what you share with him and perhaps be willing to drop the whole thing if there isn't an obvious answer. Avoid the temptation to keep digging simply to find nothing there," he finished as Stuart banged on the glass window, signaling to Gil that they were leaving.

Mason was baffled.

"I mean, we want to be sensitive to everyone's feelings. As Cici just said to me, if there's a question, there has to be an answer—even if that answer is 'nothing.' We still need to look."

"I totally get that," agreed Gil as he walked toward the door, "but just think about it for me if you don't mind. 'Don't go chasing waterfalls,' as they say," he smiled. "Thanks both! Love you guys, and see you tomorrow," he added before closing the door behind him.

"That was odd," said Mason to Cici while watching Gil through the pane of glass.

"Beyond odd."

"I might stay up here for a few extra days. Just to keep watch," suggested Mason, still holding a stack of empty cups.

"Are you sure you're ok to be here alone?" asked Cici.

"I've spent many nights up here alone. I'll be just fine."

"You've spent many nights alone when things were normal. Or as normal as Highclere has ever been. What will you do if Aida's lawyer reappears?"

"Obfuscate?" Mason replied with a light laugh. "I don't know Cici. Probably let them in. We have the right to be here until the Victoria Day weekend in May, which they told us."

"Ok, but I'll come back on Thursday, and we'll keep knocking through all the questions until we have answers."

"Deal," agreed Mason. "Can you take this inside?" he asked, handing Cici a tower of cups. "I wouldn't mind a moment to myself."

Cordelia unburdened Mason of his glassware before disappearing inside Athabasca Cottage.

Mason sat on a blue Muskoka chair and tried to relax. His breathing fell in rhythm with the sounds of the small waves lapping against the shore.

Nature's melody had softened over the years. The chirping of birds, the scattering of deer, and the alto croak of frogs were no longer a part of Highclere's earthly tune. It became an environmental curiosity why, of the four Muskoka Lakes, Lake Belvedere's animal inhabitants had moved away. A migration that locals noticed after a seismic rainfall flooded a significant portion inland during the mid-2000s. The forest couldn't provide rapid enough absorption or drainage of the water overtaking the region, and many trees and animals were drowned. Those that survived either went away or suffered root rot, causing death. Many acres of Highclere's back 39 never recovered, and her musical tune was also forever altered.

After a few quiet minutes, Mason stood and walked toward the sliding doors to join the rest of his family.

Chapter Twenty

"It's nowhere! Stop looking! It's nowhere! Don't crank it—it's nowhere! Mason!" an aggressive female voice shouted in a siren pitch while the animatronic Labia Chorus of the United Kingdom sang a tinkling version of The Twelve Days of Christmas in the background.

Mason couldn't see who was yelling at him. What was nowhere? He could see in the dim light that he was wearing his favorite ugly Christmas sweater, yet the voice was in shadow. Darkness encroached on his surroundings. A black hole swallowed the siren's voice, the singing chorus, then...

BANG!

* * *

Mason's eyes flew open, his heart racing. Sweat poured from him, soaking his sheets. What time was it? He rolled over to see it was 10:22 am.

He'd been having the weirdest dreams since Labor Day about his grandmother, shrieking voices, gold music boxes, and the Twelve Days of Christmas.

Wiping the sweat off his chest, he heard a horn honking outside. Worried Aida's lawyers had already returned, he threw on his crimson monogrammed robe, a hat, and a pair of black Crocs and went to investigate. He followed the horn across the footbridges, up from the beach to the circular loop in front of the inn.

"You're alive!" shouted Skye Cadieux as Mason came into view.

"Skye!" Mason sighed with relief. "What are you doing here?" he asked as he approached her.

"Cordelia called and told me what happened. She didn't like the idea of you being up here alone, so I told her I'd stay with you until she returns on Thursday. And..." Skye paused as she walked to the trunk of her car before contorting herself into a hilarious Madonna "Vogue" pose. "...I brought some reading material from the archives of Louella Stone!"

Upon peering into the hold of her sedan, Mason saw the four banker's boxes Louella brought to his office.

"You think the answers we're looking for are in those boxes?" asked Mason.

"'If there is a question, there has to be an answer…'" Skye began before Mason cut her off.

"Yea, yea. I've heard that line already. Ok, let me put some clothes on, and I'll meet you back here in a few minutes."

"What's wrong with what you're wearing?" asked Skye.

"I sleep naked," said Mason, pointing to his bare legs beneath his robe.

* * *

"Please submit your papers online no later than 11:59 pm on Friday, or it will be considered incomplete. If you don't include your reference material and sources, the assignment will also be considered incomplete with a grade of zero," barked Cici to her students as they hustled to close their computers and exit the theater-style lecture hall at the University of Toronto.

Cici struggled to focus during her lecture. She was eager to check her phone as often as possible for updates from Mason or Skye but withheld the urge using immense willpower. As the last of her students exited through the light wooden doors of the room, she opened her computer and pulled her phone out of her bag.

One missed text message. Cici swiped up to read it.

Hi Cordelia, I wanted to check in as I didn't hear from you after Labor Day. I hope you had a wonderful Thanksgiving. I'd still very much love to get together and talk about what happened at Highclere at the end of the summer. I'm sure you've also heard the other news about the decision Uncle Tank made re: Highclere's future. I don't want any of this to hurt our friendship, and I'd appreciate the opportunity to get together and talk. Please let me know. Love Laverna.

"Is she clueless or trying to manipulate me?" mumbled Cici to herself.

"Pardon?" said a meek voice coming from behind her.

Cici swung her chair to find Marko, the student who volunteered to help research Tank's mystery property before the proverbial shoe dropped over the weekend.

"Sorry, Marko. I was talking to myself. Strong habit in my family…history of insanity," Cici semi-joked. "What's up?"

"Most of my family was away over Thanksgiving, so it gave me time to continue my records search…"

"Oh, Marko," Cici cut him off. "That was extremely kind of you, but we found out what the property is. I'm so sorry you wasted your long weekend on this!" said Cici, touched.

"It's quite alright, Ms. Bradshaw. Can I ask, was it Highclere Inn & Carriage House on Lake Belvedere in Muskoka?"

Marko, who was no older than eighteen, wore a black-and-white striped sweatshirt with skinny jeans and glasses akin to Harry Potter. His tan complexion defused his acne, and his eyes were kind, emitting wisdom unusual in someone so young. Cici had liked him instantly.

"Unfortunately, yes. The property in question is Highclere Inn & Carriage House. My family hadn't thought it possible, but in hindsight, we were probably naïve—if not in complete denial about the possibility."

"In that case, Ms. Bradshaw. I think there is something I better show you."

* * *

"As they say, *'if you want my body and you think I'm sexy,'*" sang Mason as he jetéd into the office of the inn-come-investigative headquarters.

Skye had taped enhanced copies of interior carriage house photos provided by Drusilla to the evidence boards. As Mason sang the tune, Skye pushed out her booty and shook her tush to the beat. She turned around and saw her friend dressed in the most out-of-character "farmer chic" attire she'd ever seen. A red plaid button-up shirt over a white tee matched with dark bleach-stained sweatpants, Timberland boots, and a hat.

"If you're looking for a back-ho or tractor, I think you've entered the wrong building," laughed Skye.

"Not really. The place looks like a barn, and in fact, was one. However, sadly, my clothing options are rather limited. I hadn't planned on staying longer than the weekend, and the clothes I brought are in the wash. When I tried to fit into an older sweatshirt, it was a bit snug and gave the illusion of 'bat nipples,' so I raided my dad's closet instead."

"Bat-nipples...?" Skye repeated—confused.

"Yes. Bat-nipples. You know, the nipples on the bat suit from *Batman Forever* and *Batman & Robin*. You're staring at me blankly. Why are you blinking so much? Skye—have you never seen those movies or heard of the controversy about the suits?"

Skye's expression continued to be perplexed.

"Forget it. Someone will hear that comparison and find great humor in it!"

"You say that, but sometimes your references are so obscure I have to quietly ask Siri for explanations."

Mason, taking on a jokingly condescending tone, put his hand on his friend's shoulder and said, "I do often forget that you were well into your senior citizen years by the time I was born and, therefore, likely missed all the vital pop-culture moments of my youth since you spent most of those years gluing your dentures in."

"And now the only thing that pops out of me is dust from every orifice."

"Ew, gross!"

"Wait until you turn 50, and one of your nieces and nephews makes the same jokes to you!"

"I will welcome it with the same great humor and dignity displayed by you, my friend," smiled Mason with a wink.

"Let's get to work!" clapped Skye, her braided tail of purple hair bouncing as she plopped onto the corduroy chair while Mason sat at the desk to continue his Google search from the night before.

"Can you write the year on each enlargement of the carriage house interior photos Aunt Drew gave me? It might help me correlate the photos with happenings amongst the family and diary dates."

"No problemo, boss!" answered Skye. "How's your online search for Farnsworth Marble & Designs?"

"According to Companies House in England, Farnsworth Marble & Designs was incorporated in 1886. It was a family business that ceased manufacturing in 1990. While marble was their original specialty, they added fine gold, stones, diamonds, jewelry, pearls, light fixtures, clocks, and 'special projects' in 1910.

"Here's the weird thing—this filing says that the company didn't manufacture products after 1990 but remained incorporated until 2015, when it was closed and rolled into a holding company. I can't tell if it was sold to someone outside the family or if the holding company is owned by a Farnsworth. The directors are redacted, and numbers aren't my thing. Still, their filings show that the company's revenue was mostly through investments during the twenty-five years between ceasing operations and shutting down, which begs the question: what were Gran's 1993 and 2002 checks for if they weren't manufacturing products?" Mason wondered.

"When you say manufacture, do you mean they had a factory of employees? Mass production?" asked Skye.

"No, I don't think so. From what I can tell on auction sites, most pieces are one of a kind. Costly one-of-a-kind items at that—designed with intention. Think about the cufflinks, for example, the sixteen blue and white gemstones seem to be in a pattern of significance—I just don't know what that is," said Mason before he clicked on another website.

"'*The key to the success of the Farnsworth family's operation has been because of the inherited craftsmanship and skills of successive generations. Items were rarely outsourced, and only in a handful of situations were outside contractors hired to complete projects. Lady Rosamond Farnsworth-Ford noted that every legitimate Farnsworth product contains proof of authenticity.*'" Mason read aloud.

"So, if it's a generational skill set, then it would make sense that the Farnsworth family made the gold box, gold sphere, and cufflinks over decades. How do we prove it? What if the cufflinks and gold sphere are forgeries?" queried Skye.

"That's a good question. I inherited a china set from my other grandparents, Piper's mom and dad, and the set's era is noted with a symbol. I wonder if the Farnsworth family did something similar to their pieces. Perhaps that's the proof of authenticity Rosamond Farnsworth-Ford was referring to."

"It would be noticeable, though, wouldn't it? After all, there weren't lasers back then."

"True. There seems to be a Farnsworth enthusiast in London who specializes in authentication and resale of Farnsworth designs. I'll send her a note to see if she's willing to speak with me and share where the…I guess…'signature,' for lack of a better word, can be found and examples of it."

Mason spent a few moments typing out a quick email to jewelry expert Andrea Romero, an authority on Farnsworth products, then tapped out a quick note to Baroness Margot Ambrosia asking if Stellan or his team noticed anything minuscule embedded in the dead man's cufflinks.

"What I'm finding frustrating is whether anything with the Farnsworth family is of any importance now that we know Highclere was given to Aida and is now for sale. I'm wondering if the gold box and spheres might have been a ploy to send us on a wild goose chase while Highclere was being snatched from under us?"

* * *

Marko opened his laptop, and after a few moments of clicking, he nodded to himself. He mirrored his computer screen using AirPlay so Cici could watch on the lecture hall's television.

"How did you know it was Highclere Inn & Carriage House?" Cici asked as the image stabilized on the TV.

"When you asked me to search properties either purchased, sold, or valued around the $14 million dollar price range, I was originally cross-referencing the names Miles Valentine, Jean Fernsby, Jean Fernsby-Valentine, Aida Clifton, and Aida Clifton-Valentine with property transactions and census data. Then it occurred to me that if Mr. Miles Valentine tried to hide a property from his family, he wouldn't do the transaction under his name…"

Cici nodded while keeping her eyes on the screen.

"…or the name of one of his children," Marko added. A comment that made Cici turn her head with muscle-pulling force.

"Using Mr. Valentine's obituary as a reference, I searched properties against the names of his grandchildren, great-grandchildren, in-laws, and so forth, and that's when I found it."

"Found what?" asked Cordelia.

Marko moved his cursor to the top of his browser and pasted a link into the address bar. No longer looking at the lecture hall's monitor, Cici moved to stand behind Marko; their intensity and anticipation were electrifying. The page was buried deep in an online archive, which slowed its loading. Moments later, a scanned PDF of a property listing appeared on the screen reading "Beautiful Family-Owned Muskoka Compound (49 Acres), Lake Belvedere—For Sale," priced at $14,900,000 and dated April 10th, 2013.

"He listed it ten years ago?" Cici whispered in disbelief.

"The listing was private, and the realtor was given instructions to pass it to prospective buyers in person rather than circulating the property on the usual real-estate websites," Marko added.

"How do you know?" asked Cici.

Marko scrolled down to the bottom of the multi-paged PDF and, using his mouse, highlighted "Terms and Conditions of Listing and Sale."

"Condition number two is about viewings being done when the family is off property, but condition three, I think, is the most interesting," said Marko, zooming in and highlighting the line in question.

"'*Buyer must agree that the current owner will maintain a lease on the property for uninhibited use during his lifetime. The rent will be calculated based on fair market pricing. The lease will terminate upon the current owner's death, and the remaining family members domiciled at the property will be given twelve months to vacate,*'" read Cici. "Jesus—Uncle Tank could be underhanded," she added.

"However, it obviously didn't sell Ms. Bradshaw," noted Marko

"Do you know why?" asked Cici.

"I do," Marko said with confidence.

Cici was sufficiently impressed with him.

"My boyfriend's dad is a realtor," said Marko, "and I asked him to run the listing number through software only realtors can access. He said that the listing was terminated due to, and I'm paraphrasing, 'inspectors and surveyors deeming the property to be listed significantly above value.' I can get you the proper wording," Marko added.

Cici was perplexed.

"I've spent my entire life visiting Highclere, and 49 or 50 acres of prime waterfront real estate in the Muskoka region—even on a lesser lake—would be worth more than $14 million dollars especially today."

Cici sat in the empty chair behind Marko and talked through her thoughts.

"Uncle Tank revoked the trust in 2012, per his lawyer. In 2013, he listed Highclere for sale, with what I'm sure most buyers would consider unrealistic conditions. He doesn't tell his family. However, that point becomes moot because it doesn't sell. It doesn't sell because it's determined that the listing is heavily inflated—which means a prospective buyer must have surveyed the property. But why did the surveyor deem Highclere worth less than $14 million? Why didn't he invoke the trust again?"

"I'm sorry, Ms. Bradshaw, I'm not following," Marko said, flushing slightly, thinking he should know what she was talking about.

"No, no—sorry. I'm trying to connect the dots out loud again. I'd do it if you were here or not..."

"Right! History of insanity," winked Marko.

Cici smiled. They sat in silence while she kept trying to wrap her head around Tank's logic in listing the property for sale at that time. What was the motivation? If real, why leave the 2018 letter if Highclere was part of his estate at that point? He must have needed the money as early as 2013 or 2012—the year of the revocation. With no sale and in need of cash, then it could explain the mortgage! Cici jumped up.

"Marko, you've done amazing work on this. I can't thank you enough," said Cici, throwing on her navy-blue trench coat and packing up—coming off frazzled. "If you can send a note to students canceling my lectures for the rest of the week, I'd appreciate it."

"Consider it done!" said Marko, smiling wide.

"Thanks, Marko!" shouted Cici, taking out her phone and using her back to open the exit door. She was already in the hall when something occurred to her. She put her foot between the door and the frame to prop it open. Shouldering her way back into the lecture hall, she asked a surprised Marko, "By the way, which of my uncle's family members was the name that linked you to the listing?"

Running to her car in disbelief at who Marko had just named, Cici threw her purse and laptop into the backseat and typed out a message to Mason before turning on the engine.

I'm coming back up NOW. Have news that I can't type. Needs to be in person. Meet you at the inn. X

Chapter Twenty-One

Mason watched Cordelia park beneath an ancient birch tree. With swift purpose, she retrieved a large black plastic bin from the trunk before making her way to the inn. Mason went to open the door for her.

"What's with the bin? You moving *INN*? Ha!" Mason fake laughed at his pun and smacked his knee. "I'm just *soooo* hilarious," he said facetiously, looking at his nails while Cici walked past him.

Placing the black bin on the floor, Cici turned to Mason and Skye, raised her right index finger to her lips, and indicated that they shouldn't say another word. She then motioned for them to sit, which they did.

Cici shimmied out of her blue trench coat then walked to the Wi-Fi router and unplugged it—surprising Mason with theatrics. She then went to the bin and pulled out what looked like a walkie-talkie but wasn't. She flicked a switch, which illuminated a red light before speaking.

"Look at your phones and tell me if you have a cell signal," Cici asked.

Mason and Skye did so.

"No, I've lost cellular," said Mason.

"Me too," said Skye.

"Good. This," she said, waving the device in her hand, "is a cell jammer. I went to my storage unit to pick up my investigation bin before driving up because I think we'll need it."

"I'm curious to know what you've learned that necessitates unleashing your inner Q," wondered Mason, referring to the James Bond character.

Cici took a deep breath.

"My student who was researching property transactions came to me this morning to say he found the property in question."

"He knew it was Highclere?" asked Mason.

"He did. When I asked him how he pulled up an archived PDF property listing from 2013."

Cici pulled the document from her bag. She handed it to Mason.

"Uncle Tank listed Highclere for sale ten years ago with bizarre conditions, including the Valentines having use of the property until Tank's death."

Mason was astonished.

"How did we not know this?" he whispered while glancing over the listing.

"He didn't want you to. It's clear in the conditions that the transaction was meant to be secret, including restrictions on when the property could be viewed."

"We wouldn't have had security installed at that point, meaning there could have been a hundred showings, and we'd be none the wiser. At least today, we'd have caught it on camera."

"Not necessarily," pointed out Skye. "Didn't you tell me that the system melted the night the Senator fell?"

"Good point," conceded Mason. "But the cameras being taken down because of a power outage is one thing—they have backup power and an independent server. The power surge melting the system—which it did—is another. It was a literal 'perfect storm.'"

"Unless it wasn't," said Cici, raising her eyebrows before lowering her voice to a whisper, "and this is why I'm blocking cell service. Remember my former colleague, Kate Sampson, who was assigned to investigate online chatter spearheaded by the 'Leader of The Tanks'? The Leader claimed to have 'intimate' knowledge of a conspiracy to assassinate Uncle Tank?"

Mason and Skye nodded.

"Kate dug into the possibility that Uncle Tank's fall into the electric fencing wasn't an accident. She spoke to Aida and Laverna, who became quite defensive at the suggestion that something sinister happened. Kate then spoke to Bianca, who was Uncle Tank's private nurse during his final months. She said that while in her heart she knows it was a tragic accident, she remains puzzled about how a power surge could produce enough voltage to electrocute a human. A surge occurring at the exact moment Tank's head hit the fence was almost implausible. The cameras frying might have been a one-in-a-million incident, but Uncle Tank falling into the fence right when the power surged would be one in a trillion."

"Right, but as I've said before, the police looked into that—they said it was old faulty wiring, and it didn't matter who or what connected with the fence. It was always going to violently surge because it was deficient," reminded Mason.

"By that logic, though, a leaf should've set fire once it touched the fence."

"How does this connect to the sale?" Skye asked.

"Essentially, Kate concluded, based on research and conversations with specialists, that there must have been foul play. She spoke to a forensic electrical engineer and tossed around ideas about how the fence would know to surge at a specific moment. They eventually landed on the most realistic scenario: the fence had to have been rigged with a pressure sensor that would activate a high-voltage power supply to electrify the fence at the perfect moment. Don't forget, hydro wasn't restored to the lake until several hours after Uncle Tank fell. The surge had to be manufactured."

"Fuck," said a dazed Mason. "That would explain why a leaf or light object wouldn't have fried. No pressure to activate it, but a human body would. Can she prove it?" he asked.

"No. She snuck up to the inn with the engineer, but no pressure sensor or remanence of rigging was found. The faulty wires have also been fixed. There isn't enough evidence to back her hypothesis, so the outlet dropped the story."

"If the fence was rigged to harm Tank, then the person who planned it would've had to be sure there'd be a power outage that would require Tank to go into the garden to turn on the carriage house generator," Mason nodded as he rubbed his temples.

"Exactly," confirmed Cici, "this was in the works long before the weekend he fell. How long is now the question."

"How would the Leader of The Tanks know this?" asked Skye.

"I doubt they do. The entire cult of Tank is based on conspiracies. It could've just been a wild guess," said Mason.

"Maybe. The online chatter doesn't say how Tank was assassinated, just that he was. They might have formed a theory around the fencing based on the obituary," added Cici.

"Who would know enough about the workings of the inn to install a sensor rigging without being noticed—not to mention engineer a power outage?" wondered Skye.

"That brings me to my next discovery," started Cici.

"Go on," Mason urged.

"When Marko, my student, found the 2013 listing for Highclere, he told me he came across it after searching the names of Uncle Tank's relatives. The words 'Highclere Inn & Carriage House' don't appear anywhere on the PDF, and neither does the name 'Valentine,' which is why it was easily buried online. Since it didn't sell, no legal paperwork was filed, again obscuring the fact it was ever listed."

"If our neighbor, Trent Callahan, knew Highclere was for sale, he'd have bought it in an instant regardless of the price," added Mason, "it should've been an easy sale."

"So then, why didn't it sell? The conditions? Maybe Trent didn't want Gramps Valentine to be a tenant?" asked Skye.

"It didn't sell because surveyors found it was overpriced," answered Cici, who could see the confusion on both of their faces.

"Wait!" said Mason, holding up his hand, his voice above a whisper now. "If 'Valentine' wasn't anywhere on the listing, then whose name was it?"

"Guillaume Regan, husband of Stuart Valentine and 'engineer extraordinaire!'"

Chapter Twenty-Two

"Gil?" asked Mason in disbelief. "Gil?" he repeated. "I suppose besides being named in the listing, he'd also be the most likely person to know how to rig a pressure sensor to a fence—a fence he installed—and to engineer a power outage. He was also the person who fixed the faulty wiring," noted Mason. "This is nuts," he concluded, removing his hat and running his hands through his ever-thinning hair.

Cici and Skye nodded in agreement.

"Why do you need to jam our phones?" asked Skye.

"Gil installed the original security system," replied Cordelia. "If—and this is a *BIG* if—a pressure sensor was used to electrocute the body of whoever fell into the fence, it would take a particular skill set and knowledge of the property to do so and be confident you wouldn't get caught—"

"—the only way you'd be confident about not being seen is if you either took out the cameras or knew how to delete the footage. Both would require an awareness of the system," noted Mason, interrupting his cousin.

"Are you sure the security system fried the night of the accident and not earlier?" Skye asked.

"Yeesh. I don't know. The police tried to review video from the system, but the hard drive had melted, and the footage hadn't been uploaded to the cloud for months. Which I suppose is a little convenient now that I'm saying this out loud."

"My guess is it was taken offline weeks before Uncle Tank's fall. Plus, I've been around long enough to know that an in-house saboteur often installs their own surveillance to get ahead of anyone with suspicions. If Gil is involved, I'd bet he has a second security unit, which is why I'm jamming signals. Best to be cautious."

"Gil did try to convince us to give up at Thanksgiving," reminded Mason.

"Plus, Tank wouldn't attempt to sell Highclere during his lifetime if he wasn't desperate for money. Instead of a sale, he'd have needed the mortgage or loan to stay afloat," Cici added.

"Hang on a second," interrupted Skye, "didn't we just agree that Trent Callahan would've bought the place without a second thought? Isn't owning Highclere his obsession?"

"The listing was so heavily buried that maybe Trent never knew," Cici suggested. "And whoever was ready to put in an offer reneged after being told the property value had been inflated."

"Either way, I think we can agree that the general gist is Tank needed money, and selling Highclere was his only means to get that money without owing a debt after he died. That plan obviously failed. The question is, did anyone else in the family know about the sale besides Gil, and does he know the reason Tank was desperate for cash?" asked Mason.

"I wonder why the property was considered overpriced. I know Belvedere isn't the sexiest of Muskoka lakes, but property values are still astronomical—and we have 49 acres!" he added.

Cici shrugged, "I don't know, but I'm going to assume Uncle Tank took out the mortgage in 2013 to help with his cash problems."

"So, I guess we need to figure out why Tank was hemorrhaging money," suggested Mason.

"And if it had something to do with Gil," added Skye.

"Also, if it was worth killing him over," added Cici, causing Mason to inhale.

"But Gil loved Tank. He was Tank's go-to engineer for decades. He and Granny V paid for his schooling through a scholarship. Not to mention he married his son, for God's sake," explained Mason. "Why would he want him dead?"

"I don't know. Truthfully. I also didn't know Uncle Tank and Gil had that kind of history," said Cici.

"Who's the head honcho of 'The Tanks' fan club?" asked Skye, looking at a perplexed Mason and Cordelia.

"No idea. When I did some research on Labor Day, I read that the Leader's first Tank fan club began in 1987 or 88. Pre-digital revolution," replied Cici.

"I assume they're just some nut on the internet, why?" added Mason.

"I was just thinking about their boast about having 'intimate knowledge' of Highclere and Gramps Valentine," continued Skye.

"Are you thinking the 'Leader of The Tanks' is Gil?" asked Cici, following Skye's train of thought.

"'Intimate' is a strange boast if it was someone outside of the family's orbit," Skye noted.

"People exaggerate on the internet all the time. According to my Tinder profile, I'm an athletic build with a shockingly full head of hair," replied Mason, noticing yet another hair follicle floating to its death.

"Plus, if Gil's the Leader of The Tanks, he wouldn't want attention drawn to the fence," added Cici, also watching Mason's deceased hair follicle float to the ground.

The trio sat in silence, placing their new information into a timeline of events that still didn't make sense.

"Should we be looking to confirm the fence was rigged with a pressure sensor?" asked Mason.

"I'm not sure it's worth it or how we'd confirm it. Kate dropped the story, and the police don't believe anything about his accident was untoward. There was no autopsy. Unless we had security footage, which we don't, I think our priority is to figure out why Uncle Tank needed the money from Highclere's sale and why Gil was in the know. Those answers might lead us to the fence."

"Then I suppose we need to investigate Tank's cash position from 2013—and probably 2012 as well—and determine if Aida and Laverna knew about it. I guess it's time for me to dive into the diaries, but his emails would be more helpful and easier to search through. I have no doubt there is a digital trail of activity surrounding his finances and the aborted sale," Mason pointed out.

"Do you know his password?" asked Skye.

"I do, or at least I did—I doubt he changed it. I activated dual authentication several years ago when Tank was convinced the Russians were trying to hack him."

"Who does the authentication code go to?" asked Cici.

"Aida, Laverna, and his assistant Norah Tripplehorn. While I would be comfortable asking Norah for the code under a ruse of some kind, Aida and Laverna might still be notified that someone was attempting to log into Tank's emails. It would be best to intercept the code from Aida or Laverna, but how do we do that?" Mason shrugged.

"By the way, you're looking very honky tonk today," said Cici, noticing her cousin's farmer-chic attire.

Mason smiled before continuing to think through how to get into Tank's emails. He admitted there was a possibility that Tank's laptop was on or plugged into power. Aida wouldn't think to open the computer to see if the battery was depleted before tucking it into a drawer. Even if the computer had been charged in May, it was now October, and the battery would have drained despite being unused for months. Of course, maybe it had been used. Aida and Laverna would have had to calculate Tank's net worth using various means, and while the financial advisors could provide information on investments, other information might have had to be accessed by his computer.

What if, thought Mason, *someone was still checking his emails*? If they were, then there was a strong likelihood Tank's laptop would be on and his Outlook open and logged in.

"Cici, plug in the Wi-Fi, and when I tell you to, disengage the jammer," instructed Mason as he stood and walked to the desk to grab his computer before sitting again and placing it on his lap. He typed.

"What are you doing?" Cici asked.

"I'm wondering if Tank's emails are being monitored. If they are, then his laptop is likely either open or on, which means we might avoid having to trigger the dual authentication requirement of logging in remotely. If his Outlook is sitting idle, we just need access to his computer. I'm going to send an email from a fake email account with a tracking pixel to see what happens."

Mason continued to tap keys, his brow furrowed but his heart racing with anticipation. After a few moments, he was ready.

"Cici...disengage," Mason said slowly.

Deliberately.

He raised his finger to his lips to encourage everyone to keep quiet, in case Cici was right and Gil was monitoring less obvious places on the property.

Mason pressed send and waited.

The trio sat in silence, looking at each other with eager anticipation or intolerable constipation.

Less than four minutes later, Mason's computer dinged. He turned off the speaker, then turned his screen to reveal the message that had come through. The email to Tank's account had been opened.

Curious whether it was opened remotely, on a cell phone, or a machine, Mason logged into his email tracking software and clicked on the details of who received the email. It was opened using Outlook, installed on a laptop, and running an Apple operating system at a location containing the postal code M8W. He copied and pasted the postal code of the receiving device into Google. Within seconds, the laptop's location appeared on a map, and Mason smiled. He once again turned his computer to face Cici and Skye. Pointing to the dot on the map, he mouthed the words "Tank and Aida's house." The Senator's laptop was on and being monitored.

Cici jammed cellular service and Wi-Fi once more to provide time to discuss next steps. No one was to know about the 2013 sale who didn't already.

"I have an idea about how to get to Tank's laptop," announced Mason after a moment of thought. "It will require you to reply to Laverna's text messages and suggest a lunch date—and make sure she brings Aida," he instructed Cici, who grunted her agreement.

"I'll text her and suggest a date in mid-November. Is that enough time?"

"That's plenty of time for me to plan what we'll refer to as Operation PITA!" exclaimed Mason.

"PITA?" asked Skye

"Acronym for 'Pain in the Ass,'" winked Mason.

Chapter Twenty-Three

"This is Tinker Niner Niner coming at you live," Skye said into the two-way earbud she had surreptitiously placed into her left ear and connected to her phone.

Her ears were covered by a dark brown wig she'd borrowed from her friend's "late-night missionary box," which housed items for anything but the missionary position. She wasn't sure whether to be disgusted, impressed, or jealous of the collection, which was hidden beneath a blanket held in place by a ceramic Virgin Mary. For a fleeting moment, Skye also wanted to borrow the riding crop. It contained a lubrication projectile, which she thought could be loaded with bear spray in the projectile's orifice to use should trouble arise. After briefly considering it, she reminded herself that the goal was to project a sense of normalcy, and a riding crop may indicate otherwise to her passengers.

Outfitted with blue contact lenses and a fake scar added to her right cheek for recognition deflection, she sat in a beat-up gold Buick belonging to her grandson. She waited in position—two blocks from the home of Laverna Clifton-Lehrman.

"Niner niner? You aren't a trucker!" replied Mason, who was sitting in a panel van rented in Roland Mast's name 500 feet from the gated community of his late grandfather, Senator Miles Valentine.

"I told you I wanted code names or aliases!" retorted Skye.

"Niner niner is a frequency, not a name. You need something like Louisa Bullock or Jolly Come-Stinker," joked Mason.

"You're both disgusting," interjected Cici, who was also on the line, waiting in the bathroom of the restaurant Il Cornuto at Danforth and Broadview Avenues in Toronto.

Chosen for its distance from Aida and Tank's house and the enclosed bathroom stalls with soundproof paneling, Cici had used it for several investigations throughout her career.

"Ha! Louisa Bullock it is then. Maybe. Actually, no—I'm conflicted," said Skye.

"I'm getting anxious. I hope this works," said Mason.

"It will," answered Cici with cautious confidence.

Skye lifted a custom-made wood shelf with five burner phones attached to it. All five phones were logged into the driver's end of different ride-hailing service apps.

"It won't be long now," confirmed Cici.

* * *

"B! Are you still home?" shouted Laverna to her best friend as she gathered her leather purse and car keys from the console table in the foyer.

"I am, but I'm leaving soon!" came Bianca Anders' cheery reply echoing from upstairs.

"Ok—I'll leave the door unlocked. I'm going to pick up my mom now. See you tonight!" replied a hurried Laverna as she slid on her aviator sunglasses.

Laverna, dressed in white slacks and a baby blue cashmere sweater, exited her beautiful stained glass front door. Using her fob to unlock her car doors, she slid into the leather driver's seat and threw her purse onto the passenger side floor. Pushing her right foot down on the brake, she nudged the start button to engage the engine before shifting the gear into reverse. With seatbelt fastened, she put her dyed blond locks into a messy bun, and without looking behind her—or at the backup camera—she pushed down the gas. Almost instantly, Laverna's head smacked against the lifted headrest, and a loud *clunk* could be heard from the rear of the vehicle.

Startled, the adrenaline rush caused her face to flush and beads of sweat to appear on her lined brow. She looked at the rear-view camera, panicked she'd run someone or something over. She toggled through the camera views to see empty pavement behind her.

* * *

"By the way. What did you do to her car to ensure it would be out of service?" asked Cici.

"My strong recommendation is you don't know," answered Skye.

"Oh joy," replied Cici, "hopefully you weren't caught on camera."

"Please! Light vehicle sabotage is child's play. Constructing a situation where your enemies are entrapped with sex workers...that's another story," chuckled Skye.

* * *

That's odd, thought Laverna.

She eased her foot off the brake and reversed down the driveway once again when the familiar clunking sound erupted, causing her head to jerk against the headrest for the second time. Shifting the car into park, she stepped out and discovered that both of her rear tires were flat.

* * *

"No one told me that pickup requests come through as anonymous! I've accepted and canceled seven different people!" shouted Skye in frustration, running her hands between each phone in a movement akin to a concert pianist.

"Well...we didn't tell you because we didn't know that," sighed Mason in response, rubbing his forehead with his fingers.

"Shit," said Cici.

* * *

Laverna rubbed her temples before looking at her watch. She was going to be late if she had to wait for roadside assistance. Instead, she went to the passenger door, snapped up her purse, and ran back inside.

"B!" Laverna shouted, somewhat breathless, slamming the door behind her.

"I thought you'd left?" Bianca answered while walking into the kitchen in her nurse's scrubs.

"I have two flat tires. What time do you have to get to work?"

"1:00 pm. Transit takes 45 minutes, though. Do you need me to call roadside?"

"Would you mind?" asked a grateful Laverna.

"No problem, I'll call work and tell them I'll be late."

* * *

"*I am accepting...and then denying...Ya no puede caminar,*" Skye sang out to the tune of "La Cucaracha," throwing in the real lyrics at the end for kicks.

"What does La Cucaracha mean?" asked Mason.

"The Cockroach!" replied Skye, still singing the same three lines.

"Seriously?" erupted Cici.

"Yuppers!" answered Skye.

"Weird. By the way, what fictional name did you settle on, Skye?" asked Cici.

"Never you mind," she replied with a low chuckle.

* * *

Laverna slid open her phone and cycled through her apps, opening and closing various ride-hailing platforms to gauge which would best provide a driver toot suite. She chose the world's most popular ride app and input her address as the pickup location, with one stop at her mother's house en route to Il Cornuto.

Seconds later, her phone buzzed and said, "*Jolly is two minutes away.*"

Chapter Twenty-Four

Laverna stood anxiously at the foot of her driveway, waiting for her driver to appear. Playing with the band of her Apple Watch, she scanned east and west before opening her phone to check the driver's ETA. She had a keen distaste for ride-hailing apps, finding the drivers dodgy and unaware of the smells embedded in their vehicles' fabric.

She glanced down at her home screen as a notification appeared. It read, *"Jolly is arriving in a blue Honda HR-V with license plate number ZWA 981."* Laverna looked up to see a beat-up gold Buick with a license plate matching the one on her screen.

Fuck, thought Laverna. This is why she hated the apps. What you order is rarely what you get.

* * *

"Ok, I see her. I'm pulling up," murmured Skye into her earpiece.

"Great! We'll be listening but won't say much in case she can hear us. Just act casual. Don't talk too much, and don't draw attention to yourself," instructed Cordelia from the toilet at Il Cornuto.

"Ten-four, big mamma," she replied.

"Never say that again," replied Cici.

"Copy that lil' daddy," agreed Skye.

"Ick. That's even worse!"

"How about Roxy Rider?"

"Not wildly better, but I'll take it," laughed Cici.

Overshooting Laverna by a few feet, Skye pumped the brakes before reaching behind her to unlock the door by popping up the old-fashioned car lock. Laverna ignored this and walked around to sit behind the passenger seat. She pulled the handle a few times before knocking on the window. Skye put the car in park, turned off the engine, and exited to unlock the door for her passenger.

"Aanni! Hello!" Skye cheerfully greeted Laverna outside the car. The wind had picked up, and she could feel her wig shift.

"Hi," responded Laverna, not looking Skye in the eye.

"I'm so sorry! This clunker doesn't have automatic locks! Crazy, eh? I can't reach that far, so I just need to open the door with the key."

"No problem," replied Laverna, unsuccessfully containing her irritation—if she was trying to at all.

Skye inserted the key into the lock, which required a little muscle to turn. She heard the door unlatch, which she then opened for Laverna, who entered the vehicle after a moment of noticeable hesitation. Wondering why she paused, Skye looked at the floor to find an open condom wrapper shining in the early winter sun. Contemplating whether or not to ignore the litter, she confronted the awkward situation and bent down to retrieve the discarded wrapper.

"Oh goodness!" smiled Skye, "I'm sorry again! Obviously, this isn't mine. I'm practically asphalt down there now. You could easily strike a match on my hoo-ha in an emergency," she laughed boisterously while praying Laverna would be amused.

Laverna, unmoving, furrowed her brow as Skye held the condom wrapper—which she noticed was an impressive XL, ruling out its belonging to anyone in her immediate family—and placed it in her pocket. Closing the door, she skipped back to the driver's seat.

"No. More. Vagina. References!" whispered Mason into his phone. "That's not normal! I didn't think I'd have to say that again after the Eye of the Vulva exhibit."

The vehicle started. Skye drove a few feet forward.

"Oops. I forgot to make sure your name is Vagina! My training vanished when I saw the condom. Embarrassment, you know!"

"Oh, for fucks sake! *VERNA*, not VAGINA!" said Mason loud enough to make sure Skye heard him.

"I've never experienced so much going so wrong in such a short period of time," added Cici.

"Hey, hey, hey! Cici, I'm the only one who can quote *The Birdcage* movie, thank you very much," said Mason. "RIP Robin!"

"That's from *The Birdcage*?"

"I mean Verna!" Skye laughed rambunctiously again.

A tear slid down her cheek, which she hoped was from laughter rather than crying.

"I am," replied Laverna more amiably than she had moments before. You are—" she looked down at her phone, "—Jolly?"

"Christ, Mason! Why did you have to give her that idea?" asked Cici.

"My general buffoonery?" answered Mason.

"Shhhh," whispered Skye, confusing Laverna.

"Excuse me?"

"Oops! Apologies. I just looked at the GPS and noticed there is a blockage, and I wanted to swear but thought against it," she lied.

"Your name is Jolly?" asked Laverna again.

Skye, flustered, darted her eyes left then right before she answered. Was this a trick? Did she put her name as Jolly in the app? Or was it Louisa? Was Louisa the youngest Von Trapp girl or the middle? What's the difference between the etymology of Louise and Louisa?...

"The answer is yes!" Cici encouraged Skye.

"Yes! It is. I am indeed Jolly!" she laughed again.

"It's always nice when a name matches a demeanor," responded Laverna with a warmth and sincerity that puzzled all three of them.

"That's very kind of you," smiled Skye. "I'm a believer that names should be intentional and meaningful. My ex-husband and I thought a lot about what to name our children. We hoped their personalities would grow to correspond with their names."

"That's lovely," said Laverna.

* * *

Eighteen minutes and twenty-eight excruciating seconds later, Jolly Come-Stinker, aka Skye Cadieux, passed the panel van holding Mason as she turned left onto Governor Boulevard, the aptly named street where Senator Miles Valentine had lived for forty-two years. Mason had installed a microscopic camera in the "I" of the admittedly piss-poor, fake company name he had decaled on the side of the van—Security Technicians Inc., or STI.

Crawling toward the entrance of the manned gatehouse, Skye cranked down the old-fashioned window to speak with the security guard as Mason watched through his tablet.

"Good morning," greeted the guard with zero personality or flare. He stood five foot eleven with a slim and toned build. He was obviously proud of his body and wore his uniform tailored to best accentuate his figure. His dark hair was long on top, gelled into place, and highlighted with a misjudged fade from the crown of his head down.

"Aanii! I've got Laverna Clifton-Lehrman. We're here to pick up her mother at number eight. The home of Senator Valentine."

"Senator Valentine is dead. It's the home of Aida Valentine now. I'll need to speak with Mrs. Lehrman," said the guard as he walked around to Laverna's window.

"Skye! She didn't tell you her full name or who she was visiting!" warned Mason through the earbud. He could see his friend slouch in disbelief through the camera.

"Oh no!" whispered Cici.

Fuck thought Skye.

"Hi Truman!" said Laverna with more charm and enthusiasm than she'd had during the entire car ride.

"Mrs. Lehrman. Wonderful to see you, as always. Why are you in this shit box?" he asked.

Rude! Thought Skye. Her breathing elevated, beating herself up for her mistake.

"Truman! Stop—you! Such a naughty, naughty boy," laughed Laverna in an alarmingly high pitch while caressing her bosom. She was circling a tone verging on flirtation, which was disorienting and slightly nauseating for both Mason and Cordelia. "Two flat tires. I was running late, so I needed a lift. You know these apps, they never send what you ask for."

"I guess she thinks you've become deaf, Jolly," joked Cici.

Skye could feel sweat descend from the line of her wig and worried her fake scar would become smeared.

"I understand, Mrs. Lehrman. Please tell your driver to go through. I'll call your mother to inform her you've arrived. Have a fabulous day," he smiled.

"You're wonderful, Truman. Thank you!"

Having heard Truman's go-ahead, Skye decided not to wait for instruction from Miss Daisy. She placed her foot on the gas and drove through the opening iron gates. Mason watched through the camera as the car disappeared behind the gatehouse and rolled down the street.

Governor Boulevard was a gated enclave perched on the shores of Lake Ontario. A community of nine houses, Senator and Lady Valentine had fallen in love with the area during a weekend trip to Toronto and moved from Ottawa to a much larger home where they'd spend the rest of their lives. The community was in pre-build when the Valentines bought their house and completed eighteen months later. Decorated by an interior designer with limited imagination, it remained unchanged for over four decades. When Aida married Tank and moved in, the only thing to change was the wife living in the house. Tank wouldn't allow her to redecorate or put her stamp on their marital home. Instead, she lived amongst the ghost and possessions of the woman who came before her.

Skye noticed security drones overhead as she drove down the brick-laid road. She knew which house was Senator Valentine's, having been there once before. However, she waited for Laverna to tell her where to go in an effort to avoid repeating the same mistake from earlier. A mistake that seemed to go over Laverna's head.

"It's the next house on the left. Right after the four black potted urns," instructed Laverna.

Skye turned into the driveway and was once again overwhelmed by the beauty of the home. The house was a large two-story white limestone mansion with nine-foot front arched windows and decorative columns attached to a simple portico. Standing in front of the commanding walnut-colored doors with baroque gold knockers was the recent widow of Senator Miles Valentine.

Aida was a surprisingly squat woman. To Skye's eye, she was no more than five feet tall, hefty with meaty arms but slim legs. She was dressed in her typical shapeless crewneck black tunic with a cream turtleneck underneath and a square white hat on top of her neon red hair, giving her the aura of someone who had rolled Whoopi Goldberg for her costume from *Sister Act*. Her half-moon Dumbledore-esque glasses sat on her nose while a vibrant pink satchel was draped across her body. While Skye couldn't see her footwear, she assumed she was wearing something meek and practical, like sneakers.

"Good afternoon!" Skye greeted Aida after parking the car and jumping out to open the door.

"Blessings, child!" replied Aida.

"Jesus. I mean Christ. No...I mean...no, I do mean Jesus! She sounds like she's about to break out a rendition of 'Climb Ev'ry Mountain,'" quipped Mason.

"Thank you?" said Skye, confused though polite.

Aida tried to enter the vehicle, but her tunic prevented her legs from spreading wide enough to step into the interior. Instead, she held the roof of the Buick to steady herself, then appeared to heave her body "habit" first into the car—her head falling into the lap of her daughter while her legs flailed in the air. Sure, she could have simply sat and swiveled, but why do something the easy way when you can put on a show?

"Hello, you," said Laverna as she kissed her mother on both cheeks after she'd sat up straight and fastened her seat belt.

"Grace and peace, my darling," said Aida in a breathless tone. "Grace and peace," she repeated.

Skye rolled her eyes and wondered if Aida might actually be a biblical character who was cryogenically frozen. One thing was confirmed for her, however—Gramps Valentine hadn't gotten laid in over twenty years.

"Are we still meeting Cordelia at Il Cuntory?" asked Aida as she adjusted her tunic.

"It's Il Cornuto, Mom. Yes, we are."

"Any strategy to consider darling?"

"Follow my lead. When I reached out to Cordelia after Labor Day, my goal was to find out if they knew the Highclere trust had been revoked and to see if she'd been approached about Uncle Miles dying by foul play. I think in light of the video that was provided to us, we..."

"Not to interrupt you, my dear, but should we be talking about this with..." Aida pointed her white hat at the driver's seat.

"Good point," agreed Laverna, who changed the subject.

* * *

"Crap! What video?" grunted Cici.

"No idea, but you can still control the conversation," said Mason as the gate to Governor Boulevard opened and Jolly's car exited.

Truman waved after them.

"If the computer is logged out of Outlook, I'll try inputting a password at 12:30 pm. If I'm unsuccessful, I'll attempt once more at 12:45 pm."

"Fingers crossed, I can read the authentication code upside down," said Cici. "I'll text you as soon as I have it."

"Remember, the code is only valid for fifteen minutes. If I don't get it in that window, we're cooked."

"I know," sighed Cici.

Skye coughed down the line—their signal she had made it onto the highway.

"Alright, as they say, it's showtime!" said Mason as he slid into the front seat of his STI rental. "Time to hang up."

"Good luck," said Cici.

Cough, cough, phlegm'd Skye.

Chapter Twenty-Five

Mason put the van into drive and wheeled from the curb toward Truman, his fitted shirt, and the gatehouse.

Deep inhale, deep exhale, he said to himself, pulling his ball cap further down his forehead while adjusting his sunglasses.

He, Skye, and Cici had planned "Operation PITA" the best they could. However, there were still elements they had no choice but to leave to chance. The first had been Skye procuring Laverna's ride request, which she did. The next unknown was whether Mason's old gate fob his grandfather had "loaned" him years earlier was still programmed. Mason wasn't sure he'd ever used it before, but according to the security drone footage Roland Mast had weaseled from a contact, the security guard at the gate of Governor Boulevard rarely stopped any vehicle that had an operational fob and never surveyed security vans either.

While Mason expected he might have to speak to the guard—he hoped that wouldn't happen. If it did, he prayed he could charm his and the unfortunately titled STI truck through the gate.

Having circled the block, Mason arrived at the entrance gate and extracted the fob from his breast pocket. He pointed it at the cast-iron barrier in front of him, pushed down, and saw the small red indicator light illuminate the fob's black surface. Nothing happened.

"Shit," said Mason under his breath. He wondered if he was too far away and crept forward. He pushed down again—still nothing.

He took another deep breath and moved the truck even closer to the gate. Before he could push the button for a third time, Truman walked out and gestured for Mason to roll down the window. Busted!

Panic rising, Mason felt sweat drip down his sides. He tried the fob once more in a "Hail Mary" before cracking the window to speak with the guard. With one eye closed, Mason pushed down and could hear a small engine start and the faint sound of iron beginning to wheel into the decorative hedge.

YIPPE!! Mason cheered in his head, a wide grin plastered on his face.

His elation was disappointingly brief as the handsome Truman knocked on the window before STI could drive ahead.

Shit!

He parked the van and pushed down the automatic window, resisting the urge to ask, "Is anything the matter, officer?" while cutely biting his finger and batting his eyelashes.

"Good morning," said Mason cheerily.

"Good morning!" replied Truman in a pleasant tone. "I see an owner has provided you with a fob, but since I've never seen a vehicle for Security Technicians Inc., I'll need some information."

Mason could see apprehension in Truman's manner. He had interviewed enough people on his podcast to know when someone was being less than forthcoming. There was a shift in their movements, sudden muscle jets, and rapid breathing. Aware it could backfire spectacularly, Mason followed his gut.

"You must be new then!" Mason fired.

Truman's cheeks flushed.

Bing!

"I've been here for three months. I'm still getting to know everyone," Truman said sheepishly before adding, "but don't worry, I never forget cute faces."

GAY! thought Mason. Poor Laverna she'll be heartbroken when she finds out, but Mason's gaydar piqued when Truman said "fabulous" in conversation with her.

"Awe. Don't make me blush," Mason replied.

"Who are you here to see?"

"I'm here to visit the Valentine residence. Mrs. Valentine called to say she'd be out but asked that we send someone to reset the alarm codes. Her housekeeper Geneviève is expecting me."

"I thought the Valentines used our company?"

Shit.

Think. Think.

"Nope! She's always had STI," Mason said.

Truman paused, looked at Mason, and smiled, "I hope she has an ointment for that."

Mason was impressed with Truman's quick humor. He prayed he wouldn't lose his job over this.

"Don't worry. She's been prescribed penicillin," Mason joked back.

"Please go ahead through," instructed Truman, stepping back and gesturing for Mason to drive through the gates.

"Thank you! I'll see you on the way out."

"I hope so," winked Truman.

Mason drove forward and turned into the driveway of the home that had once belonged to his grandparents. He'd barely visited after Tank married Aida. The memories of his grandmother were amplified by the frozen in time décor—Mason found the lack of change discombobulating.

Mason parked STI in a security blind spot between the ten-foot hedges and the hydroelectric meter. Switching his ball cap for a wide-brimmed fedora, Mason exited the panel van and removed the fleece jacket Cici had made, which displayed the fictional logo of Security Technicians Inc.

It was time for Mason to shake his fictional personality and settle back into himself. While role-playing what could happen next, Cici and Mason felt it essential that he used goodwill and charm as Mason Valentine to gain entry to his late grandfather's home.

Briskly walking toward the imposing front door, Mason lifted the ornate knocker and banged it as loudly as possible. His fedora shielded his face from the camera above the door, and he avoided using the doorbell, which would record him with an independent camera once it was activated. He waited.

No answer.

Checking his watch to see it was almost noon, he resisted the temptation to look up at the camera. Like an itch, it was difficult not to scratch. He lifted the knocker and banged it against its gold base. The force he put into it made his ears ring. If that didn't get the door answered, he wasn't sure what would!

After several anxious moments, he heard the various locks recoil within the doors, and the chestnut panels opened.

Chapter Twenty-Six

Jolly Come-Stinker rolled to a stop outside Il Cornuto at 12:01 pm. Skye was delighted that she'd arrived almost on time and without the car stalling or any further distractions in the form of sexual contraception. The drive from Governor Boulevard was primarily quiet, with Aida periodically pointing out newly strung Christmas décor and making inane comments about how the city had changed since she married Tank.

Skye exited the Buick to open the door for Aida.

"Crap," Skye muttered after realizing Aida had locked the door with her arm. Skye knocked on the window, and Aida opened the door on her own. Having learned the lesson from her graceless entrance, she pivoted in her seat and put both feet firmly on the ground before reaching for Skye's hand to help her out. Laverna exited the car at the same time. Neither said thank you to Skye before walking through the red-framed door of the restaurant. Skye pulled out her phone and texted Cordelia and Mason before driving off.

Delivered! They better tip me! Good luck. I'll be eager to hear what you discover! –Jolly ;)

* * *

Cici stood when she saw Aida and Laverna enter Il Cornuto and waved energetically to them as they adjusted their vision to the darker interior. She braced herself and prepared to put on the most enthusiastic performance of her career. It was one thing when she acted to deceive someone for a story; faking conversation with two people you've known your entire life wasn't as simple as it might seem. Cici knew she had to be calculating but charming, evasive yet friendly, familiar but distant. Her husband encouraged her to add "sexy yet demure" to her repertoire, but Cici ignored that advice.

Mother and daughter wore bright smiles on their faces and opened their arms wide when they were within feet of Cici. Checking the time, Cordelia noted it was 12:05 pm. She had 25 minutes until Mason's first attempt at logging into Tank's email. However, she had only 30 seconds to wonder what the fuck Aida Clifton was wearing.

* * *

"Mr. Mason! Mr. Mason, it's so nice to see you!" sang out Geneviève Talbot, Tank's housekeeper who had been with him since the day he moved in. She rocked her unexpected visitor side to side in one of the most expressive hugs Mason had ever received.

"Mrs. Talbot!" beamed Mason back at her.

Much like his affection for Tank's assistant Norah Tripplehorn, Mason also had a soft spot for Geneviève Talbot. While Tank tended to surround himself with inadequate lackeys, Norah and Gen were two of the good ones.

"What are you doing here, Mr. Mason? I didn't think I'd ever see any of you again," she said in her French lilt while eyeing Mason up and down with the flash of a tear in her eyes.

"I need your help, and I was wondering if I could come in?"

"Anything Mr. Mason! Your family has been so good to me. I miss Lady Valentine, and I pray for her each day. She was a mother figure to me, and I'd do anything to help you. Does the second Mrs. Valentine know you're here?" asked Gen.

Mason shook his head.

Gen smiled, stood back, and said, "Good," before she invited Mason inside.

Conscious time was ticking by, Mason stood still and drew a serious expression.

"You can't tell anyone I was here."

"Your secret is very safe with me."

"Mrs. Talbot, I am concerned that my grandfather's money was siphoned from him eleven years ago in what we suspect to be a criminal act."

Mason had no proof of that, nor was he sure he believed it. It wasn't even his point of greatest concern, but he was eager to get Mrs. Talbot on his side—and fast.

"I know," replied Gen.

Mason was stunned.

"Excuse me?"

"The second, Mrs. Valentine and her daughter always think I can't hear them talking. But I can. I know a mortgage was taken out on the house years ago. Senator Valentine did lose a lot of money. The second, Mrs. Valentine, and her daughter weren't upset. They said Senator Valentine's 'money was safe' for them."

Mason took a step forward, becoming serious.

"How long ago did this happen?"

"I heard them talk about it six or seven years ago."

"You are confident that's what you heard. That they knew the money was safe for them?"

"Yes."

"Mrs. Talbot, I need to access my grandfather's computer to transfer his emails to an external hard drive. We—" Mason used "we" to make Geneviève feel like she was part of an exclusive and important group "—need to confirm that my grandfather's money was, in fact, stolen from him and find evidence that Aida and Laverna knew about it."

While Mason was sure Geneviève Talbot was telling the truth, he was less confident that she had correctly interpreted Aida's meaning. Still, it was promising that Gen knew about the house's mortgage and the missing mullah.

"Of course, Mr. Mason! His computer is in the top left drawer of his desk. I dusted it this morning."

"Thank you! I won't be long," said Mason, already walking toward his grandfather's office.

Geneviève nodded and waved at him as he marched down the hall.

Chapter Twenty-Seven

Cordelia noted the time was 12:17 pm. With drinks ordered, she lulled the Clifton girls into a sense of ease with tactile friendliness.

Reaching out, she scooped their hands in hers, smiled so wide she could feel it in her neck, and cooed, "I'm so, *SO* happy you reached out. We've known each other for so long I was worried our friendship would now be over."

"Never!" replied Aida.

"We understand that your allegiance is to Uncle Miles's family," said Laverna, "but as you said, we've been friends for so long it would've been a shame to become estranged now. You mean a lot to us, Cordelia and we're happy you feel the same."

Bullshit, thought Cici. They were all there for the same reason—information.

Neither of the Cliftons had their cell phones in sight. It was time to start the investigative "to and fro," and fingers crossed, get the phones on the table before 12:30 pm.

"How's wrapping up the estate?" asked Cici.

"Difficult," replied Laverna before taking a deliberate pause by sipping her water. "Have you spoken to Uncle Miles's family at all?"

"Not as much as I'd like," lied Cici.

"They haven't been making this process easy for us."

"How so?" asked Cici, playing dumb.

"They sent Roland Mast to my mother's house looking for Lady Valentine's jewels, acting as if we'd stolen them. It was ridiculous. My mother is the closest thing to a saint on Earth. Her faith would never allow her to do something so awful," said Laverna.

"Right..." Cici replied, desperate not to laugh. "Well..." she coughed, "I'm so sorry they did that. It must have been upsetting to be ambushed that way," Cici smiled.

"Laverna tells me you know about Highclere," said Aida with a grin.

"Yes. I must admit it surprised me," replied Cici.

Laverna sighed.

"The problem is, Uncle Miles asked us to let his family stay at Highclere for another six months. Until then, we can't close a sale," complained Laverna.

"Really? Why not?" asked Cici, confused.

Highclere belonged to Tank outright, and as his wife, it was now Aida's fair and square. The Valentines needn't vacate to close a sale.

"Something having to do with the legalities around insurance and occupancy," replied Laverna.

That doesn't make sense, thought Cici. *They're hiding something in that statement.*

"Are you comfortable accepting Highclere from Uncle Tank? Knowing its history and legacy?"

"Yes," the Cliftons replied in unison.

12:21 pm.

* * *

Mason opened the door to Tank's office, only to see most of its contents had been packed into boxes marked "garbage" or "storage." With little time to be nosey, he sat in his late grandfather's oversized desk chair and opened his laptop drawer. Mason knew Tank didn't have a passcode to open his computer because Mason disabled it after one too many instances of Tank forgetting what it was and his touchpad no longer recognizing his aged fingerprint. He scrolled to Outlook and clicked to open the application.

"Come on, be logged in," Mason whispered to himself.

The multicolored wheel turned and turned and turned as the app loaded.

"Come on," urged Mason.

Moments later, Outlook filled Tank's computer screen.

"Fuck," Mason said to himself.

He was being asked to log in. Mason pulled out his phone and fired a message to Cici:

Logged out. Need SMS verifier. Advise which phone –M.

Mason looked down at a piece of paper taped to Tank's desk that contained the phone numbers of the entire Valentine and Clifton families. Mason cross-referenced the last four digits of Aida, Laverna, and Norah Tripplehorn's numbers. Once he attempted to log into Tank's email account, he'd be presented with three options for an SMS verification code, and he wanted to make sure it'd go to either Aida or Laverna by way of Cici's intervention.

12:24 pm.

With six minutes left, Mason looked around the room without leaving the desk chair when he spotted a box on the couch labeled differently than the others. Maybe there was time for nosiness after all.

* * *

"You don't feel Highclere rightly belongs to them?" pushed Cici.

"It belonged to Miles, and Miles made his wishes clear. He wanted it to be left to us. We aren't ones to argue with a dead man's wishes, Cordelia. He must have had a reason for not leaving it to the family, but it's not our responsibility to interpret the man's bequests, just execute them. He needed to leave us something after all," soothed Aida as Laverna shot her a sharp look.

Mother and daughter discord, thought Cici.

"I understand. Did you know before Labor Day that you were inheriting the inn?" asked Cici.

"Yes, we've known for some time," confirmed Aida, spreading butter onto a roll.

"Then why did you share Uncle Tank's letter after the funeral if the content wasn't accurate?"

Silence.

"Sorry—investigative brain! Forget I asked. I'm sure you'll miss Highclere, though," added Cici.

"We will miss Lake Belvedere specifically, but there are other lakes, and we can always visit Norah Tripplehorn," noted Aida.

"Visit Norah Tripplehorn where?" asked Cici.

"Belvedere, she has a charming cottage on a rock cliff."

Cordelia was taken aback. It wasn't in her nature to cast aspersions, but she couldn't fathom how Norah Tripplehorn could afford a cottage in the area. She pushed that to the back of her mind and refocused.

"Do you have a buyer?" asked Cici, taking a sip of water.

"We do, yes. An eager one," said Laverna.

"Will it be a profitable deal?" Cici asked, knowing the 2013 offer was withdrawn because Highclere was considered overpriced.

"We aren't ones to boast, but it will make us very comfortable," answered Aida.

"You got the asking price?" Cici faked excitement.

"And then some," winked Laverna, "but we do need to close this deal as quickly as possible, which is why waiting until May is so bothersome."

"How come?"

Laverna squirmed.

"Oh, just to get one of the big jobs done, I suppose," she replied while looking at her fork.

Liars thought Cici. The Cliftons were obviously aware that the offer from ten years earlier exploded after an inspection, and they wanted the check before they suffered the same fate. *What is knocking millions of dollars off Highclere's value?* Wondered Cici, who realized she'd lost track of time and glanced at the clock on the restaurant wall.

12:27 pm.
Shit.

Mason was about to make his first attempt at sending the SMS code—Cordelia needed one of their phones. In a rush of thoughts, Cici brainstormed possible strategies, considering Aida and Laverna's recent social media posts. She wondered if there was a topic she could bring up to distract them, from scenic lake pictures to heartfelt tributes for Tank, or even foodie-type posts about their extravagant meals or...Jesus Christ! That's it! Jesus. Christ!

"Aida, I saw you presented a sermon about grief at your church, but you didn't post a video. Was it recorded? I'd love to see it."

"Sadly, the file was too big to post online, so we settled for photographs instead. I felt it went well overall. It's such a shared experience. Grief, I mean."

Aida lifted her bag onto her lap and rummaged through the contents. Cici was elated. Aida was so predictable.

"I have a video on my phone, though."

"Would you mind if I AirDrop it to mine?" asked Cici, heart racing.

* * *

Mason sat back down after his swift but fruitful box rummage to see Cordelia's message on his phone.

Aida's phone. Pretending to transfer a video —C

12:30 pm.

The moment of truth.

Mason went to Outlook, where a window with Tank's email address and password prefilled—but blacked out—appeared on the screen. He moved the cursor under the redacted password and pressed login. Within a blink, a second window appeared with two phone numbers—only their last four digits showing. Mason looked at the taped contact sheet again to ensure he chose Aida's phone number. Temporarily curious why Norah was no longer an authentication option, Mason double-checked and triple-checked that he'd clicked Aida's and pressed send.

* * *

12:32 pm.

"Gosh, this is a big file. How long did you speak for?" asked Cici, wondering where the hell the SMS code was.

"About thirty-five minutes. When the Lord speaks through me, I answer Him by sharing His wisdom in my voice. It's always been my calling to speak for the Lord, a gift that I think Miles also had. We could both become silent and converse with the Father about issues in our lives or the world. Miles would often make decisions based on what God would tell him. It helped guide his political life, as well as how he engaged with his family. A true, true gift."

Stifling the urge to perform the biggest eye roll in the history of over-exaggerated gestures, Cici nodded as Laverna's phone vibrated.

Shit.

* * *

Mason waited.

12:37 pm.

"What the fuck," he said under his breath.

He again cross-referenced the four digits on the screen with the phone numbers on the desk. Mason felt the box waiting for the SMS code was becoming increasingly judgmental and hostile as he stared at it. A timer next to the box counted down. Less than eight minutes until the code expired.

Mason picked up his phone and sent his cousin a question mark. She responded with a thumbs-down emoji.

Shit. Fuck. God damn.

* * *

12:40 pm.

"Sorry. The Wi-Fi is so slow here!" apologized Cici.

Their meals arrived as Cici continued to hold Aida's phone. Pretending the video was still transferring through AirDrop, Cici had instead enacted her backup plan—a plan she didn't tell Mason about—when Laverna jolted her.

"What do you know about the Dawn girl?" asked Laverna.

"Makayla? I love her grandfather," answered Cici, wondering where the hell this was going.

"Do you trust her?"

"I've never thought about it. I trust Ahren, and Ahren trusts Makayla. Are you considering keeping her on at Highclere until the closing date?"

12:42 pm.

"No. That family adored Uncle Miles. They'd never do as we asked," grunted Laverna.

"They adore Highclere, not Uncle Tank specifically," noted Cordelia, who worked closely with Ahren when she was the resort manager.

While she didn't know Makayla, she had no reason to doubt her ability or ethics.

"Why are you asking? Did she do something?"

Laverna hesitated before picking up her phone again and typing out a message.

Please, God, say the codes didn't go to Laverna's phone, Cici prayed.

"A few...I guess you'd say curious...actions...taken by the Dawn girl have been brought to our attention."

"Like?" asked Cici, forgetting to monitor the time or the operational cul-de-sac of the fake video transfer.

"There's reason to believe that she's the one who has stolen Jean Valentine's belongings.

12:46 pm.

* * *

With the first code having expired, Mason—confused and anxious—requested a new SMS code sent to Aida's phone. He hadn't heard from Cici but assumed she must have the situation in hand. He swiveled the chair to look at the empty shelves behind him, taking a deep breath and stretching. Footsteps then echoed in the hall before entering the office.

"Mason?"

* * *

"Where are you getting your information from?" asked Cici, befuddled by the random accusation thrown at Makayla Dawn.

"The authorities. They have evidence that the girl absconded with items following Uncle Miles's death."

"The poor dear. Following the way of sinners at such a young age," added Aida.

12:50 pm.

Still no code.

Chapter Twenty-Eight

"Bianca!" Mason said as he sheepishly greeted Laverna's best friend, who had unexpectedly walked into Tank's office, catching Mason in a compromising position.

Though, perhaps not the compromising position he feared.

"Were you just pleasuring yourself in Uncle Tank's chair?" asked the jovial Nordic nurse.

"What?"

"You were groaning and looking at the wall while your hand went up and down."

"Oh!" laughed Mason. "I was doing a breathing exercise, and I like to do hand gestures as if I'm conducting music for good measure. I mean, you've seen me clap before. It's akin to a seal—I get overly ambulatory with my limbs," he flushed a slight pink hue, attempting to charm her and lean into their warm relationship, hoping to avoid potential trouble.

"Oh, thank God," laughed Bianca, putting down a letter-sized envelope addressed to Aida.

"Oops!" laughed Mason in return while shrugging.

"Are you supposed to be here, Mason?" Bianca asked in a kindergarten teacher's voice, complete with hands on hips.

"Mr. Mason! Mr. Mason! Quick, close down! Ms. Anders is here!" shouted Geneviève as she barreled into the office, stopping dead when she saw Bianca looking at her.

* * *

"Do you know what Makayla has allegedly taken?" asked Cici.

Upon realizing that Operation PITA had failed, she returned Aida's phone—however, not until she was sure her plan B had been successful—which it had. Then, she focused on the unexpected twist concerning Makayla Dawn.

"We don't. The police have video evidence showing her leaving the carriage house with items the morning after the burial."

So, that's the video? But the cameras were down, thought Cici. *How can there be footage unless the system remained operational? Or maybe there is indeed a second system—set up by whom? Gil? Things pointed in that direction.*

"When were you told about this?"

"I think the Father told us some weeks back, but I wasn't able to interpret the message," responded Aida, adjusting her habit-like hat, which had slipped backward.

"Her father is dead," noted Cici.

"*THE* Father," said Aida—pointing up.

Oh, for fucks sake.

"When did the police tell you this?"

"Last night," said Laverna, signaling the server for their bill.

* * *

Mason stood and asked Bianca to sit down, a not altogether simple task considering every seat held boxes for storage except for the desk chair. While Bianca was a lovely woman, her heft would be no match for any box's light fibers. She grabbed a folding chair from the cupboard and positioned it next to Mason, who remained seated at the desk.

Mason broke the silence, carefully considering what he was about to say.

"Bianca. You and I have always had a lovely and, I'd argue, loving relationship. I admire what you did for my grandfather in his final months—leaving your job to care for him. It was a selfless act that endeared you to me and my family for a lifetime."

He was laying it on thick, but flattery was his best weapon—a weapon which Bianca seemed to appreciate as she flushed at the compliment, a smile appearing on her pale face.

"That's very kind of you to say, Mason. But what are you doing here?"

Mason sighed.

"I'm not going to bull shit you, Bianca. The truth—" *or a fraction thereof,* thought Mason bull shitting her, "—is we are rather desperate to get my Granny V's things back. I know my grandfather didn't leave them specifically to us in his will. I also know that the police couldn't find them either."

"Which was a major error in judgment, Mason. Huge error sending them in," interrupted Bianca.

"It was. However, withholding the will and springing a 'For Sale' sign on us at Thanksgiving was also an error in judgment, though I understand it was in line with what we did."

Bianca nodded.

"I'm trying to get into my grandfather's emails to see if there's any mention, documentation, or inquiries surrounding my grandmother's things. That's it. I promise," he lied.

Bianca hesitated. With Tank dead, Mason had no right to be in his house, let alone snooping through things that belonged to Aida.

"This has nothing to do with his money?" asked Bianca.

"Nothing. We have more than anyone could ever need in life. We'd never contest anything having to do with his wealth."

"And nothing to do with Highclere?"

Mason gulped.

"Ok, I admit, if I stumbled across something related to Highclere, I'd probably have read it. Right now, though, all I'm looking for are my grandmother's belongings. That's it. I'm not beneath begging."

He smiled.

Bianca stood, pushed Mason's chair aside, and walked to Tank's computer. She took her phone out of her pocket and sent a message. Moments later, her message was returned, accompanied by a vibration that rattled the rings on her fingers. Two clicks of the mouse later, Bianca again waited a few moments for her phone to vibrate. Once it did, she typed in six digits and pressed enter. She moved out of the way to reveal a successful login screen displaying the emails of the late Miles "The Tank" Valentine.

"Mason, you have ten minutes and ten minutes only. I'm going to be waiting outside the door. There will be no printing or forwarding of emails. If there is something of note, take a picture on your phone. No screen grabs. Understand? I'm already late for work. I'm just here to drop off Verna's car. Then I'm heading to the hospital."

"Of course!" Mason smiled wide. "I can't thank you enough for this!"

Bianca walked to the door, then turned back to Mason.

"I never knew my grandmother, and my mother died young. The only family I've ever felt a part of was Tank's and the Clifton clan. I doubt I'll have children, but if I were to, I'd do anything to have heirlooms and family history to pass down from one generation to the next. You could call it the proverbial connective tissue that defies DNA. It forms who we are and who we become by telling us where we came from. No family should be denied what's theirs by their birthright. Aida and Laverna will never know about this. I hope you find what you're looking for—within ten minutes. I love you, Mason, but don't do this again."

Bianca nodded and left the room, closing the heavy door behind her and leaving Mason to find his needle in the haystack. Mason didn't need ten minutes. He only needed three. Discarding the idea of saving the emails to a hard drive—which would require more than his granted time, he moved the cursor over an icon that read "Inbox Rules." After a click, a window opened, and he scrolled down to an automated action titled "PC Office—Fwrd." He opened the action and clicked further before selecting "Run Rule." He logged out of his grandfather's emails and closed the laptop. Placing it back into the drawer where he found it.

Seven minutes left.

No harm in a bit more light snooping thought Mason. He was becoming more and more like his nosey Aunt Drusilla every minute.

* * *

Cordelia Bradshaw hugged Aida and Laverna outside the restaurant. "It was so nice seeing you both," Cici said.

"Can we please do this more often?" asked Laverna.

"Of course! Bygone's, etcetera," Cici smiled. "Are you taking an Uber?"

"No!" shouted Laverna. "The one we had on the way here was brutal. We're taking public transit. Our driver's name was Jolly, but she was anything but!"

With that, mother and daughter walked down the cold, wintery Toronto street toward the underground entrance to the subway.

Once out of sight, Cici pulled out her phone to see a message marked urgent from Mason.

Oh fuck! Cici—I know what's killing Highclere's value. Msg me when you can.

Cici's eyes widened as she typed back.

We need to get to Highclere ASAP. Something is up with Makayla Dawn. If I'm right, the police will get to her tonight or tomorrow if they haven't already. I'll pick you up at your place in 45 minutes. Tell Mack to meet us at the office of the old inn, and you can fill me in on what you found on the drive-up.

Chapter Twenty-Nine

"If a hunch had a punch, it'd be spiked with Dom for my lunch," Lady Margot Ambrosia recited to herself in a sing-song voice. She took another swig from her alcohol-free flask while watching the front door of 201 Elizabeth Street, just off Eaton Square in London. She told her husband she'd stay out of it and not meddle in an active investigation. Curiosity, however, had been firmly piqued, and after a conversation with Mason Valentine, a quick Google, and seven calls to various disconnected phone lines, she sat in the shambles of a Valentino outfit, waiting for the roses.

At 6:12 pm British Standard Time, Margot Ambrosia finally saw the white delivery vehicle emblazoned with pickaflower.co.uk in large floral writing on each side. Lady Ambrosia had to admit to herself that she was rather embarrassed to buy flowers for a stranger from such a common website, but expediency was the game's name in this instance.

The jauntily dressed delivery boy exited the van and slid open the panel door, pulling out a cellophane-wrapped bouquet of white roses. White, thought Margot, would signal good intent, peace, and friendship. A card, poking out from the depths of the roses, was written in dark cursive writing.

The delivery boy—well, he was an adult man, but Margot called anyone without facial hair a boy—approached the door of 201 Elizabeth Street and pressed the bell.

Margot watched with suspense, wondering if she'd see movement inside the home.

Feeling tense and guilty about going against Stellan's wishes and nervous that her mission would be in vain, Lady Ambrosia couldn't contain her glee when an elderly woman using a steel gray walker opened the door to receive her surprise delivery of white roses.

* * *

Stuart Valentine closed the frost-covered sliding door behind him and looked at the sky. The snow fell onto his face, giving the sensation of pin pricks before melting against his warm skin. He sought moments where he could feel. Feel what, he was never sure. Feel something is all he could ever say.

Carrying a brown woven basket complete with a fancy lid, Stuart walked a few paces from the house toward his companion, who sat next to the roaring fire emanating from a decorative fire pit.

"We might be underestimating your family by thinking things will change if they ever found out," she said.

"I know. I love them—I truly do. But it gives them a reason not to stand by me when they learn about Dad's money."

"You're speaking as if the money and what happened to it isn't distinct from who you are. It's not mutually exclusive, Stuart. Love finds a way. Families find ways. They won't think less of you. They're more likely to be angry with your father for putting you in this position."

"He didn't put me here alone."

Stuart's companion hesitated.

"No. He didn't," she whispered. "If we burn these—the story dies with us. Are you sure that's what you want?"

Stuart stood in the cold, his hand holding the top of the woven basket.

"Your mother wouldn't have wanted you to do this."

"Well," he paused, "she's not here to help me decide."

"Yes, she is, Stuart. Always."

He sighed.

"I just feel a lie is easier than the truth. I know where you're coming from, Louella, but I want to get this over with."

Stuart handed the lid to Louella Stone. Her backyard smelled like a Christmas fireplace, the embers of cedar and balsam flavoring the sky with a festive jolt running counter to the joyless activity the two were undertaking.

He stepped toward the fire pit and flipped over the box. The contents spilled atop the fire; their fibers quickly caught in the dancing flames. Stuart and Louella watched as the blue flames cascaded from one paper to another, slowly engulfing decades of secrets until nothing remained but the soot of a lie.

Chapter Thirty

To: Mason Valentine
From: Baroness Margaret Ambrosia MBE
Date: November 18, 2023
Re: Farnsworth Marble & Designs

Dearest Mason,

I've returned from my impromptu (though I do admit theatrical) visit to Farnsworth Marble & Designs expert Andrea Romero, who confirmed to me she's not just an enthusiast but did indeed purchase the company after Rosamond Farnsworth-Ford's death some years ago. The transaction was done via the solicitors of the elusive Joyce Redstone, who inherited the company. They never met in person; thus, she couldn't describe Mrs. Redstone to me.

Oh, before I forget, Mrs. Romero doesn't check emails, which is why you haven't received a response from her. She apologized for appearing rude, and I said you'd, without question, accept her apologies.

Anyway, evidently, there is a lucrative business in the resale of early (or vintage) Farnsworth designs. When Mrs. Romero bought the company, she became the owner of everything, including prototypes, unsold and returned products. Rosamond Farnsworth-Ford started the tradition, now continued by Mrs. Romero, of buying back Farnsworth items from inheritors for exhibition or resale.

And here is where things get very interesting!?!:

When the sale of Farnsworth Marble & Designs was finalized, Mrs. Romero went through each piece she acquired and placed select items for sale. Some weeks later, she received a seemingly random telephone call from someone called Maxwell, asking if she had a pair of silver cufflinks engraved with the Fernsby family crest on them. Mrs. Romero divulged that she had the item in question. However, since it was a personalized family piece, it would only be sold to relatives of the Fernsby family. He revealed to her that his full name was Maxwell *Fernsby*, and he wished to repurchase the item for sentimental reasons. He rang round 201 Elizabeth Street and bought the cufflinks with cash.

The Farnsworth family and Mrs. Romero have kept an impeccable register of each design since their incorporation including the name of who commissioned it, the year it was created, and (where possible) who currently owns it. In addition, as suspected, each design does contain a signature of sorts—a microscopic rectangle with a dot in the center. Once I figure out how to break it to Stellan that I've interfered with an investigation, I will ask him to have the cufflinks checked for the signature to confirm authenticity.

Mason, out of curiosity, I checked to see where Maxwell Fernsby falls in your family tree; however, as far as I can deduce, no Maxwell Fernsby has ever existed. I suppose it was a pseudonym in order to gain Mrs. Romero's trust. The address he provided for the register doesn't exist either and never has. As the purchase was made with cash, there is no cheque that can be cross-referenced to confirm identity. Could the dead man in Fernsby House be the alleged Maxwell Fernsby? If so, how does he fit into this saga?

Speaking of cheques, Mrs. Romero and I went through the register to check the dates associated with the canceled cheques you found amongst Senator Valentine's belongings. There is indeed a description associated with Lady Valentine's purchase in 1993—she bought a pocket watch for her son, Stuart. However, no such description exists for the 2002 cheque. This is peculiar for obvious reasons but also because prior purchases by your grandmother were itemized correctly in the ledger, and as far as the register is concerned, the items remain in the possession of Lady Valentine and have not appeared for sale anywhere else or claimed by another owner wishing to authenticate them.

The outlier being a gold and pearl box containing four

circular indents in a velvet lining and four gold spheres, each with laser-etched geometric shapes on one side. The register correctly reflects that Lady Valentine commissioned these objects. However, there is no purchase date, and the items are noted as being returned in trust to Farnsworth Marble & Designs in the year 2004. It's possible that your grandmother's 2002 purchase was the gold box and spheres, but the dimensions in the memo of the cheque don't make any sense to Mrs. Romero in connection to those items.

As I said, Mrs. Romero does not have any forwarding information for Joyce Redstone except some vague memory of being told that she and her husband would relocate to the continent after the company's sale.

I have attached the purchase register as a PDF to this email. If nothing else, perhaps it will help you itemize the pieces you deem to be missing from your grandmother's estate, which could then be searched through online resources by the MET (pending I'm still married in the morning) or Canadian authorities.

Much Love,
Margot

PS—I sent Mrs. Romero white roses as a gesture of friendship, which arrived moments before I "ambushed" her on her doorstep. In hindsight (and as Mrs. Romero herself pointed out), since I had her address, I could've just knocked rather than resorting to a theatrical stunt to get her attention. I have indeed enjoyed one too many cheesy spy novels, and my new motto is "simpler is better" in real-life espionage.

Chapter Thirty-One

Mason printed the email and ancient register of Farnsworth designs as Cordelia flipped through the report that Mason had found—and taken—from Tank's study in Toronto.

"Even though I'm reading the words, I still can't believe it," Cici sighed while focused on the bound report. "'*The findings reveal that Highclere Inn & Carriage House is sitting on top of a highly toxic ecological biohazard, which, based on certain assumptions of Muskoka's local hydrogeology, has likely been ongoing since approximately 2005. As a result, we have concluded that the value of Highclere Inn & Carriage House has significantly diminished,*'" Cici read aloud.

"That's the report that canceled Highclere's prospective sale in 2013," said Mason as he tacked the register to the evidence board. "That said, it also indicates that the toxic soil is isolated to the back 39 acres; however, keep in mind the report is ten years old. My worry is the biohazard could've spread to the waterfront by now," he added, turning back to his cousin.

"This means Uncle Tank and Gil have known about the toxic soil for ten years and kept it from the family—I assume doing nothing about it. At lunch, I got the distinct impression that Aida and Laverna were fully up to speed about what killed the 2013 sale. I hate to say it, but I'd wager Stuart is in the loop too. Why not tell everyone else?" wondered Cici.

"It would've outed their efforts to sell without the family's permission."

"True. I can't decide if this is connected to everything else," admitted Cici, closing the report and tucking it into the desk drawer. "Did a municipal pipe burst during the flood of 2005, causing a toxic leak, and that's what has caused the slow death we've seen the back 39 go through in real-time? Or was the poisoning deliberate?"

Mason shrugged.

"The report says it's a toxic soup of over 100 different poisons, including petroleum, lead, and arsenic, which seems pretty deliberate to me, but I don't know enough about it. Keep in mind, the report says the seepage started around 2005, which would've been shortly after Tank married Aida. Considering we weren't super welcoming toward her, perhaps she and Laverna plotted revenge by destroying the value of the one thing we fought for?" he added.

"Until Labor Day, I wouldn't have believed that possible, but their behavior has been sneaky and underhanded. I can agree that it's a deliberate poisoning. That said, we need our own report. If the soil is of similar or a higher degree of toxicity than in 2013, then I don't think the Cliftons are the perpetrators since they stood to inherit Highclere. Killing the value would be the equivalent of shooting themselves in the foot. If the toxicity level has diminished, they might have been the perps but pulled back once they learned the property was theirs. Are you going to share this with the rest of the family?" she asked.

"I have to, even though there is one person on our side who would have the technical know-how to engineer a toxic leak," Mason pointed out.

"Gil," Cici nodded.

"But what's his motive?" asked Mason. "There is nothing from my experience with him that would lead me to believe he'd want to harm Tank or the family."

"That is the more worrisome question," Cordelia admitted when Makayla Dawn knocked on the office door of the old inn.

Cici covered their bulletin board of evidence using an old, moth-eaten (or mouse-nibbled) duvet from one of the guest cabins and pushed the boxes from Louella Stone out of sight. With the blinds partially drawn, she opened the door. A blast of the frigid winter night air smacked her in the face.

"Hi, Mack!" Mason said warmly to Makayla from behind Cici. "Please come in and sit down," he said, pointing her to the corduroy chair.

Makayla removed her homemade toque, and two short blond pigtails tumbled out to dangle behind her ears.

"We appreciate you coming here so late. I'm sure you must be apprehensive about why we wanted to talk to you so urgently," Mason said.

"I've had butterflies since your message. I seem to be getting myself into trouble these days," replied Makayla.

"What kind of trouble?" asked Cici.

Makayla looked down at the worn-out wood floor, tracing the top of her boot along the gaps between the old oak boards.

"My guess is the kind of trouble that brought me here tonight." She looked up at Mason. "You know what I've done?"

"Mack, this afternoon we found out that there is a video of you leaving the carriage house after Tank's fall—or death—and in that video, you are seen stealing items that belonged to my late grandmother. Have you heard about this?" Mason asked, his eyes as warm as possible, given his anxiety.

Makayla looked back down to the floor, her breathing beginning to increase. The silence felt thick between them. Cici could feel the build-up of an emotional wave about to tsunami out of the girl, a wave she needed to hold back.

Placing Makayla's hands into her own, Cici said, "I know what it's like to get yourself into trouble. One of the pesky things about being human is that we are born with overactive survival instincts. Desperation causes even the most rational person to do irrational things. When we feel boxed into a corner, our instinct is to fight our way back out, and almost every time, that fight is in the dark. We claw and punch without knowing what we're doing until we see that small light of hope. Our way out. Let us be that light for you, Makayla. Stop punching in the dark."

Makayla looked up at Cici, tears trickling down her porcelain, youthful face. Her lips quivered but were calmed by a subtle smile, the body's external sign of hope.

"Have you seen the video, Mack?" asked Mason.

"I have the video," she answered.

"How do you have it?" wondered Cici with a smile.

"It was sent to me."

"Do you know by whom?" she asked.

"No. It—they—came through a blocked number."

"They?" noted Mason.

"There's been more than one video," confirmed Makayla.

"How many?"

"Three in total."

"Why do you think whoever sent them wanted you to see them?"

Mack paused. Larger tears slid down her face. The truth, she so wanted the truth to set her free.

"Because the sender said they'd go to the police if I didn't do what they asked. I was scared and didn't want to let my grandfather down."

"They blackmailed you," commented Cici.

"Guess so," agreed Makayla.

"Mack, what did you take from the carriage house?" asked Mason.

"Nothing!" Makayla reacted strongly.

Mason and Cici looked at each other.

"But Mack. There's a video of you leaving the house with my grandparents' belongings. A video you saw and agreed is incriminating enough to be blackmailed for."

"I don't remember doing it," sighed Makayla, shaking her head, "and I couldn't find anything in my house that I allegedly stole. I looked everywhere."

"You think the video is a fake?" asked Cici.

"I don't know. It looked real to me, and I've been known to sleepwalk. I don't remember stealing anything, but I also can't be 100% sure it didn't happen either."

"Makayla, the blackmailer didn't keep their word. They handed the video evidence to the police—"

"Oh my God," Makayla muttered.

"—and the police are investigating. They've spoken to Aida and Laverna, and my friend at the Royal Canadian Mounted Police said local law enforcement has been brought in, and they requested a warrant for your arrest today."

"Holy shit," said Makayla louder. "What am I going to do? Why would the blackmailer send it to the police? I did what they asked of me!"

"Mack, we can't help you if you don't tell us everything," urged Cordelia.

"Do you think they found out I warned you?"

"You warned us?" asked Mason.

"Oh my God. Oh my God," repeated Makayla.

"Mack," said Cici, "you need to focus and tell us all you know."

Makayla stopped her spinning thoughts and looked at the investigative journalist.

"Ok," said Makayla with a sigh.

"You said there are multiple videos. When were you sent the first one?" asked Cordelia.

"On July 30th, just over two months after Senator Valentine fell, but he wasn't dead yet," answered Makayla. Calm and focused.

"Can we see the video?" asked Mason, to which Makayla agreed by pulling her phone from her jacket pocket. She opened the video and handed it to Mason.

Cici leaned in. It was a black and white video, the lens of the cameras set on infrared due to the time of night, which the date stamp showed was 2:18 am on May 31st—almost a week after the security system allegedly fried. The video was 45 seconds, spliced with footage from multiple cameras. Mason and Cici watched Makayla exit through a garage stall of the carriage house, carrying what looked like a heavy loot bag. Lady Valentine's loonie-sized ruby brooch, framed by magnificent white diamonds and gold sprigs, was visible. Drusilla Brisbane had listed the brooch as missing alongside her mother's other belongings.

As the video ended, a black screen appeared with the words, "We require your help. Please respond ASAP."

Cici looked back to Makayla.

"Did you reply?"

"No. I was too scared. First, I wanted to see if I had the items I'd allegedly stolen. But I couldn't find them. I was praying the video was a prank, and if I ignored it, it would all go away. Two days later, another video came through…" she trailed off as she took her phone back from Mason, scrolled through her messages, and pressed play before handing it back to the cousins.

Mason and Cici watched. At first with confusion, then disbelief and shock.

Recalibrating their focus, they stopped and watched again, checking the date and time stamp to confirm the day of the video. They started from the beginning once more, watching the video at half speed before handing it back to Makayla.

"Fuuuuuuuuccccck," sighed Mason.

"Makayla. I...I..." Cici started.

"It's not me, Ms. Bradshaw. The first video might have been, but I know that's not me in the second video. It's a fake, or computer-generated, or AI or something."

"Why didn't you show it to the police?" asked Mason.

"Well...if the first video is real, which I don't think it is, then I truly stole valuable pieces from Lady Valentine's collection. The cops would arrest me for that."

"You are 100% certain the second video is a forgery?" asked Cici.

"I am. Maybe parts of it are real, but the bits with me aren't."

"Can you AirDrop me the videos?" asked Mason.

Makayla nodded and did so.

"I'll send you all three," she added.

"What happened next?" asked Cici.

"I got a call from a blocked number. The voice was being messed with like a Cher song—"

A Cher reference! Mason smiled.

"—I couldn't tell if it was a man or a lady. The first thing they told me to do was to make sure the security system was toast. They said it busted during the storm the night Senator Valentine fell, but I was told to take a blowtorch to the DVR and ensure the hard drive, buttons, cables, and wall outlet were all fried. For good measure, I ran a drill through the ethernet ports at the back of the DVR."

"This was the beginning of August?" asked Cici.

"Yes," confirmed Makayla.

"Mason, are you sure the system failed the night Uncle Tank fell?" asked Cici. "The footage Mack just showed us is date-stamped before and after his fall."

"Well...I was. The police and security firm confirmed it. Now I'm not so sure," he sighed. "I'll have to take a closer look at the camera angles to see if the footage is truly from our system or if there is indeed an unsanctioned second IP security unit somewhere." Mason turned to Makayla, "When did you hear from the blackmailer again?" he asked.

"That was the strange thing...it was near the end of August before I heard from them again. I was anxious for weeks every time my phone rang. But as time passed and there was no call, I thought maybe I'd outrun them?" Makayla said as a question while acknowledging her naïveté.

"What were you doing in the meantime?"

"The inn was open again, so I was busy keeping the place running with Pa—which is what I call my grandfather. With the legacy guests coming and going and no one here to manage—the responsibility fell on us. We didn't complain, though. We're happy to help. It was cool to see Highclere full of people. I'd never seen it like that before. Unique bunch of folks you get here, that's for sure," she laughed.

"A box of frogs," agreed Mason.

"Other than running the inn, was anything else going on that seemed strange?" wondered Cici.

"Just preparing for Senator Valentine's funeral and burial," answered Makayla while still thinking.

"What preparation went into that, other than digging the world's most narcissistic hole?" mused Mason.

"A fair bit, to be honest," answered Makayla.

"Why?"

"Well, Pa got a call from Laverna at the end of June telling him that the prognosis for Senator Valentine was not good. He was unlikely to survive his wounds, and she was preparing for the services and burial. She asked that we locate the plans for the burial grounds to reconfirm the space available to the Senator so they didn't get too big of a casket."

"I thought that problem was licked when Uncle Tank and Laverna redesigned the burial plot ten or twelve years ago?" asked Cici. "Wasn't the whole point to ensure his casket would fit?"

"Don't get me started," began Mason. "But yes. He redesigned his monument and decided that, despite the county ordinance limiting the burial plot to only urns, he would seek special approval for one casket—his own. There are special regulations about caskets versus urns. A casket must be a certain distance from potential drinking water sources, particular vegetation, and animal life. Also, in our case, it couldn't be too close to the walls of the old septic tank on the north side of the burial plot. Anyways, it was his casket that started the domino effect of having to unearth—har har, literally in this case—everybody buried there to accommodate his ego. Apparently, even doing that didn't give him enough space to rest in peace."

Cici and Makayla stared at Mason.

"To be clear, you got yourself started on that one, Mace," pointed out Cici.

"Well, it just pisses me off—still! Vanity. Blarg," Mason added.

"So," said Cici, turning back to Makayla, "Laverna asked you and Ahren to find the plans at the start of the summer?"

"Yup. There's a box in the basement here labeled 'The Burial Plot.' I'd seen it hundreds of times. Inside it were the blueprints for the redesign from 2010. It confirmed the maximum dimensions for the casket and the dimensions for the vault that needed to be dug. We wanted all the headstones to look smart for the funeral, so we began polishing them at the start of the summer for whenever the sad day came. I laugh because we did over-shovel for the casket and accidentally went into the perimeter of two of Lady Valentine's Golden Retrievers. Not far enough to disturb the urns, though."

Makayla blushed.

"You'd done nothing to upset anyone before the videos came in? It's a lot of effort for someone to go to out of petty malice," asked Cici. "What they've sent you took time to piece together if they're indeed fabrications."

The "if" in Cici's sentence made Makayla blush even more.

"Well. I had two other personal projects I'd started, but I don't see how they'd have upset anyone."

"What were they?" asked Mason.

"The box with the burial plot blueprints had a lot of old papers in it. Obituaries of those buried, headstone designs, pictures of the different dogs, and their names on the back. Nothing super exciting, except for two things."

Makayla leaned forward out of instinct.

"The first was a letter sent to Mr. Valentine from Muskoka Lakes, dated around the time of the redesign, saying that they had declined Mr. Valentine's request for a casket exemption because the grounds were deemed unfit for purpose."

"Did they say why?" questioned Mason.

"From what I could understand, and the legal language did go over my head, geological surveyors did a site visit to assess where a casket could be appropriately buried. They did some measuring and drilled deep into the soil, looking for well water. I guess the soil sample was analyzed and had traces of toxins."

Mason and Cici looked at each other in disbelief.

"Including arsenic, lead, and petroleum?" asked Cici.

"Yes! You know!" sighed Makayla.

"We literally found out about it today," replied Mason, "and are still wrapping our heads around it."

"I wasn't sure if any of you knew. So, after I found that letter, I started researching and talked to a few experts to find out what it meant. I sent some soil samples to a professor at the University of Waterloo who was curious to learn more."

Cici and Mason sat silently for a moment before looking at each other, thinking the same thing.

"Mack, who else knows you were looking into this?" asked Mason with some urgency.

"No one. You were all going through too much, and I didn't want to mention it. Just people online, a few chat boards, the professor at Waterloo. That's it."

"When did you send the samples to Waterloo?" asked Mason as Makayla's phone rang.

"Right before the August 1st long weekend. It's Pa calling. I better let him know where I am," said Makayla, standing up and leaving the office to take the call outside.

Cici turned to Mason.

"She's being blackmailed because she stumbled across the biohazard," Cordelia said.

"I agree. We were going to find out about the poisoned soil today regardless of whether I found the report," suggested Mason. "Which seems a bit too coincidental, to be honest."

"True," Cici nodded. "I wonder if Uncle Tank was blackmailed for the same thing."

"If Tank's financial problems were from an extortion plot, then it would make sense that he'd revoke the Highclere trust to sell and recoup his losses so he and the Cliftons could live the life of grandness they'd come to enjoy. The timeline works. The soil is discovered to be toxic in 2010, and he's blackmailed before 2013, then lists Highclere for sale."

Cici nodded as Mason continued to weigh options.

"Maybe," he started, "Tank was responsible for the biohazard and ignored it. I wonder if someone got sick, or worse—died?"

"I will ask Marko to look into professors at the University of Waterloo. There has to be a connection between someone there and Uncle Tank," said Cici, tapping out a quick message on her phone to her new investigative protégé.

"It might not be the UofW professor who outed Mack. It could be someone from an online forum where she left a question," suggested Mason.

"Could be, but I'd bet my vintage Manolo Blahnik Mary Jane's that the link is the professor."

Mason over-exaggerated, sinking into his chair.

"Then you MUST be certain! Carrie Bradshaw had to steal those from the Vogue closet, lest we forget!"

"I've always loved her last name," winked Cici. "Also, great *Sex and the City* deep-cut reference. Bravo you!"

"Guys!" called Makayla, running back into the office distressed.

Both Mason and Cordelia stood up. Out of the corner of her eye, Cici saw the faint whirl of blue and red police lights bouncing against the snow-covered trees of the driveway.

"Oh shit," said Mason.

"What do I do?" asked Makayla.

"Listen to me. Makayla. I don't believe you've done anything wrong. I need you to confirm a timeline for me quickly. OK?" said Cici, focused but firm.

"Ok," she agreed.

"Uncle Tank fell on Victoria Day weekend?"

"Yes!"

"Laverna called you to check the burial plans at the end of June?"

"Yes!"

"You sent the soil samples to Waterloo at the end of July, right before the long weekend in August?"

"Yes," Makayla said, whimpering.

The police vehicles were almost at the door.

"The first video was sent to you a few days later?"

Makayla nodded.

"I'm going to need a yes, Mack."

"Yes!"

"You then took a blowtorch to the security system to ensure it was fried?"

"Yes."

"Then?"

"I had to install eight hidden deer cameras in the trees."

The police had parked and exited their cars, moving on foot toward the inn door.

"Where are they?"

"All over!"

"Are they Wi-Fi?" jumped in Mason.

"No! Card read."

"Then?" pushed Cici.

"I had to steal items from the carriage house the night of Mr. Valentine's funeral."

"Why?"

"I don't know."

"Where are they?"

"I was told to bury them."

"Did they call again?"

"Yes, but I hung up on them right before Thanksgiving. They were very angry with me."

"You said you warned us," asked a frantic Cici, interrupted by the knock on the inn door.

The police announced their presence from outside. Makayla looked from Cici to Mason, then out the window again. Terror stitched on her face.

"Makayla, how did you warn us?" pressed Cici.

Bang, bang, bang.

"Police! We have a warrant for Ms. Makayla Dawn."

"I...I," Makayla stuttered.

Tears streamed down her face.

The police entered the inn and walked toward the office door, their spooky silhouettes projected from the officers' wandering flashlight beams against the door's cracked pane insert.

"Mack. How did you warn us? Where did you bury them? What was the second item you found in the box?" Mason asked in an aggressive whisper.

"It's all..." she started.

"Mack!" urged Mason.

The door to the office opened. Makayla, in terror, turned to Mason and whispered.

"The burial plot."

Chapter Thirty-Two

A Christmas nut since he was a kid, Mason popped his daily chocolate puzzle piece from his Advent calendar before drinking a cup of tea. This year's calendar was special to him, having been sourced by his friend Skye from an underground sex shop during her recent trip to Winnipeg. The *"Celebrity Dick-in-a-Box Christmas Spectacular"* Advent calendar promised that by the birth of Christ, the owner will have assembled a famous male appendage using daily chocolate puzzle pieces. On this, the 14th day of Advent, Mason had long discovered that the dick in his box belonged to Michael Fassbender—and it was going to be delicious! (Mason was also mildly surprised that the manufacturer didn't have to extend Advent to the New Year to create enough pieces to do Fassbender justice).

"Ding dong merrily on high!" Skye sang out as she knocked on Mason's office door.

"And a delicious dong it will be, darling," Mason retorted, looking at his chocolate puzzle. "Truly one of the best gifts you've ever given me, and you're the person who bought me wrapping paper with my face on it! Genius!"

"I know what you like, boss, just don't tell HR," said Skye, closing the door. "Maybe the narcissism apple didn't fall far from the Gramps tree," she winked while sitting across Mason's desk.

"Oh, ouch!" Mason fake cried, campily taking an imaginary dagger and piercing his heart. "How could you do this to me?"

"Oh, shush it, ego boy," she retorted. "Have you sent your Christmas list to Santa yet?"

"I have," Mason replied, rubbing his hands together.

"Annnddd? What did we ask for?"

"Oh, the usual. Evidence that my grandfather's money was stolen from him in an extortion plot surrounding the malicious poisoning of my family's Muskoka resort while dropping reindeer pellets in the correct direction of my late grandmother's missing jewelry in addition to giving me the GPS coordinates of the still MIA Joyce Redstone topped off with the discovery of a magical clause in the Highclere trust that would legally prevent Tank from revoking it in favor of his late in life second wife and the birth certificate of the dead man found at Fernsby House in my stocking."

"You have excellent breath control," noted Skye.

"And world peace," Mason smiled.

"How's Makayla doing? The poor thing—I just want to give her the biggest hug!"

"Have you met her?"

"No! It's just awful to go through that so young. I spent my share of time behind bars at her age, and it hardens you."

"She was in for one night!"

"Well, still. The slammer sticks with you."

Mason gave a sarcastic nod.

"Right. Well, as far as I know, she's doing ok, but we haven't spoken to her since that night—almost a month ago now—and we aren't allowed to see her while she's under house arrest."

"Any luck finding the items she buried the night of Grampy V's funeral?"

"We haven't tried to look for them. Her blackmailer instructed her to install deer cameras around the property. They don't emit a signal of any kind, so we can't scramble them from a distance or find them using a radio controller. The best option is to wander the property with infrared LED goggles, which Cici and I plan to do over Christmas."

"Won't that be obvious?"

"Not if it looks like we're cross-country skiing."

"Why not install your own cameras to catch them when they change SD cards?"

"They seem to have the property well surveilled with deer cameras and a likely second security system. We don't know where their blind spots are, so they're likely to see us before we see them. Whoever 'they' are."

"I've been thinking about your theory that the people who are blackmailing Makayla also extorted mullah from Grampy V over the ground poisoning. What I can't wrap my head around is, why would toxic soil be threatening enough to a Canadian Senator to blackmail him out of millions?"

Mason gave an honest, pensive nod this time.

"The issue, Skye, is we can't figure out what other skeleton they'd blackmail him for. We are still assuming that Tank's accounts were siphoned shortly before he put Highclere for sale in 2013, which would have been three years after the county notified Tank that toxins were in the soil. It's hard to imagine his financial depletion could have happened between 2010 and 2013 for any reason other than extortion resulting from the toxic soil. The timing connects."

"I still don't think it's a big enough reason to give into extortion."

Mason held back his theory that someone may have died from the poisoned ground. A death that would've been embarrassing and a career-ender for a Senator—as ancient as he already was at the time—but legacies still matter, and any deadly mischief Tank got up to would tar the rest of the family as well. He had yet to find evidence to prove or disprove his guess, and until he had more concrete information, he and Cici kept the notion to themselves.

"Time will tell! Once I have the emails, we might glean a bit more information. I'm going to Ottawa the day after tomorrow and will finally have them in my hot little hands."

"Why are they in Ottawa?" asked Skye.

"Oh God, here we go!" laughed Cici, walking into Mason's office. "He's about to gloat ONCE more about what a brilliant idea this was. Go for it, Mason!"

"Thank you, Cici," said Mason as he cleared his throat before slipping into a deep, pretentious broadcaster's voice. "Well, Skye, because Tank was a Canadian Senator, the Privy Council's office requires all electronic communication about state matters be housed at the National Archives for historical and governance preservation. They prefer PCs to use a government account, but like nearly all of them, Tank would flip willy-nilly between his personal and senate accounts. I set up an automated rule in Outlook during the early aughts to keep him out of trouble. Any incoming or outgoing email containing specific keywords from Tank's personal account would be automatically forwarded to the archives. That rule has been in effect for 18 years and was never turned off. Which also means the poor archivist whose job it is to read all that crap has likely been trudging through a pile of Tank Valentine conspiracy horseshit since he stepped down from the Senate."

"Why would that be sent to them?" asked Skye.

"The filters used to identify government-related businesses were very broad. All he had to do was reference government documents in an email or attach a PDF with a parliamentary email listed in the file, and it would trigger the forward."

"Ah," understood Skye.

"How*everrrrrrr*," smiled Cici. "Come on, Mason. Tell her the real brilliant bit."

Mason glared at his cousin. "Have you taken double the dose of your uppers today, Cici? I'm not enjoying this type of levity coming from you."

Cici gave a coy smile and shrugged.

"Yes, well. Again, thank you, Cici. Whenever a new e-mail rule is created, an alert is sent to me, Laverna, and Tank's longtime assistant, Norah Tripplehorn. This security measure was implemented because hackers like to use inbox rules to hide the comings and goings of nefarious communication, which keeps the 'hacked' in the dark. However, an adjustment to an existing rule does not trigger an alert. Therefore, I turned off the trigger words and made it so that every single bloody email ever sent or received by Miles 'The Tank' Valentine has now been forwarded to the Privy Council's office."

"And little Mason Wayson...how does this genius plan finish?" asked Cici, still smiling, blinking her eyes rapidly to annoy her cousin.

"Yes. Thank you again, Cici...one final God damn time. The trick now is to get the emails back from the PC office. This part of the plan seemed simpler in the moment. However, it is proving difficult..." he smiled facetiously at his cousin, white teeth blinding his two guests, "...but I am not one for giving up, and I shall use my winsome charm to get them back."

"How?" asked Skye.

"Well...conveniently, I found the only gay archivist there and have booked an appointment," Mason said, beaming.

"You did?" Skye laughed.

"He did!" confirmed Cici.

"I want you both to know it wasn't as easy as it sounds. It took me HOURS of cross-referencing LinkedIn with Grindr—which I admit the Grindr piece could be a bit distracting—with the government website and Hinge, Tinder, and Match. I have more dates lined up for the New Year than I have had in ten years, and they all expect me to look like I'm 25, so I'm very stressed about that and can't stop eating. So, bite me—both of you! You do it next time," Mason said, crossing his arms in a huff.

"'Tis the season to be jolly," started singing Skye.

"Fa la la la la, la la la la," joined in Cici.

"I hate you both. Especially you, Jolly Come-Stinker. Live up to your name!" Mason yelled at them.

"May I change the subject?" asked Cici.

"Fine," said Mason, pulling out a box of his favorite Christmas nosh, Almond Florentines, from his bag and decidedly not sharing with the ladies.

"I spoke with my movie editor friend last night, and he confirmed what your colleague said, Mason. The first and third videos sent to Makayla aren't fabrications. Admittedly, they haven't been forensically reviewed, but to his eye, and the various mechanics of the videos he could manipulate using his software, they're authentic."

"No surprise. Also, on that topic, thanks to the blackmailer's use of multiple cameras to piece together the incriminating evidence, I can confirm that the footage did not come from Highclere's security system. The angles don't match where our cameras were. That said, two clips seem to have been recorded off-property," Mason noted.

"Drone?" asked Skye.

"No. My guess is they're from Trent Callahan's security system."

"That name is certainly appearing more and more," noted Skye.

"Indeed! What about video two?" asked Mason.

"Also authentic," Cici replied.

"What's she doing in the second?" wondered Skye.

Cici sighed.

"We trust you completely, but it's best we don't share it. The police only have the first video and the third from Labor Day—both of which are legit. From what we can tell, the second video Mack showed us, which is also in our possession, hasn't been given to the police. We want to keep it that way because everything will become even more complicated if it gets out."

The three sat silently, listening to the sound of Christmas bells and a musician on the street corner playing "O Holy Night" on the trumpet.

"By the way, did you see the email from my forensic data scraper re: Mack?" asked Cici.

"Don't you mean your hacker," chuckled Skye as Cici nodded her agreement with a wink.

"I did. I agree we've got our Christmas Eve narrative between the videos being legitimate and the information he sent," Mason answered.

"Perfect! Then, let's go!" said Cici, standing up and signaling Mason to grab his things. "We're off to meet Marko. He has some information for us." She turned to Skye. "Wishing you a very Merry Christmas, Skye!" Cici said, leaning into Skye for a hug.

"What? I don't see you again before Christmas?" asked Skye.

"Not me, at least," answered Cici.

"Nor I, sadly. I've got meetings and have to get packed for Ottawa, then I'm heading straight to Highclere until the New Year. I'm giving myself a few days of silence to cross-reference emails with the diaries. I'm struggling to read Tank's writing and struggling to care about what he's saying. I'm hoping the emails pinpoint me to certain dates in the diaries," added Mason.

"Aww. Merry Christmas to you both! I love you lots, and if you need any sleuthing done over the holidays, just let me know! Otherwise, I'll spend half the time eating and the rest of it replacing the lotion and tissues next to the computers so my grandkids can cleanly occupy their time!"

Chapter Thirty-Three

To: Lawrence Valentine; Jocelyn Valentine; Stuart Valentine; Drusilla Valentine-Brisbane
CC: Cordelia Bradshaw; Roland Mast KC
From: Mason Valentine
Date: December 16, 2023
Re: Highclere Ground Poisoning

Lovers and cheap shaggers,

Cici and I reviewed the urgent ecology report we commissioned to confirm the findings of the document I "found"(shhhh) at Aida's dated 2013. We then had a huddle with her student, Marko (who was wearing the worst ugly Christmas sweater known to humankind—the poor kid. It was dark yellow with white sleeves accented with gold rings around the biceps. If you crossed your eyes, it looked like he was cosplaying the Michelin Man after discovering Ozempic and puking all over himself…but I digress).

Anyway, here's what we know from the new report. Firstly, it's a near certainty that the poisoning of Highclere's back 39 acres was deliberate. While there are what is considered "organic" biohazardous materials—such as arsenic—in many soil beds in the area and are considered "safe," the level of toxicity Highclere is experiencing is categorized as "inorganic." That, compounded with about a hundred other different toxins identified in the samples, has made for one mighty toxic soup.

The samples were taken at various soil depths and radii. The depth samples we commissioned reveal that the poison level is 175 parts per million two feet underground, which is highly toxic—and would also indicate that the poisonous seepage is coming from ground level (or roughly a foot under). These levels are all 135% higher than the 2013 report.

The highest concentration reading is about 25 feet northwest of the burial plot (close to the old septic tank) and is more than five acres from the waterfront, meaning it is unlikely toxic runoff has moved into the lake (and therefore not endangering us or our drinking water).

After mapping out where the samples were taken, we've determined that 24 acres of the back 39 acres of Highclere are largely toxic (though to varying degrees).

How long has this been going on, you may be asking? Well, using farming irrigation averages coupled with assumptions of Highclere's local hydrogeology, as well as taking into consideration the climate of winters, natural barriers such as tree roots, and surface absorption (don't I sound brilliant!), the best guess is that it has taken between 15 and 20 years for the toxic stew to infect and spread to its current concentrations. This aligns with the 2013 report and tacitly substantiates Makayla's theory that Tank's casket was denied in 2010 because of poison found in the ground.

The human effects of ingesting this concoction of toxins directly would be death; however, it indirectly mimics about fifty common illnesses. Symptoms are usually of the "tummy trouble" variety in the beginning and stay in the human body for several days to weeks but exit when you take a shit.

However, since most of the homes in the area are seasonal, if residents were drinking toxic water while on the lake for a weekend or for a few weeks at a time (for example), it would be out of their system within days of returning home with symptoms only reappearing when up north. It would only kill you if you drank it undiluted and directly—which, sadly, many animals and vegetation have been for years and are now dead.

Long-term exposure can lead to cardiovascular disease, diabetes, and cancer, two of which are the most significant contributors to death in the world.

All that to say, there is no way to identify if anyone

has died as a result of the poisoning at Highclere—but chances are extremely remote, unless (as Cici wonders) someone stumbled across the dissemination point—the most toxic spot—and became sick and died. She suggests that if a Senator were implicated in such a death, it would end any legacy he'd hope to leave—meaning easy blackmail material (which is the first likely theory we've come up with about why Tank was successfully extorted).

Next step is to find the dissemination point.

With the ground being frozen, it is safe for us to be up at Christmas.

Marko did more research and pulled a report of a similar deliberate ground poisoning in Manitoba, which provides insight into administration and clean-up.

We will see what comes of it. I'm off to Ottawa tomorrow!

SEE YOU ALL REAL SOON!!
Mason

PS- Cici has asked if she, Tobias, and the kids can join us at Highclere for Christmas. I've said YES; however, should any of you disagree, please reply all so your darling cousin can understand why you hate her so—especially during this festive season of love and joy.

* * *

To: Cordelia Bradshaw
From: Mason Valentine
Re: re: Highclere Ground Poisoning

UMMM CORDELIA—flip to the last page of the report Marko gave us re: the deliberate farm poisoning in Manitoba. An extremely interesting and recognizable name appears…
I have an idea.
X M

PS- LET IT SNOW, LET IT SNOW, LET IT SNOW!!!!!

Chapter Thirty-Four

"Hi! I'm Mason Valentine, and I'm here to see William Marshall," announced Mason with such intense festive enthusiasm he felt as though he might burst a blood vessel in his eye.

Focused on the fact that William Marshall, the archivist, could be anyone or anywhere, Mason wanted to ensure he was at his delightful best from the moment he stepped into the Office of the Privy Council of Canada. A sandstone building just outside the Parliament Hill complex, it was known for its "Second Empire" style of architecture—an architectural type that Mason would have zero ability to discern or identify outside of Wikipedia telling him of its existence.

More importantly, the building also housed the Office of the Prime Minister, and while Mason had visited many corridors of the gothic Canadian government complex during his lifetime, he'd never set foot into this specific building.

Dressed in an olive-green military-style winter overcoat, black skinny dress pants, and his signature Chelsea boots, Mason felt confident.

Mason felt sure of himself.

Mason felt William Marshall would be putty in his hands at the sight of the stylish man candy appearing before him.

Mason also knew that he was one hat short of being accused of a complete style rip-off from the Princess of Wales, as seen on the cover of a recent glossy—a glossy that was awkwardly facing him amongst a stack of papers and magazines on the table next to the guest waiting chair. However, should anyone ask, he would claim the Princess stole the look from *him*.

"Who?" asked the plexiglass-imprisoned security guard without looking Mason in the eyes.

"Mason Valentine," he repeated.

"No, that part I got. Who're you here to see?"

"William Marshall," Mason said.

"ID, please," requested the guard, stretching her hand through a banana-sized hole in the partition. Mason handed over his passport, which the guard scanned into the computer using an open-top flatbed digitizer.

The guard paused.

She looked at her computer screen, then at Mason.

Confused, Mason plastered on a smile. Was there a federal warrant out for his arrest he wasn't aware of? Was he about to be taken into custody? Or, worst of all, is she the first to notice the obvious similarities between his outfit and that of Kate Middleton and was about to call him out?

The guard stood and held Mason's passport next to his face.

"You're a Senator?" she asked with a mix of shock, confusion, and irritation.

"What!" Mason replied with unexpected intensity, causing the guard to take an instinctive step backward.

"My system says you are Senator Miles Valentine?"

"I most certainly AM NOT!" Mason responded indignantly, emphasizing the final two words definitively and bitchily.

"Your passport says Miles Mason Valentine; my system says you're a member of the Senate. Are you saying my system isn't accurate, sir?" she questioned.

Oh, for the love of God, thought Mason.

"No. I'm Mason Miles Valentine. Miles is my middle name. Miles Valentine was my grandfather; he was indeed a Canadian Senator but retired in 2010. He died this past August."

"Sorry for your loss," the guard said, sounding as sincere as Amazon's Alexa. Which Mason would have to admit was all the sincerity the gesture warranted about this particular death anyway. "I was about to give you a full access pass!" guffawed the guard, who Mason could now see was named Edna.

"You still could," Mason smiled back.

"No," Edna scolded. "Who are you here to see again?"

Government efficiency at its best.

"William Marshall. He's an archivist for the Privy Council's Office," he repeated with slight exasperation, checking his watch to ensure he wouldn't be late for his meeting.

Edna scrolled and scrolled and scrolled before BINGO!

"Ah," Edna sighed. "Please have a seat and feel free to flip through the magazines to find other outfits you can steal from Royalty."

Damn it! Edna had no irony in her voice either. Monotone as can be, which made the exposure of Mason's fashion thievery all the worse!

Mason affixed his visitor pass to his coat and sat down.

* * *

"Anni, hello. I'm Jolly Puanteur, and I have an appointment with Lois Rudan for a massage," announced Skye with a smidge more boosterism than the situation warranted.

Having again adopted her pseudonym of Jolly and a more family-friendly surname, she was decked out in a blond wig, green contact lenses, and Chanel caftan.

"Welcome," responded the red-headed receptionist dressed head to toe in white and with a complexion so pale you could see the inner workings of her blood vessels under the LED lights. Skye hoped her name was Casper, and if it wasn't, Skye would call her that anyway. "Do you have your membership card with you?" Casper asked.

"Umm," said Skye, beginning to feel her face warm.

"It's in your phone! I sent it last night," announced Cordelia through the surreptitious earpiece Skye was wearing.

Cici was in the Security Technicians Inc.—or STI—van outside of the decadent and elite Spa Fab in Yorkville. She was listening and coaching Skye, aka Jolly, through their latest ruse.

"Of course, treasure! It's in my phone," Skye replied to Casper.

She pulled out her phone to find her entrance pass.

"You're sure she'll be here?" Skye asked into her two-way earpiece once she was alone in the plush ladies' locker room of Spa Fab.

"I am," confirmed Cici. "She mentioned in an email to Aida Clifton that she has a standing appointment at this time. I've followed her to confirm, and she's kept it for the last few weeks. I'm confident she'll be here and not out holiday shopping."

Skye sighed.

"I'm still not sure we're doing the right thing keeping this hoax from Mason. I felt strange lying about not seeing you both again until the new year," she confessed.

"I know. It sits funky with me, too. He knows I cloned Aida's phone at lunch in November as a 'plan B,' so he's not completely in the dark. He just doesn't know what we've found and what we're doing about it. Look, I hate keeping things from him, but in this case, I know he'd get worked up and jump to conclusions before we have answers. I'll drop it if we don't get any new information. I have a hunch that she'll have loose lips if we work her properly. Or find her a cocktail."

"Ok, ok. I trust you," said Skye as she tightened her white robe and readjusted her wig, which had become loose while changing.

"You'll recognize her when she comes in?" asked Cici.

"I think so."

* * *

Mason continued to wait for William Marshall. Having finished his twenty-third back-to-back game of solitaire on his phone, he worried he would miss his afternoon flight back to Toronto if William continued to be delayed. Or worse, his time to review the archive of emails would be too limited to give fruit to any answers Mason was looking for.

Wondering the time, Mason slid the game app up his screen to check the clock—1:30 pm.

Mason hoped William Marshall would give him a hard drive filled with digital copies of Tank's emails to review during the holidays. However, he knew deep down that he would likely be given limited time to flip through physical papers under supervision. It wasn't his preferred option, but he knew which years to prioritize if the emails were organized by date.

Mason stood to talk to Edna as his anxiety rose while the "Hallelujah Chorus" from Handel's Messiah played through a small black Bluetooth speaker on her desk.

Hallelujah! Hallelujah!
Hallelujah! Hallelujah! Halle—lujah!
Smile on, boy!
"Edna!" Mason said jovially.
Hallelujah! Hallelujah!
Hallelujah! Hallelujah! Halle—lujah!
"Yes?" she replied with a quick shuffle of papers on her desk.
For the Lord God omnipotent reigneth
Hallelujah! Hallelujah!

Mason peered through the plexiglass to see what state secrets Edna was hiding from him. From what he could tell, officially, she was cross-referencing two visitor logs. However, unofficially, Mason could easily see the glow of her phone screen beneath the papers, revealing the captivating world of Candy Crush. Edna's sheepishness in trying to hide her phone was surprisingly endearing.

Hallelujah! Hallelujah!

"I hate to be a bother, but I'm worried I'll miss my transfer back to Toronto this afternoon if Mr. Marshall is much longer. Do you have an ETA for him?" Mason asked, smiling wide but with his eyes showing a dollop of casual concern.

Hallelujah! Hallelujah!
Hallelujah! Hallelujah!

"I'm so sorry for the wait. He'll be out in a moment," reassured Edna, who was assessing her computer monitor. "I see his fob just opened the security door down the hall," she explained with a newfound compassion clearly attributed to being busted with her phone out.

The kingdom of this world, and His of Christ

"Thank you so much! I love this song, by the way. It reminds me of one of my favorite episodes of the old show *Touched by An Angel*."

"Oh! I loved that show too!" replied Edna, who leaned to her left and increased the speaker's volume.

A resounding buzz captured Mason's attention, leading him to watch the gradual opening of a massive brown wooden door. The room beyond emitted a radiant glow of afternoon sunlight, causing Mason to squint his eyes. The figure who emerged from behind the door was nothing but a silhouette. His heart filled with anticipation, and Mason hoped that the approaching person was none other than William Marshall.

And he shall reign for ever and ever
King of kings, and Lord of lords.

As Mason's eyes adapted to the light, they locked onto a man with a beaming white smile, dimpled cheeks, and thick, tousled brown hair approaching him.

And he shall reign for ever and ever
King of kings, and Lord of lords.

The door closed, and Mason could now see William Marshall.

Hallelujah! Hallelujah!

His picture on LinkedIn didn't do the man justice. With his electric smile, he exuded confidence and warmth.

Hallelujah! Hallelujah!

He was adorably preppy with his button-up blue shirt tucked into his tan chinos. Mason looked to the floor to see William was also sporting his favorite footwear—Chelsea Boots.

Hallelujah! Hallelujah!
Hallelujah! Hallelujah!

For the first time in forever, Mason felt unbalanced. He could feel his heart beating. His palms became sweaty. His face flushed a slight red, and if he was being honest, there was a tightness stirring in his pants, which was happily covered by his overcoat. The "Hallelujah Chorus" blasted in his ear, the sunlight perfectly diffused by the closing door; Mason wasn't sure whether time had slowed down or if he had died and gone to heaven. Either way, he wasn't opposed to the sight.

Ha....lle....lu....jah!!!!!!!!

The song rang out at its musical finish.

Hallelujah indeed, thought Mason.

"Hi! I'm William," he introduced himself, extending his right hand.

* * *

Skye exited her hour-long massage with Lois Rudan and entered the ladies' locker room.

There she was. Her target. She was sitting on the plush lavender ottoman, staring at her phone while wearing a large white fleece robe. Skye took a breath, regained her courage, and went for it.

"Louise Fucking Harris!?" Skye yelled as she walked toward Tank's long-time lawyer, projecting a look of wonder, familiarity, and excitement at seeing someone she hadn't seen in eons.

The reality, of course, is that they'd never met before.

Louise wore her snow-white hair in a ponytail held in place by a red ribbon. The unforgiving overhead lighting revealed awkward shadows on her narrow face, revealing the hard contours of her bone structure.

Louise looked at Skye, puzzled. A look, which Cici explained earlier, could be used to their advantage, considering Louise Harris had had hundreds of clients, co-workers, friends, and sorority sisters over her sixty-ish years, which she'd never recognize in a line-up without a facial recognition program.

Despite Louise's tentative look, Skye embraced her in a big bear hug. Louise stood, plastered a smile on her face, and faked a sincerity she'd hoped wouldn't have to be repeated so soon after her weekly nighttime ritual with her husband the night before.

"Why hello, YOU!" Louise said as she leaned in and squeezed Skye in return.

"I honestly can't believe it!" said Skye, holding Louise tight and rocking her back and forth.

Louise's arms had become limp, but Skye kept her close. Squeezing. Louise's eyes bulged slightly.

"I saw you sitting over there, and I was like, 'OH. EM. GEE! There is Louise Fucking Harris! I haven't seen her since first year law school,' but I'd recognize you anywhere. You look the exact same. I'm sure if you looked up Jolly Puanteur in our yearbook, you'd be like, 'What the hell has she done to her body?' but you know, aging seems to go better for some people than others! The rest of us melt and expand," Skye rhymed off, almost shouting. She released Louise once Louise gave her a not-so-subtle and rather hard double pat on the back.

Louise and Skye held each other at arm's length, both wearing smiles, eyes wide.

"Jolly, you haven't changed a God damned bit!" lied Louise. "Honest to God. Where has the time gone?" she asked, making small talk.

"Beats the hell out of me! What time is your massage?" asked Skye.

"I just finished. Quick one today. You?" replied Louise.

"Just walked out! That Damian...prrr!!!" Skye lied. "Anyways, it's just such a treat to see you, plus it's the festive season. What do you say about a quick drink? Could use your advice on something," Skye asked, hoping to all hell that Louise's ego would be too big to say no.

Louise stepped back to her open locker, looking at her phone and then at Skye.

"Let's do it!" she answered.

Cici, listening to the entire conversation, pumped her fists in the air with joy. This was going to work.

Chapter Thirty-Five

"Hire. I'm Taston Malentine," Mason said as he extended his hand to clasp William's.

What!?

"Sorry! Hi, I'm Mason Valentine," he corrected himself, regaining his composure.

As stupidly handsome as William Marshall was, Mason reminded himself he had a mission to accomplish with little time. He didn't have the luxury of googly-eyed time.

Well, one or two seconds of googly-eyeing won't hurt anyone, he thought.

"It's a pleasure to meet you! I read two of your books and did a bit of a Google stalk before you came," admitted William, still smiling.

His dimples indented so dreamily that Mason wondered if they were surgically created.

"You say some hilarious stuff on your podcast, too! A bit risky...but I laughed out loud!"

"Oh God! I often cringe at what I say. Also, don't believe everything you read about me!" replied Mason.

"Follow me," William instructed, though Mason would've followed him anywhere.

William pulled out his ID badge and fobbed open the brown door once more, holding it open for Mason as he placed his hand on his upper back to guide him through.

Shiver...

Slight stiffening...

Shit...

"I appreciate you taking the time today," Mason said, trying to take control of his manner.

"Oh, it's my pleasure. I appreciate you reaching out about this. I've set us up in a conference room down the hall."

Mason hoped that wasn't code for, "I've put all the documents in a conference room, and you'll have five minutes to flip through them while I adorably watch you."

William and Mason walked in companionable silence through a labyrinth of working civil servants hunched over computers in their cubicles. Moments later, William swiped his ID badge to open a sliding glass door to a medium-sized conference room with windows running across the entire width. William walked ahead of Mason to turn on the lights, and Mason couldn't help but notice that William's ass was perfectly cupped by his pants.

It was going to be hard...er...tough to focus.

With the lights up, Mason eyed the frosted conference table and became deflated upon seeing it was empty except for three brown banker boxes and a laptop. He felt his heart sink. Either a career's worth of emails and documents could fit into three unassuming boxes, or he was about to be let down.

"Please have a seat," William said, pointing to a chair next to the laptop computer. He then poured Mason a glass of water and handed it to him.

William situated himself in front of his screen and turned to face Mason.

God damn, his hair and smile were bloody perfect. It almost made Mason want instant hair plugs, a few shots of Botox, and to experiment with nipple Skims.

"So, how can I help you, Mr. Valentine?" William asked.

His green eyes fixated on Mason's.

"Call me Mason. As I said in my email, we are organizing my late grandfather's estate and need some emails and documents to help us with this process. Which, I'm sure you can imagine, has been an utter delight," Mason smiled while rolling his eyes with great exaggeration to confer facetiousness. "Unfortunately, his assistant closed his account too soon after he died, and his history of correspondences was deleted," Mason lied.

"Do you have a copy of Senator Valentine's will with you? I'll need to confirm you're an executor."

Shit. Fuck.

Beautiful dimples, though...

Shit. Fuck again!

"I don't, but I'd be happy to send you a PDF when I return to the city."

Better find a decent photoshoper ASAP.

"Without it, I'm not sure what I can show you today," William admitted, though he didn't look happy about it.

"You can't show me anything? I'm his grandson."

"I know you are Mr. Valentine—"

"—Mason!"

"—sorry! Mason. But there are certain protocols we have to follow to release archived information ahead of the unsealing date."

"When's the unsealing date?"

"It depends. We can provide a limited amount of information in legal circumstances to family, and if someone files an Access to Information Act request. However, most files, correspondences, and official documentation about a deceased member of the Privy Council remain under the privy seal for fifty years. It takes an act of parliament, or the Crown, to release them sooner."

"So I'd have to wait until the year 2073?"

William laughed—a twinkle in his eyes. He leaned toward Mason, putting his hand on his.

"No. I'm not going to make you wait. I just need to come up with a reasonable explanation about why I'm turning over documents to you."

Mason could see the kindness and warmth in William's eyes—he wanted to help, and Mason could tell he was a trustworthy person. Mason had planned to flirt his way into going home with all the records he could, but perhaps this was a time for the unvarnished truth rather than charismatic subterfuge. There was a connection between the two, an immediate spark. Maybe that was enough to get what he wanted. Though he had to admit Cici wouldn't be too thrilled about anything other than being wittily devious in case William wasn't what he appeared.

Mason took a sip of water and looked up at the stucco ceiling. Keeping his eyes fixed on the tiny white chunks, he told William the truth.

"I'm not an executor."

Mason moved his eyes down to William, who was still smiling at him. He wasn't phased.

"I suspected that much," William admitted before closing his laptop. "Why are you really here, Mason?"

Mason wasn't sure what he was about to say was the right thing to do, but he went for it anyway.

"Since my grandfather died, there have been several mysteries surrounding my family that we can't make sense of. From what I can tell, my grandfather lost the lion's share of his fortune about twelve years ago for reasons we can't figure out. My late grandmother, who died two decades ago, had many priceless heirlooms that have gone missing, and we're curious to know if the Senator knew what happened to them or was aware of their disappearance. There are other oddities concerning ownership of a family property and what appears to be a calculated plot to poison our land. William," Mason leaned forward and lowered his voice above a whisper, assuming the Government was listening, "there are a lot of serious things happening to the Valentine family at the moment, including a mysterious death at an ancestral home in the UK, blackmail plots against our staff, and more that I shouldn't implicate you in. I don't know if there's anything amongst my grandfather's correspondences that will help, but I'd like to skim through specific periods, cross-reference with his diaries that I am in possession of, and see if I can piece together what the hell is going on."

He bit his lip.

William kept his eyes on Mason as he listened. His smile faded—his face became serious. Absorbing everything this relative stranger had just revealed to him, William sat back, placing his hands behind his head before taking a deep breath.

Mason couldn't help but notice William's toned arms as he did so.

"Are you in danger?" William asked, concern in his voice.

Mason also sat back in his chair. He shrugged.

"I don't know for sure. I think my family could be in some kind of danger."

"Are the authorities involved? The RCMP or the Canadian Security Intelligence Service?" asked William.

Mason shook his head again.

"No. We're working alone. My cousin and I have assembled a bit of a variegated group of curious but loving oddballs to see what's what."

William smiled.

"Why am I picturing the A-Team?"

"Think more circus performer types," replied Mason.

"You're sure the authorities aren't involved?" William asked again with an expression that indicated he knew something.

Mason was surprised.

"We haven't involved them, though the Ontario Provincial Police arrested a staff member of ours after being provided with what we believe to be disingenuous evidence. For various other reasons, the Metropolitan Police in the United Kingdom are also on the periphery. Besides some threats and our assumptions of criminal behavior, we don't have enough facts to bring in police yet."

Which was the truth.

"Even with the poisoning?"

"Even with the poisoning. We don't know where it came from or why."

The two sat in silence once more. William rubbed his eyes and leaned forward. A light curl fell from his bushy hair down his forehead.

"Cordelia Bradshaw is the cousin you're referring to? One of the carnival performers?" William asked.

"She is," Mason agreed, though surprised.

"Talented investigator."

"She is. William, why did you ask if I was sure the security services weren't involved? Your manner signaled you know more," Mason wondered.

William hesitated before standing and moving to the banker's boxes. Opening a lid, he pulled out several file folders.

"We archive all files about privy councilors, including notices of security threats. We don't store them digitally. When I received your inquiries, I downloaded and compressed the entire archive of Senator Valentine's emails for you but decided to satiate my curiosity about what's in the paper files. I found this."

William handed him a file titled *"Hon. Senator M. Valentine - RCMP Dispatch 2012."*

Mason opened the file and read the top sheet.

"Shit," he said under his breath.

Mason looked up to see that William had retaken his seat.

"This is legit?" Mason asked.

"Of course."

"Am I reading this correctly? My grandfather called the RCMP in 2012 because of a blackmail threat?"

"That's how I understand it," William agreed.

"But by the time dispatch had sent officers to speak with him, he recanted his claim?"

"Correct, but to be safe, the RCMP monitored his bank accounts in case he was being threatened into lying. They noticed significant sums of money being transferred but couldn't follow the transfers to a recipient. The endpoint was cloaked. They spoke to Senator Valentine again by phone to re-confirm his assertion that he wasn't being blackmailed, and he once more denied it—said a prank had been played on him, nothing to worry about. They couldn't reasonably continue investigating and closed the case."

"Did they stop monitoring his accounts?"

"It doesn't say, or at least not from what I read. The FBI was involved, but that was to monitor incoming foreign transfers that might match the amount the Senator sent. I'm not an expert in bank fraud," he laughed, "but I'm sure the money was splintered and washed."

"Well. I guess you've confirmed it. He was being blackmailed and successfully at that. Now, the question is why and by whom?"

Chapter Thirty-Six

Jolly Puanteur and Louise Harris squeezed into a small red leather booth in the back corner of Sassy's Sauce, a cocktail lounge on the outskirts of Toronto's fashionable Yorkville area and an easy one block away from Spa Fab.

Cordelia continued to monitor the conversation from STI, which remained parked in the same position as earlier. Thankfully, it was close enough to Sassy's to maintain a strong connection with Skye's earpiece.

"Mrs. Harris, welcome back," greeted the young server with a distinct Spanish accent. His soft, blemish-free, tanned skin perfectly accentuated his chiseled features.

"Hello, Tristian. I'll have the usual, please," said Louise.

Louise turned to Skye. "Jolly, what will you have? Wait—no—let me guess. I want to see if I can remember your drink of choice!" said Louise, scrunching her face, trying to think back and find memories that were so non-existent that Skye almost felt embarrassed.

"This should be wildly entertaining," whispered Cici into Skye's earpiece. "I wish I brought popcorn!"

"It was something strange..." Louise said before brightening up and looking at Skye, smiling.

"It was a Pink Pantie Drop!" she declared.

"Oh my God. Play along," instructed Cici.

"Oh goodness!" Skye chuckled. "You're so, so close. It was actually an Adios Motherfucker. Remember? With vodka, tequila, rum, gin, and Blue Curacao?"

"That's it!" agreed Louise, lying so convincingly that Skye believed they could fake an entire friendship and get away with it.

"So, one gin and tonic and one Adios Motherfucker?" confirmed Tristian while taking their menus.

"She'll have an Adios Motherfucker also," said Skye to Tristian before turning to Louise and winking.

"Oh, sure, why not?" agreed Louise. "It's Christmas, after all!"

"This is going to be child's play," squealed Cici to Skye.

Fifteen minutes later, after their first sips of Adios Motherfuckers, Louise Harris' lips were floppier than an untied shoelace.

"...I mean. Who knew you'd need Viagra at such a young age? Also, the ads are misleading, aren't they? You think, 'Oh well, he'll take a pill, and forty minutes later, he'll have a raging hard-on,' but the truth is you still have to get him worked up! It's exhausting! I thought modern science would help me keep that time of the week down to a few quick minutes. Nope! I'm still required to put in effort. Typical. Clearly designed by a man," ranted Louise as she sipped the blue liquid further down her cylinder glass.

Skye nodded, took a sip, and looked at her watch.

"Louise, do you mind if I jump into the advice I mentioned earlier?" she asked.

"Of courth," was Louise's lushy, lispy reply.

"Skye, I'll ask anything in your ear you forget, so don't worry, just be casual and curious," assured Cici.

"As you know, I'm in the resort business. My husband and I have opened several over the last thirty years, and they've been massive successes," Skye started.

"I knew that. I read an article in the Star or Globe about it. Good for you, truly!" lied Louise.

"This bitch is good," said Cici to Skye, who nodded in unseen agreement.

"Anyways, I know you're well connected within the Muskoka region, and I was wondering if you knew of any properties of scale—perhaps on quieter lakes—that might be worth development?"

Louise sat silently, taking another sip of the blue concoction before shaking her head, "Not off-hand, unfortunately. There was a larger-than-usual parcel on Lake Muskoka a few years back and another at Georgian Bay earlier in the year, but they sold rather quickly. Which is normal in the region."

"No other lakes? The main four maybe—Muskoka, Joseph, Rosseau, and Belvedere?" pushed Skye.

"I don't think so."

"That's a shame," Skye said, looking forlorn, "We wanted to open an inn on a nice, yet underdeveloped, though exclusive lake and—"

"—actually," interjected Louise, leaning to pick up her phone, "there is one. Do you remember an old politician named Miles Valentine?" she asked.

Skye shook her head.

"Not at all. Was he high ranking?"

"He was. Very senior cabinet minister in the sixties and seventies before becoming a senator. Anyway, he died recently, and his prized treasure of a property was a dump of a resort on Lake Belvedere called Highclere Spa & Stables or something to that effect."

"Bitch," whispered Cici.

"If it's a dump, I'm sure the family must be selling it on the cheap," mused Skye.

"How long has it been in the family?" asked Cici.

"Any idea how long it's been in the family?" regurgitated Skye to Louise, who was still scrolling through her phone.

"Oh, a long, long time. I think Mr. Valentine once told me it had been in the family for over one hundred and fifty years?" she guessed.

"Why are they selling?" prompted Cici.

"Goodness! Why would the family decide to sell a legacy property like that?" asked Skye.

"They wouldn't if it was the family's decision, but he didn't leave it to them. He left it to his wife."

"A second marriage?" asked Skye.

"Yes, after his first wife died, he quickly remarried to have a queen for his kingdom."

"Your tone makes me feel like it was a marriage of convenience," suggested Skye.

"More for one than the other," winked Louise as she passed her phone to Skye. "That's the property listing."

"Looks beautiful. Definitely a fixer-upper. Why didn't he leave it to his family?"

"He said they didn't deserve it."

"How come?" asked Skye while pretending to scroll.

"Family dynamics. I get the impression he wasn't the world's greatest father, if I'm being honest. I also suspect he was having some financial issues at the end of his life, and if a woman is going to marry a man for money, you better be able to pay at the end of that agreement, come hell or high water. I think this property is all he had."

"Isn't this the guy people think was assassinated? The conspiracy guy?" fed Cici to Skye.

"Oh wait, you know! I do remember this, Miles Valentine. He was big into conspiracies, right? I feel like I read somewhere that his fans think he was assassinated?" asked Skye while handing the phone back to Louise.

"Lots of nuts out there," Louise answered, putting her phone in her purse.

"You don't believe he was?" asked Skye.

"I doubt it. He was one hundred years old," replied Louise, polishing off her drink.

"When did you last see him?" Cici prompted again after a moment passed.

"Did you see him often?" Skye asked Louise, who was pink in the face from her Adios Motherfucker.

"A fair bit. He was a good and long-standing client. Difficult at times. Inconsistent, I guess, is a better way to put it. He was easily swayed by whoever was in favor, and I guess, in the end, he favored his wife's family the most. I'd like to have said goodbye to him," she answered, waving to Tristian for the bill.

"It can happen so suddenly," agreed Skye

"Especially with Miles. We spoke by phone on a Wednesday because he wanted to sign an updated will we drafted months earlier at his request. We were supposed to meet the following Tuesday to sign it, but he fell the day before, so I didn't get to see him."

"Falling before signing a new will? That's suspicious," said Skye, "maybe his fans have a point about assassination?" she mused.

Louise laughed.

"His wife is many things, but a killer she is not. Of course, from an ethical standpoint, the amended will would've done the right thing. But that's not for me to talk about."

"Did he get an electronic copy?" Cici wondered.

"Our lawyers always refuse to send draft documents to us via email. Only through an encryption portal. How does your firm handle it?" asked Skye.

"It depends on the client. Mr. Valentine liked things on paper, so we couriered the draft will to his home about four months before he fell."

"And you're sure the will changes wouldn't have made someone push him to his death?" asked Skye.

Louise laughed again.

"Maybe it could've. His stepdaughter had a lucrative non-binding sales agreement drawn up with a buyer ten or eleven years ago, which would've fallen through once the new will was fully executed."

Louise paused, considering whether to share more.

"Let me put it this way," she continued in a whisper, "and God knows I shouldn't say this, but we're old friends. If the Senator had gotten to sign his new will, it wouldn't be his wife you'd be negotiating with for his resort."

"Intrigue," sang Skye as they both stood from the booth.

"What do you think of the humble dump? I don't know the status of the non-binding agreement, but I sense it's in flux. I know my colleagues have been canvassing it to commercial real estate companies for Mrs. Valentine, but I can get you a tour if you're interested in seeing it?" offered Louise.

"Would love to! Give me your card, and I'll give you a call," said Skye.

* * *

Cici watched through STI's spy hole as Jolly said goodbye to her fictional longtime friend Louise Harris, KC. Skye winked at Cici's van while walking in the opposite direction from Louise.

Cici leaned back, her suspicions confirmed. She had cloned email conversations from Aida's phone and discovered a thread discussing the cancellation of an "estate meeting" with Louise, which was scheduled for the day after Tank's accident. It was clear why the meeting never occurred—Tank was unable to sign new documents because of his brain injury.

But what about Highclere's ownership? Had Tank experienced a change of heart and passed down the beloved resort to his children? Or was there a third party set to become the new beneficiary of Highclere Inn & Carriage House?

If Laverna had a non-binding sales agreement drawn up ten-plus years ago—an agreement that would've become moot with the will change—was it possible that the Cliftons had resorted to violence to ensure their inheritance of the property?

Chapter Thirty-Seven

To: Mason Valentine
From: Baroness Margaret Ambrosia MBE
Date: December 20, 2023
Re: Re: Farnsworth Marble & Designs

Darling Mason,

Stellan wishes me to tell you that his DI was able to speak with Mrs. Romero (the owner of Farnsworth Marble & Designs), and she largely reasserted the information I previously relayed to you. She went through the grisly ordeal of being shown a photograph of the deceased, and while she couldn't be 100% confident in her assertion, she did agree that the man in the photograph resembled the alleged "Maxwell Fernsby" who bought the cufflinks from her some years ago.

Sadly, this doesn't get us any further, as "Maxwell Fernsby" is a phantom of which there is no historical record.

Lastly, the cufflinks "Maxwell Fernsby" was wearing are authentic. Mrs. Romero was able to show the DI where to find the "signature." It's located on the bullet (the narrow cylinder that secures the cufflink in place), and indeed, it is a microscopic upright rectangle with a dot in the middle. Please find attached a picture the boys in the lab took for your perusal.

That's all from me.

Love to you, and Happy Christmas!

Xx
Margot

* * *

```
To: Lawrence Valentine; Stuart Valentine; Drusilla Valen-
tine; Jocelyn Valentine
CC: Mason Valentine; Cici Bradshaw
From: Roland Mast
Date: December 21, 2023
Re: Highclere Family Trust
```

Troops,
My office has done some investigating, and I've gone through the entire historical record of the Highclere trust, and I'm irritated by what I have to report back.

The original trust was created in 1923 upon the birth of the bulldozer known as Tank. His father, Hollis Valentine, is listed as the settler who created the trust. He and his wife were the trustees until Tank and his two sisters came of age, and then they became trustees and beneficiaries. When Hollis died (from what I can tell), Tank swindled his sisters out of the property by buying their shares using his inheritance from his father. Get this, the shit had the property appraised in 1973, right after his dear ol' daddy died, and was told that it was worth a conservative $105,000. Through our research, we have calculated the 1973 value of Highclere to actually be around $207,000, so his estimate was HIGHLY conservative, to the point of being unconscionably low. However, that wasn't low enough for Tank, as he told his sisters that it was worth no more than $90,000 and he'd pay each of them $10,000 in cash plus a share of the resort's profits. But since Highclere never *EVER* made a profit during its operational years, the sisters collected just $10,000 dollars. Not a loonie more.

When they were bought out, the trust was dissolved, and Highclere became privately owned by Tank. This, of course, is at odds with what Tank wrote in the letter he left y'all. However, based on paperwork, that is the truth.
I also understand that the original trust from 1923 was used as the basis for the future trust despite not being applicable. The current governing trust was created in 1993 once Tank and Lady V had all of their grand-ankle biters,

and the term "settler"—creator of the trust—is still used in the 1993 version but is not defined by name. The settler is simply noted as "the owner of the property known as Highclere Inn & Carriage House prior to being placed in trust"—obnoxiously—in this instance, that person is, in fact, Tank. If it were a continuation of the 1923 trust, then Hollis would be the settler, but legally, that's not and can't be the case since that trust wound up in the early 1970s. A revocation clause has been in every version of the trust since 1923.

I confronted Tank's underachieving lawyer, Louise Harris, about the settler nuance, and while she asserted privilege, she mused that "the family should have read the trust a bit closer. However, it would be understandable if family members wrongly assumed the settler to be Hollis from a quick scan." Pissingly (not a word, just made it up), Tank has been the settler for fifty years. Legally…it's all been kosher.

So…we're SOL.

That said, the 2005 trust, where you specifically state that Mega Rip-off is not a beneficiary, still describes the property as being "Fifty Acres on Lake Belvedere, Muskoka—Land Parcel ML182391," which is incorrect. In 2002, the county bought one acre from the trust at a cost of $200,000 for hydro administration purposes, meaning ML182391 is not correctly described. The correct property description should read "Forty-Nine Acres on Lake Belvedere, Muskoka—Land Parcel ML182391." We could go to court and try to split hairs, but my instinct says the understanding between the parties was clear that the agreement pertains to the remaining 49 acres even if incorrectly administered. I doubt the result would change, but I can try. You still have until May 24th to get it back—then you're sunk.

Think about it over Xmas and let me know if you want me to peruse it.

Feliz Navidad to y'all.
Rolly

Chapter Thirty-Eight

The halls of Athabasca Cottage were decked, with no surprise, literal boughs of holly (though for most of Mason Valentine's life, he believed the song lyric was "bells of holly").

Every year, Mason traveled to Highclere Inn & Carriage House ahead of the rest of his family to festivize and create a Christmas wonderland for all to enjoy. While Mason's drive north was mostly uneventful, he was bizarrely held up at the inn's old gatehouse because three black and white Holstein Friesian cows were blocking the road.

Mason had no idea where they came from. They were without ear tags and seemed in no rush to move out of the way. After trying to reason with the cows for several minutes—including an embarrassing attempt at mooing—Mason positioned himself behind one of the heifer's robust bottoms and endeavored to push the cow out of the way. All Mason succeeded in doing was face-planting into the snow before noticing that one of the poor dears desperately needed a significant milking. Ahren Dawn happened to be driving onto the property a short time later, and he—with annoying ease—led the cows off the road. While it was commonplace to see a host of wild turkeys running around at Christmas—the cows were a confusing first.

Once Mason was settled and dry, he went to work, ensuring Athabasca reflected its role as the centerpiece of the family's festive happenings. A 9-foot balsam fir sat in the middle of the double-floor living room, decorated with sentimental ornaments of family pictures, trinkets from travels, and heirlooms passed down the generations. A simple handmade angel sat atop the tree, her wings aglow from the fifteen hundred lights illuminating the magnificent fir. Its smell wafted through the rooms with a rich, thick balsam scent that even the lamest of nostrils could deduce as soon as they entered the home.

The fireplace was dressed with garlands and coordinated stockings alongside vases of twinkle lights and festive florals.

The expanded dining table was draped in Lady Valentine's ancient holiday tablecloth, which she gifted to Mason the Christmas before she died. White cloth with intricate hand-sewn silver quilting brought dynamism and magic to the fabric. The stitching reflected the light of the candles and garlands around the room. The center of the tablecloth was a large needle-point Christmas tree with sixteen blue and silver ornaments on the boughs and six red and yellow wrapped gifts around the base. Further individual needle-point images of each of the Twelve Days of Christmas surrounded the tree, starting with a single partridge along with its pear tree all the way to twelve drummers drumming. Behind each scene of the twelve days was a unique background of patterned red and white snowflakes. The shape and sequence of which were never repeated.

Shooting star lights were tucked into the branches of the naked trees between Athabasca and the lake, which had recently frozen. It was the Christmas house of children's dreams, and Mason achieved endless pleasure by ensuring a magical atmosphere for the happiest time of year.

Mason's older brother Oliver felt the décor was akin to Santa having a case of runny shits, but what did he know?

A large fire roared as Mason sat on the comfy brown sofa with a cup of caffeine-free tea. Next to him sat Tank's infamous diaries, and on this the 22nd of December, he had no choice but to work his way through the thoughts of his grandfather, but this time with a new methodology, thanks to recent evidence found by Makayla, William Marshall, Marko, and Cici. Seventy years of Tank's one hundred had been diligently chronicled nearly every day in his own hand.

The most pressing issue was the toxic soil—who knew when, and what did they, or did they not, do about it? More importantly, was anyone harmed because of it? The first known date of its discovery was a letter from the county in 2010 during the burial plot redesign per Makayla, so that's where Mason began. He had sourced the redesign blueprints amongst the contents of the boxes Louella had kept. The placement drawings were dated August 9, 2010—Mason's starting point.

* * *

August 9, 2010,

Laverna has done a stellar job with the burial plot. I've been touched by her spiritual consideration toward each person buried there. All the urns have been exhumed, and they, along with their headstones, are stored on the carriage house's third floor. We are waiting for the county to give us the coordinates of where my casket can rest. I admit, I didn't think there would be this much red tape to make it happen. The surveyors measured the burial plot's distance from the old septic system, took soil samples, and isolated spots where a water well could exist should it ever be needed. A casket must be buried lower than urns, so I suppose I understand the environmental worries. However, my theory is that it's my property, my casket, and, ultimately, my choice. However, I'll let the county do their job.

Laverna has proposed that Jean's Golden Retrievers not be re-buried. She argues it would be helpful for the measuring and placement of the humans. She thinks we could make one large plaque with all their names, birth and death dates to honor them—then either scatter their ashes or keep them in storage. I'm not opposed since I didn't think the bloody dogs should be buried there, to begin with!! It was one of Jean's foolish ideas. I'll leave the decision up to L and B. The most important part of this project is where my enlarged monument will go and where my casket will rest.

* * *

August 10, 2010,
OUTRAGEOUS!
We received a notice from the county DENYING MY right to have a casket for MY funeral and MY burial at MY property!! They claim that the land is "not fit for purpose." Whatever that means! This is an outrage and an utter slap in the face. For everything I have done for this county, and this country, they refuse me, is utter balderdash.
Laverna and I will call them tomorrow.

* * *

August 11, 2010,
L and I spoke with the county, and they claim that the soil samples they took from the burial plot contained traces of toxins. This has caused them to pause their agreement for a casket until further tests can be done. They are also concerned that the old septic tank is leaking.
It made me shudder.

* * *

August 12, 2010,
Many back and forths with the county about steps we could take. We've agreed to remove the septic tank and plant specific foliage around the burial plot, which would absorb any toxin that might be excreted from it. Gil, Laverna & Bianca will take care of it. We're keeping it on the QT. There were also questions about the 1969 issue. I thought that took care of itself when we had the land designated as a burial ground. I reiterated we have since and always will do things by the book...99% of the time, anyway.

* * *

"That's curious," Mason said as Michael Bublé sang "Holly Jolly Christmas" through the speaker system. "What's the 1969 issue, and what did that have to do with creating the burial plot?"

Mason placed a tissue between the pages of the 2010 diary to mark where he'd left off before rummaging through the boxes looking for 1969. Mason continued to process the brief passages. Tank wrote the septic tank was to be removed in 2010 out of concern that it might be the source of the toxic seepage. If so, why was it still noted as being in place in the 2013 survey that the prospective buyer initiated? Did Tank lie to the county about its removal? Or did Gil, Laverna, and Bianca tell him it had been removed, and he didn't question them? This also means that Laverna knew the ground had toxic traces as long ago as 2010. Therefore, the 2013 report couldn't have surprised her. No wonder Aida and Laverna are keen to get the check for Highclere as soon as possible—its value is crumbling every day.

The diaries' lack of chronological order made searching for a specific year difficult, but he finally found 1969. Its outside was identical to 2010 and every other diary—a chocolate brown leather cover with silver spiral binding—the only difference being the gold embossed year.

Where to start, though? This would've been a critical political time in Tank's life, and an issue surrounding Highclere would be unlikely to take up as much space as it would after he retired.

When in doubt, start at a date when Tank would be talking about and celebrating himself and would've been at Highclere. Mason flipped to July 31, 1969—Tank's 46th birthday, and if he had no luck, he'd skip to December—the next period Tank would be at Highclere.

Ninety minutes later, he found what he was looking for.

* * *

December 22, 1969,

Arrived at Highclere for Christmas! It was a long, snowy drive from Ottawa, so I will keep my thoughts brief before I go to sleep. My office secured a conclusion to the ordinance violation we received. We've agreed to pay a hefty fine and designate the specified area as a graveyard. I will travel to town hall tomorrow and enter the back entrance to complete the transaction. The designation will take some time, but I hope to have it finished for Jean's 50th birthday. The site hasn't been further disturbed. I'll deal with that once the paperwork is final and the ground is no longer frozen. Either way, we will do our annual Christmas wish to him as usual.

* * *

Mason reread the paragraph. There it was, the answer he was looking for, written 54 years to the day earlier. What was the ordinance violation? Aren't those usually a fine? Why would there have to be a negotiation between Tank's parliamentary office and Muskoka Lakes?

Mason ran upstairs to grab his phone. Upon returning to the sofa, he snapped a picture of the passage and added it to a text message.

Cici—Read this passage. Can Marko find the noted ordinance violation in a database somewhere? Tank seems to have had to negotiate something concerning it...which I find odd. Since the county was aware of the issue in 2010, I doubt the paperwork has been destroyed. Thoughts?

Mason pressed send and again sat with his thoughts, watching the heavier flakes of snow fall outside while humming along to the carols he could sing verbatim in his sleep. His phone vibrated.

Hello hello darling Mason! Don't worry, I'm not up in the middle of the night! We're in Vermont for Christmas with Stellan's family. I wanted to give you a quick tickle and let you know that the autopsy of the man known as Maxwell Fernsby is finished and released. While he did tragically die by suicide (may he rest, of course), he also had an aggressive form of bone and blood cancer. The coroner was quite puzzled by how the man had the strength to "do the deed," but there were no signs of foul play, and he didn't intimate as such. The theory is that "MF" must have known he was dying and wanted a quick exit from his pain. We suppose he must have had some connection with Fernsby House (besides borrowing the name), but it's not enough to warrant further investigative time. The case is now closed, and work on Fernsby House will start next year. With love and best wishes—Margot X.

Shit thought Mason. Maxwell Fernsby and the happenings at Fernsby House could be unconnected after all. Mason was so sure they were tied to the mysteries in Canada, but that was proving to be less and less likely each time Margot sent an update. Mason placed his phone face down when it vibrated once more. He flipped it over.

PS—Oh dear. I just reread and realized "MF" could be "mother fucker," which I assure you I am not calling anyone. I meant to simplify "Maxwell Fernsby," but I suppose I should've just typed his name anyway. Oops! X

Mason laughed out loud. Those were the messages that made him love Lady Ambrosia even more.

Looking at the clock it was almost midnight. Mason stood and went to turn off the music when he realized it was playing the "Hallelujah Chorus," and a silly, goofy grin was suddenly upon his face as he thought of William Marshall. He wondered whether it would be too weird to send a message saying, "Guess what song is playing?" since William probably didn't notice it was the theme to their first meeting, and Mason didn't want to come off too assuming and flirtatious. What did he know about him after all, other than he had magnificent hair and his ass rocked a pair of khaki-colored chinos?

Instead, Mason switched off the audio, and as he turned off the last table lamp, he caught sight of two enormous eyes in the window staring at him. Shocked, he jumped back, losing his footing and falling ass-first onto the floor. He was being watched—by one of the Goddamn cows! Its nose was right against the windowpane, fogging and defogging as it breathed.

"How the hell did you get over the bridges?" Mason asked, only partially expecting an answer.

He hoped it wasn't the girl in need of milking—that said, he did forget to buy milk for his morning tea. Perhaps nature was solving his problem.

Beep beep went his phone.

Marko's on it —C

Chapter Thirty-Nine

"There's eleven of them now!" cried Mason into his phone while looking out the window. "No, I don't know where they're coming from, but we'd like them removed," he said to the person on the other end of the call.

"No, no one in my family has a cattle fetish or history of livestock thievery," he replied, rolling his eyes at the question. "No, we were never a slaughterhouse, though we were a farm for many years a century ago," he sighed. "So, you're suggesting the cows are on a pilgrimage of some sort to discover their ancestry?"

He snorted.

"Yes, I do think it's ridiculous. Cows aren't like homing pigeons nor are they interested in where they hail from! Our groundskeeper is trying to keep them warm and safe, but we'd rather they be moved to a farm," Mason noted, banging his head with his fist.

"No! The 27th is not soon enough—we have children coming. We need them gone."

Mason shook his head while walking into the kitchen.

"Ok. If you could, I'd appreciate it. Merry Christmas to you," he said while hanging up.

For whatever reason, the Christmas cattle invasion of Highclere Inn & Carriage House was multiplying every 12 hours for reasons Mason couldn't understand. It was one of the strangest things to happen at a place where the odd was *de rigueur*.

After taking a cleansing breath, Mason released the last chocolate puzzle piece from his Michael Fassbender penial Advent calendar and diligently assembled it to reveal what he believed to be a true masterpiece.

"A thing of beauty!" Mason said to himself as he snapped a picture with his phone to send to Skye before devouring the celebrity penis in all its glory!

This was when the "Hallelujah Chorus" should've been playing in the background. *He shall reign forever and ever—indeed!*

"I hope they take suggestions for next year's celebrity penis."

Christmas Eve was Mason's favorite part of the Christmas season. To him, everything about Christmas Eve was joyful. Starting with his colorful ugly Christmas sweater, to his annual viewing of *The Muppet Christmas Carol*, the arrival of the entire family to take part in the celebrations, and of course, the candlelight church service at Valentine Chapel presided over by none other than the eminent Reverend Bernard St. Joy.

Mason spent the previous day herding cattle—literally—and continuing to work his way through Tank's diaries, taking pictures of different passages of note to share with Cordelia. Cici and her family would arrive later that morning to provide ample time to huddle with Mason at the inn before their "Operation: Mrs. Doubtfire" went into action.

Drusilla Brisbane had flown in from her home in Italy a week earlier but only arrived at Highclere with Stuart and Gil the day before. Aunt Drew situated herself at the old inn, which she would share with Cici and Tobias along with their children, as well as Bernard St. Joy. Mason's uncles retreated to their cottage—known as Gay Acres—which they decorated with jaunty gay trimmings (including suggestively shaped bubble lights on their tree, which would've complimented Mason's Advent calendar rather well), and a kitschy blow-up Santa Claus and heavenly angel positioned on their dock.

The rest of the great unwashed would drip in as the day progressed.

Mason made a cup of tea before reading a few more pages of Tank's diaries, which were now stacked in chronological order on his dresser.

Placing his tea on the table, he once again took 2013 from the stack of diaries and sat on his bed with it.

He had read the entire diary the night before and was perplexed to find only a single reference to the sale of Highclere. For most people with normal emotions, selling a beloved and long-time family property, one rich with memories, traditions, love, and friendship, would be an exercise filled with distress. An option only taken when all others had been exhausted. 2013 was one of several years with large swaths of dates not written about—2012 was the other year with significant gaps. Tank went weeks and, in one case, an entire month without writing a word. Silence, as they say, speaks louder sometimes. Mason, along with Cici via text, determined that those weeks and month must have been when the sale and behind-the-scenes machinations were happening. Apparently too difficult to write about, or more likely, too sensitive to put into writing for fear of being caught.

The solitary reference to the sale, obscured amongst plans for a conference about government corruption in monetary reform (yawn), provided one tantalizing piece of helpful information.

* * *

October 21, 2013,

Had a buyer for HI—a development company that was prepared to meet the conditions—but had to take it off the market after they deemed it uninhabitable, unexpandable, and overpriced. When they explained why, I realized I was facing the same problem of several years ago. I'm running out of options and wish that Stuart didn't get us into this predicament to begin with. I reminded him that this was his mistake that I was solving, but he hung up. Then Gil sent an angry email saying I was deflecting blame because, ultimately, it was MY fault.

Incredible really.

You give a boy a chance for a future, you furnish him, love him, and provide him with all he wouldn't have had without us, and he holds you responsible for loose lips. I'll probably regret writing this, but the kids need to know why the Cliftons will come looking for handouts once I'm gone. I'll talk to Louella tomorrow.

Off to the land of nod.

* * *

Stuart was fully aware that Highclere had been listed for sale in 2013, and according to Tank, it was because of a situation that Stuart had brought into the family. This removed any possibility that Tank and Gil were working behind Stuart's back to offload the inn—Stuart was in on it. Could the troublesome situation Tank mentioned be Gil, Mason wondered? The passage alone confirmed that Tank knew as late as 2013 that Highclere was still toxic, yet he seemed to indicate some surprise. He must have believed Gil and Laverna when they said they removed the old septic tank three years earlier.

It was also curious that Tank intended to call Louella Stone the following day. Has Louella known for ten years that Highclere was taken from the family and placed for sale? Why wouldn't she say something? She was as surprised at Thanksgiving as the family.

Mason's phone vibrated. He closed the diary and unlocked his phone.

Holy God. Marko found the citation from the county. The name was redacted—he had to search the land parcel number to find it. Are you sure you want to read it today? It might not make for a merry Christmas –C.

Mason raised his eyebrows, then closed his eyes. The voice of Frank Sinatra singing with his children about Christmases past leaked into the bedroom as Mason sat in contemplation, his thoughts interrupted by the periodic audible moo from outside. Did he really want to know? On his most favorite holiday of them all?

He wrote back.

Tell me everything.

Chapter Forty

"Human fucking remains!" Mason said in wonder as he plopped himself onto the corduroy chair across from Cordelia, who was sipping an early afternoon mimosa Drusilla had waiting for her.

"Human remains!" Cici confirmed in a higher-than-usual pitch.

"I'm baffled. Stunned. Shocked. Surprised!"

"I can tell. All those words mean the same thing," Cici retorted, taking another sip. Thankfully, Drusilla always used the best champagne, so the mimosa was delightfully made with Cristal, also Cici's favorite. She wished she'd done Christmas at Highclere more often.

"So let me get this straight," Mason said, adjusting one of the bells dangling from his ugly Christmas sweater, which had been bouncing on his un-Spanxed man boobs, ringing an annoying tune in the process. "Tank gets a citation in 1969 because a neighbor's dog—super fucking cliché, by the way..."

"Don't I know it!" Cici interjected, tipping her drink toward Mason theatrically.

"—finds a human bone in the area now known as the burial plot. He doesn't deny it, meaning he knew it was there. He uses his parliamentary office to make the problem go away, which he successfully does by paying a huge fine through a holding company—having his name redacted from public records and agreeing to formally designate the land a graveyard. I assume he then re-interned the body after the site had been zoned correctly," Mason concluded, looking out the window to see two new wide-eyed cows slipping and sliding down the icy slope of the driveway without a caretaker.

"That's how I read it," agreed Cici. "Also, Mason, Uncle Tank seemed to know who the bone belonged to."

Mason shot her a look.

"What makes you say that?" he asked, a titch incredulous, though he wasn't sure why.

Cici picked up her purse and released her phone from a collection of Christmas tinsel.

"The kids thought the tinsel would be cute," she explained somewhat apologetically. She opened her phone, and after a few moments of scrolling, she said, "In the passage you sent me from 1969, Uncle Tank writes, '*We will do our annual Christmas wish to him as usual.*' He obviously knew it was a '*him*' and that the bones had been there for some time since he wrote '*annual Christmas wish...as usual,*' an act that had gone on long enough to become a tradition. I guess Auntie V also knew who it was. It must have been someone close enough that they'd feel it important to visit on a holiday."

"An important enough person in their lives that they'd go out of their way to protect by paying off the county," Mason added.

"Or," Cici countered while downing the last of her mimosa, "Uncle Tank and Auntie V had to pay the county to protect themselves."

Cici let that statement linger between them for a moment. Mason leaned forward and rubbed his temples.

"You think they put the body there?" he asked with some disbelief, but Cordelia's logic was sound.

"Or they knew who did."

"A family member?"

"Maybe."

"Were the police ever brought in?" asked Mason.

"I don't know, but I wondered the same thing. It's weird that a human bone was found, and it became a disposal violation rather than a death or murder inquiry."

"What circumstances would stop the police from becoming involved?"

"Things in 1969 weren't as sophisticated as they are today. It was also a simpler, more innocent time. If no one had reported a missing person in the area, or there wasn't an open, active case about a murder or suspicious death, then I'd imagine that it was deemed a fluke and only investigated through by-law. A homeless vagrant, perhaps? Highclere was also an active working farm nearly a century earlier—"

She paused, also noticing the latest livestock migrants' shocked looks as they slipped into place.

"—of course, it may be becoming one again. Anyway, many animals could be buried in strange places. Farm hands without family might have died at work, and Hollis Valentine or his father Bertram before him dug their final resting place. Foul play wouldn't have been the instinctual first step in that era," Cici explained.

"I guess human remains found on a cabinet minister's property would still be a scandal, even in 1969," Mason suggested.

"I think it could've been a big one, which is why Uncle Tank settled the matter quietly. Avoid bad press."

"Which is all well and good, but it's clear to us that Tank and Granny V knew the body was there, knew who it was, and while they could deflect to all the innocent possibilities you just described to keep out of trouble, the truth is, they needed it kept quiet because there is some darker underlying reason the body is there."

"Exactly," Cici agreed.

Mason stood and looked at the corkboard of evidence they had collected over the previous four months. A random collection of threats, death, symbols, letters, "Doors to Nowhere," jewelry, purchase ledgers, news clippings, pictures of missing strangers, and puzzle pieces he wished pieced together as gallantly as Fassbender's festive chocolate penis puzzle.

He turned to Cici, who handed him a printout of the ordinance violation Marko had sent her. He placed it against the board but stepped back before tacking it into place.

"Cici?" Mason asked, almost in a sing-song. "Do you think the threatening note knifed into the carriage house wall had to do with the bones in the burial plot from 1969? The one on Fernsby House letterhead?"

Cici stood and joined Mason at the board, reading the letter out loud for the first time in months.

"'*Do you think your treachery will be ignored? Do you think people who do what you did deserve to have it all? We don't. We're reclaiming what's rightfully ours. Piece by piece. Sleep with your eyes open. Lock your doors. Board your windows. Nothing will stop us. Watch it. We're coming for all of you.*'"

Cici sighed and twirled her loose red locks into a bun atop her head.

"I don't know," she confessed. "'*Do you think people who do what you did deserve to have it all?*' feels like it could be connected to the unsanctioned burial of an unknown man. But '*We're reclaiming what's rightfully ours. Piece by piece*' feels like there is more than one 'thing'—for lack of a better word—that the author was pissed about and wanted back."

"I suppose the threats in the TIC file are more in line with the 1969 issue," suggested Mason.

"'*You've been a piggy at the trough for years. Abusing your power to imprison your enemies...you disgust me...I wouldn't rest too easily, sir,*'" Cici read out loud. "Maybe. But I'm not convinced either are connected to each other or the human remains."

Mason and Cici stood in silence. Their thoughts were broken by the subtle sound of wood creaks coming from outside the office door. A knock followed before Drusilla let herself in, holding a mimosa in each hand.

"Knocky, knocky," she said despite having already entered the room, boundaries never quite being her strong suit. "Cordelia, I thought you might be able to use a refill on the mimosa front. Not to get you too pixilated before church. Bernard just arrived wearing hip waders painted red, which he claims is part of his Father Christmas costume. He apparently has a special, though 'practical' festive outfit for the service, so you might need to steel yourself before we go."

Cici took the champagne glass out of her cousin Drusilla's hand.

"You don't have to ask me twice. Thank you!"

"Mason, did you tell Cordelia about our adventure to the 'Eye of the Vulva' exhibit?" Drusilla asked with girlish delight.

"I did. Yes. She thought it was a great thing to take me to," Mason replied without expression.

"I really do think the vagina is one of God's most beautiful creations, even if it's not always the most illustrious of art subjects," Drusilla said in her otherworldly accent.

"Yes. Super beautiful. Like a peony," added Mason, rolling his eyes.

"I'd be perfectly pleased to see an exhibition called 'The Eye of the Dorsal Nerve' with you, too, should one exist," she said while laughing at her comment. "In fact, I thought of you when I picked up this flyer," she said, handing her nephew a trifold glossy from her pocket. "It's for an exhibit called 'Apropos of the Anus.'"

She smiled.

"'Apropos of the Anus' made you think of me?" Mason deadpanned.

"Well, I do suggest that the chocolate willy puzzle you nibbled on could be considered a soupçon Freudian and rather apropos of an anus!" Drusilla suggested while performing what appeared to be jazz hands.

"Uh huh," Mason sighed, scanning the flyer, slightly tantalized by the subject.

"I think it fits like a glove," Cici said, laughing.

"That's the name of one of the talks," replied Mason, turning to show her the lecture title.

Cici sneezed some of her mimosa out of her nose while laughing.

"Well, I'll let you two have your fun," said Drusilla as she turned to exit the door of the office when her eye caught sight of the corkboard of clues.

She stopped.

"Gracious," she uttered while staring at it.

"I suppose you haven't seen any of this before," Mason noted.

"Indeed, I have not. I'm not sure I've wanted to know. I dare not speak ill of my dead father, of course, and Mrs. Clifton doesn't deserve any due thought or consideration in my mind either, especially since she pulled Highclere out from under us. I suppose I was playing dumb. Just how I like it," she said, nodding her head with a slight smile.

"Have you looked at the Farnsworth Marble & Designs purchase ledger?" Mason asked.

"No, but Stuart gave me an overview."

Mason pulled the multi-page document from the board and handed it to her. Drusilla sat in one of the extra chairs while Cici retook her place at the desk and Mason on the corduroy chair. The door to the office remained open. Christmas church hymns sung by a children's choir filtered in from the lounge. The voices of children—the Bradshaw/Neuman children—were audible in the distance while whispers of "come on, Bessie" and cow bells dinging crept through the thin windows.

"Obviously, not every piece of Granny V's jewelry was made by Farnsworth, but a good chunk was. It's all noted as being in the family's possession, other than the gold box and spheres that Joyce Redstone brought us. The ledger indicates that they were returned in trust to Rosamond Farnsworth-Ford before her death," Mason said while his aunt perused the document.

"Who on earth is Maxwell Fernsby?" Drusilla asked.

Mason saw her finger tapping on the line item pertaining to the cufflinks.

"A phantom," said Cici, polishing off her second mimosa and still wiping the snotty remanence of her sneeze from her shirt.

"In what way?" asked Drew.

"From what we can tell, no Maxwell Fernsby has ever existed. Certainly not as a member of our immediate family, anyway. According to Andrea Romero, who bought the Farnsworth patents, Maxwell Fernsby was the name of the man who bought the cufflinks etched with the Fernsby crest on one side and a pattern of sixteen gemstones on the other. The cufflinks were on the body of the man who killed himself at Fernsby House around Labor Day. Andrea Romero confirmed to the police that the man who identified himself as Maxwell Fernsby was the same man who took his life."

"He's not related to us?"

"His DNA didn't match mine," confirmed Mason.

"It's strange. If I didn't know better, I'd almost think it was Maxwell *Farnsworth* we were talking about."

Cici and Mason looked at each other, then back at Drusilla.

"Who is Maxwell Farnsworth?" asked Cici.

"The first and probably true love of my mother's life."

Chapter Forty-One

"I'm confused," said Mason, his head about to explode from the onslaught of information that'd come at him in the last forty-eight hours. "How was Maxwell Farnsworth related to the family?" he asked.

"Maxwell Farnsworth was Rosamond Farnsworth's brother," said Drusilla.

Mason had a clear look of confusion on his face.

"That can't be right," said Cici, taking up Mason's train of thought before standing and walking to the evidence board. "I have Rosamond's obituary right here, and there is no Maxwell Farnsworth listed as a brother," Cici pulled the print-out from the board and handed it to Drusilla, who quickly reviewed it.

"Hmm. Well, that's shameful," said Drusilla. "But, I guess not all that surprising."

"There was Farnsworth DNA on the cufflinks 'Maxwell Fernsby' was wearing when he died, but the DNA of 'Maxwell Fernsby' didn't match the Farnsworth DNA either," pointed out Mason.

"Well, it wouldn't, would it? Maxwell Farnsworth was adopted and died during the Second World War," said Drusilla.

The group sat in silence for the briefest of moments.

"Keep the story going, Auntie Drew. You can't just stop there. Start from the beginning, please," prodded Mason, whose bouncing bell continued to dance on his moobs.

"I only know what my mother shared with me over the years. As I understand it, Maxwell joined the Farnsworth family as an infant, but I believe it made for an awkward childhood because he was the same age as Rosamond. They were both one year older than Mom, according to the obituary. Despite having no genetic connection, Rosamond and Maxwell effectively grew up as twins, but from what my mother told me, Maxwell never quite felt like he was part of the family. He and his sister would have joint birthdays and celebrations, but he was treated ever so slightly less than Rosamond. As you know, the Farnsworth estate was the neighbor to Fernsby House, and Maxwell became sweet on Mom when they were in their early teens. I think—and this might be wrong—but I think he and Mom were together for five years. He joined up with the armed forces when he turned

18, which was after the war started. He left for the battlefront and never came home. He was officially declared dead in 1944. Mom was in Canada at that point with her sisters and mother, while Papa was still in England. At the end of that same year, Jean Fernsby met Miles Valentine, and the rest, as they say, is history."

"You're sure he died?" asked Cordelia.

"I have no reason to believe otherwise. I guess the Farnsworths decided to erase him from history, which is a shame. Especially considering what he meant to Mom."

"Why would you say he was Gran's 'true love?'" asked Mason.

"She often said so. Also, she gave her first son 'Maxwell' as a middle name, so that's pretty telling!" said Drusilla.

"Who has Maxwell as their middle name?" asked Mason, confused.

"Stuart," Drusilla answered, seemingly annoyed at the question.

"Stuart's middle name is Hollis," Mason retorted, equally annoyed by her answer.

"It isn't," confirmed Drusilla before looking upwards and back at Mason. "Actually, you're right. He was Stuart *Hollis* Valentine at birth, but his middle name was changed to Maxwell a short time later. I guess Mom had become angry with Dad for something and decided to stick it to him by changing their son's name from a family name to her first love's."

Cici sat back down and took her notebook from her purse.

"Funny that both Uncle Tank and Auntie V's first loves have popped up over the last few months," she said while looking at her notes. "Do you know anything about Caroline Monroe?" she asked.

Drusilla thought for a moment before shaking her head.

"No, he didn't say much to me about Caroline. I'm not sure I knew her last name before now."

Mason pulled over one of the boxes Louella Stone had brought him and pulled out the old, broken framed picture of Tank and Caroline. He blew off the accumulated dust and wood flakes before handing it to his aunt.

"This was Caroline Monroe," said Mason as Drusilla gazed at the sepia photo.

She ran her fingers between the shards of glass, touching the gloss of the picture, feeling for signs of life or memories from the past.

"She looked ever so much like Mom," she said.

"I thought that's who it was at first," agreed Mason.

"Are there any other pictures of Ms. Monroe?" asked Drusilla.

"No. That's the only one."

Drusilla turned the frame over to read the faded writing on the back. Mason hadn't reattached the backing after he did the same at his office.

"'*Caroline and Miles 1944.*' He must have met Mom shortly thereafter."

"As Louella explained, Caroline—who was American—was on her way to Canada to finish planning her wedding to Tank when he sent a telegram telling her not to come as he'd met someone else."

"He could be a shit," Drusilla smiled before adding, "What a terrible thing to do to someone. I imagine that sort of rejection isn't something you'd quickly move beyond."

"He was a shit, and you're right about the devastation. I hope she went on to have a pleasant life," nodded Mason.

"He never did care how his reckless whims affected other people. As long as he got what he wanted," added Drusilla before fading off with her thoughts.

Mason nodded.

"Is she still alive?" she asked.

"No idea. We haven't thought much about her," said Cordelia.

"I'd be curious to know more about her when you have the time, of course. A newly recognized member of the 'Miles Valentine Survival Club!' We should send her a membership card," joked Drusilla, still looking at the back of the photograph. "How did you know her name was Monroe?"

"The writing on the back," said Mason.

Drusilla shook her head.

"It's only her first name," she pointed out before handing the picture back to Mason.

Mason bit his lip and crunched his face. She was right.

"That's a good question then. I guess Louella must have told me," said Mason.

"Good for her to remember at her age. I hope my memory is that pristine in my nineties," said Drusilla. "Also, is there a page missing from the Farnsworth ledger?" she asked.

"No, that's the full PDF Margot Ambrosia sent. Why?" replied Mason.

"I was hoping it might say where Mom's jewelry box was."

Mason sat up straight, the bells on his sweater dinging against his man tits. Cici noticed his change in demeanor.

"What jewelry box?" asked Cici.

"Dad had one made for her by Farnsworth early in their marriage. It looked very similar to the one in which Mrs. Redstone delivered the spheres. Except, this one had a miniature alfresco dining scene on the top. A man and a woman seated at a white table, with what I remember to be a partial house façade—mostly a door—behind them. I believe the figures were made of clay. It was very pretty."

Cordelia looked at Mason. He was deep in thought. Trying to remember something, but what?

"Mason?" asked Cici.

He blinked a few times before looking at her and smiled.

"Aunt Drew just triggered the memory of a few dreams I've had about Granny V and a music box. They started at Thanksgiving," he said while biting his lower lip, still thinking. "But it must have been something else."

"The box did play music when it opened," said Drusilla. "Perhaps you were dreaming about it. Just not in the correct context."

"You don't know what happened to it?" asked Mason.

"No. I asked Dad many years ago, after Mom died, where it was, but he didn't care to look."

"It's not listed on the register—at all?" asked Mason, holding out his hand, signaling his Aunt Drew to pass him the printout.

She belatedly took the hint, and he flipped to the earliest date he could find. Nothing.

"You're sure it was a Farnsworth piece?" asked Cici.

"Absolutely. As I say, it was almost identical to the gold box with the spheres."

Mason looked up.

"She kept the jewelry box here, didn't she—at Highclere?" he asked, processing his thoughts.

"She did," confirmed his Aunt Drew.

"In the hutch by the dining table!" Mason said, standing up and going to the evidence board.

Briefly startled, Cici and Drusilla joined him. He knew what he was looking for, just not where it was. He scanned the board and couldn't find it. He rolled the boards to the side and practically leaped on top of the box he knew it would be in. Sweater bells jingling the entire time.

Pulling off the lid, Mason shuffled through papers until he found it.

"Look at this," he said after standing, rejoining his aunt and cousin.

Mason held a picture from Christmas 2003 showing Tank and Lady Valentine seated at their dark wood dining room table with an assortment of desserts showcased and all their grandchildren seated around them. In the background, amongst the various platters and vases in the glass cabinet, was the musically inclined jewelry box, with the alfresco figures visible and seated, enjoying their outdoor meal.

"That's indeed it," agreed Drusilla. "I just don't know where it went."

"Or when it vanished," added Cici.

Drusilla nodded.

"I wish we had other pictures of the hutch from the in-between years," confessed Mason.

"Didn't I give you a picture from Easter 2004?" asked Drusilla.

"You did, but I meant between 2003 and 2023," he clarified.

"Well, that I can't help you with," sighed Drusilla as she stepped back toward the door.

She turned around.

"Well, thank you both tremendously for all you're doing to help find Mom's things and come up with a way to keep Highclere in the family. I better get ready to jingle all the way! Oh, and according to Bernard, the internet says the cows are aliens who've come to Earth to provide a Christmas message to the family of Miles Valentine. It's good of them to do so!" she said with a flourish and exited the office.

Mason returned the photograph to the box while Cici took position in the corduroy chair, pulling out her phone.

"Holy shit, he's right!" Cici laughed, reading from her phone. "There's an entire Reddit thread about how an alien race that couldn't travel to Earth for Senator Valentine's funeral will take the form of cows and bring festive cheer to the Valentine family at their resort. That's hilarious!" she laughed again.

"Oh sure, that's a sensible explanation," nodded Mason. "It's clearly a prank."

Cici nodded.

"Probably, but they don't seem to have wranglers, and none have ear tags. I wonder if the aliens transform into cows or if they're transferring their consciousness to the heifers."

"Should I call the windowless van?" Mason joked.

Cici laughed.

"Probably. We should just have it on standby." She sighed. "Mason. To Drew's point about our 'efforts' to keep Highclere. You and I combined haven't been focused too closely on that. After the handwriting sample of Uncle Tank's letter and the trust revocation were confirmed to be authentic, we kind of left it. Roland Mast has been doing most of the leg work while we've been following blackmailers, soil samples, lost jewelry, doctored videos, and now human remains."

Mason was crouched and flipping through additional pictures in the box. He stopped and thought about what Cici had just said. He had to agree.

"You know, I guess I just assumed that once we solved the whole shebang, Highclere reverting back to us would be an outcome. The revocation clause in the trust was legit. It was signed by all parties, perhaps not in good faith considering the fuzziness around 'the settler,' but it was signed."

"Uncle Tank could've been coerced into it by the Cliftons, and if he changed his mind about who inherits the inn, maybe greed led to anger and that led to Uncle Tank's death?"

"That's a leap, don't you think? While I've been convinced that Tank's fall was no accident, we don't have anyone with a motive for zapping him. Gil is our prime suspect for rigging the fence with a pressure sensor, but we don't know what would've precipitated him doing that or if Tank was even the intended target," acknowledged Mason.

"Well...there is something I haven't told you," replied Cici, who then told Mason about Jolly's drinks charade at Sassy's Sauce with Louise Harris from a week earlier.

"So, you're saying the pressure sensor on the fence and Tank's fall were orchestrated because he had decided to change his will and leave Highclere to someone other than Aida?" asked Mason.

"I think it's possible."

Mason bit his lower lip. Thinking.

"Knowing what we know from the two toxicology reports, almost any offer to buy Highclere would be reneged after ecological testing," added Cordelia.

"Meaning if Highclere was ever listed for sale down the line, as long as the ground stayed poisoned, the value would continue to nosedive, and it could be bought at a steal," nodded along Mason. "And we most certainly have one or two people in our coterie of crazies who could ensure the soil stayed toxic to keep the property value down. We also have someone who would love nothing more than to buy the place on the cheap if it meant undercutting Tank or his heirs...Trent Callahan."

"Plus, there'd only be one absolute, guaranteed, 100 percent method of ensuring Highclere would be listed for sale in the future," suggested Cici.

"If Aida Clifton-Valentine were to inherit it," Mason nodded. "Shit," he added.

"Then the question is who was he leaving it to in the unsigned will, who knew, and who would it affect?" posited Cici. "Louise told Skye that Laverna had a non-binding sales agreement drawn up years ago. If money has already been exchanged and she can't repay it, then she'd be desperate to ensure Highclere went to them and usher through the sale."

"I can check the emails for communications with Louise and see who was in the loop," suggested Mason.

"You won't find any. Louise confirmed to Skye that she and Tank spoke by phone and that the draft was couriered to his home in January."

"Could that be what the Cliftons were looking for in the boxes at Louella's? The will?"

"I'd say it's a safe bet. If a draft copy of the updated will was in the boxes, then there would be reason to suspect the Cliftons had motive to incapacitate Uncle Tank," Cici said as she stood to look out the window when she heard voices of excited children bundled in their snowsuits throwing themselves into plowed banks of snow.

Ahren, meanwhile, continued to move cattle to the warmth of the carriage house, and to keep them away from the children.

"Ok. So now I'm really wondering—especially in light of the 1969 disposal violation—if we are way off base about the blackmail being about the toxic soil," Cici admitted before looking at her watch. "Shit. Mason, what time do we have to be at the chapel?" she asked. "I have to sort our getups."

Mason didn't answer her.

"Mason?" she asked, peering around the corkboard. Mason was now standing, holding two photographs side by side. Cici walked over to join him.

"What are you looking at?" she asked him.

"This photo is from Easter 2004. Granny V was still alive then," he reminded her.

He then pointed to several spots in the picture.

"It's all already gone."

Chapter Forty-Two

"As the Lord said, *'when we teach a man to fish, he shall provide protein, but if we teach a man to leaven bread, a sandwich he will make.'* In the Lord's name, we pray. Amen," said the Rev. Bernard St. Joy from the beautifully decorated festive pulpit of Valentine Chapel.

The tiny clapboard building was lit by individual candles being held by the 75 local parishioners who had come for a mix of Christmas spirit and farcical entertainment.

Bernard St. Joy, a noted sufferer of pyrophobia, preached the lessons of the birth of Christ while adorned in a firefighter's uniform he had purchased from the internet without understanding what type of store he was ordering from. His Christmas-red leather spiked tank top, with accompanying green leash, accentuated his aggressively hairy chest and surprisingly obvious pierced right nipple. His top was tucked into flame-retardant navy-blue pants with yellow reflective accents on each leg, the fabric flimsily being held together by Velcro.

A fire extinguisher on a rope was draped across Bernard's body, and his yellow helmet displayed a sticker of a man using a reproductive organ as a hose, which Cordelia turned into a man holding a Christmas cracker using red, silver, and green markers before the service began.

Additional ambiance was provided by the whirring red lights of an ambulance parked outside of the stained-glass windows. Rev. St. Joy had called the paramedics once he realized he hadn't cast anyone to deliver the baby Jesus during his annual re-enactment, for which he hoped a paramedic could provide some modern-day realism. The honor of playing the newborn went to a robotic vacuum with doll arms taped to it named Melanie, who exited the legs of the woman playing its mother right on cue and then helpfully hoovered up the sparkle dust Bernard's leash was leaving in his wake while the congregation sang "Silent Night."

All in all, it was a pretty tame Christmas Eve service as far as the Valentines were concerned. After all, it was almost impossible to top the year a farmer's donkey, who was assigned the role of a camel, gave birth to an experimental Zebra crossbreed called a "Zebrass" from beneath Joseph's coat of many colors while the choir sang "What Child is This?"

Christmas Eve at Valentine Chapel had become a thing of legend, and the family was even beginning to wonder if Rev. St. Joy was more lucid than he led on and was leaning into his festive fame by upping the ante each year—Zebrass excluded.

The pews were filled with locals and imports alike, who traveled to cottage country to spend the holiday season away from frenzied urban centers and instead implant themselves within the setting of a tranquil Rockwellian Christmas.

Tank's long-time assistant, Norah Tripplehorn, joined the congregation for the first time at Mason's urging, bringing along her daughter, who was staying with her for Christmas. Ahren and Makayla Dawn sat in the third row, closest to the emergency exit, and next to Highclere's neighbor Trent Callahan and his wife, Kendell. All were decked out in the colors of the season and singing and laughing along with the rest of the crowd.

During the second round of Bernard leading the congregation in "The Song that Never Ends," Mason and Cici snuck out from behind the boisterous vocalists, clapping youngsters and banging bells to take their positions.

* * *

Valentine Chapel cleared once the service came to a close, leaving only the scent of extinguished candles and peppermint lingering in the air as Ahren and Makayla Dawn went to work discarding left-behind programs and tossing winter tarps over the pews. Together, they'd tuck the old chapel in for her long winter's slumber to awaken in the spring with the return of the residents of Lake Belvedere.

"Excuse me," came a meek voice from the door of the chapel.

Surprised, Makayla and Ahren turned to see two old women dressed in their warmest winter clothes approaching them. Stout in stature and made wider by their parkas, the two women's toques hid most of their short, silvery curls. Large Sophia Petrillo-style glasses sat perched on their noses, and wicker purses dangled from the crook of their arms. Their wrinkled jowls, red from the cold, glowed under the fluorescent lanterns of the entrance.

"Have we missed the service?" continued the same voice as before, the shorter of the two.

"Indeedy, Ma'am," answered Ahren, who all but tipped an invisible hat in their direction. "It started at seven and ended a short while ago."

"Balderdash! I told you the man on the phone said seven," complained the second, taller woman to her friend.

"Seven didn't seem right though, Euphegenia. I've been to this service before, and it has always been at eight-thirty," replied the shorter woman.

"That doesn't matter, does it, Dorothy? Events can change times over the years, wouldn't you agree?" asked Euphegenia.

"Agreed," said a sullen Dorothy.

"You wouldn't happen to know of any other services in the region we could attend? It wouldn't be Christmas without a little faith," Euphegenia asked Ahren.

"I dunno, to be truthful," Ahren replied, then turned to Makayla. "Honey, what other churches are open?"

Mack walked toward the trio. "There is a 9:00 p.m. service at Belvedere United tonight that you'd be able to make if you hustle. How long would the drive from here be, Pa?" asked Makayla.

"Twenty minutes. No more than that," Ahren replied.

"That sounds ideal then," said Euphegenia. "Would you be able to give us directions?"

"I'd be pleased to," answered Mack before turning to Ahren and saying, "Pa, why don't you go turn the taps off and close up the basement while I give these lovely ladies some directions?"

Ahren turned and smiled at Dorothy and Euphegenia.

"Don't let the limp fool you ladies. I'm still quite sprightly," he said almost flirtatiously before heading toward the carpet-lined stairs and descending into the bowels of the chapel.

"You're going to leave him broken-hearted," winked Makayla as Cici and Mason removed their fitted latex masks, wigs, and fake glasses.

"If he was fooled, then anyone watching the place will be too," argued Cici.

"Even I wasn't sure it was you," confessed Mack, who was wearing a Christmas-themed cardigan and green leggings. "This has to be quick. I'm not allowed to be seen with you two," she added while marveling at the realism of their masks.

"We know and appreciate you taking the risk. We just have a few questions," responded Mason as the three of them sat in a single white pew.

"I'll tell you what I can, but not if it's going to risk my trial," stipulated Mack.

"Completely fair," agreed Cici, who opened her wicker handbag and flicked on her trusty cell jammer. "First things first, where are the infrared deer cameras you were told to install around Highclere? What direction are they facing?" she asked.

"The majority of them are around the burial plot, but there are two facing the main inn and two facing the carriage house. There's also one on the transmission tower on the county-owned acre behind Highclere's back 39."

"Are there any facing the personal cottages? Athabasca or any?" asked Mason.

"None, or at least, none put up by me. But I can't be sure."

"To your knowledge, has anyone ever physically collected the SD cards from the cameras?" asked Cici.

"I've never seen anyone, but I have changed the batteries of a few cameras, and the cards have been gone."

"Not replaced? Just gone?"

"Yes."

"Can the cameras see each other? As in, would they be recording the face of the person who is swapping the SD cards?" added Mason.

"Probably, but if someone knew the right sequence to remove, erase, and reinstall the cameras, you could hide or create blind spots, I suppose."

"Mack, you said the night you were arrested that there was a second item you were looking into besides the toxic soil. What was that?" asked Cici.

Makayla opened her mouth but stopped when she heard what sounded like footsteps. Mason and Cici haphazardly threw their masks and wigs back on and waited, but no one appeared.

Conscious of the time, Cici pointed to her watch and gave a hand signal telling the two they had to speed up.

"It's silly, and to be clear, I'm not like a Tank Valentine superfan or anything. I just find...or I guess I found him interesting as he's the only famous person I'll probably ever meet in my life. I've been a member of various Miles Valentine fan clubs online for a few years. They're all moderated by someone called the 'Leader of the Tanks.' 'The Tanks' being Mr. Valentine's superfans—"

"Oh, we know of them," interrupted Mason.

"—anyways, the 'Leader of the Tanks' was pushing this idea that Mr. Valentine's accident wasn't an accident but a planned execution, which is dark and creepy for sure, but I also had questions about how the fence surged during a power outage. The Leader of the Tanks tried to get the media to investigate, but I guess no one thought there was a story there. So, I DM'd the Leader and said I could maybe help because I lived nearby and could investigate."

"And they took you up on your offer?" asked Mason.

"They did," confirmed Makayla.

"When?" asked Cici.

"Early August?" replied Mack, not sure.

"Good, that's very helpful," said Cordelia.

"How so?" asked Makayla.

"We've finally found the intersection of your lies."

Chapter Forty-Three

"I've been telling you the truth!" exclaimed Makayla, panicking.

"No, you haven't. None of what you've just said or said to us last month is true," confirmed Mason.

"Makayla, of the three videos you showed us the night you were arrested, the second one, the most startling one, depicted you installing a device to the fence outside the carriage house two days before Uncle Tank fell," said Cici.

"That wasn't me! I admitted to being blackmailed into stealing on Labor Day and am willing to admit I did so in the first video—I just don't remember doing it. The second video is a fake. I'd never hurt Senator Valentine."

"It's not a fake, Mack," said Mason, leaning in. "We had several experts check it repeatedly, and every single one of them confirmed the footage to be authentic. You attached something to the fence before my grandfather fell into it. A friend of Cici's, who is a digital mastermind, scraped all conversations amongst Tank's fan sites online and found a public discussion between the Leader of the Tanks and the user 'Mackmuskoka,' which we've been able to identify as you, dated June of this year. You told the Leader that you'd been forced to attach something to Tank's electric fence before moving the discussion into a private chat room. Thanks to some light hacking, we read that conversation. You identified the object as a pressure sensor and added that someone anonymous forced you to install a fish-line trip wire. You were worried that you had been the one to effectively kill Miles Valentine and didn't know what to do."

"Oh my God. How were you able..." asked Makayla as tears trickled down her face, "how did I get myself into this?"

"The Leader of the Tanks then targeted you and threatened to reveal what you'd done unless you followed their instructions. Correct?" asked Mason.

"Yes," confirmed Makayla.

"You didn't find a document about toxic soil in the burial plot box, did you?" asked Mason.

"No."

"There are no deer cameras set up to watch us?"

"No."

"You didn't take soil samples and send them to a professor at Waterloo, did you?"

"No."

"How long have you been selling prescription drugs?" asked Cici, who had sympathy and kindness in her eyes.

Makayla knew lying was only going to make it worse. Out of the corner of her eye, she saw her grandfather standing in the frame of the chapel door, the wings of a stained-glass angel illuminated by the outdoor sconces behind him. His eyes looked at the ceiling, tears visible on his lined cheeks while his distinguished, aged lips trembled in disbelief.

"Two years," Makayla whispered, using her sleeves to wipe her eyes. "How did you know?"

"Nothing stays hidden on the internet," said Mason.

"I'm assuming your supplier recruited you. Contacted you to work for them out of the blue?" asked Cici.

"Yes," wept Mack.

"Your supplier then needed some 'favors?'"

"Yes."

"One of them was to lay the pressure sensor and trip wire?"

"Yes."

"Then, when Uncle Tank fell, you felt guilty and told the Leader of the Tanks what you'd done because you thought the Leader would understand—or was your friend?"

Mack nodded in agreement.

"But then they, too, asked for favors to ensure their silence?" asked Mason.

"The Leader found my phone number. I couldn't escape them. They seemed to know so much about Mr. Valentine and the inn…I had to do what I was told. I couldn't figure out how the Leader had camera footage to use as blackmail since the system had been torched, and according to the DVR log, there hadn't been a remote download of footage in months."

"We've determined that a second, unsanctioned security system exists on the property. That's how the Leader had the footage. We just don't know where the cameras are or what they're recording to," noted Mason.

"That makes sense," Makayla sniffled. "The first video of me stealing from the carriage house was actual footage, but the items were computer generated. I was told that if the Leader could make me look like a thief that easily, how easy would it be to make me look even worse? But they wouldn't report me if I managed to get some mementos from the carriage house the night of Mr. Valentine's funeral."

"Which you buried in the burial plot?" asked Mason.

"Yes, on top of Mr. Valentine's casket. The items were gone the next day. They'd been dug up. Then, when I thought about it, I realized that messages from my drug supplier and the Leader were getting mixed together. They seemed to know what the other one was asking me to do and confusing themselves," said Mack.

"They're working together?" asked Mason.

"They're the same person," replied Cordelia, scratching at the mask adhesive on her chin.

"I'm pretty sure, yeah. When I figured that out, I yelled at them to leave me alone. I knew then I was done for. That's when they sent the footage of me messing with the fence. Murder, they said."

"So, why were you fed all the information and given an elaborate story about toxic soil and Waterloo professors the night you were arrested? We'd only found out about the soil a few hours earlier," asked Mason, still looking like Euphegenia Doubtfire.

"They wanted you to know. Said it was important. Something you guys did that day spooked them, I think, so they told me about the casket refusal because of the soil and that if all went to plan, you'd be on your way up to see me, and I was to tell you about it. Said if I didn't, they'd send the videos to the police, which they'd already done anyway," explained Makayla before crying. "I'm such a fool. Why do I fall for these things!?"

"Oh, Mack," said Cici, leaning in and giving Makayla a tight hug while Ahren stepped forward and sat in the pew behind them.

"You're not a fool. You were set up to point us away from whoever has been messing with the family. The toxic soil is very real and deliberate, which has been going on for a long time. There are other serious matters, which will all come out in time," she said, releasing Mack but still holding her shoulders and looking at her in the eyes. "My journalism career was derailed a decade ago because a tech genius had advanced artificial intelligence past the point of Hollywood quality image generation. He created a convincing fake evidence trail, which caused me to lead a bunch of very bad people to a very innocent teenager. I'm a professional investigative journalist. I spent decades learning to detect a truth from a lie, to know when pulling a string will drop a clue or an anvil," laughed Cici, and so did Makayla. "And I fell for it. I pulled the string, and the anvil dropped on someone other than me.

"An old colleague of mine named Kate Sampson looked into Uncle Tank's death in September after she got a tip from the Leader of the Tanks about foul play. Our friend Skye pointed out that the tip seemed too convenient and too knowledgeable; it had become clear that someone was trying to point us in a specific direction.

"From what a forensic electrical engineer can tell based on the video quality, the device you attached to the fence was not in any way, shape, or form a pressure sensor. He said it was probably just an old scale," winked Cici with a smile. "There would've been wires and digging and all that good stuff needed to harm Uncle Tank. The location of the trip wire you installed would've also been too low. It was the same height as a rock, which Uncle Tank needed to step over anyway, so your wire didn't trip him either. What I'm trying to say, Makayla is—you didn't cause any harm to Miles Valentine. Someone did—that's clearer than ever because of the Leader—but it wasn't you. They just wanted you to believe you had to set you up as a patsy."

Makayla collapsed her head into her hands, her sobs uncontrollable, her tears seeping through the cracks of her fingers dripping to the floor. Her grandfather led his tired body to the pew to console the one family member he had left. The one person he loved more than anyone in the world.

"I was about ready to say I'd done it!" Ahren half laughed, half cried.

Cici turned to Mason, both wiping tears from their glassy eyes as they watched the relief and love felt between granddaughter and grandfather. If only they weren't dressed like obese old women, which sullied the touching Christmas miracle just a titch.

"The drug selling has to stop," said Mason to Mack.

"It will, I promise," she said, wiping her nose.

"We will need all your communication with your supplier, contacts, empty parcels, etc.," Cici said.

"No problem."

"This stays between us for a while longer," added Mason. "We still have to figure out who targeted and blackmailed you and how they connect back to the problems at Highclere."

"Our lips will not be pried open even by the toughest pliers," smiled Ahren.

"There's one more thing you need to know," Makayla whispered. "The night of Mr. Valentine's funeral—I wasn't the only person secretly sneaking in and out of the carriage house."

* * *

Mason and Cici walked beneath the zenith of bright stars while absorbing the brisk winter air, peeling off their prosthetic wrinkles and jowls en route back to the inn just in time for the reading of *The Night Before Christmas*.

"I'm almost sad there aren't any deer cameras," said Mason as he tried to peel off what he thought was a fake third chin—but was actually his own. "We went to such effort to conceal ourselves!"

"It was better to be safe. Plus, there is a second security system well hidden somewhere. Thankfully, our industrial jammer scrambles it, even if we don't know where the cameras are," said Cici, walking slowly, thinking, and enjoying the burst of cold on her face after she scrubbed off some of the mask adhesive with a wet wipe.

She could hear the faintest of Christmas tunes being played on a piano in the distance, vibrating through the sleeping trees, all snug under their duvets of snow.

"Mack was targeted for the Leader to have a fall guy at the ready," said Mason.

"Yup. Which means the Leader is someone with pre-existing knowledge of the people and their roles up here," added Cici. "Not some stranger. Skye was right—they're familiar."

"The Leader told Mack about the toxic soil the day of Operation PITA because we spooked them. They knew we would run to Highclere to talk to Makayla because 'they' had planned for the Cliftons to tell us about the video. If the Leader and the supplier are the same person, I'd be willing to assume they're also the poisoner and blackmailer. They're all our 'Person X.'"

"I agree. Especially since the Leader knew about the toxic soil and specifically asked Mack to tell us about it, it would be one thing to know about the pressure sensor. The soil is another," replied Cici.

"Keep in mind, the only people we interacted with that day, other than each other, were Laverna, Aida, Tank's former housekeeper Geneviève Talbot, and Bianca."

"I thought of that. Could the Cliftons or Laverna specifically have done this?" wondered Cici.

"Well, according to the diaries, Laverna was on the phone with Tank when the county reminded him of the 1969 disposal violation," added Mason.

"Strike two, for sure, that would've given her something to use against him," agreed Cici.

"If she signed a non-binding sales agreement, and money had been exchanged—she and her family would have the most to lose if Tank changed his mind about giving them Highclere. As you always say, humans have an overactive survival instinct," Mason reminded her.

"What doesn't fit for me is why they'd kill the value of something they stood to inherit. I can't make that fit within our current context of the case. That said, Gil is also proving troublesome. He installed the electric fence and security system; his name was on the 2013 secret Highclere listing, and he tried to get us to drop the investigation at Thanksgiving. Plus, he's known about the toxic soil since 2010; he was asked to fix it, and as far as we can tell, he didn't."

"Maybe he got tired of the secrets and abuse Tank was heaping on Stuart and snapped. The diaries indicate that Gil stood up to Tank when he blamed Stuart for the blackmail. Perhaps Gil tried with simple poison and got caught, so that plan didn't work, which led him to set the fence to end Stuart's pain. The motivation having nothing to do with the will change. He could easily be the Leader of the Tanks based on his access—obviously a group less benign than we thought," suggested Mason.

"Maybe," whispered Cici, "but I'm not sure that feels quite right. Before we go there, let's see how your conversation goes tomorrow with our newest member of the 'Toxic Soil Club.'"

Mason and Cici abruptly stopped at the inn's main entrance when unexpected warm puffs of condensation blew at them with a sneeze from one side of the road.

"No! No, no! Not more," cried Mason as he saw six new cows standing confused and cold—making a total of twenty-three. "Where are they coming from?" he asked in frustration, jumping up and down toddler-like.

Cici stepped toward one and looked her in the eye.

"What planet are you from?" she asked like a robot—or E.T.

No response.

"I do say, what. Planet. Are. You. From? Do you transform into cows, or are you controlling them telepathically?" Cici asked the cow again, their noses almost touching.

Mason's jaw slacked as he moved his face into Cici's peripheral view.

"Please, God, tell me you're joking."

Cici shrugged.

"I dunno, Mason. Maybe it's not so crazy. Maybe they are aliens who've come to provide festive greetings to the family of Miles Valentine. They are appearing from nowhere," she smiled.

"It's happened, Cordelia," Mason said, shaking his head. "You're officially a box of frogs," he smiled.

"Ha, ha," replied Cici. "By the way, I might have an idea about the differences between the Christmas 2003 and Easter 2004 pictures from earlier," Cordelia teased as the two left their livestock pals to join the family for the final hours of Christmas Eve.

Chapter Forty-Four

The residents of Highclere Inn & Carriage House were up before dawn to exchange gifts and watch the wonder in the kids' expressions as they first eyed what Father Christmas had left for them the night before.

The sun rose alongside a beautiful orange and red sky, revealing soft snowflakes falling. The inviting warmth of festive fireplaces started in the early morning and emanated a smell of pine with notes of maple while the sounds of jingling bells, remote control motors, popping boxes, and "slamming sloo-slonkers"—to quote the Grinch—reverberated all around the property.

At "Gay Acres," Guillaume "Gil" Regan had just finished reading an archived news story written by his cousin-in-law Cordelia Bradshaw when his husband Stuart roared through their front door, kicking off his tan ankle boots and tossing his winter coat onto the newel of the banister.

"She's an absolute nightmare today," grunted Stuart as he walked toward his husband's easy chair.

Gil slowly closed his laptop, careful not to arouse suspicion.

"How can she be? It's Christmas!" Gil replied as Stuart sat on the rocking chair beside him.

"She's upset because this is our last Christmas at Highclere, and she's upset because she wants to know where Mom's things are before we go, and she's upset that 'Mrs. Clifton' has won the long game to get Dad's assets," said Stuart of his twin sister Drusilla.

"There wasn't much left for Aida to get," pointed out Gil in a conspiratorial voice. "And if she didn't get Highclere, then she'd have had almost nothing but the house."

"I know," said Stuart, his green eyes fixed on the slim bay of frozen water that separated the small island of his cottage from Athabasca's. "If you'd asked me a week ago," sighed Stuart, "I'd have said I could easily live with this secret for the rest of my life. Today," he paused, "it feels heavy."

Stuart and Gil sat in silence. They could hear laughter and the joyful screams of their great-nieces and nephews who had bundled up in their winter best to roll around in the snow at the inn's little beach. Gil stood at the window to watch the fun, his breath fogging and un-fogging the pane of glass in front of him.

"I don't think it's a good idea," Gil responded, continuing to look out, not turning to face Stuart.

"Why, though? You always say that to me and never tell me why. This is my family. MY family..." Stuart trailed off.

"You've made that very clear to me over the past few months. Of course, I think you're trying to convince yourself of that more than you're trying to separate me from them," snapped Gil.

"It's been ten years, Gil. I'm seventy-three years old. I'm in the final phase of my life. It's not like it isn't going to be figured out eventually. I think you underestimate Cordelia if you think she won't get to the truth."

"I just wish I knew what she's discovered," Gil sighed.

"Then let's just help her by telling her what happened. Or ask her what she knows? She'll find out soon enough. Why can't we be the ones to tell her?"

"If you tell her, it breaks the dam before I'm ready to have it broken," said Gil, turning to Stuart, anger etched on his face.

The lines of his dark skin deepened, his bald head beginning to glisten as he worked to control his temper.

"I've gotten us this far. If we show our hand too soon, the long game we've been playing will be done prematurely. We'll be uncloaked. While I know you need to get certain other lies off your chest, I want to remind you they weren't your lies to begin with. They belonged to Tank. You're the victim of his bullshit. The way he made you feel like it was your fault, as if you had any choice in the matter? The way he had Laverna dangle it over your head for the last ten years. It just makes me seethe. I'm glad the bastard is dead if I'm being honest. Good riddance! He left a fucking mess, and he knew he was leaving a mess, the narcissistic shit. He played us against each other. He played you against your siblings and let this madness into our lives. All because of his fucking ego."

Gil took several deep breaths and sat back down in his easy chair. Stuart's expression was unmoving. He sat staring straight ahead. Gil reached to grab Stuart's hand.

"Stu," Gil trembled with immediate regret, rolling his shoulders forward. "I'm sorry. I shouldn't have spoken to you like that, and I shouldn't have spoken about your dad that way."

"I always knew you wanted him dead," said Stuart, flicking Gil's hand away.

"Only because I knew life would be easier without him," replied Gil, his rejected left hand now holding his right as his eyes became teary.

"You've become obsessed," said Stuart, whose eyes were equally misty and tired. "You've spent all of our money on this. I've had to ask my sister for help...twice! I can't do it again! We're broke!"

"I know," agreed Gil, looking pained and upset.

Stuart reached and took Gil's hand into his own.

"Ok then. It's Christmas. This is your family, too, and I'm sorry if I've made you feel otherwise. Why don't we forget about this for today and pick it back up tomorrow?" offered Stuart before adding, "Or never, because I'm happy to move on."

He smiled.

Gil smiled back.

"Ok. Let's go attempt to cheer up your sister before caroling since she always has top-shelf booze, and I need a stiff drink. Especially if I'm going to have to move cattle around."

"Plus, Bernard is there, so it'll be drinks and a show!" laughed Stuart as he and Gil rose from their chairs.

"Oh my God!" said Gil, his body frozen after a quick stretch.

"What?" asked Stuart.

"Do you think old Rev. Bernie and Drew are banging?" asked Gil with a joyfully horrified look on his face.

"What?" shouted Stuart with a laugh.

"I'm just saying, his outfit last night proved he is still in bangable physical condition, even if mentally he's not on this planet."

"Or is he somewhere over the rainbow?" winked Stuart.

"You know, he could be! I always thought he was checking me out. He also has always had a thing for snakes."

"Don't flatter yourself."

"Seriously. Big, black snakes."

"Ha, ha," said Stuart facetiously as the two climbed into their outdoor winter gear. "Oh shit!" Stuart said, popping up from zipping his boot. "You're serious! I forgot he used to collect Gray Ratsnakes!"

"I know!" laughed Gil. "What is it with you people and your reptiles? Pet snakes and alligators galore at Highclere."

"And squirrels," added Stuart.

"That's not a reptile."

"But having one as a pet is weird."

"I think we should all just be hauled off in straitjackets at this point."

"I'd start with hauling the cows, frankly."

"Agreed."

"Do you think their color and skin patterns reveal which planet they're from?"

Chapter Forty-Five

"Oh, for the love of God—what's happened now?" whined Mason as he crossed the icy bridges to see throngs of festive singers in multicolored parkas gathered around one of the slim basement windows of the inn.

"Well...Bernard tried to get to the basement to find the carol books, but two cows were blocking the outside *Wizard of Oz* doors. So, instead, the Rev decided he could reach the booklets by going through the window, and now we have a bit of *Winnie the Pooh* situation. Half of Bernard is inside, and the back half..."

"Back three-quarters," Mason sneered.

"...the back half is outside. Ahren thinks he can get him out," laughed Stuart. "Gil and Drew are pouring drinks, so the revelers have refreshments for the show. Oh, and three more cows showed up. They walked in from the woods! We're up to 41."

The traditional carol sing at Highclere dated back to when Tank's parents, Hollis and Bea Valentine, first funded the building of Valentine Chapel as a place for locals to congregate and worship during the summer months and on Christmas Eve. Proponents of community spirit they also instituted the annual Christmas Day carol sing where neighbors—a group often resembling the congregation of the Christmas Eve service—were welcomed to Highclere to sing festive tunes with the Valentine crew.

Mason noted to Cordelia that there was a stronger-than-usual turnout. They suspected it was because of curious friends and property owners wondering how the Valentines were adjusting to their post-Tank era and looking for gossip about why Highclere was for sale—a discussion point that Drusilla was delighted to natter ad nauseam about with anyone who simply wanted to wish her a Merry Christmas. Some also learned of the cow invasion online and wanted to see it themselves.

With several heave hoes, Bernard was free, and the singing began.

Reverend Bernard St. Joy assigned himself the role of choir leader, a position traditionally taken by Tank. With the note picked, Bernard's arms flailed out of rhythm, and Cordelia couldn't help but notice that in the winter's light, he had an uncanny resemblance to Ethel Merman.

Mason was delighted to see first-time caroler—and Tank's long-time assistant—Norah Tripplehorn amongst the chilly group of festive singers. He'd invited Norah to carol and the Christmas Eve service the night before. They'd had a mutual fondness for each other since Mason was a child. Norah welcomed his rambunctious ways and definitive personality. She also appreciated that Mason didn't take shit from his grandfather and approved of his talking back to Tank when his level of absurdity teetered off a cliff.

Norah was not obtuse to Tank's flaws, didn't suffer fools, and didn't ascribe to blind loyalty either. Nor was she unaware of his strained connection with his children. Mason always assumed that Norah, who was also close with Lady Valentine, was one of the many people who saw through Aida's forced charm and wishy-washy motives for marrying a man who'd lost his wife of 60 years just weeks earlier.

Yet Cici, in particular, couldn't help but feel Norah was the one person in the best position to bide her time until useful intel floated along that she could use to betray her employer. Norah Tripplehorn was privy to all of Tank's emails, letter correspondences, family antics, and banking information. She'd know as much—if not more—about Tank's life as Tank did, and despite being a well-paid government employee—come—personal assistant, it was puzzling how she could afford a property on a pricy lake such as Lake Belvedere. A matter that was so quiet he wasn't sure Tank knew. Norah also ran Tank's official social media accounts, meaning it wasn't unreasonable to assume she could take one step further and be the 'Leader of the Tanks.' The Leader had a pre-existing, intimate knowledge of Highclere to target Makayla. Who better to know about Mack than the woman who mailed her paycheck?

However, Mason's gut instinct wasn't often wrong when it came to people, and he struggled to believe she could be connected to the family's strange goings-on. Sadly, his instincts were plunged into self-doubt when Norah's name popped up in the most unexpected of places. As Mason was reminded earlier that day after scanning Tank's diaries once more, sometimes human behavior was simple. It's action and reaction, one step in front of the other. Imagination and the unknown are the lethal combination for the mind. The simple answer is often the right one.

"*Then all the reindeer loved him, as they shouted out with glee.*"

"*With glee!*" replied the children.

"*Rudolf, the red-nosed reindeer, you'll go down in history!*"

"*History!*"

The song ended and with a loud, boisterous shout of "Merry Christmas!" the carolers departed.

"I think I better do this alone," said Mason to Cici as he spotted Norah walking toward them.

Cici nodded her agreement.

"Thank you so much for the kind invitation, Mason," said Norah, leaning in for a bear hug.

"Had I known this was a tradition of yours, I'd have forced Mr. Valentine to invite me years ago," she said, smiling wide, her face still youthful for a woman in her mid-seventies—her pencil gray bob tucked beneath her furry toque.

She released Mason and turned to Cordelia.

"So nice seeing you again, Cordelia."

"Please call me Cici, and it was very nice seeing you too," Cordelia responded, leaning in for a less forceful hug than Mason received.

"Where are you parked?" Mason asked.

"Just outside the front gate, on the county road. I wasn't sure if you were plowed to the inn door or not, but it turns out all your parking is taken up with cattle."

"Yeesh, that's a bit of a hike. Let me walk you to your car," insisted Mason. "Maybe we should give out cows as party favors," he joked.

"I'd take one!" Norah laughed. "That's kind of you, Mason, but really not necessary. I can walk alone," she replied, her smile warm.

"It would be my pleasure. I don't want you to slip," replied Mason.

"Alright then," nodded Norah, who put her right arm through Mason's, and with an enthusiastic wave goodbye to the rest of the Valentine family, Mason and Norah headed up the hill.

* * *

Guillaume Regan's gaze lingered on Norah and Mason as they made their way, arm in arm, up the snow-dusted slope toward the inn's driveway. Whether it was the sight of the duo or the gin and tonics warming his insides, unease crept over him, his pulse picking up pace.

Gil spun to check if Cordelia was still nearby.

She was.

A wave of relief washed over him, along with the realization that he might be overthinking.

Mason was being polite.

Nothing was amiss.

* * *

Trent Callahan and his wife Kendell, brimming with merriment, exchanged farewells with the Valentines and others. With their scarves pulled tight, they trekked toward home through the mattress of fallen snow. To hasten their journey, they marched a path toward the carriage house—the current refuge of the ever-arriving livestock—and crossed the frosted forest hemming Highclere from their property.

Trent paused, fog having clouded his sunglasses. He wiped his lenses just in time to see Norah and Mason, arms linked, striding toward the county roads. A distinct unease crept over Trent for the first time since Senator Valentine's burial. Lurking in the shadows of his mind was the gnawing fear that he might soon be exposed.

* * *

"This snow is deep!" exclaimed Norah as she and Mason took turns pulling each other through the more densely packed areas of the property.

While the little ones and cattle had well-trodden the snow, the wind had picked up in the afternoon, blowing the less stable sheaths into awkward mounds that needed to be forged to reach the county roads.

"I'm so out of shape," huffed Mason, almost embarrassed by his shortness of breath.

"Ok, let's stop for a second," suggested Norah, who was full-lunged but could hear Mason's need for a breather.

"Only if you insist!" said Mason, nodding his thanks for the gesture.

"It gives me a moment to share some news," said Norah looking past Mason, watching the disbursement of the carolers.

She noted Gil was hanging back longer than the rest before heading back to Gay Acres.

"Oh?" said Mason, taking deep breaths.

"I told Mrs. Clifton and Mrs. Lehrman that I'll be retiring at the start of the new year," she said, now looking at Mason, whose eyes were obstructed by sunglasses.

"Really?"

"I'm sure it can't be surprising to you. I was hired by Mr. and Lady Valentine over fifty-five years ago, I have a wonderful government pension, and I've viewed the terms of my employment to be for their lifetime, not for that of the Senator's second wife," she noted with slight force.

"No, I'm not surprised," agreed Mason, "but you sound frustrated," he paused.

The two stood in brief silence, Mason having his breathing back under control.

"I'm not," Norah lied. "Transitions in life are always difficult."

"Shall we keep going?" asked Mason, pointing toward the old gatehouse.

"Absolutely," Norah agreed, and again, they linked arms as they booted their way off the property.

"In light of this news, would you mind if I asked you a few questions?" asked Mason.

Norah smiled.

"I assumed I was invited here for more than my mezzo-soprano voice," she winked.

"To preface what I'm about to ask, I just want to say that I know over the decades your allegiance has been to my grandparents, and it was not your responsibility or job to warn or share information with their children and family regardless of how you viewed certain situations," Mason said, choosing his words carefully.

"I understand," Norah replied.

"But, taking into account certain discoveries, I'd find it helpful if you could tell me what, if anything, you know."

Norah stopped walking and turned to Mason.

"Mason, Senator Valentine, and your family have been nothing but kind and supportive to me. I found myself, on occasion, in difficult circumstances, especially since Lady Valentine died, but I always offered my candor and advice to Mr. Valentine whether he asked for it or not. He has now died. I am unemployed. I'm not bound by any further allegiance," she confirmed.

Mason nodded his thanks before diving in.

"Were you aware that my grandfather revoked the Highclere trust in 2012?" he asked.

"I was."

"Cordelia and I have since discovered that my grandfather was successfully blackmailed around that time. We assume he lost the lion's share of his fortune and felt obligated to ensure Aida was provided for financially and therefore chose to leave her Highclere."

"Not originally," Norah stated without hesitation. "He was blackmailed, and from what I understand, he lost millions of dollars because of it. He was under significant pressure from Laverna, in particular, to ensure the future financial comfort of her mother. It was Laverna's idea to sell Highclere in 2013 and then rent it back for the rest of the Senator's life."

"So, Laverna knew he was being blackmailed," Mason confirmed.

"She was an active part of everything that happened over that time."

"Why didn't he fight the blackmailer? The security services knew it was happening."

"Your grandfather said it wouldn't be to his benefit to have it investigated."

"Why not?"

"He said it was too damaging."

"So, the blackmailer had evidence?"

"Mr. Valentine believed so. Or he was spooked into believing there was no other option than to pay."

"Norah, did someone die up here from the poisoning of the back 39 acres?"

Norah's jaw slacked.

"What?" she asked, confusion displayed on her face.

"One of our theories is that the blackmailer knew of a brewing biohazard on this property and either used that information against my grandfather or knew of a tragedy that resulted from the ground poisoning," said Mason.

"The ground had nothing to do with the blackmail," she confirmed.

Mason jolted his head.

"It didn't?" he asked with some disbelief.

"No."

"Then what did the blackmailer have on Tank?" asked Mason.

"Something to do with Stuart."

Chapter Forty-Six

"Christ," said Cici, dropping her head into her hands. She and Mason snuck up to his bedroom at Athabasca Cottage during a brief respite before dessert.

Cici was in a long red dress with cranberry edging and a wide black belt that had belonged to Lady Valentine. Her red locks were in a ponytail, with a twig of holly behind her right ear. Mason was dressed like an extra from *Xanadu*, sporting a green and red sequined shirt and skinny green chinos. A yellow paper crown sat on his head.

"So, Uncle Tank was correct in blaming Stuart in his diary," said Cici.

"Norah didn't say the blackmail material was Stuart's fault. It just had to do with him; she was never told what the blackmailer had on Tank, but Laverna and Aida know. So do Stuart and Gil."

"Then ground poisoning is out as blackmail material, but the downside is the motive for it could be a lot more sinister than we hoped. If it wasn't being done to blackmail someone, it might have been done to hurt someone."

"I don't know Cici. I still think the purpose of the biohazard was to kill the value of the property for the family. I'm not convinced someone was meant to die. That said, if the blackmail was about Stuart, it confirms that Uncles Stuart and Gil are being less than forthcoming."

"Which we've suspected about Gil for a while, but I had hoped Stuart wasn't deeply involved," confessed Cici. "By the way, and off-topic, did you see that Laverna's husband Phil was brought home today?" she asked.

"No, where did you see that?"

"Bianca Anders posted online," shared Cici as she searched her phone's social media apps for the video. "Here," she said, handing it to Mason.

Mason watched as Bianca narrated the arrival of an ambulance pulling into the driveway of Tank and Aida's home. Laverna and Phil's children jumped into the frame and banged on the ambulance's back door, which opened from the inside, revealing a tearful Laverna holding hands with her husband. Twenty years after his accident forced him to live in an assisted living facility, Phil Lehrman could now be cared for at home.

The medical technician lowered the ramp, allowing Laverna to push Phil's wheelchair out of the vehicle and into the house. Aida Clifton-Valentine, wearing what looked to be a circus tent and an 'Etch a Sketch' around her neck, danced toward her son-in-law, giving him a long, teary hug.

Bianca turned the camera to herself and cried, "It's a Christmas miracle!" between sobs, before recording the family reunited, walking into the house, and their future. The video then went black.

"Well," Mason said, surprisingly choked up as he returned Cici's phone. "It's hard to begrudge someone a con if their endgame was this," he said. "I'm glad for Phil that they can afford to have him home, which is where family should be."

"Money can't buy you happiness, but it can buy you options," Cici agreed. "And I think, despite the benefactor, Phil being home is money well spent."

Mason nodded before remembering he had something for her. He opened his dresser drawer and handed his cousin a small red box with a green bow.

"Merry Christmas!" said Mason as he passed it to her. "I was going to give it to you later, but we need an excuse for disappearing."

Cici untied the bow and removed the lid. Her lineless brow furrowed as she comprehended what the gift was.

"Ah!" she said, laughing. "It's a great-looking keychain," she added, lifting it out of the box and dangling it from her index finger. "I thought, for a second, it was a real gift," she smiled.

"What you talkin' about 'foo! It is a real gift. You're touching it, aren't you?"

"I meant something from Tiffany, not this," she said, gently mocking her new accessory.

"You say that now, but when the day comes you need it, you'll be all like, 'Oh, my cousin Mason is brilliant!'" he joshed. "It's all set up and ready to go," he added.

"Thank you. I'll treasure it forever," she replied, returning it to the gift box.

"You're welcome," Mason said, walking toward the door to rejoin the chaos downstairs.

"Wait!" shouted Cici, pushing the door closed again. "What did she have to say about Manitoba?"

* * *

Norah and Mason reached her black compact car, sitting all by its lonesome with a subtle film of blowing snow circling the hood.

"A few more really quick questions," said Mason as Norah fumbled for her keys.

"Do you know our neighbor, Trent Callahan?" he asked.

Norah's body stiffened. Her hand, fumbling inside her purse's darkness, stopped moving. She stood still.

"How do you mean?" she asked, resuming her efforts to find her keys, her voice pitched upwards.

"I mean, do you know Mr. Callahan?" Mason repeated. "He and his wife were two of the carolers."

Norah looked up, then to the right. Clearly thinking, but Mason wasn't sure whether she was about to lie, run, or was contemplating telling the truth.

"You know…" she began, returning her focus toward Mason, "…I'm not sure. I know Mr. Valentine spoke of him. I understand they had some kind of feud. I don't think I've met him before today," she shrugged.

"Oh, Norah," said Mason, looking up toward the ever-clouding sky.

Fresh snow floated toward his face—the cold biting his sensitive cheeks.

Norah breathed deeply, her warm breath momentarily obscuring her reaction to Mason's exasperation. She sniffled.

"You know, don't you?" she asked, a warble in her voice.

Mason removed his sunglasses and looked Norah in the eyes.

"I know something," he agreed. "But it would be easier if you told me. I understand it will be difficult for you."

"Well…I…" Norah's emotions caught in her throat.

Mason's warm, kind eyes focused on Norah as she composed herself.

She realized he was showing no judgment nor eagerness. He wasn't being unkind or voyeuristic. If anything, he was allowing her to lighten the burden of her truth.

"My brother," she started, speaking slowly. "Well, we grew up in Manitoba. My father was a farmer, and my mother died when I was just about to turn 11. It was a different era when we were young, especially in rural Manitoba. While I was always interested in agriculture and my brother in politics, our life paths were a fait accompli. A son was to take on the farm, and a daughter to be a wife or an executive assistant of some kind. My brother and I used to laugh that I ended up in politics and he in farming when it should've been the reverse. He was a good brother…" she trailed off, collecting her thoughts.

Her nose was running, but Mason wasn't sure whether it was because of emotion or the cold. Either way, he scrounged a tissue out of his coat pocket for her while she took a moment.

"I'm sorry, I never talk about him," she laughed nervously before blowing her nose. "As you know, I never married, and my daughter is adopted, so I've never had a big family or many relations to reminisce about my brother with. When my dad died, my brother took over the farm. Our neighbors, the Owens, had a long-standing immovable disagreement with us about the ownership of a small acreage between our properties. After our father passed, Scott Owens, who is my generation and had taken over their farm from his father, made it his mission to claim the disputed acres as his. The government stepped in around 1978 and decided that the fair decision would be to split the disputed land into two. Scott Owens thought this was a travesty of justice and tried to appeal it, but the politics weren't on his side. Scott wasn't a good man. Morally bankrupt since he was a child. He seemed to fester and breed hate and directed it toward my brother."

"Your brother's name was Henley? Henley Tripplehorn?" Mason asked.

Norah smiled.

"That's correct. See, you know more than you let on," she said once more with nervous laughter and a sniffle.

"Why did Mr. Owens feel the politics wouldn't have been on his side if he appealed?" asked Mason—assuming he could guess the answer.

"Because Miles Valentine was the Minister of Agriculture at the time, and Henley's sister—moi—was personal secretary to the minister."

"So, Mr. Owens ostensibly let it go," suggested Mason.

"He did. After the land was divided in two, things seemed to quiet down between Scott and Henley. The few times I went to visit, I felt they were getting along almost like friends or brothers, even. They'd meet at the picket fence between the properties in the morning for coffee and at sundown for a beer. I'd go so far as to say it seemed affectionate.

"Two years later, our crops struggled. We'd cultivated and sowed that land for fifty years before then and never had a problem, but almost half of the harvest was destroyed. Henley chalked it up to a fluke. He developed a plan to get two rounds of crops harvested the following year to make up for the loss. It didn't work. This time, the entire crop failed. Henley was distraught and became unwell. He was pale and gaunt. Extremely thin. I thought he was depressed, and it was manifesting physically, but then he became weaker and weaker. Several years went by, and his organs started to give up. He had no income, no family, no money saved. If it weren't for your grandmother, who gifted me a sum to keep the family land, my brother would've been without a home, too.

"Seven years after the land dispute was settled, Henley died. He died from arsenic poisoning. He'd been drinking it for years because the aquifers and well water had become toxic, and that water also killed our farm soil. Deliberately."

"By Scott Owens..."

"Yes," she confirmed.

"As I understand it from a decontamination report I read, the Crown Attorney at the time refused to file murder charges against Scott for poisoning Henley?"

"That's correct," confirmed Norah as she wiped crystalline tears from her eyes.

"Why?" asked Mason.

"They said there wasn't enough evidence to prove the poisoning was intentional and not a natural phenomenon. Arsenic can occur naturally—though rarely in Manitoba, and to that level of toxicity."

"What happened to Scott Owens, then?" asked Mason.

"Eventually, the local Crown Attorney was pressured to charge Scott with murder. A bench trial was ordered—which was unusual for a murder case, but a speedy resolution was requested—he was jailed for manslaughter."

"Did he appeal?" wondered Mason.

"Over and over and over again. The amount of money he spent trying to overturn his manslaughter conviction was incredible. It was a never-ending fount of money."

"Was he wealthy?"

"No, he wasn't, but his cousin—who he grew up with—was. Still is. He is a lawyer but also inherited a fortune from his parents."

"...and his cousin is?" urged Mason.

"Trent Callahan."

* * *

"So, Trent has a family history of poisoning properties to make a point," noted a tipsy Cici as Mason walked with her to the inn.

"Yup. Scott Owens died in prison, and Trent blamed it squarely on Tank because he's the person who pressured the Crown to bring charges. I showed Norah some of the threatening letters in the TIC file—T.I.C. apparently being Trent's initials—and she recognized them as being from Trent, though she doesn't know who cut off his signature. The letters were being kept in case Trent became violent. She feels a lot of anguish about being responsible for the Callahans becoming a part of our lives.

"After Scott was convicted, Norah—at Tank's urging—sued for damages and won a considerable sum, which Trent paid on Scott's behalf. It was invested for years until she used a portion to buy her cottage. She told me it's on a typical rocky Muskoka ledge with two small buildings—she lives in one and rents out the other for income. The second was meant to be an art studio or bungalow for her daughter, but they preferred to use the main house together," Mason added.

"It's amazing that Trent's anger could lead him to spend years trying to make Uncle Tank pay for his political heavy-handedness against Scott. First by moving in next door, then buying all the land surrounding Highclere and being a general pain in the ass about by-law violations, noise complaints and the like," said Cici before adding, "If the blackmail was about Stuart, like Norah said, then in my experience the motive for extortion circles punishment or revenge territory. I don't think the blackmail was an act of financial greed or an effort to deplete Uncle Tank's finances to force a sale of Highclere."

"That's a leap of logic, don't you think?" asked Mason.

"Not at all. It's science. While the brain's reward center controls both revenge and greed, revenge is personal and emotional. Whereas greed is abstract and material. Going after the son is emotional. Person X could've demanded Uncle Tank hand over Highclere as part of the blackmail. They didn't—they wanted to destroy the place to inflict pain. That's revenge."

"Well...if you remove greed from the mix, then a deliberate electrocution and poisoning of the soil also scream revenge," thought Mason.

"Obviously, Trent Callahan is the person with the clearest motive—and behavior pattern—for revenge, plus he has a history of being around contested properties that become biohazards," noted Cici.

"But Norah told me that Tank and Gil confronted Trent after Muskoka Lakes reported the toxic soil samples during the casket debacle of 2010. Tank always knew who Trent was and his relationship to Norah. If it wasn't Trent, then it would be the world's most monumental coincidence that the recipient of Trent's written threats and ire had his property befall the same fate as the Tripplehorn farm. Trent denied he was responsible for the poisoning, apparently becoming an almost inconsolable blubbing mess—he worried that the soil samples, coupled with the letters, could get him arrested. Tank believed him, and they agreed to a détente. Norah said Tank told her Gil solved the soil problem, and they never discussed it again," added Mason.

"Monumental coincidence would be an understatement, and while Trent was angry, he isn't stupid—so it's unlikely he tried to be oh-so poetic and mimic his cousin's shenanigans to turn Highclere into a biohazard," said Cici.

"Exactly. Trent is too convenient of a baddie—he's too obvious—he might as well have a gigantic neon sign saying, 'I did it' hanging over him."

"I agree, in which case my darling cousin, someone with knowledge of Trent's history with Norah, is using him as a smoke screen by setting him up to look guilty as F," said Cici.

"Or they're daring us to point the finger at Norah, who is, after all, the keeper of Tank's buried bodies—in this case, literally," Mason paused. "She said one more interesting thing; apparently, the night Tank fell, she lost access to his email account."

"What?" Cordelia marveled.

"Yup, Tank fell around 8:30 pm, and she received notice that her remote access to his email was revoked by 8:50 pm. She went to Tank's house the next day, but his computer had been logged out of Outlook, and while the password had not been changed, she had been removed as a recipient of the dual authentication code, which locked her out completely."

"Jesus!" Cici roared before adding, "...I wish you a very happy birthday," while looking at the sky. "We don't need another electrocution," she laughed, turning back to Mason. "The level of premeditation is becoming more and more obvious. The ground poisoning has likely been going on for seventeen years. The blackmail was ten years ago, the Highclere trust was revoked in 2012, and Makayla was targeted less than two years ago. Person X has been at this for longer than twelve months. As greedy as the Cliftons often appear, this plan was put into place long before Miles Valentine decided to change his will."

"Why good evening, Betsie, Elsie, Gilda, Lemon, Bessie, Boston, Marge, Grace, Daisy, Bella, Buttercup, and the rest of you," nodded Mason to the lineup of cows being kept warm by blankets and space heaters provided by Ahren. "Where did you come from?" Mason asked irritably before refocusing. "There is now something I'm more curious to know than ever," he added as the cousins stood in the soft glow of twinkling outdoor Christmas lights hanging from the inn's eaves. "Who did Laverna sign the sales agreement with in 2013? Trent knew the soil was toxic for three years at that point—he wouldn't buy it—or not for the asking price at least."

Cici nodded.

"Unless he felt coerced. However, I think based on all we've learned in the last few days, this case comes down to four questions. One, what is it about Stuart that was blackmail worthy, and who knows about it? Two, does it connect to the human remains found in the pre-designated burial plot—which feels more like a blackmailable situation? Three, why was it important to go after Uncle Tank for it specifically and not Stuart? Lastly—and in that same vein—what was the blackmailer's motive other than taking the money? This will prove or disprove our revenge versus greed theory. That said, I am confident there's more to 'why' Person X has done what they've done—and revenge is the name of this game."

* * *

With the dinner guests having left and Christmas ticking away its final minutes, Mason tucked himself into bed and scrolled through the pictures he had taken during the day.

His favorite photo was one he'd taken before dinner of his niece Mika and her cousin Harrison playing their seven hundredth game of the new and improved Connect Four. Mason hadn't realized that Connect Four was still a thing, but indeed, the classic game where people take turns dropping colored disks into a six-by-seven blue grid was still thriving! The new version, however, contained a box suspended below the grid, which magically popped open to reveal a prize to whoever got four of their disks connected in a row first.

The set came with several prizes to load in the box, but by the end of the day, the magical box was out of treats, so Mason inserted a Post-it that said "IOU," which Mika had won. She stuck the paper to her forehead while sticking out her tongue.

The light in the picture was perfect. The sky had cleared, and the sun was setting in the windows behind his niece with a sublime honey glow reflecting off Lady Valentine's Twelve Days of Christmas tablecloth.

Mason color-balanced the photo and saved it to his favorites before turning off his phone. He then pulled two printed pictures from a drawer next to his bed: one from Christmas 2003, with the jewelry box visible in the hutch at the carriage house, and one from Easter 2004, when it was already gone—months before Lady Valentine had died.

Where had it gone? He still didn't know, but thankfully, Cici's theory from the night before proved true. Mason searched the diaries and found their answer. They knew who had removed Lady Valentine's belongings and why. It was simple, really—human behavior at its most predictable.

Placing the photos back in his drawer, he looked at the stack of diaries on the dresser in front of him. All of them identical in look but varied in content. Tank's dedication to his daily writing was more sporadic than Mason had been led to believe. While they gave tacit answers to unintended questions, the purposeful ones were censored out. However, he'd worry about that the next day.

Mason rolled to the other side of his bed to turn on his sound machine and flick off the light. As he slid under the covers with his eyes closed, the stack of diaries continued floating in his mind's eye. He could see them all sitting one on top of each other and one next to the other.

All symmetrical. All the same.

All that was different was the year etched on the front cover.

Except.

Except.

They weren't.

Mason opened his eyes and turned on the light. He stared at the diaries.

He hadn't noticed it before.

He jumped out of bed and put on his red robe and glasses.

He crouched down until his nose practically touched the pages. His eyes had fooled him—of course, they had—he had no reason to assume anything was different or unique.

Yet, there was.

He took the oldest diary from the stack, dated 1949.

Mason opened the front leather cover and started to count.

* * *

The next morning, the cows were gone.

Chapter Forty-Seven

To: Louise Harris
From: Roland Mast, KC
Date: January 4, 2024
Subject: Last Will & Testament of Senator Miles Valentine

Louise,
Happy New Year.
We've received credible information that Miles Valentine was scheduled to meet with you at your law office on Tuesday, May 23, 2023, to amend his Last Will & Testament. As you know, that would have been 48 hours after Mr. Valentine's accident.
You and I have been colleagues for a long time. I'm not trying to cause trouble, but I'd appreciate if you could verify this intel as it would be helpful to his family.
-Roland

* * *

To: Roland Mast, KC
From: Louise Harris
Date: January 5, 2024
Subject: Re: re: Last Will & Testament of Senator Miles Valentine

No idea what you're talking about.
-L

* * *

To: Louise Harris
From: Roland Mast, KC
Date: January 5, 2024
Subject: Re: re: re: Last Will & Testament of Senator Miles Valentine

Oh, Louise.
Yes, you do.
-Roland

* * *

To: Roland Mast, KC
From: Louise Harris
CC: Aida Valentine
Date: January 12, 2024
Subject: Re: re: re: re: Last Will & Testament of Senator Miles Valentine

No, Roland, I don't, and I certainly do not appreciate your intimation of impropriety. I caution you not to disseminate any baseless accusations about me unless you want me to hit back.
I checked with my assistant, who confirmed that Mr. Valentine did not have an appointment scheduled for May 23rd or any other day that month. He had not requested any amendments to his will.
I have cc'd Mrs. Valentine on this email who can also confirm that no meeting had been scheduled and no changes to Mr. Valentine's Last Will & Testament made.
-Louise

* * *

To: Cordelia 'Cici' Bradshaw; Mason Valentine
From: Roland Mast, KC

Date: January 12, 2024
Subject: Fw: re: re: re: re: Last Will & Testament of Senator Miles Valentine

Well, kids, she and old lady Ripoff are hiding something. Between Louise telling Skye that the will was going to be changed and you guys having some email correspondences of Tank's confirming that in your hot little hands, I think we can lean into the idea that Granny no-bucks or her spawn stood to lose big and needed to fry their way to financial freedom.
Still nothin' legally I can do about Highclere with this information yet. If you can find a draft of the changed will or prove they rammed the old man down to avoid the teat going dry, we'll have something criminal to work with (we need to avoid being accused of stealing emails, too).
-R

* * *

To: Mason Valentine
From: Cordelia 'Cici' Bradshaw
Date: January 21, 2024
Subject: Callahan Security

M – I spoke with my friend who works at the security firm the Callahan's use at their cottage. I asked him to pull their camera footage from Labor Day in case their system caught the two people Mack saw removing objects from the carriage house. No footage exists from that day.
-C

* * *

To: Cordelia 'Cici' Bradshaw
From: Mason Valentine
Date: January 21, 2024
Subject: Re: Callahan Security

Huh…was it deleted or corrupted?
-M

* * *

To: Mason Valentine
From: Cordelia 'Cici' Bradshaw
Date: January 22, 2024
Subject: Re: re: Callahan Security

It never existed! The system was off. However, all footage up to June 30, 2023, was deleted with no cloud backup. Someone has been messing with their system. It's a tough one to break into…
-C

* * *

To: Cordelia 'Cici' Bradshaw
From: Mason Valentine
Date: January 21, 2024
Subject: Re: re: re: Callahan Security

Creepy!!! I guess that explains how Person X got footage of Mack from the Callahan's cameras—they seem to have full access to their system. I better move hackable cameras out of my bedroom and bathroom in case we're being watched, too.
-M

* * *

To: Mason Valentine
From: Cordelia 'Cici' Bradshaw
Date: January 22, 2024
Subject: Re: re: re: re: Callahan Security

Yes…I'm sure Person X has been desperate to watch your weird sleeping habits and beauty regime. Compelling viewing…lol.

I will let you know when I hear from Muskoka Hydro. They're being PITAs.
-C

* * *

To: Mason Valentine
From: Cordelia 'Cici' Bradshaw
Date: February 3, 2024
Subject: Hydro

Mace—Hydro finally confirmed which power line and transmitter went down on May 21st (the night Uncle Tank fell). I was able to "borrow" doorbell camera footage from the neighboring properties (don't ask). At 7:58 pm that night, several cameras picked up two audible "popping" sounds before going offline. One property's generator kicked in almost instantly, and you can see a massive (thick) branch sitting on the fallen hydro lines. When I checked the video from earlier in the day, the branch seemed perilously attached to the trunk. You can see a gap between the trunk and the branch. Out of curiosity, I went back in time, and as recent as three weeks earlier, that branch was FIRMLY attached to the rest of the tree—it looked very sturdy. However, on the night of May 14th (7 days before his fall), all local cameras distorted for just over two hours—after which you can see the branch had become compromised—deliberately. My money says the first "popping" noise was a small charge explosive to ensure the branch fell, followed by a second charge frying the transmitter for safekeeping. The next day, after Hydro had repaired the lines, the cameras once more became disrupted, and when the picture returned, the branch was gone. Storm or not, power was going to go down.
-C

* * *

To: Cordelia 'Cici' Bradshaw
From: Mason Valentine
Date: February 3, 2024
Subject: Re: re: Hydro

Alright, fine. I can admit when I'm wrong. I had assumed that it would be hard to plan a power outage, but apparently, it can be done quite easily! If it was a remote explosive, what would the radius be?
-M

* * *

To: Mason Valentine
From: Cordelia 'Cici' Bradshaw
Date: February 5, 2024
Subject: Re: re: re: Hydro

25km at most. Person X would've had to be on the lake somewhere.
-C

Chapter Forty-Eight

"I'm not sure how to say this with love," said Skye, attempting to hold her laughter, "but you've never looked more pathetic in your life. And this is coming from the woman who watched you run and scream like a beheaded turkey after you lit your umbrella on fire during that big rain storm a few years ago. Remember? Wait—how does a beheaded turkey scream? Either way, that storm was predicted days in advance, but you still insisted on wearing head-to-toe white in homage to Ginger Spice. All we could see were your Spanx and black undies once you got soaked," she reminisced, laughing her cacklish giggle, strands of her purple hair loosening from beneath her wide-brimmed hat while she chuckled.

"Man! You were so flipping pathetic that day! Soaked through! I still have visions of you filling the car with gas, looking like you'd just gone for a swim. You looked like a chump," she finished with a sigh. "But this could be worse."

Mere moments earlier, Skye—who had returned from a month in Manitoba that morning—stopped outside of Mason's office when she heard what sounded like a quiet baritone singing "The Fifth Dimension." Surprised, she looked through the glass pane of his office door, but Mason wasn't sitting at his desk.

"It must be a radio somewhere," she said to herself, turning to look at reception, which was also empty, having closed early for Valentine's Day. Deciding to think nothing of it, Skye continued her walk down the hall, just as an oddly confident bellow of "*ONE less...BELL to answER. ONE less...egG TO fry! ONE LESS...man...to pick-UPpp after...*" boomed from Mason's office, with emphasis on the least likely syllables.

Skye opened the door, and there was Mason lying on the floor and singing with pathetic vigor. His feet rested on the seat of his desk chair. His computer sat next to his head, an empty glass of alcohol-free champagne by his side, along with an empty box of Valentine's Day chocolates. Another heart-shaped box sat on his stomach, the cellophane still in place except for a small portion with a knife dangling.

Mason's pink sweater had spots of red blood on his chest, his left hand closed over a crumpled ball of tissues, which were becoming a violent shade of crimson.

"I am a chump!" Mason shouted at Skye while over-pretending to be upset and fake, crying for the fun of it. "I'm going to be alone *FOR...EV...EVER!!*" he whined and mock-cried even louder, ever so similar to Fran Drescher's *The Nanny*. His face was scrunched, and his lip quivering.

"Honest to Creator, this is pathetic," Skye repeated with nonplussed sympathy while taking out her phone and snapping a few pictures to use against Mason next she needed to. "Will you please stand up!"

"No!" Mason cried back feebly. "I'm bleeding. And I'm all *allllooon-nnneeeeeeeee*," he croaked at his friend and colleague, elongating the word to garner additional pitiful points.

"Stand up!" Skye demanded.

"Fine!" Mason responded before getting to his feet and removing the ball of tissue to see if his cut had stopped bleeding.

"What happened?" she asked, sitting in the guest chair across from Mason's desk.

"I cut myself," he replied irritably, showing her his hand while maneuvering his face into an expression that meant "duh."

"Oh yes. You poor, poor thing! No one has nicked their hand before with a knife! I wonder if this will be a turning point in the history of medicine. They'll name a knife cut after you, 'the Mason,'" she said mockingly, speaking to Mason as if he were a preschooler.

Mason put his computer back on his desk and pulled a bandage out of his bag.

"Social media stalking will be my downfall in life," Mason confessed to Skye, this time looking legitimately sad.

"Why?"

Mason turned his computer screen around, which revealed an Instagram post by William Marshall published earlier in the day.

Skye looked with increasing confusion.

"I thought you said he was gay and single?" she said, perplexed.

"That's what I thought! But he must be bi and dating this leggy blond hussy," Mason spat out before petulantly crossing his arms, giving his chest the illusion of busty man boobs. He really needed to hit the gym.

Skye re-read the caption beneath the loved-up photo of William Marshall hugging a beautiful, slim, fair-skinned, blond girl sporting deep red lipstick, dynamo eyes, and a smile that screamed happiness. "My Valentine. Always and forever. #Blessed #ValentinesDay #Love," the caption said.

"I hate today," said Mason, "and I shouldn't because it's literally *MY* day!"

"Valentine's Day has never been my *thang* either," Skye agreed, swiveling the laptop back toward Mason. "I thought you vetted him before going to Ottawa at Christmas?"

"I did! His official staff photo was cute. I looked him up on LinkedIn, and it mentioned he was a part of various LGBTQ2S+ groups inside and outside the Government. I then scrolled through three dating apps, and he was on two of them as a 'man seeking man.'"

"Catfish?" wondered Skye.

"Oh," said Mason, leaning back in his chair, his head almost hitting the frosted glass behind him. "That didn't occur to me," he admitted, now looking dazed.

"It could be worse, though. Remember that fella who sent you a card that said, 'Mason, I want you to know that my fountain is flowing through you, both deep and wide?'"

"Oh yeah. Huh," Mason said, his elbows on the desk, his face resting in his hands like a cherub. "That was kind of romantic," he added with childlike eyes.

"Romantic?! He was arrested for stalking you!"

"Well," Mason grouched at Skye while playfully throwing his ball of bloody tissue at her, "maybe I was too judgmental? It's not like the pickings are being carted in on a gold palanquin à la Cleopatra. It's hard to meet people at my age. Way harder than I thought it would be. Though," he added with a sigh, "a palanquin would be pleasant."

"So what?" said Skye with the apparent enthusiasm of an emerging pep talk. "It's his loss! Maybe he's straight, maybe he's gay, maybe, as you said, he's bi, but either way, it doesn't seem meant to be. Who cares? He would be so lucky to have you."

Mason smiled.

"Thanks, Skye," he said while leaning forward again. "I guess I got my hopes up," he admitted.

"Well. You got your imagination active. I'm not sure about 'hope,'" she replied. "You met him two months ago, and as far as I know, besides a few investigations-related emails, you've done nothing to pursue him."

Mason nodded.

"I know. I just...struggle in that department...I guess. Being single after over a decade of...not being single...is discombobulating. I suppose it's been easier to dream and imagine than leap."

"Well, you got burned," added Skye, referring to the sad end of the relationship Mason thought would last a lifetime.

"No," Mason replied, "we burned each other."

Skye nodded her agreement before changing the subject.

"So, where are we with Person X?" she asked.

"Ugh," sighed Mason, pulling his chair forward. "Mostly dog tail. I told you we realized at Christmas that 474 pages from Tank's diaries were ripped out before I got them?"

"You did!" Skye marveled.

"Just as I was going to bed Christmas night, I realized the diaries varied in thickness. I hadn't noticed it before because why would I? I was told all the diaries were identical except for the year, and I never questioned it. Then it clicked. I started counting, and 474 pages were gone."

"Any idea who did the censoring?" asked Skye.

"Oh, we know who it was. Very few people could do so, and the thinnest diaries are the years we need the most information from," replied Mason. "What are the odds?" he shouted à la Regis Philbin.

"Well, ain't that the pits!" laughed Skye.

"We also haven't been able to pinpoint who Laverna made the sales agreement with in 2013—though we're putting money on Trent Callahan despite his knowing about the toxic soil. We suspect he was coerced into it. Speaking of which, we also can't find anything that Stuart has done that would be worth blackmailing a Canadian Senator. Since Christmas, we have gone through his medical, education, and dating history. We've checked to see if he hadn't paid his taxes or had bad debts or outstanding warrants for his arrest in this or any other country. There's not even a hint, the tiniest sliver of a possible 'something' he's done that could make Tank look bad."

"Nothing in the emails?" asked Skye.

"Nope. We've itemized all the emails and have comprehensive search technology that uses AI to know if Stuart is referred to by a different name or spoken of as 'he or him.' Nothing. The most likely source of information was the diaries, but again, the pages we need are gone. Marko is digitizing Tank's official expense ledgers, which were in the boxes with the diaries. He's doing the same to all the tax, insurance, and checkbooks I conveniently 'borrowed' during Operation PITA. Who knows what we'll find in there?"

* * *

"That's everything for today! If you're in love, or even if you're not—scram! Get outta here! Go enjoy what's left of Valentine's Day," Cordelia instructed her class with a warm smile.

Always keen to dress for the season, Cici was decked out in a red cashmere sweater with pink and white heart patterns down the sleeves. Her white silk dress pants were pleated and accented with red jeweled pumps.

Cici was using Valentine's Day as a ruse to get rid of her students thirty minutes early. Per usual, Tobias had dreamed up a big romantic celebration set to begin at 6:00 p.m. on the dot, which didn't give her much time to follow up with Marko before meeting Tobias. Marko emailed Cici the night before, suggesting he had some news, but it needed to be shared in person.

The class continued to empty the lecture hall as Cici sat at her desk and lifted her laptop open to glance at her messages.

Nothing—except an email from her mother.

Cici moved her cursor over the unopened email, the subject line reading "Old Picture Digitization," and clicked to open it. Once she read it, she forwarded it to Mason.

* * *

```
To: Cordelia J. Bradshaw
From: Diane Bradshaw
Subject: Old Picture Digitization

Dearest Cici, I took a trip down memory lane and found
some interesting pictures that your grandmother had given
us years ago. I thought you'd be fascinated by the very
old photos taken at Fernsby House. Perhaps the preservation
group might like them for a display or exhibition? I've
scanned them the best I can, but you know how hopeless I am
with computers. I might ask one of your nephews to help me
do it better. Love Mom
```

* * *

"So sorry I'm late Ms. Bradshaw," Marko half whispered while bounding down the stairs of the lecture hall, his cheeks red both from the cold and mild embarrassment at being tardy.

"I've told you to call me Cici when we're outside class," she reminded him.

Marko looked around.

"But we are in class, Ms. Bradshaw," he noted before picking up a black plastic folding chair and moving it beside his professor.

Cici rolled her eyes at herself.

"You're right. Forgive me!"

Marko nodded and smiled without comment as he opened his computer.

"I'll cut to the chase, Ms. Bradshaw. The AI I've been using to analyze Senator Valentine's emails, financial ledgers, taxes, insurance claims, and checkbooks has been programmed to flag entries that are out of the ordinary. For example, Senator Valentine gave his grandchildren checks every year on their birthdays, which are noted and consistent. Therefore, they aren't deemed 'out of the ordinary,' and the program skips them. However, one-time or similar transactions done years apart are considered 'out of the ordinary.' Mostly, the flags have been charitable gifts, political donations, and off-pattern bill payments," Marko said, turning to face his professor, who nodded her understanding.

"In the last month and a half, the AI protocol has scanned Senator Valentine's emails and expenditures about seventy times, each time perfecting and rethinking what is or isn't abnormal. Last night's scan output included a series of checks written in 1993 that hadn't been flagged before because the payees weren't deemed abnormal, but the memo descriptions have been."

Marko paused again as Cici straightened her back in anticipation.

"The first is check number 1142 from August 4, 1993. It's a payment to what I assume was Senator Valentine's long-time travel agency, as the name of the company appears most years. The total is $2,941 dollars with the memo reading '*Round trip flight from ZHR to YYZ re: AB-neg,*'" Marko brought the entry up on his screen so Cordelia could read the description for herself.

"Ok, I see that," she agreed while nodding.

"From what I can tell, 'ZHR' refers to Zurich International Airport, and 'YYZ' refers to Toronto International Airport. 'AB-neg' I assumed was referring to the blood type, but I did some research in case it's a little-known acronym for something else. While 'AB' is a common abbreviation, the 'neg' or 'negative' is specific to blood plasma."

"So, what you're suggesting is that Uncle Tank either flew bags of AB-negative blood from Zurich to Toronto in August 1993 or, more likely, paid to fly someone with the blood type AB-negative overseas for something?" asked Cici.

"That's how it reads to me. Was there any need for a blood transfusion in the family?" wondered Marko.

"I don't know. If there was, there's no reason another family member couldn't have donated blood to whoever needed it. I'll ask Mason," she replied while leaning over to take out her phone.

* * *

"By the way I don't think 'dog-tailing' is an actual saying," pointed out Skye as she opened Mason's second box of chocolates, cutting through the cellophane without injuring herself.

"Yes, it is. It's when a dog grabs its tail and runs itself around in circles," Mason retorted as he unfolded the Godiva guide to make sure he wasn't about to eat a chocolate with a gross fruit center.

"I know what you think it means, but I'm saying that I don't believe it's actually a commonly used phrase," Skye countered as Mason's computer sounded the familiar ding of an incoming email. "Prairie dogging, however, THAT is a real term," she added.

"Every fiber of my fragile being wants to know what prairie dogging is, but I'm worried it's something only you people from Winnipeg will truly understand," Mason winked with a wry smile as he opened the first of his new emails—this one from his Aunt Drusilla.

"You're thinking of 'snagging,'" Skye laughed.

"I don't think I'm thinking anything you're thinking!" Mason fired back without a smile before one manifested on his face anyway.

"Good news?" Skye asked.

"Not really 'good news,' but Aunt Drew found a clear, detailed photo of my grandmother's missing jewelry box."

"The one you've been dreaming about?" asked Skye.

"Yea. I thought it was a music box, but Aunt Drew confirmed it's a jewelry box that plays music when it's open. So, I guess it's a bit of both. It's similar to the box Joyce brought from the UK, except the jewelry box has a clay alfresco dining scene on the top with two people and a partial house façade behind them. I'm going to print this for my evidence table. Would you be a lamb and grab it from the reception printer?" asked Mason.

"I'll be more of a dog than a lamb. Dogs are eager to please. Lambs are simply delicious," laughed Skye as she stood and walked toward the reception desk.

Mason chuckled, "Also, your mail from last month is at reception. I flipped through the 'Muskoka Realtor' magazine sent to you. Some gorgeous spots!" he added as he opened the email Cici had forwarded from her mother. As he decompressed the picture files, he felt his phone vibrate in his pocket. Mason fished it out to see a text from his cousin.

Did anything happen in 1993 that would require a blood transfusion? -C

* * *

"The second check is number 1148, dated August 11, 1993," Marko continued. "The payee is a car service company for $310 dollars. The corresponding memo description in the checkbook reads '*YYZ—36 Queen St—home—YYZ,*'" Marko stopped mid-breath when he heard Cordelia's phone vibrate on her lap.

She flipped it over to see Mason's response.

Stuart's boating accident? He nearly died. Drew's breast cancer? All that year. -M

Cici turned the phone's screen off and again placed it face down in her lap. She sat back in her chair, looking into the empty lecture hall. She could see dust floating in the late afternoon sunlight streaming through the multicolored stained-glass windows. Cici's eyes followed the fractals of color projected from the windows against the pale walls just as a thought seeped into her brain. Though it was a foggy thought, it niggled at her. It lacked edging, clarity, and scope, but it was there. What was she beginning to think?

"Ms. Bradshaw?" said Marko, interrupting Cici's contemplation.

"Sorry!" she said with a smile. "My message was from Mason. He reminded me that in 1993, my cousin Stuart was involved in a boating accident at the family resort. He was out in a sailboat when a massive motorboat, being driven by a drunk driver, came upon him," she recalled. "I'll never forget how the crash echoed through the bay. I can still hear the propellor splintering the sailboat."

"Jesus," Marko said, his mouth hanging open in horror.

Cici nodded.

"From what I remember, he was flown by helicopter to Toronto. He lost a lot of blood. It floated like a film on the lake for a day or two. He needed many transfusions. I don't think anyone from the family was abroad. I remember Drusilla being in Canada because she was being treated for breast cancer. She wanted to do that in Toronto so she could recuperate at Highclere. She'd be the most likely to be out of the country—she and her late husband had homes around the world—but she was here."

"Interestingly, the address in the check's memo, 36 Queen Street, is the entrance to St. Michael's Hospital in Toronto," Marko noted.

"So, Uncle Tank flies someone to Toronto from Zurich. That person is taken directly to St. Mike's, which I'd wager a guess is where Stuart was being treated, presumably to give blood. Wouldn't any of his siblings have been able to donate?" asked Cici.

"Not necessarily. One sibling can be AB negative, and the others just A or B, depending on their parent's blood type. I'd assume that his twin sister would be AB negative as well, but if she was being treated for cancer, then she wouldn't have been a clean match. Less than 1% of individuals are AB negative, and it's tough to find."

Cici leaned forward again, placing her elbows on her desk.

"Do you think you can figure out the identity of the donor flown from Zurich?" Cici asked.

"I think I already have."

* * *

"Here you go!" said Skye as she placed the printout of the jewelry box in front of Mason. "It's beautiful, oh my gosh! Also, there were black and white photos in the printer tray."

"Oh, thank you," smiled Mason. "Cici's mom sent old pictures of Fernsby House from when the family lived there. I was curious to see what they looked like printed."

Mason flipped through the black and white images before placing the jewelry box photo on top of the stack.

Skye snagged another chocolate from the heart-shaped box and moved behind Mason's desk chair to peer over his shoulder.

"There isn't a key slot for that box, eh?" noted Skye.

"Well spotted, Granny," replied Mason.

"Har, har. You're hilarious! Riddle me this: if there isn't room for a key, how does it work, Grandpa?" Skye responded, nibbling at her dark chocolate truffle.

"Hey, hey! I'm still a 'daddy' at best!" Mason joked.

"Oh sure," responded Skye with an eye roll, chocolate dust attractively floating out of her mouth.

"The figurines are the lock system. The bistro table, two diners, and the door behind them are on some kind of swivel mechanism that opens and closes the box. The decorative crystals on the door—there are sixteen of them—are buttons. You push in the code to unlock the swivel mechanism, then turn the entire dining scene ninety degrees to the left, and presto, she's open!"

"Wow," Skye marveled. "That's sophisticated for such an old piece. What's the power source? Battery?"

"Nope, a crank system like old-fashioned music boxes. However, I don't understand how that works. Something about a cog and a drum," Mason admitted.

"Does anyone know the code?" asked Skye.

"I do," said Mason, "or at least I did."

"Do you have it written down?"

"No, but I should. Can you grab me the blue and silver Sharpies from my evidence table? I'm going to show the code by coloring the trigger buttons blue and the dummy buttons silver. I'll also number them with input order using a pen."

Skye walked to Mason's boardroom table turned Toronto evidence display. While the office at Highclere remained Mason and Cici's main headquarters, with three corkboards and several shelves full of evidence, clues, and puzzle pieces, they realized after Christmas that a similar setup would be helpful in the city. Mason had a conference table moved into his office to display copies of evidence. He also installed a protective plexiglass cover on the table, which could switch from transparent to opaque white at the press of a button, ensuring the contents remained hidden from the prying eyes of unexpected visitors.

Skye pushed the circular white button on the side of the table, which turned the plexiglass clear, revealing the contents of the investigation beneath its shielding. She pulled a blue and silver Sharpie from a mug of markers and pens. She handed them to Mason before returning her attention to the assortment of pictures, printouts, diary pages, threatening letters, and maps that had been gathered since Labor Day. A digital frame displaying Mason's photos also sat atop the plexiglass, which she moved aside to fully appreciate the table's contents.

"You're due for a breakthrough," Skye announced as she ran her fingers along the glass.

"Ha! From your lips to Creator's ears," Mason replied as he finished coloring the final crystal blue and numbered the order in which they needed to be keyed.

"How do you remember the code for the jewelry box after all this time?" she asked.

"It's the sort of thing I don't seem to forget. I think it's muscle memory. I still know my locker combination from high school," he added as he double-checked to ensure he correctly numbered the buttons.

"That crazy memory and overactive brain of yours!" Skye commented, shaking her head.

"Blessing and curse," said Mason before tapping the edge of the picture on the table to get Skye's attention. "Can you put this under the glass, please?"

"Of course," she said, taking the flimsy paper while Mason looked at the black and white pictures of Fernsby House.

"Cameras from the late 1800s and early 1900s were remarkable. This picture is of family members playing soccer in the forecourt, yet in the background, there are two people sitting at a table in front of the 'Door to Nowhere,' and they are just as crisp, clear, and in-focus as those playing the game closer to the lens. The detail is extraordinary. I wonder if Cici can get the originals for me?" thought Mason, still focused on the century-old images.

His query was met with silence. Curious, he looked up to see Skye still holding the jewelry box photo while shifting her gaze from the picture to the table.

"Skye?" Mason asked, laying the pictures down on his desk and standing up.

"Mason. You better see this."

* * *

"The third and final check is check number 1151, dated September 1, 1993," said Marko, again displaying the digitized checkbook on his computer screen. "The payee is the '*InterContinental Hotel 8050*,' and the memo says, '*Folio 0291*' with something else written next to the folio number—but as you can see, it's blacked out," he noted while pointing to the thick black line running the rest of the memo line.

"Shit," said Cici before asking, "Where is Hotel 8050?"

"It took a bit of digging, but in the early 1990s, some franchise hotels were incorporated under the brand name with the postal or zip code included in the title of the legal entity as a property differentiator. Nowadays, a hotel would be known as 'The InterContinental Barclays,' for example, but thirty years ago, it was brand name plus postcode."

Cici could see Marko was getting increasingly animated.

"And postal code 8050 is?" she asked, already knowing the answer.

"Zurich," he replied, spitting on his laptop. "Sorry," he said sheepishly, cleaning his saliva.

"Can we get folio number 0291 to find out who stayed there?"

"No," he said undeterred. "They don't keep that information for thirty years. Also, it was a primitive computer era."

"Not so primitive, Marko. We had Windows and MS-Dos!" Cici proclaimed.

"MS what?" asked Marko.

"Never mind. So, presumably, the name of the person associated with that folio number is written in the memo and blacked out?"

"That was my thinking, too," Marko agreed.

"Damn it," Cici shouted as she put her hands behind her head to stretch.

"No, no. No need to get upset, Ms. Bradshaw—I know the name."

Cici dropped her arms like anvils and pivoted her chair to face Marko. Her face was a mix of shock and excitement.

"How?" she asked.

"I took the physical checkbook out of the box and went to that entry. Senator Valentine, or his assistant, wrote the name in pen before redacting it with a marker. I just flipped the page over, and you can read the name from the back," Marko said while lifting his backpack onto his lap and pulling out the checkbook. "I've noted the page with a Post-it," he added while handing the slim booklet to Cici.

Cordelia felt her hands shake as she flipped to the page the Post-it was beckoning her to. Who had her Uncle Tank needed to fly to Canada after Stuart's accident to give blood? Why couldn't a family member do it, and why the secrecy? She took a deep breath and ran her fingers across the line of black marker, feeling the indentation of letters roll against her skin while smelling the chemical aroma of the Sharpie emanating from the paper.

Cici turned the page over to read the name deemed too sensitive to be revealed. She narrowed and focused her eyes, struggling to make out what was written. She picked up her phone and turned on the flashlight, which she slid beneath the page to illuminate the letters.

She gasped.

"No!" she whispered, staring at the backward name for several moments before placing the checkbook on her desk.

She sat back, her right hand covering her mouth, her left still holding the illuminated phone. Her niggling thought had taken shape and curve.

"No..." she said again under her breath as she stared into the darkening lecture hall, the sun setting outside.

Cordelia wanted to convince herself it couldn't be true. It was impossible to have perpetuated this heartbreaking of a lie for so long. She wanted to believe that Miles "The Tank" Valentine would never have even tried to do it. Yet because of all her years in investigative journalism and all she'd learned about her uncle's hubris and narcissism since he died, she had to admit that the glove fit. Was she surprised at Tank? Or were her feelings of distress coming from the apparent truth she was struggling to admit to herself—that her Aunty V was in on the lie as well?

Maybe she didn't know Lady Jean Valentine as well as she thought. Perhaps she didn't know Jean or Miles Valentine at all.

Then, as she shifted her gaze to look again at the plastic cover of the closed checkbook, another realization crystallized. Another fear proved true.

Shit.

Cici jumped when her phone rang. Marko had closed his computer, giving her a few moments to process her thoughts. She looked at the screen to see Tobias calling.

"Oh shit," she said to Marko. "This is my husband. I'm going to be late for dinner at Ozone. Shit! FYI, the restaurant locks cell phones away on Valentine's Day, so can you message Mason and tell him I have to talk to him first thing tomorrow? Tell him it's the break we needed!"

"Of course, Ms. Bradshaw," Marko replied as Cici scrambled to pack her things and run.

Cici smiled and gave a half-wave before disappearing from the door.

Chapter Forty-Nine

"Do you think you've made a mistake? Just repeated something you've seen a lot recently?" asked Skye. She held up a picture of the Farnsworth-made jewelry box next to a printout of the gemstone side of the cufflinks worn by the alleged 'Maxwell Fernsby' when he died. The pattern of the cufflink's sixteen micro-cut sapphires and white diamonds matched the blue trigger and silver dummy buttons Mason had colored on the jewelry box's keypad.

"Maybe, but I don't think so," Mason replied, breathily and confused. "This doesn't make sense. Why would the gemstone design of the cufflinks be the same as the code for the jewelry box? They were both made by Farnsworth. Perhaps it's just a common pattern for them?" he wondered.

"I don't know Mace. Why would a jewelry box keypad require sixteen buttons? Ten would be normal. Five would be doable. I could see the logic in a dozen, but sixteen? It seems intentional, and the trigger keys are where the blue sapphires are on the cufflinks," Skye added.

"I agree. We know the care Farnsworth put into their designs and products. Maybe the cufflinks are a key or a reminder for how to open the jewelry box?"

"Then wouldn't they have been together?" asked Skye.

"Not if you're trying to keep the pattern from getting into the wrong hands. But those cufflinks were never in Canada as far as the Farnsworth ledger shows, and they were made during the Second World War, whereas the box was made in the 1950s."

Mason and Skye stood in silence, thinking. Pictures from Christmas appeared on the digital frame Skye had pushed to the side of the table.

What could the matching patterns mean? Was one item the key to the other? Or were both the jewelry box and cufflinks a key to something else?

"Aww! Oh my gosh—how adorable!" Skye squealed with delight while looking at the picture displayed in the frame.

Mason looked to see that the photo he'd taken of Mika and Harrison playing Connect Four on Christmas Day had settled on the screen. He smiled.

"Right!? That was just before dinner. The sun's glow bouncing off my grandmother's tablecloth was pretty magical."

"You hate the phrase 'pretty magical,'" she pointed out.

"I do. But the way the honey-yellow light was streaming through the windows—it was almost like the kids had halos on. Even though Mika is sticking her tongue out and looks more devilish than angelic. Also, the light almost makes the blue and silver ornaments on the needlepoint Christmas tree shimmer," he noted.

"That's your grandmother's tablecloth? With the 'twelve days' and Christmas tree?" asked Skye, pulling the frame toward her face.

"Yup! She gave it to me the Christmas before she died. We used it on Christmas Day 2003, and then she wrapped it up and gave it to me on Boxing Day. I guess I should've known then that it would be her last Christmas. She seemed to know, at least."

Skye looked from the frame to the conference table and then back to the frame again.

"I love that she updated it for you."

Mason turned to his friend, perplexed.

"What?" he asked.

"The changes she made to it. They're great!" Skye answered, uncertain if she was assuring Mason about the quality of the changes or if she was sharing something he'd never noticed before.

"Give me that," Mason said as he snatched the picture frame from Skye's hand. He looked at the picture. "That's how it's always looked," he said, absolute.

Skye looked back to the table.

"But it doesn't match the tablecloth in this picture," she said, pointing to the picture of Lady Valentine with Tank and their grandchildren at Christmas 2003, the jewelry box visible in the cabinet behind them.

"Holy shit," said Mason, glancing from the digital frame to the 2003 picture and back again. "Holy shit!" he repeated before handing the frame back to Skye and then picking up his phone from his desk.

He opened his photos and scrolled to a picture of his decorative table setting taken just before Christmas dinner a mere fifty days earlier.

"How have I missed this?" he asked himself.

"You saw the same tablecloth for almost twenty years. Why would you ever think she'd have updated it before giving it to you?" Skye replied, knowing Mason wasn't looking for an answer.

"She didn't update it. That's an entirely different tablecloth. That picture," he said, pointing again to the 2003 Christmas photo, "was taken the day before she gave it to me. There wouldn't have been time to update it. She had a near replica made."

Mason placed his phone on top of the conference table next to the 2003 photo, and after pausing the digital frame, he put that next to his phone.

"Look," Mason said, pointing to the center of the original tablecloth. "The bulbs on the tree are silver and gold here, whereas they are blue and silver on the one she gave me."

"Also," Skye added, "there are nine bulbs on the original center tree and sixteen on the new one."

"Sixteen..." Mason whispered. "SIXTEEN!" he then shouted, grabbing the top of his head with both hands, "Skye! Sixteen silver and blue bulbs...or...rather...sixteen white and blue whatevers, where have we seen those!?" he said in disbelief.

Skye gasped.

Mason placed the cufflink and the jewelry box printouts next to his phone, which was still displaying the tablecloth. Each had a pattern of sixteen blue and white circular objects arranged identically.

"Unbelievable!" Mason shouted. "Holy shit, Skye! This is unbelievable! Am I dreaming? Is this a dream?" Mason asked her, his eyes wide, cheeks red, and his thinning hair mussed by his hands.

"I'm not sure," said Skye, who grabbed a glass of water and threw it at Mason's face. "Did you feel that?" she asked with a smile.

"I hate you," Mason replied, water dripping from his hair down his nose and lips.

"It will get the blood out of your sweater, at least," Skye said, laughing.

Mason wiped the water from his face on his sleeve.

"If we hadn't just discovered something massive, I would be angry with you," he said, "but this is just too fucking exciting!" he said with electric energy.

They both turned once more to the table.

"Ok. The jewelry box code, the cufflink gemstones, and the bulbs on the tablecloth all have the same pattern. But why? Is it reasonable to assume that there has to be something else that uses that pattern or sequence? Something that we are being pointed toward?" Mason asked.

Skye shrugged.

"I don't know. Also, did you notice that the new tablecloth has red and white snowflakes behind each Twelve Days of Christmas scene? They aren't in the original. Maybe those are codes for something also? Maybe they're all codes?"

"Codes," Mason repeated. "Why codes, though?"

"Well, the jewelry box uses a code, and I assume the bulbs and the gemstones are reminders of the code."

"Where else would a code be needed?"

"A safe? A vault? A locked door? A drawer?" Skye suggested.

Mason looked from the jewelry box to the cufflinks to the paused picture of the kids playing Connect Four on the digital frame.

"A safe, a vault, a locked door, or a drawer," Mason said again out loud, his eyes shifting from the jewelry box to the cufflinks to the digital frame.

A safe, a vault, a locked door, or a drawer.

Jewelry box, cufflinks, digital frame.

There was an idea, a connection, an answer sloshing around in his subconscious. Mason could feel it. He was willing it to come to him. He knew he was standing at the precipice of something—but what?

A safe, a vault, a locked door, or a drawer.

Jewelry box, cufflinks, digital frame.

A safe, a vault, a locked door, or a drawer.

Jewelry box, cufflinks, digital frame.

No, that's not it, Mason thought. *Jewelry box, cufflinks, AND Connect Four? Is that it? Are those the objects connecting in my brain?*

A safe, a vault, a locked door, or a drawer.

Jewelry box, cufflinks...and Connect Four.

Yes, that's it!

Jewelry box, cufflinks, Connect Four. Jewelry box, cufflinks, Connect Four.

A safe for jewels.

A locked box for jewels?

The cufflinks could be considered jewelry, and the box needs a code to open, almost like that silly drawer that pops open after playing Connect Four.

Mason closed his eyes, thinking.

A safe, a vault, a locked door. Jewelry box, cufflinks, Connect Four.

Mason stood silent. Still. One word was working its way through his subconscious, elbowing its way to the front.

One word.

He stood silent.

Then he had it.

Mason's eyes shot open. He turned and looked at Skye.

"You see the alfresco setting with the figurines in front of the door on top of the jewelry box?" he asked Skye as he pointed to the picture.

"Yes," nodded Skye, noticing water still dripping down Mason's forehead.

"I've seen that exact scene today. I think you're right. The pattern is a code, and I'm 99% sure I know what it opens and where," he said, walking to his desk. I need to talk to Cici."

Still standing, he woke his computer to find a message from Marko at the top of his inbox.

* * *

```
To: Mason Valentine
From: Marko (Cici's Student)
Subject: Ms. Bradshaw needs to speak tomorrow!

Mr. Valentine,
Ms. Bradshaw asked me to tell you she needs to speak to you
first thing tomorrow. She and her husband are at Ozone for
dinner tonight, and the restaurant has a no-cellphone policy
on Valentine's Day, which is why I'm reaching out to you.
She says it's a break in the case.
Marko
```

* * *

"Shit," Mason said, closing his laptop. "Do you have plans tonight?" he asked Skye while packing his computer.

"Nope. Why?"

"I might need you to tackle a maître d'"

"What makes you think I'd do that?" Skye asked.

"You're from Winnipeg," Mason said, putting on his coat.

"Alright, you got me there. You're paying my bail, though! Again," she said, running toward her office to collect her things.

Chapter Fifty

"Is the clientele getting younger, or are we getting older?" asked Cordelia as she settled into her seat.

Tobias had reserved the exclusive corner table of Toronto hotspot Ozone, a restaurant with intense scenic views of Toronto's Skyline, including the CN Tower, lit up in festive pink and red. The candlelight atmosphere, along with the glow emanating from the downtown skyscrapers, provided a romantic ambiance and magical lighting that optically erased visible wrinkles and fine lines without the need for last-minute Botox.

A Valentine's Day miracle!

"Getting older!? How dare you! The clientele is definitely younger. It's that whole Gen Z thing of 'why should we have to wait until we are financially stable to eat at a Michelin-star restaurant? We want it now!'" Tobias winked at his wife as the server poured champagne.

"Wow. You're normally terrible with quick retorts, but that one was pretty good!" she said while taking her first sip of bubbly.

"I practiced that line for any number of scenarios that might arise tonight," he said with a smile, moving the dangling ribbon of one of the 700 heart-shaped balloons floating against the ceiling. It was tickling his nose.

"Balloons are a bit much," Cici suggested while removing a long string that had wafted into her water glass.

"Without a doubt," Tobias nodded. "Oh. You'll never guess who I saw today," he said while reading the menu.

"Oh? Who?" replied Cici.

"Laverna and Gil."

Cici closed her menu and looked at Tobias.

"Gil? Gil Regan?" she asked.

"That's the one," he agreed while eyeing the appetizers.

"Tob...Tobias," Cici said while using her finger to lower his menu. "Just...can we focus on this for a second."

"Why? What's the big deal?"

"What's the big deal? You know the big deal. They are two of the only people who know what it is about Stuart that is blackmail worthy, and they're hanging out? Isn't that strange to you?"

"Not really. Aida hired my firm to renovate her house on Governor Boulevard, and Gil was the engineer who oversaw the upgrades and minor renovations during Tank's life," said Tobias, his eyebrows raised with a facial expression suggesting it wasn't a scandalous situation.

"Why your firm?" asked Cici.

"Why not my firm? We're one of the best."

"I know that, but you'd think that if they were going to hire your firm, they'd ask for you specifically to be the architect on the project."

"It would be a conflict of interest."

"Does Gil have a relationship with your company?" wondered Cici.

"Other than me? Not that I know of," answered Tobias, picking up his menu again and trying not to succumb to his growing irritation.

Cici turned to look out the window.

"Why would they want *you* to see *them*?" she asked.

"Hmmm?" grunted Tobias, not looking at his wife.

"No, nothing. I'm just wondering why they'd want you to see them together. I'm not sure what they're trying to prove by teaming up."

"Maybe they aren't trying to prove anything, and I saw them together because they are simply renovating a house."

"The Cliftons have been nothing but calculating for decades. Aida hires your firm but then sends Laverna, who invites Gil? It was obvious they wanted you to see them together."

Tobias placed his menu down on the table and stared at his wife.

"Well, next time, I'll just ask them what the deal is with Stuart and why, whatever it is, Tank could be blackmailed out of millions for it. Would that help?"

"Kind of, actually," Cici laughed as Tobias, smiling, ripped a multigrain bread roll open and buttered it.

"I'll ask around tomorrow and see what I can find out," agreed Tobias.

"Cordelia! Tobias!" called an excited voice from behind several pink balloons.

"Hello?" Cici called back to the faceless, voluptuous woman in a skin-tight yellow dress who was walking toward them.

"Happy V-Day!" beamed a joyful Bianca Anders, squeezing her head through two heart-shaped balloons entering like Jack Nicolson in *The Shining*.

"Why hello, B!" Tobias greeted while standing to hug their unexpected guest followed by Cici doing the same.

"Are you on a hot date?" asked Cici in a girlish tone.

"Ha! I wish," said Bianca, turning her head to look for her companions. "You can't see a thing through these lovely balloons, though!"

"Who are you here with?" asked Tobias.

"Aida and Laverna. With it being Aida's first Valentine's Day without Uncle Miles, we thought it would be nice to go out and celebrate in style," she declared while doing a twirl to show off her dress.

"I think I have the same dress in blue," said Cici.

"Oh, probably—I get most of my fashion ideas from you," laughed Bianca, placing her hand on Cordelia's shoulder.

Tobias looked to Cici, then back to Bianca.

"Are Aida and Laverna going to say hi?" he asked.

"I suspect not because of who just made a conspicuous entrance behind us," Bianca grimaced.

"Who?" asked Cici seconds before she heard the distinctive voice of the person in question.

"Yes, hello! Happy Valentine's Day. Lovely night, isn't it? Voulez-vous—aha, as Abba sings. Are you fans of Abba? Don't worry. I'm not embarrassed or sweaty. I'm just wearing man Spanx," said Mason to various tables while excusing his need to weave between tight chairs to get to Cici and Tobias's table.

"What's a man spank?" asked one of the diners.

"Depends on the context. A spank or Spanx? Two very different things, you see, spanking is when..."

"He's not sweaty! He's wet," shouted Skye from the maître d's station, cutting Mason off, "I threw water at him!"

"She did indeed. I'll tell you what Spanx are on my way out," he said to the curious patron while continuing to meander through the tables. "Yes, I'm Mason Valentine. What? Never heard of me? That's not unusual. I'm really a lovely person, it's just. It's a big night. Oh! Great looking dessert, can I have a bite?"

"Mason!" Cordelia said firmly as he picked up a stranger's fork to taste a bit of cheesecake.

"What?" he asked with the fork in midair.

"There's an open aisle right there," Cici said, pointing to the simple through-way. "You didn't have to disturb these happy people out for Valentine's Day."

"What kind of entrance would that have been?" Mason shrugged as he reached Tobias, Cici, and Bianca.

"It'd have been no entrance at all! No pizzazz!" shouted Skye.

"I can take it from here!" Mason yelled back.

"Hello, Bianca! Surprise seeing you here," said Mason, leaning in for a hug. "Hot date?" he winked and nudged her with his shoulder while smirking.

"No. I'm here with friends," Bianca replied, still jovial and ever-pleasant.

"Handsome friends?" Mason teased. "With robust bank accounts and all-night stamina?" he winked.

"I've always thought Aida was a handsome woman," nodded Tobias, letting the air out of Mason's chatty exuberance.

"Oh," Mason said, nodding. "And...where might Aida be?" he asked, his voice in a pitch not dissimilar to a pre-pubescent boy.

"She's seated with Laverna, and I should get back to them. So, lots of love from me to you three, and Happy Valentine's Day!" waved Bianca, taking a few steps backward before turning and knocking balloon strings out of her way.

"I didn't expect them to be here," Mason said, speaking out of the side of his mouth.

"To be fair, we didn't expect you here," said Cici as she and Tobias sat down.

"I know, I'm sorry! But I *HAVE* to tell you something," he said, getting down on his knees.

"Cici, it's huge," said Mason, stopping and turning to Cici. "Wait, Marko said you have a break in the case, too. Let's start there," urged Mason.

Cici smiled.

"I actually have two. I was going to tell you both tomorrow, but I'll say what I can now. Considering Laverna, Aida, and Bianca are in the same room, it might not be much."

The three of them leaned in and talked in hushed voices.

"The AI program Marko was running on the emails, checkbooks, financial statements, insurance policies, expenditures, and the like, came back with a few entries it deemed out of pattern. They were three checks, all issued shortly after Stuart's accident in 1993. The first, to Uncle Tank's travel agent for a round-trip flight from Zurich to Toronto, next a car service from Toronto airport to St. Michael's Hospital, then to an unknown address, and lastly, a payment to a hotel in Zurich, not far from the airport. The first check was noted as having to do with AB negative..."

"The blood type?" asked Tobias.

"Yes," confirmed Cici.

"Whose blood type is AB negative? I'm O," questioned Mason.

"Stuart is AB negative," said Cici. "Or at least I think he is. It's a rare blood type and often difficult to come by, especially in large quantities. Especially in 1993."

"Tank flew a blood donor from Europe to ensure Stuart had sufficient supply?" asked Mason.

"Yes," whispered Cici.

"Do you have the name of the donor?" asked Tobias.

Cici nodded.

"The memo section was redacted, but we could read it from the back. Do either of you have a pen?" she asked.

Moments later, a blue felt tip appeared in Mason's hand, along with a Post-it note.

"This note will not leave this table. I'm going to soak the ink off as soon as you've both read it," she said before scanning the room to ensure Laverna, Aida, and Bianca weren't within hearing range.

Cici pulled the cap off and maneuvered her glass and salad plate to act as a barrier while scribbling out the first and last name—twelve letters, twelve letters that knocked the door off several what-and-why questions.

Cici again checked her surroundings before showing the Post-it to Mason. Mason unfolded the paper.

"What!?" he heaved after reading the familiar name. "You're sure?" he asked.

"Yes," replied Cici, who then slid the note in front of Tobias before ripping it up and dropping it into her glass of champagne, the bubbles wiping the ink from existence.

"I don't get it," admitted Mason. "What does it mean?" he asked.

"Think, Mason, think," urged Cici, hoping he'd race to her same conclusion.

"Drusilla wouldn't have been able to donate blood. She was undergoing chemo," said Mason.

"Yes, but why this person specifically?" she pushed. "Come on, Mason. Think. Think about Maxwell Farnsworth."

Mason sat in silence, replaying their conversation with Drusilla from Christmas Eve. The words running through his head, the smells, the sounds, the cows, the sights of the discussion racing along his memory, every nuance being pulled from one end of his consciousness to the other.

And then.

"Oh shit," said Mason, covering his mouth and looking up at Cordelia. "You think?" he asked in less disbelief than he would have if it hadn't been his second shock discovery of the day.

"I do," she confirmed.

"That they're..."

"Yup," she smiled.

"For this long?" Mason asked, still in wonder.

"Yes."

"I'm lost," said Tobias, grabbing another bread roll.

"I'll fill you in at home," Cici smiled, passing him the butter.

"Well, if that's not mind-blowing enough for one day, ready for my monumental news?" asked Mason.

Cordelia and Tobias pivoted their bodies to face Mason, ready for whatever he was about to say. Yet, nothing could've prepared them for it.

Chapter Fifty-One

"Golly goodness! This is exciting indeed, isn't it?" trilled a bouncy Baroness, Margaret "Margot" Ambrosia, as she adjusted the camera she'd attached to a thin tripod after it fell over in the wind. "Is the image at all clear on your end? Or did I damage it?" she added while waving her pink gloved hands to the screen, smiling wide.

"It's perfect," replied Mason, who had squeezed the corduroy chair next to Cici at the old desk of the inn's office. Mason's laptop was mirrored onto a large TV screen next to them to give a more detailed picture of what they were about to watch unfold in the United Kingdom.

"You're sure this is solid?" reconfirmed Margot, whose face was against the camera's lens, leaving a blush mark while she planted the tripod deeper into the gravel.

"I'm not sure about solid, but you do have a wonderful complexion for your age," noted Mason from Canada. "If you can clean off the lens, that would be helpful too," Mason winked.

"Oopsie! Tremendous apologies, darling. I forgot for a second that you would become intimate with my pores as I did this," she said.

Mason and Cici heard a shoe moving gravel on top of the tripod's base to hold it in place. Margot then took several steps from the camera and turned to face the action behind her.

"I'll move out of the way. However, do confirm you can see ahead," she added before leaving the frame.

On the screen in front of them, Mason and Cici saw an assembled group of construction workers, several police officers including Stellan McManus, and a few tottery old people. The assemblage looked to Mason like a geriatric-led Village People tribute band. All were standing around the fabled "Door to Nowhere" at Fernsby House.

"It's perfect Margot. You can hear my voice next to the door?" asked Mason.

"Let me check," said Margot, who skipped toward the door with light movements. "Check, check 1, 2, 3," said Margot.

"We can hear you, Margot," said Mason.

"And I you in return, dear Mason," said Margot before retracing her steps to the camera.

"Shall we get this show on the road?" asked Mason.

"Indeed, we shall. First, let me introduce you to a few important individuals who have kindly agreed to give us their time today. I suspect you'll find everyone is as much a buzz with nerves and excitement as we lot are!" noted Margot, clapping her hands together.

"Right. First, the group over there," said Margot, moving toward the elderly contingent, "are part of the preservation society."

They waved to the camera, and Cici and Mason waved back. Margot returned to the center of their screen.

"Next, Mason Valentine, Cordelia Bradshaw, I'd like for you to meet, well virtually meet, Mrs. Andrea Romero," said Margot as an older, short woman with gray hair and a walking stick moved toward the camera."

"Good day to you," smiled Andrea Romero, waving to the camera.

"So lovely to meet you!" replied Cici.

"As you both know, Mrs. Romero is the industry expert and owner of Farnsworth Marble & Designs' patents and products. She'll be able to authenticate anything we find today and will also ensure that we don't accidentally distress or damage the door during this effort," explained Margot.

"Thirdly," she continued while grabbing a middle-aged man by the arm. "This is Mr. Milton Hague," she said of the handsome, slim fellow with wispy gray hair and a smart pinstriped suit. "He is from the War Museum and was the kind benefactor who funded our deep soil radar expedition several weeks ago. If he hadn't generously agreed to do so, we wouldn't be able to embark on our experiment today. Mr. Hauge is also one of the nation's best art restorers, and he, along with his white gloves, will be the person following your instructions, Mason."

"Thank you, Mr. Hague. We appreciate you doing this," Mason waved.

"My immense pleasure. This is the sort of thing we history and art buffs dream of finding," Milton said through a slight cough.

"You, of course, know Stellan and his officers. We also have various workers to help with any lifting or pulling that may be needed since we don't know how well-maintained the gears and springs may be," Margot concluded.

"I guess this is the moment we've all been waiting for," said Mason, his anxiety appearing through the restlessness of his right leg. "Mr. Hague, if you're ready, we are."

"Absolutely, sir," agreed Milton.

"Perfect. Mr. Hague, please go toward the 'Door to Nowhere' and please remove the false front and back of the door to reveal the interior glass bulbs," instructed Mason.

"Righto," waved Milton who marched toward the Fernsby's eccentric piece of art come historical war memento.

"Margot, I suggest everyone move off the concrete surface around the door other than Mr. Hague," said Mason.

"No problem," agreed Margot, who hurried everyone onto the grass.

"Mr. Hague, each side has sixteen bulbs. We'll start on the east side of the door and go from left to right of each row, starting at the top. Ready?" called Mason.

"Oui, oui," said Milton, almost jumping up and down.

"Ok. Mr. Hague. Turn bulb two to the left," instructed Mason.

"Number two to the left," repeated Milton as he did so with his white gloves.

"Number five to the left."

"Copy number five to the left!"

"Number eight to the left."

"Righto, number eight to the left!"

"Number 11 to the left."

"Number 11!"

"Number 14 to the left."

"Numero 14!"

"Number 15 to the left."

"Number 15!"

"Ok, the moment of truth," Mason said, turning to look at Cici. "Please turn number 16 to the left."

"Number 16," called back Milton Hague, who turned the bulb in the lowest right corner of the door.

Everyone held their breath and waited.

* * *

"Nothing happened?" Mason asked Margot, who had just finished walking the perimeter of the "Door to Nowhere," to see if there had been a shift.

"I'm afraid not," confirmed Margot. "We could hear what sounded like iron poles going up and down after each bulb turn, but nothing else. Shall we try from the west side?" she asked.

"Yes," agreed Mason. "First, bring the bulbs back to center," he added, which she did.

"Mr. Hague, here we go. The west side, please," shouted Mason.

Mason read off each number again and watched with growing anxiety as Milton turned the specified bulbs to the left. Upon reaching the sixteenth and final bulb, the group held their breath again to listen for signs of movement.

Nothing.

"Shit!" said Mason, pounding his hand on the desk.

"Take a beat," advised Cici. "We know you're right. The deep soil radar proved it. There has to be something we're not doing," she suggested.

Mason thought. What was he doing wrong? Did the "Door to Nowhere" follow a unique pattern to the cufflinks, jewelry box, and tablecloth? It was possible, but he felt unlikely, considering how frequently the same sequence of sixteen appeared.

Think about the jewelry box, Mason, he thought to himself. *What else is unique about it?* Mason tapped his fingers on the desk, his right leg jumping up and down with anticipation, thinking.

Thinking.

Wait.

What did Skye ask me? Mason wondered. *What was it?*

Mason jumped out of his chair.

"Margot!" he called.

"An idea, dear Mason?" Margot asked.

"Power, we need a power supply. Is there something resembling a crank nearby? It might be further afield. Closer to the perimeter of the property?" he asked, willing the answer to be yes.

"I'm not sure we've seen anything of the like, but let me canvas the group," Margot suggested before stepping away to speak to the elderly delegates from the preservation society.

Mason and Cici sat as they watched Margot and her group gesticulate to each other and mime a crank. They pointed to several locations of the property before folding their arms in front of themselves again and speaking less animatedly than before. They were clearly deep in thought.

Then, one of the old men started speaking with broad gestures. Mason and Cici felt like they were watching a game of charades as the man drew a box in the air with his fingers while tapping his forearm and pointing to his head. He then swung his hips from side to side before turning around on the spot. Putting his arms in the air—almost doing jazz hands—the rest of the group enthusiastically applauded him as Margot trotted over to a worker.

Margot pointed the man in a yellow hat toward the main house. Both looked upward.

The bell tower? Mason wondered.

The burly worker ran toward the house and out of the camera's view. Margot walked back to the tripod.

"We suspect we know where a crank might be," she confirmed with glee.

"Really?" asked Mason.

"Indeed. There is what we thought to be a decorative life-sized marble statue of the crucifixion at the top of Fernsby House, right at the bell tower. Leonard, over there," Margot pointed to the man who had been doing his smoothest hip swinging seconds earlier, "remembered he was surprised to see it was on some kind of 'Lazy Susan' and turned it a few times during an early inspection and in doing so, he heard a click and what sounded like a fan starting. He thought little of it at the time, but we've sent someone to give it some cranks."

"Alright, your ladyship!" yelled a distant voice to Margot, who looked heavenward. "I've turned it as far as it will go!"

"Right-o!" Margot shouted back. "Mason darling, I can confirm the sound of a fan or barrel circling is now audible. So, back to you and Milton."

Mason took his position, a thrill charging him. This was it.

"Ready, Mr. Hague?" called Mason.

"Indeed!" confirmed Milton.

Mason and Milton once more made their way through the sixteen large, custom-crafted bulbs that had once shone secret messages to British vessels, allowing them to maneuver their way inland safely. Emerald Fernsby's eccentric "Door to Nowhere," a symbol to most locals of a woman unwell, was a piece of British history, a piece of war history, a piece of Mason and Cici's history. A piece that had one more secret left in her.

"Number sixteen to the left," confirmed Milton Hague as he gently turned the bulb to the left, accompanied by the sound of a metal pole lowering.

Mason stopped breathing.

He watched.

Listened.

He hoped that his hunch was correct.

Silence.

Then, bulb sixteen became lit, followed quickly by 15, 14, 11, 8, 5, and 2. Milton ran from the door as it sprung to life. The sound of a motor roaring awake could be heard in the distance.

The "Door to Nowhere" shook and wiggled.

Cracks could be heard as the door started to turn ninety degrees, moving gently as if it knew her old bones were brittle and tired.

The door came to an abrupt stop.

The sound of the motor slowed as the lights in the door returned to their natural state of glass.

A loud click ricocheted into the camera's microphone, followed by a second, third, and fourth. The group at Fernsby House covered their ears to protect them from the assaulting decibels.

Silence once more befell the scene as Margot Ambrosia walked toward the "Door to Nowhere," confirming that three sides of the concrete slab beneath the door had popped open and lifted from the ground.

Margot used her phone's flashlight to peer between the concrete seam and the grass's edge. Squinting, she mainly saw dust and darkness until her light illuminated the edge of another structure hidden below the surface.

Chapter Fifty-Two

"Heigh hooooooo!" Mason sang out, ready to belt out the entire song from *Snow White*.

"As in 'hi hoe?' or are we back to 'felt green frog with a hand up its ass' territory?" asked Skye Cadieux as she locked her car, having just arrived at Highclere Inn & Carriage House. "We need new material!"

"We do! This bit is stale. Ready to do some grave robbing? Woot woot!" Mason asked, fist-pumping while doing so. "I'm so glad we could call in an expert," he winked.

"Ha, ha. You dig up one or two graves in your life, and suddenly, you're the 'go-to' for it. I could start a business," she joked as they walked toward the door of the inn.

Mason and Cici had called Skye earlier and asked her to join them at Highclere for a few days while they navigated the latest developments surrounding the Valentine family.

"This is starting to feel more and more like we're in a movie," said Skye as Mason held the inn door open for her.

"Or a book!" he smiled.

As the door slammed behind them, they could hear the loud thud of Cici's work boots as she bounced down the stairs carrying work gloves, a rake, and a hoe.

"Nice hoe," said Skye, who turned to give Mason a high-five for her joke. "Two hoe references in five minutes. Yay me! I want a prize," she laughed.

"We'll get you a cookie when we're done," replied Cici. "Ok, I put the shovel and pickaxe outside. I also have a rake and Skye's big hoe," Cici said as she looked down at Skye's feet, which were adorned with delightful moccasins embellished with beaded turtles. "You might need sturdier footwear," she advised.

"Oh, no worries. I have boots," Skye confirmed.

"Ok, let's grab them en route," said Cici, and the trio left the inn.

Amid the mid-March silence, the outdoors lay hushed and mysterious. The muddy crunch of dirty snow and a gentle breeze filled the air as Cici, Skye, and Mason ventured through the darkness of Highclere's expansive back 39 acres.

The cool minus-ten degrees Celsius temperature painted a frigid backdrop. Warm clouds billowed from their breath—visible in the glow of the headlamps fastened to their toques.

"So, are you going to tell me what you found beneath the 'Door to Nowhere,' or are you going to keep me in suspense?" asked Skye, eager to hear the update that Cici and Mason deemed too sensitive to discuss over the phone.

"Here goes," began Mason.

* * *

"It's astoundingly beautiful!" radiated Baroness Margot Ambrosia, holding Lady Valentine's missing jewelry box in her gloved hands.

It was in perfect condition. The gold plating was polished and exquisite. The figurines of the alfresco dining scene had been painted and looked as if no time had passed since their creation. The box's pearled edges, white and divine, melted into the design, creating a seamless masterpiece of craftsmanship and care.

Margot and Andrea set the box on a high, cloth-covered table in front of the camera. With excitement and wonder, the duo turned the crank on the back of the box and entered the passcode supplied by Mason. Andrea's face mirrored childlike delight as she examined the hidden treasure.

"I still don't understand how you knew it would be in there," commented Andrea, never taking her eyes off the box.

"I didn't," replied Mason. "Once I realized that the scene on top of the jewelry box was a recreation of a typical summer evening for our ancestors—sitting at a bistro table in front of the 'Door to Nowhere'—it struck me that Rosamond Farnsworth and her family were intentional with every single element of the pieces they created. This made the alfresco scene in front of the 'door' undoubtedly purposeful. I assumed that the 'Door to Nowhere,' much like the jewelry box, must also open to some kind of safe or vault below. Margot and Mr. Hauge explored the area with deep soil radar and discovered the outline of a concrete room beneath the door. The same sequence or pattern of sixteen consistently appeared throughout our evidence gathering, making it a solid bet that it, too, was the code to the 'Door to Nowhere.' It was beyond my wildest imagination that the jewelry box would be there," Mason concluded, his chin resting on his hand, his thoughts racing in multiple directions.

"Mason, there was a letter with the box, which Stellan and the police are reviewing and documenting. He'll bring it over shortly," said Margot.

"Mr. Valentine! Ms. Bradshaw!" called Milton Hague as he stomped toward the camera setup. "What an absolutely extraordinary day! My mind is boggled, absolutely boggled," Milton said while wiping his brow with a hanky. "I've taken photographs for you, which I'll have Lady Ambrosia pass along," he nodded while looking at Margot, who did a small curtsy. "What a truly remarkable mechanism.

Once the code was activated, the concrete base of the door popped open. The base is equipped with large hinges on the north side, allowing the concrete to lift effortlessly. The whole thing works like a human-sized music box. Upon opening, we descended the stairs—rather rickety and unsafe, in my opinion—into a room lined with concrete, measuring approximately 650 square feet. To our surprise, the room provided access to a hidden tunnel that stretched across the entire property and conveniently led to the old Farnsworth estate. Remarkably, the exit door at the Farnsworth end was rather skillfully concealed with foliage and rocks, making it virtually indistinguishable as a secret entrance!"

He stopped to take a breath.

"Does anyone have water? Or a vodka?" he asked.

"Of course," assured Margot before turning back to Milton once more. "A water, I mean," she smiled and walked out of frame.

"Would you grab my bag as well?" Milton hollered after her.

"Mr. Hauge, is the room beneath the 'Door to Nowhere' some kind of bunker?" asked Cici.

"Partially, yes! It could very well have been built to protect locals from potential air raids. It has a similar design aesthetic to the type of underground air-raid shelters at Stockport—outside of Manchester—but it also might have been inspired by and used as a military pillbox. I noticed there appear to be several closed loopholes right below the concrete hatch. However, in this instance, if I'm correct, I believe it's actually a vault," he said, his eyes wide, hands clasped together.

"I'm assuming that the tunnel entrance is how the dead man accessed the property the night he died?" asked Cici. "It would be the only way CCTV cameras wouldn't have seen him."

"Exactly," confirmed Milton. "There is another mechanism that unlocks the concrete base from the inside. Other than the noise, which I suspect was audible on the cameras, no one would know how one could trespass so secretively."

Margot re-entered the frame, handing Milton a bottle of water and his sleek brown leather briefcase.

"Lady Ambrosia, mind if I borrow you for a moment?" Andrea Romero asked, holding several folded papers that Mason assumed came from the jewelry box.

Margot nodded in agreement, and they disappeared from the camera's view.

"Now," said Milton, unlatching his bag, "I even believe I know what that room was for." He pulled out a large red-bound book called *An Oral History of Sussex—Fact or Myth?*

"You do?" asked Mason.

Milton was quiet as he flipped to a page marked with a ripped piece of paper. His eyes scanned the text back and forth until he found the paragraph he was looking for.

"Ah! Here it is," Milton said. "If I may read a few lines to you from this book, I'd appreciate it."

"Of course," agreed Cici.

"*Some decades after the Second World War, there were murmurs amongst long-time residents of Sussex that a vault of significant size and protection was built beneath one of the area's great houses and was used to store priceless artifacts of prominent area homeowners from 1939 to 1945. 'Before the start of the war, I have a memory of father moving expensive silver, art, and heirlooms from our house to something he referred to as The Treasure Chest,' recalled Lady Sybil Landsford. 'I was never told where the safe, or treasure chest, was located, but I've been told that many top families stored their valuable belongings there for the duration of the war to protect from invading soldiers or bombs.'*

"'*Lord Frederick Baxter said that he too was told of a special unground vault. However, he indicated that not all was what it seemed, 'it was a con job by the Germans,' says Baxter. 'There was indeed an underground vault or safe storage space somewhere in the area, but it was built by a double agent, a traitor to his country who was exiled from Britain when the war concluded.'*

"'*While many believe the existence of the vault to be a myth, Lord Baxter and Lady Landsford agree that its existence was a FACT, not a tall tale, despite neither knowing where it was built or if it has since been destroyed.'*

"'*I'll never forget when the community learned of the deceit by the double agent. My father, in particular, was disgusted at how this man could turn on the United Kingdom. Father is the one who led the campaign to rid us of the traitor and his family. He had the traitor's hereditary title stripped,' remembers Lord Baxter, who, with a laugh, added, 'he even wrote a—I guess you could describe it as a "menacing" letter—on gilded letter stock belonging to the traitor's family about how we would take back what's rightfully ours.'*

"'*Despite the warning about "taking back what is rightfully [theirs]," neither Lord Baxter, Lady Landsford or others alive during that era are aware of any priceless pieces from their families' collections having gone astray,*'" Milton finished reading, closing the book with a thud.

"The community pushed our family out," Cordelia said as a fact, not a question.

"If what I just read to you is true, then your great-grandfather built the vault alongside the Farnsworths with the express purpose of keeping the possessions of his neighbors safe during the war. However, once Nazi Germany fell and the locals learned that Lord Fernsby was a double agent, they deemed him a traitor and exiled the Fernsby family to Canada. Rumor would have been impossible to control in 1945. While he was a double agent, he did so for Britain, not against her. History has proven that. And as I'm sure you know, your family's title became extinct at the request of Lord Fernsby—not as retaliation."

Mason and Cici looked at each other before twisting their gaze to the corkboard in front of them.

"Oh my God," said Cici as she stood to untack the item they were both eyeing.

"Something the matter?" Milton Hague asked through the camera just as Cici sat down.

"Mr. Hague, the line in your excerpt about a menacing letter written by Lord Baxter is true," announced Cici as she held up a copy of the Fernsby House notecard she and Drusilla found knifed to a carriage house wall.

"Extraordinary," sighed Milton. He moved closer to the screen to read what Cici was holding up. "Where did you find this?"

"We found it after my grandfather's burial. It was impaled into a wall using a steak knife. We thought it was a newly written note directed at us. I guess," Mason paused, "it was the threat that forced the Fernsbys to move to Canada. My grandmother must have kept it all these years," he added, shaking his head.

Makayla Dawn admitted to leaving the sinister message for Mason or Cordelia to discover, claiming it was a warning about the existence of Person X and a brewing conspiracy. However, they assumed she had written the note using old Fernsby House stationery. Little did they know, she had embedded an existing note into the wall's grain instead.

"Well, that explains some things," nodded Cici, massaging her closed eyes.

"Why would anyone wish to leave the two of you a threatening note?" asked Milton.

Mason laughed.

"Oh, Mr. Hauge. Next time I'm in the UK, I'll take you for dinner and tell you one hell of a story."

"Milton, are you still talking to Mason Valentine?" asked Stellan McManus, coming from behind Mr. Hague.

"Indeed, I am," Milton bowed.

"We're still here, Stellan," Mason called.

"Excellent," said Stellan as he maneuvered his husky body and remarkable head of silver hair into the camera's frame. "Mason, we've found two more items that you'll find of interest. Two letters. The first was outside of the jewelry box and written by the deceased. It is addressed to the family of Lady Valentine. We need to keep it for evidence, but I'm about to send you a photograph of it," he said while doing so.

"And the second?" asked Mason.

"Mrs. Romero found it inside of the jewelry box. It's from Lady Valentine herself."

* * *

My Darling Family,

Oh, how I hope you aren't reading this letter. If you are, it means my concerns regarding Miles's behavior have come to pass, and Miles failed to keep his most important promise to you.

The gold spherical objects Rosamond brought you are keys and will open a custom marble cargo box buried in the back 39 acres of Highclere, close to the burial plot. I have included a map alongside this letter showing where it is. Please be careful when opening the box, as it contains one-fifth of my most treasured possessions alongside the paperwork.

I'm sorry, my loves that your father betrayed you. I wish I could say I'm surprised, but obviously, I'm not since his way of operating is why I've had to ensure your interests are safe from beyond the grave. I know this treasure hunt will feel melodramatic and camp, but if it were simple, Miles and his hangers-on could've gotten everything without issue. That is what I've tried to stop from happening.

Also, please ensure nothing changes with Stuart once you open the marble box. It doesn't need to.

Love,

Mom, Gran, Jean

Chapter Fifty-Three

Lady Valentine included a hand-drawn bird's-eye map of Highclere, which outlined the location of the buried marble cargo box.

"Do you know what's in the box?" asked Skye, careful not to slip on icy patches while avoiding being hit in the face by naked tree limbs.

"No, just what's written in the letter. She said it holds one-fifth of her most treasured possessions—I'm not sure what that is. I'm also wary about the paperwork she referred to," said Mason.

"We are now positive that Joyce Redstone and the spheres were intercepted before making their way to the family," said Cici, breathing heavily in the cold.

"Why is that?" asked Skye as Cici stopped and handed her a printout of the document sent by Stellan McManus.

They all paused for a breather.

**

CREATED USING: VOICE-TO-TEXT DICTATION SERVICE

August 31, 2023,
To: The Family of Lady Jean Valentine,
Hello. My name is Harold Mendoza, and I'm the husband of the late Maxwell Farnsworth who in life went by the name Marvin Faulk. He took the name Marvin when he returned from the Second World War, and I'll refer to him as Marvin in this letter. I'm ill and not a gifted storyteller, so forgive me if I'm missing details—I'll try my best.

I met Marvin in 1977 in Boston, Massachusetts. He had been living there since the end of the war. I often traveled there for business. I was the president of an American company that engaged Marvin's consulting firm in the early development of fiber optic technology. Despite being twenty years younger than Marvin, it was love at first sight when such love was misunderstood. We became life partners and lived in Boston until moving to the United Kingdom in 1982.

Marvin was the adopted brother of Rosamond Farnsworth—later Ford. Because they were born the same year (though several months apart), their parents raised Rosamond and Marvin as twins. Marvin maintained his whole life that the

Farnsworths were decent, honorable people. However, he felt he was a burden and excluded from being viewed as a legitimate part of the Farnsworth family. He felt like an "other," and after being injured and left for dead during the war, he decided that should he survive his injuries, he'd move to North America and start a new life—leaving Maxwell Farnsworth behind and forging his own path. Allied troops found him nearly dead and nursed him to health. He gave a fake name to the medical team, and therefore, the British Armed Forces assumed him dead in 1944.

This might seem cruel to those who loved him, and in truth, it was. However, emotional healing came with time. Love was remembered, and Marvin reconnected with his sister in the late 1960s. In both of their hearts, they were family and became an important part of each other's lives until Rosamond died in a plane accident.

Several years after Marvin moved to North America, he read a newspaper article about the glamorous wife of a young politician in Canada. The article had a picture of the couple, and Marvin recognized her as Jean Fernsby. He took a train to Ottawa and met with Jean in 1952, and they remained close friends—and, in some ways, soulmates—for the rest of Jean's life.

Two years before Jean died, she asked Marvin to visit her in Canada. She gave him a gold jewelry box and said that she'd left a second box and instructions with Rosamond to deliver to the Valentine family upon the death of her husband, Senator Valentine. While she hoped it would be unlikely, Rosamond's box instructed the Valentine family to contact Marvin should the "worst come to pass." The jewelry box would provide the answers needed, and her grandson would know how to open it.

Marvin died in October 2017, leaving me responsible for the jewelry box. Unfortunately, I've been diagnosed with an aggressive form of cancer that's spread to my brain, disqualifying me from medical assistance in dying. I, therefore, decided to expedite my journey out of pain and rejoin Marvin in the afterlife.

In truth, I had forgotten about the jewelry box and wasn't keeping an active eye on the life of Senator Valentine either. I guess I assumed he was already dead and that the family did not need the jewelry box. Then, a woman claiming to be Drusilla Brisbane contacted me a few weeks ago, around August 11th, and asked for the jewelry box. She carried with her the letter written by Jean that she received alongside the gold box from Rosamond's granddaughter. I was more than happy to turn over the jewelry box; however, I became troubled when she refused to show me any identification to confirm she was Drusilla Valentine-Brisbane. At first, she said she'd forgotten it, then the next time I saw her, she advised her bag had been stolen and asked me to trust she was who she said. I didn't...

I googled a picture of Senator Valentine's family and realized the woman visiting me was an imposter. Threats were delivered to me when I refused her calls, initially in writing and then through example. My windows were smashed one night, and my car was destroyed. The violence and fear worsened my condition. I'm often paralyzed, and my eyesight comes and goes. I had long planned my transition to the afterlife for Labor Day weekend. However, I've changed the location so I can place the jewelry box in a safe place for you.

Many years ago, Marvin showed me the "Door to Nowhere." He performed annual maintenance to keep it in working condition. Over time, he forgot the passcode, but Rosamond had shared a secret—in the event Lord Artemis Fernsby was killed during the war, a pair of cufflinks had been crafted and held by the Farnsworths which revealed the code in precious gemstones. I acquired them on Marvin's behalf from Andrea Romero. And now, I have these precious artifacts in my possession.

I wish there was more I could have done to get the jewelry box to you, but I'm worried my phone is tapped or the imposter is monitoring my movements online, and I didn't want to put you all at any risk in case my cancer-filled brain was playing tricks on me (which it has been).

The rest of the information you need should be in the box itself.

Now, I shall join my love and friends as we all, finally, rest in peace.

Good luck. Please keep safe.

Yours,

Harold Mendoza

* * *

"Yikes," said Skye, finishing the letter before handing it back to Cici. "You think the imposter Harold mentioned changed the spheres before Joyce brought them to Canada?" asked Skye.

"No. He's clear: Joyce Redstone never made it to Canada. We think a woman claiming to be Drusilla went to the UK to collect the box and spheres from Joyce, only to discover that Maxwell Farnsworth held a second box via Harold. Since Harold didn't turn over the jewelry box, there would be no reason to suspect the spheres were anything other than ornamental—though expensive. I get the impression from Auntie V's note that she didn't mention the spheres were keys in the first letter Joyce was supposed to deliver alongside the box on Labor Day. Auntie V seemed determined to keep a separation between the contents of the two boxes. We suspect three of the four spheres were swapped out—which we all know to be true—and were delivered to us by someone pretending to be Joyce Redstone. It would explain why we can't find her picture online or track her down," said Cici.

"She seemed so familiar to me," said Mason, grinding his teeth. "That's what's throwing me. Why did she feel like a distant memory if she wasn't Joyce Redstone?"

"Could just be someone from central casting you've seen in TV shows or theater?" suggested Cici.

"True," agreed Mason.

"Who do you think the imposter is?" asked Skye.

"That's the troubling bit because if you were Joyce Redstone and Uncle Tank died, who would you call?" replied Cici.

"The widow," Skye replied.

"Exactly," seconded Mason. "And we know Laverna was running the ship post-Tank and could've designed a plan to get the gold box and spheres with ample time before the funeral in case it was anything of value. The only fly in that creamy ointment, however, as far as we know, is that Laverna didn't leave Canada."

"Why a creamy ointment?" asked Cici.

"Seemed grosser and funny," said Mason as he came to a halt before stopping the other two. "Ok, we are five hundred feet northwest of the burial plot. There should be a rock formation somewhere near here. There is no description of what it looks like, but we need to find it."

Mason, Cici, and Skye stepped in different directions, surveying the surface for notable rock collections.

"Do you think Laverna might have sent someone to the UK on her behalf?" asked Skye, picking up where Mason had left off.

"We wondered if she sent Bianca, but her social media during that period is filled with pictures from Canada. We also checked Laverna's children, and they, too, were in the country," replied Cici.

"Wait," Mason said, coming to a stop several yards away from the other two. "I think we're on the rock formation," he suggested.

"Really?" asked Skye.

"Yes, this seems to be rock we're standing on. The burial plot leads into a small gulley, which we just walked through. Then we climbed up that short hill," he said, pointing, "but I don't think it's a hill made by soil—I think we're standing on a mass of rock," Mason added before kicking up snow and dirt with his boot, his toe meeting moss then rock.

"You're right," added Skye. "Look, the trees only border this portion of the land. Morphed trunks, fallen trees, and chaotic branches only create the illusion we're still in the forest when we're standing on a rock."

Mason moved further away from Skye and Cici, creeping deeper into the darkness. He held one foot out to test for solid ground before stepping. Until—

"Oh shit!" yelled Mason, his boots shooting into mid-air before his entire body dropped below the surface.

"Mason!" Cordelia shouted as she and Skye linked arms, combining the power of their headlights to walk to where Mason just disappeared.

"FUCK!" shouted Mason.

"Are you ok?" asked Skye.

"Yes. Don't worry. A rock broke my fall," he said between audible 'fucks.' "I didn't want children anyway."

"The boys got tangled?" giggled Skye.

"Impaled," Mason groaned.

"We're coming," advised Cici. She and Skye lowered themselves down the side of the steep rock, holding onto tree limbs and trunks to ease their descent.

When they landed at the bottom of the rock formation, Mason stood and wiped as much excess mud and snow off his clothes as he could.

"This mystery is getting more and more painful," Mason noted as he took the drawn map out of his coat pocket once more to gauge their next steps.

"Yes, you look like you shit yourself," noted Cici as her head beam focused on Mason's ass. "Let's just snap a picture of this for William Marshall," she added while pulling out her phone.

"Oh, genius!" echoed Skye, who also snapped pictures of Mason's butt.

"Put those phones away, or this is going to get very *Blair Witch*," Mason warned while reviewing the map.

"Yes sir," said Cici facetiously, snapping one last photo.

"Ok, if I understand Gran's hen scratching correctly, we need to take 20 steps east, where we'll find a cluster of four birch trees. The marble cargo box, container, or whatever it is, is buried between them," said Mason, "the ground is still frozen, so we're safe while walking. Still, since we'll be digging, we better put respirators on to protect ourselves from inhaling traces of toxic soil. Touch nothing with your bare hands," he said, handing each of them respirators and gloves, which they put on.

Mason, Cici, and Skye walked a short distance to the bouquet of four trees. They exchanged glances and, without speaking, began their work. The frozen mid-March ground forced Mason to use a heat gun to warm the soil between the trees.

Once Cici's pickaxe could break through the earth, Mason turned the gun off and dug while his cousin and Skye worked to massage and break up the soil.

Twenty minutes later, Mason's shovel hit something solid. Cici and Skye dropped to their knees and finished the final dirt removal with their gloved hands.

They found it.

Chapter Fifty-Four

Two hours passed by the time Cordelia, Mason, and Skye had dug, scraped, hoed, and raked enough of the soil from around the—larger than expected—marble cargo box for them to lift it out.

"Before we try, I want to take a few pictures in case it gets damaged, or we hurt the integrity of the locking mechanism somehow. I want to make sure Andrea Romero will have enough detail to fix it, if need be," advised Cici as she pulled her phone out of her pocket.

"Fine by me," said a very sweaty Mason Valentine. "Gives me time to see how long it takes for my shirt to freeze."

"Stop complaining," warned Skye, who stuck her tongue out at him before remembering she was wearing a respirator.

Cici bent down and ran her gloved hand along the top of the thick, black marble, pushing aside lingering earth to ensure a clean photograph.

"It feels like a grave," said Cici spooked.

She estimated the box to be about four feet long and three feet wide. The lid was engraved with a pattern of numbers and letters—IIVMCMLIVXMCML—repeating from the top left to the bottom right, roughly 40 to 50 times.

Four circular indents ran down the middle, known by all three as the matching counterparts to the gold spheres—the actual keys to uncovering and opening the marble structure. The indents were protected by glass, presumably to shield the keys' function from years of dirt and weather.

Cici unscrewed one of the glass covers and snapped a photo of the interior. Despite the limited lighting, she could see a series of thin, intricate lines protruding from the base. Each gold sphere should have a corresponding pattern etched into one side. Once the spheres are placed into their corresponding marble indents, the locks should retract, granting them access to the hidden contents inside.

"Mason, look," called Cici as she cleared more muck from the sides of the container.

Mason kneeled beside her.

"It's covered with engraved frogs. Hundreds of them," she smiled as her cousin looked at the eccentric detail that repeated on all four sides.

"Gran literally left us a box of frogs," he laughed—his forehead still streaming sweat.

It was a remarkable display of ingenious engineering and craftsmanship. A design that Cici believed only existed in movies until a year ago. However, with the discovery of the "Door to Nowhere," the jewelry box, and now the marble box, she found herself inspired by the brilliance of the Farnsworth family's ability to create such wonders using traditional tools and ingenuity far ahead of its time.

Mason stood as Cordelia took several more pictures before retrieving a sewing needle-like object from her coat pocket and inserting it into one of the engraved letters 'M.'

"Right," she said, standing up. "Let's try to lift this bad boy, shall we?"

Mason handed Cici the end of a large, thick band that resembled a seatbelt. Together, they slid it under the bottom of the marble. Mason did the same with Skye. With the girls on one side and Mason on the other, they were ready.

"On the count of three, we lift," instructed Mason. "One, two...lift!" he hollered as the three used their limited upper body strength to lift the box out of its resting place.

"No, stop! Stop!" cried Skye, who dropped her side of the band and rotated her arm around a few times. "I think I've pulled something."

"How much does this weigh?" wondered Mason.

"Probably a few hundred pounds," suggested Cici. "Skye, are you ok?"

"This granny isn't used to this kind of physical activity," she chuckled. "Let's give it another try," Skye added while again picking up her end of the band.

"You're sure?" asked Mason.

Skye nodded.

"Ok, count of three. One. Two...lift!" Mason instructed as the three pulled and pulled until—*SNAP!*

Both bands broke in two, sending Cici and Skye flying backward into the mucky snow while Mason maintained his balance.

"Shit!" Cici shouted as she sat up but remained on the ground.

"Oh! A mud bath," Skye cooed while jokingly lifting mud and patting it on her arms. "I'll look twelve again."

"You'll also develop superpowers because of the toxic soup," Cici reminded her. "This isn't going to work."

"It's too heavy," Mason agreed. "We need to bring in supplies to help. I can order a lift and buggy, but it'll take a few days. Are either of you keen to get back to the city?"

"I can stay," said Cici.

"Me too," Skye replied as well.

"Ok, let's go back. You two stay in the inn. I'll head to Athabasca and order the gear. We'll regroup in the morning," said Mason.

"I don't understand how Lady Valentine could lift this on her own," said Skye as Mason and Cici helped her up.

"Oh, I'm sure she didn't do it alone," replied Mason. "Someone had to help her."

"Who?" asked Skye.

"Probably Ahren," answered Mason who attempted to get his footing between a tree and the rock formation to climb up.

"Wouldn't he say something?" wondered Cici.

"His discretion—and his father's before him— was invaluable to Tank through the decades. I'm sure he did a lot of strange tasks for both my grandparents and never asked questions. He might have forgotten or didn't think it was his business to question what he was burying and, therefore, doesn't have anything to tell us."

"Oh, if only these trees could talk," said Cici, pulling herself up the rock's edge, using tree branches to stabilize her.

"But they can talk," said Skye, correcting Cici's assumption. "And speak beautifully they do!"

"Ok, great. Then you have the bark for tea tomorrow, Skye, and see if they're feeling chatty," joked Mason.

"I will!"

The trio reached the top of the rock formation and continued to retrace their steps back to the inn and their beds.

* * *

Freshly showered and wrapped in his red robe, Mason looked at the mantle clock and saw it was 1:21 am. He longed for his comfortable, plush bed but instead placed his laptop on the dining room table and made his way through multiple online stores until he found what they'd need to haul the marble box back to the office of the old inn.

When done, Mason closed his computer and sat still while looking out onto the partially frozen lake. The light from the half-moon reflected off the ice, giving the thin crystallized film of frozen water the illusion that it was lit from within.

Upon seeing the black marble cargo box, Mason's mind stirred. Skye's comment on Valentine's Day, which he had initially brushed off, now held more significance after the day's events.

The original Christmas tablecloth and replica displayed identical scenes of the Twelve Days of Christmas. However, as Skye had pointed out, the replica featured red and white snowflakes behind each image, which the original did not. Skye speculated the snowflakes might be codes, like the ornaments on the needlepoint Christmas tree that opened the "Door to Nowhere." Mason agreed with her, but he had no idea where twelve locked boxes, vaults, drawers, or underground safes requiring passcodes could be.

That was until Mason, Skye, and Cici returned to the inn through the burial plot. Mason noticed two solar LED lights at the base of Lady Valentine's Golden Retrievers' headstones were on the fritz. He separated from the others to examine whether the lights were cracked or if their solar panels were malfunctioning. Mason realized that all the dogs' LED lights were outdated, so he'd order new ones for spring installation.

He would need to order twelve lights.

For twelve dogs.

The Twelve Days of Christmas.

Mason sat, deep in thought. A cascade of half-shaped ideas flickered through his mind, elusive and teasing. Then, like a video coming into focus, clarity hit him.

"She couldn't have," he muttered, weighing the reality against the possibilities.

The room was silent, punctuated only by the ticking of the clock and the drumming of his fingers. He paused, mulling over the implications before speaking louder with resolve, "Maybe she did."

Mason scrolled to the file folder on his desktop containing high-quality images of the evidence corkboard at the inn. He zoomed in and moved the pictures up and down. Re-reading the writing on old letters, documents, deeds, citations, orders, ledgers, and more.

Nothing with twelve.

Nothing with twelve.

Until.

"Got it!" Mason shouted out.

He stood and went to the kitchen to find a measuring tape.

Pulling a pencil and notebook out of his bag, he drew a vertical rectangle and a horizontal one. Using a measuring tape, he eyed what he now assumed were dimensions, "2 + 1.5 + .75 / 2 x 6 = (12) & 4 x S + B," written in the memo of Lady Valentine's 2002 check. He tried inches, centimeters, and feet—changing shapes and sizes until it made sense. Once satisfied, he wrote the corresponding integers along the lines of his drawing.

He had it.

He knew what the snowflakes opened.

* * *

Cordelia sat in the lounge of the old inn, working her way through the meaning of the letters engraved on the marble box. She parsed IIVMCMLIVXMCML into several combinations before it became clear what the basis of the inscription was—Roman numerals—of a specific date or dates.

Cici split the letters into two sections—IIVMCML and IVXMCML. She wrote them on a pad of paper and then penciled the corresponding month, day, and year above each. Since it was unclear whether the month or day was first—as they're often reversed—she tried both versions, the second of which provided a date she recognized.

She placed her pencil on the table and rubbed her eyes.

She might have been right when she said the marble box felt like a grave. In fact, she was confident that she'd just discovered the last piece of one of the most elusive puzzles she and Mason were trying to make sense of.

Oh, how she wished she'd be wrong.

* * *

Guillaume Regan stood at the roundabout and watched as the last light turned off in the inn.

He looked at his watch. It was 2:47 am. Thankfully, he still had plenty of time before sunrise.

He turned around and waved into the darkness. A car engine ignited, the headlights beaming toward him as he slowly walked to the vehicle before signaling it to follow him down the back road.

Toward the burial plot.

Chapter Fifty-Five

"Fuck!" shouted Cici looking at the now empty hole she'd dug the night before with Skye and Mason.

"Oh Jesus," added Skye.

After sleeping in, Cici and Mason huddled in the early afternoon, told each other about their overnight discoveries, and discussed the next steps.

After a late lunch, the team of three once more collected their shovels, hoes, and rakes for their next adventure in grave robbing and headed toward the burial plot to drop equipment en route to a daytime viewing of the marble box.

Mason, Cici, and Skye slid between rock and tree, lowering themselves to where the marble box had long been buried. As they neared the quartet of birch trees, Cici noticed footprints coming from different directions. Skye pointed out deep square davits and wheel tracks that weren't there the night before. Mason threw his hands against his head and shouted that the marble container was gone.

"We're being watched," Mason said with panic as he fished his phone out of his pocket and turned it off. "Turn your phones off," Mason ordered.

"Who's watching us?" asked Skye, her hands shaking as she powered hers down.

"I don't know!" said an exasperated Mason as he paced. "Person X is my guess!"

"Fuck!" Cici shouted before looking at Mason and raising her eyebrows. "We know who," Cici mouthed.

Mason's face became stone.

"Oh fuck."

He closed his eyes tight before taking a deep breath.

"What's traceable other than our phones?"

"Has the inn been bugged?" wondered Skye.

"No. We always search for bugs when we arrive, and our industrial signal jammer would wipe out everything from cell phone listening to hidden microphones and the secret second security system. Whatever is trackable took them to these exact coordinates, which means it's on us," answered Cici.

"We have to assume that whoever took the marble box knows everything we know," said Mason, no longer pacing but staring at Skye and Cici.

"I agree," nodded Cordelia. "It's one thing to be feeding us information, but taking it from us is another."

"What do you mean by that?" asked Skye.

"That we're running out of time," jumped in Mason.

"They can't get into the cargo box without the spheres, and they only have three of the four," Skye pointed out.

"They could if they took machinery to it," replied Cici.

"Where's the fourth sphere?" asked Skye.

"Tucked away," Mason smiled. "They won't find it."

"It doesn't matter if they have the fourth fucking sphere or not. They can take a core drill to it and be inside within a day," said Cici, removing her toque and running her hand through her red locks.

"Do we confront Laverna without solid facts and see what she says? We know she was looped into Tank being blackmailed—she pushed for Highclere to be left to the Cliftons. It's not unreasonable to assume she's coordinated the whole scheme through a demure smile," suggested Mason.

"We don't have a solid enough lynchpin to confront her. We'd be shooting in the dark if we cornered her. Plus, we haven't ruled out Gil—or Stuart, Norah, and Trent, for that matter. It could be any of them!" suggested Cici, her voice echoing from the trees.

"So, what do we do?" asked Mason.

"Ok, when we hid the gold sphere, I started the practice of attaching GPS tracking devices to evidence in case we were usurped," Cici divulged.

"Bad. Ass!" smiled Mason.

"I slid one into an engraved letter M on the marble box last night. As long as whoever took it isn't blocking cell signals, we should be able to track where it lands. It could lead us directly to Person X. That said, if they have been smart enough to follow us digitally, then I'm confident they are blocking cellular."

"Damn," sighed Skye.

"They can't block cellular forever. It will have to blip at some point," Mason urged. "Batteries die, and power goes out."

"True," agreed Cici.

"Easter is in ten days. The entire family will be here. We need to move forward with 'Operation BYOB,' and Cici, you need to talk to Gil. It's time to lay those cards on the table. We have to rule him in or out now. He might tell you what he and Laverna were doing on Valentine's Day," advised Mason.

"I agree," Cici replied. "I also think it's time for you to send Margot Ambrosia the package we've been sitting on," she suggested. "Once we add a few additions."

"I agree," nodded Mason.

"I'm in Ottawa for Easter, so I'll hit Gil before I leave."

"Anything for me?" asked Skye

"We need your digging skills again right now," Mason smiled as the trio found footholds to climb back up the rock formation.

"In case no one has told you this already, your 'operation' names make no sense to anyone but you," said Skye to Mason as she grabbed hold of a tree branch to steady herself.

Mason snorted his amusement—she was right—but that wouldn't stop him.

"Hey—also, you never told me why Trent Callahan asked for a copy of Tank's death certificate in September," added Skye.

Cici and Mason stopped in place, eyes wide. They turned to look at each other.

"Oh shit," they said in unison.

* * *

Person X threw another log onto the fire before checking if Mason Valentine or Cordelia Bradshaw had sent new digital data from their devices.

Nothing.

Perhaps not all that surprising, considering they'd have realized their devices had become compromised.

Stepping away from the computer, Person X walked toward the window to watch the vibrant colors of the sunset splash across the sky. They always felt like Muskoka sunsets were created by God throwing a bucket of red paint into the atmosphere, followed by a bucket of pink, then orange and blue, swirling and stirring together until there was nothing but an inky black sky waiting for the stars to wipe clean for morning. For a life that had been absent of magic, Person X liked to believe it could exist and did so in the divine.

It was quiet and cold—perfect. Just the way they preferred it.

Having opened the window to let in a light breeze, Person X heard the faint sound of their computer ding from across the room.

Sitting at Senator Valentine's storied leather desk chair, which had been nicked a few months earlier, Person X shook the computer awake. Mason's phone was on after all, and he was texting Cordelia.

C—The dimensions noted on the 2002 check to Farnsworth were to create 12 mini "Doors to Nowhere," which Gran used to intern the goldens in the burial plot. Essentially, the headstone is a marble slipcover; when removed, it should reveal a mini door with sixteen silver buttons. When the code is input, a small vault (approx 2 feet x 1.5 feet) unlocks, and the urns should be inside. Sadly, the twelve doors (meaning the twelve dogs) are gone. The marble slipcovers have been filled with concrete. Laverna most likely has them, but I'm not too worried about getting them back. I don't care about the dogs' ashes. Even if we had them, there is no way of knowing the codes—red herring.

"The buttons are for codes," whispered Person X while wheeling the chair around to look at the twelve mini-marble "Doors to Nowhere," each containing the remains of one of Lady Valentine's beloved Golden Retrievers. "I didn't expect that," they admitted before standing, "but where are the codes?"

Person X had tried to open the large frog-etched marble box—snagged earlier that morning with Gil's help—without the fourth sphere, it wouldn't. Not to worry, the fourth would arrive in due course, once the lake thawed.

The breeze from the open window felt different on their bare feet. The much-hoped-for warm front had arrived.

* * *

Mason switched his phone off, placed it on the inn's old industrial kitchen counter, and plugged in a hand drill.

"Hopefully, that keeps Person X from being interested in accessing the dogs' vaults," Mason said, putting on workman's goggles to shield his eyes.

"Fingers crossed," Cici agreed, standing back. "Either way, Person X went out of their way to ensure we knew they were tracking us. Whatever the epilogue of their scheme, it's coming."

Mason turned on the drill and, using the thickest bit he could find, drilled through the center of his phone.

"True, but we're closer than ever to IDing them. All we need is for the tracker to ping once, and we've got 'em. Next, please," he said, holding out his hand for Cici's phone, which he drilled through as well.

"We'll sweep our computers but use new ones in the meantime," said Cici.

"Agreed," Mason nodded as he unplugged the drill and threw the phones into the garbage.

"We thought we had less than two months to prove who Person X is and maybe get Highclere back as well—but based on Person X becoming carefree, I'd say we have less than two weeks."

"I'll track down Trent to have a wee chat," said Mason.

"You're going to talk while peeing?" Cici joked.

"Har, har," Mason replied, knowing Cordelia was referencing his shy bladder.

"I'll get to Gil," said Cici, "and you'll do Operation: BYOB?"

Mason nodded.

"First things first, though," he said as he went to turn off the kitchen lights. "We need new phones."

Chapter Fifty-Six

Mason stepped out of his car and breathed deeply to calm his nerves. Of everything he and Cici had uncovered since Labor Day, it was time for him to confront the most shocking—a lifetime's lie burned to the end of its wick.

Mason looked at the large, white, double doors of the beautiful mid-century home and hoped that by the time he exited later that day, the path to truth and healing would have begun.

He buttoned up his blue overcoat, the ends of his long monogrammed scarf peeking from beneath. Chelsea boots were tight and ready, and fresh Spanx in place—it was now time. He walked toward the door and pushed the large silver doorbell. He heard it ring inside and knew it would take some time to be answered, but he was patient.

After a minute or two, the door locks unlatched. The automatic door then slowly opened, revealing its owner seated in a wheelchair. She gazed at her guest through her eyelashes while positioned at the bottom of her grand staircase.

"I saw it was you on that tricky camera Stephen installed," said Louella Stone. "Welcome, Mason."

Mason entered the double-story front hall and walked toward Louella, bending down to kiss her on both cheeks before saying anything.

"Your silence is filling me with calm," she joked, patting his hand.

"Mrs. Stone..." Mason said before pausing.

He didn't know what expression was on his face—he hadn't practiced any or planned to supplant his emotions. He knew it would be futile, and his life's success was based on being expressive and honest. Instead, he crouched down and looked the old woman in the face. As Mason opened his mouth to speak, Louella cut him off.

"It's ok, Mason," she said. "You've figured it out, haven't you?" she asked.

"I have," Mason nodded.

* * *

Cordelia's Uber arrived outside of Stuart Valentine and Guillaume Regan's house just as Gil, with his arms full of groceries, was making his way to the door.

"Cordelia?" Gil asked, surprised to see her.

"Hello, Gil!" Cici greeted him, leaning in to give him a peck on the cheek. "Bad time?" she asked.

"Not at all. Stuart is out of town dealing with Drusilla, so I'm a bachelor for a few days. Can you stay for dinner?" he asked as Cici took one of the brown bags from him so he could fish out his keys.

"I'd love to," she agreed.

Gil flipped through the various keys on his keychain, looking at Cici out of the corner of his eye.

"Not that...not that I'm not pleased to see you," said Gil, "but I have trouble believing the great Cordelia Bradshaw would pay an unannounced visit unless...well...unless she had something to say."

Cici smiled.

"You knew Stuart was out of town, didn't you?" asked Gil.

"I did," Cici nodded.

"Alrighty then! Step right in. I sure hope you're into Cher because her tunes will be playing in the background while we have a chat."

* * *

"Who taught you to cook?" asked Cordelia as she wiped the last dinner plate dry and handed it to Gil.

"I taught myself. Growing up in foster care, you never knew what type of meal you would get when you changed families. A good meal could always make me feel safe as if I was 'home' even if it wasn't my home," he replied.

"I didn't know you were in foster care."

"Yes, my parents died when I was five—classic tragic cliché of getting run down by a drunk driver over Christmas. My mom was pregnant when she died, so I would've had a sibling, but that never happened. Another glass of wine?" Gil asked, turning off the kitchen lights and leading Cici to the living room.

"Yes, please," she replied.

Gil poured the remaining vintage white into Cici's generously sized wine glass before they sat on the modern ivory-colored sofa.

"When did you meet Tank?" she asked.

"I was in my twenties, so fifty years ago—give or take. Of all people, Wentworth Clifton introduced us," he laughed.

"Aida's first husband? You knew the Cliftons before Aida married Tank?"

"I did—well, one of them anyway," Gil responded, sipping his red wine. "Wentworth and I went to high school together in Ottawa, but that was long before he met Aida Dela Cruz. Anyway, Wentworth then went to university for political science, and I went into construction since I couldn't afford school. He worked for the Liberal Party for a semester before being hired full-time—which is how he and Aida met Tank. I desperately needed work when Tank and Lady

Valentine needed some adjustments done on their Ottawa home, so Wentworth made the connection. I did a few odd jobs for the Valentines, and one day, I expressed an interest in engineering but didn't think it was in the cards because I was already in my mid-twenties and time was running out. The Valentines offered to pay for my education if I was accepted to school, which I was. I couldn't have done it without them. By the time I graduated, they had moved to Toronto, and a firm in Montreal hired me. We didn't see each other much after that, but we stayed in touch. I did some light work on their home in Toronto periodically."

"You didn't meet Stuart early in your working relationship with his parents?" Cici wondered.

"No, we only met in 1997. He and Drew were out of the house by the time I met the Valentines, and our paths didn't cross until Tank asked me to build new cottages for the family at Highclere. We met and started dating, moved in together in 2000—broke up for a few years, and rekindled and married in 2006."

"Happily ever after?" Cici smiled.

"You're married," he laughed. "Periodic bliss, but 'hard work ever after?' Is that a thing?" Cici laughed.

"It is now!"

They both gulped their wine, listening to the loud grandfather clock announce the time as 10:45 pm.

"Did you keep in touch with the Cliftons?" asked Cici.

"No, I didn't meet Aida until she married Tank. Wentworth and I drifted, but because he and his family were so close to the Valentines, I heard bits and pieces about his life through Tank and Lady V."

"Ah," said Cici, checking her Apple Watch.

"So...are you going to tell me why you're here," asked Gil, "or will I have to guess?"

Cici placed her wine glass on the frosted tempered glass coffee table and positioned herself on the couch, looking Gil in the eyes.

"This isn't an easy conversation for me to have with you," she started.

"Ok," replied Gil, putting his wine on the table and facing his cousin-in-law.

"As you know, Mason and I have spent months investigating the various mysteries and unanswered questions surrounding the family since Uncle Tank died..."

Gil nodded.

"We have not updated the family since Christmas despite the amount of information, additional evidence, and a handful of answers we've discovered."

Gil nodded again.

"The icky thing throughout this process has been the number of times your name has appeared in the strangest places."

"Such as?" Gil asked, no anger in his eyes.

All Cici could see was kindness and curiosity, which didn't make the conversation any easier.

"For starters, when Highclere was listed for sale in 2013, it was your name on the listing and not Uncle Tank's. You were asked in 2010 to remove the old septic tank next to the burial plot, which Tank believed was leaking toxic chemicals into the ground—you did not. When Highclere failed to sell, you and Tank learned that a toxic soup of chemicals and poison, including arsenic and petroleum, continued to penetrate the back 39 acres of the property. An issue that you were well aware of for years, yet you failed to remove the septic tank and continued to expose your family to toxic soil for another decade. As you know, it's still leaking. You installed the security system at Highclere, which—despite it having surge protectors and a power back-up—got torched, allegedly, during the storm, the night Tank fell. We also believe that a pressure sensor and independent power supply had been attached to the electric fence, ensuring that Uncle Tank would be electrocuted once he fell into it, regardless of whether there was a power outage. An electric fence you installed," Cici finished, never taking her eyes off Gil.

"A calculated electrocution of our centenarian needed to be well plotted to ensure a power outage occurred on the May long weekend, with or without a storm. It would take a particular skill set and awareness of Lake Belvedere's infrastructure to pull off."

Gil stared at her, his eyes becoming intense, almost menacing.

"Anything else?" he whispered.

"You are also one of a handful of people who knew the truth about Stuart, a truth that would be so damaging to the family that Tank had no choice but to pay off a blackmailer. You also angrily defended Stuart when Tank railed on him for 'causing the blackmail.'"

Gil's eyes went from menacing to shock.

"You know about Stuart?" he asked.

"Yes. Mason visited Louella Stone today."

* * *

Mason glanced at the clock on his dashboard, registering the time—almost 11:07 pm—as he pulled into his office parking spot. Exhausted and bewildered by his extraordinary afternoon with Louella Stone, he had to ensure that reception had dispatched a package to Baroness Margot Ambrosia. Only then could he return home and process all he'd learned.

A warm front was rolling through Ontario, and he could feel the temperature rising as he exited his car.

Mason's phone vibrated in his hand. Once he saw who was calling, he realized his night was far from over.

Chapter Fifty-Seven

Gil looked down at his tightly clasped hands as he debated what to tell Cordelia. She had discovered everything except two critical pieces that he and no one else knew.

No one was better than Cordelia Bradshaw; she was formidable and brilliant. With Mason Valentine working alongside her, Gil knew they were days, if not hours, away from uncovering what had taken him almost fourteen years to deduce.

He wasn't ready to confess fully. Not yet. He needed more time, but time was running out. He had to do it for himself and Stuart.

"Ok," Gil said, still not looking at Cici. "You're right about almost everything. I will confess my part.

"When Muskoka Lakes informed Tank in 2010 that the ground around the burial plot was toxic, you are correct. He asked me to investigate where it came from and arrange a clean-up. Laverna and Bianca were redesigning the plot, and before Tank's casket could be approved, we had to show good faith efforts at determining how toxins were getting into the ground. At first, we thought Trent Callahan was the one creating the biohazard. Norah and Tank knew his cousin's history in Manitoba and the ripple of it—the motive was perfect. After all, he'd been sending nasty letters to Tank for years. So, we confronted Trent. He was obviously shocked and panicked that the soil, combined with his letters, would ruin him. He agreed to friendlier relations moving forward and helped pay for the clean-up."

"What did you do next?" asked Cici.

"Well, Tank and Laverna believed there must have been a leak in the old septic tank," Gil said while Cordelia listened intently. "However, I disagreed. It didn't make sense to me how the septic system could become compromised since it was no longer attached to any of Highclere's plumbing. I researched and ran tests of the area to find where the chemical readings were the highest. When I found the worst spot, I dug about ten feet and found a wide hose which siphoned off into two dozen smaller hoses going in multiple directions…"

"What?" Cici responded. "That's not how a septic system works, is it?"

"Not at all! The large hose could've been affixed to the old piping and concrete tank. But, if it fell out, it wouldn't have grown tentacles using present-day materials."

"So, sabotage?" Cici asked.

"That was my thought! I followed the large hose, which led me to the ancient pipeline that drew waste from the old staff quarters. When the new septic system was installed, the staff quarters were excluded because the inn was no longer operational, and the consensus was there would never be staff again, so we decided not to include it when we upgraded the pipes at the same time. I went into the staff bathroom where I found tens of thousands of dollars worth of major high-grade chemicals, the type of stuff that had been outlawed for a generation by that point."

"Though, it's all still available in other countries," Cici added.

"Exactly, and I assume smuggled into Canada," Gil agreed. "But the dangerous cocktail of the mix, including petroleum and arsenic, sitting in raw form by the toilet, was mind-blowing. I'm talking crude oil. If a flame had touched any of it, the entire place would've blown."

"Essentially, at this point, your gut says, 'this is not only deliberate but heinous,'" suggested Cici.

"Yes. I was extremely worried about it because it meant that the family had become a target for whatever reason. Not that Tank didn't have enemies—but he was largely out of the public eye by that time."

"What did you do?" asked Cici.

"I tried to explain to Tank what I'd discovered, and then I disconnected the staff quarters from the old pipes and looped it off. The next time someone would try to send chemicals down the toilet, it would circle back and overflow onto whoever was doing it," Gil smiled.

"You said 'tried' to explain to Uncle Tank?"

"He wasn't exactly God's gift to listening. He decided it was the old septic tank, and nothing could budge him from that belief despite what I told him."

"Typical," Cici nodded.

"You know how he was; he was always right regardless of facts or sensible arguments. He dug in his heels and told the county we found the source and would remove the old septic system ASAP."

"But you didn't remove it."

"No, because it wasn't the problem and would waste time and money."

"Did you ever wonder if Uncle Tank misled you into believing the septic system was the problem? Perhaps not deliberately, but he accepted what he'd been told by someone else?" she asked.

Gil was stunned. He'd never thought about it before.

"You're suggesting Tank might've known where the poison was coming from and wanted the leak to continue?" he asked.

"I'm suggesting that someone knew where the poison was coming from and needed Tank to point you elsewhere so the leak could continue."

Gil shook his head.

"I've never thought about that. He was insistent—aggressive almost—in his belief it was the septic tank. As you know, he judged his own thoughts to be the best, so I don't know if it was his hubris or someone whispering in his ear."

"Ok, so at this point—2010—you, Stuart, and Laverna learn of Tank's disposal violation from 1969?" redirected Cordelia.

"That's right."

"You didn't know before?" asked Cici.

"No, and neither did Stuart. He had no idea. Tank told Laverna about it, and Laverna told Stuart."

"Why the hell did she think she should be the one to tell him?"

"She said it slipped. Claimed to have thought he knew, but that was bull. She knew that wasn't true. She was just delighted to know something that none of the Valentines did. It gave her the upper hand. A behavior pattern we'd see on Labor Day."

"When did the blackmail start?" asked Cici.

"Christmas 2011. Stuart knew and had accepted the truth by this time," replied Gil.

"Was the demand sent to Stuart or Tank?"

"Stuart, whose inclination was to go to his sister for help since we couldn't afford it, but the letter stated payment would only be accepted from Miles."

"And Uncle Tank was always going to capitulate?" she asked.

"At first, no. He called in the RCMP, but when the letters became more graphic and detailed, he called them off. Though I've since learned that they kept looking into it, but Tank wouldn't cooperate, so they closed the case. If I was Tank, I think I'd pay the blackmailer too. Who'd want that information out in the world?"

"I get that," said Cici as she reached for her glass of wine to take a mouthful, noting it was just past midnight. "Did you ever think the chemicals and the blackmail were connected?"

"Of course, it was my immediate thought. It was too coincidental that 1969 came back to haunt Tank, and then just over a year later, he was blackmailed for it. I always felt there was a straight line from the chemicals to blackmail. I just couldn't prove it."

"You cleaned it up, though, correct? In 2010?"

"Yes, I cleaned up and planted vegetation that could also help maintain the soil naturally, and as I said, Trent Callahan helped pay for it. It had only been spreading for about five years and hadn't seeped as widely as it would."

"When did you realize chemicals were still being pumped into the soil of the back 39?" asked Cici.

"During the developer's inspection before the sales agreement in 2013."

"Until then, you thought it was clean?"

"I wasn't sure. I installed deer cameras to keep a close eye on anything happening in the woods, but not once did I see anyone or anything nefarious going on. I had noticed that the birds and animals remained largely absent from Highclere—nature remained quieter than normal—which was a big clue, but I was also worried I was paranoid. Once the sale was terminated, I did another search and found a fake shack on the single acre of land the county bought from Highclere. The shack was being used to disseminate the chemicals with more hoses buried beneath the surface."

"Your cameras were tampered with? Which is why you didn't see anyone?"

"Yes," Gil replied. "By this point, I was really getting worked up. I became obsessed with figuring out who was doing this. Who was blackmailing us, who was trying to poison us—or kill our property value—it felt like my life's mission."

Cici sighed.

"You've been investigating for ten years?"

"Longer than that! I've been investigating and hiring private investigators, security firms, and security drones. I've spent all our savings; we've had to be bailed out financially by Drusilla...twice. I kept feeling like I was getting close, only to lose the trail again. It has been maddening and a vicious cycle, and based on my efforts, plus my skill set, Stuart warned me it would look like I was the perpetrator, and I think the blackmailer..."

"...we use the term 'Person X,'" Cici interrupted.

"...ok, I think Person X designed their hits to point at several people, including me. There's no other way a fence could produce enough electricity to harm someone unless a pressure sensor was attached. I knew that immediately as well. Who would be most capable of that? Me! Also, I installed the fence. The security cameras got torched, as you said, despite the surge protectors and backup power system that *I* installed. Then, camera footage from a second system ended up with the police. A system I still can't find. Then..."

Gil stopped, unsure whether to go further.

"Then...?" Cici urged.

Gil sighed.

"Then, in September, one hundred thousand dollars was wired to my bank account."

Cici sat up straight.
"Do you know from whom?"

Chapter Fifty-Eight

After yet another restless sleep, an exhausted Mason swirled the contents of his mug while standing in his apartment kitchen. The doorbell rang.

"Why do they always have to be early?" Mason asked himself while carrying his vintage *Live with Regis and Kelly!* mug to answer the door.

"Hi, hi!" Cici and Skye greeted Mason in unison—not unlike the sisters from *White Christmas*—as they held up a bag of pastries.

"What is wrong with you two? Why are you both so perky this early in the day?" asked Mason irritably while moving aside to let them in.

"It's noon!" replied Cici as she hopped to the living room and kneeled on the couch with Skye joining her.

"I guess that's true," grumbled Mason as he sat down. "Well, let's get to it. Cici, what have you got to share about your evening with Gil?" asked Mason as he dug out a chocolate croissant from the bag of goodies the girls brought.

Cici then divulged everything that Gil had revealed to her the night before.

"One hundred thousand dollars from Miles Valentine?" asked Skye. "If dead men are sending money, then me want some of that!"

"Gil believes it was wired to him as a warning shot," said Cici.

"I'd accept that warning happily if it came with the mullah," Skye added.

"He thinks Person X caught on to his nosing around and wanted to point the blame at Gil as an insurance policy, like how they've pointed us to Trent. The money transfer was to make him look like he was the blackmailer by ensuring a suspiciously large sum of money was in his account. Person X is very tech savvy."

"How much did Tank pay the blackmailer?" asked Mason.

"$3.5 million dollars," Cici revealed, breaking apart a flakey warm pastry on her lap.

"It's a lot of money, but that wouldn't deplete his finances. There should've been millions left," noted Mason, his mouth full.

"Mace, you said he was spending wildly in his final years. Maybe that, combined with the blackmail, caused his financial problems," suggested Skye.

Mason nodded.

"Does he have any idea who Person X is?"

"He said no. But he's lying," replied Cici.

"You're sure?" Mason asked.

"Zero doubt. He's not Person X, but he knows who is."

"Were you able to talk to Trent Callahan?" Skye asked Mason.

"I did last night after I left Louella's. All my questions have been sufficiently answered for the time being," Mason replied.

"Do you think he's Person X?"

Mason sighed.

"I don't know."

"Ok, well...I'm excited to hear about that conversation, but first—your time with Louella?" nagged Cordelia.

"Right..."

* * *

"It's ok, Mason," Louella said. "You've figured it out, haven't you?" she asked.

"I have," Mason nodded.

"Well then," replied Louella breathily as she turned the joystick of her wheelchair to point her toward the living room. "You better come in and sit down," she added, leading Mason into the large, comfortable room.

The weathered furniture, forsaken by the sun and neglect, stood before a magnificent, gray marble fireplace adorned with intricate bespoke carvings of people, houses, and flowers upon every inch of the surface. The wood floors, sheltered by worn Persian rugs, exuded a sense of history. A grand piano displayed dozens of framed pictures in the far corner, while copious windows on every wall bestowed ample light upon the room. The white walls, adorned with art, sculptures, tapestries, and cherished family photos, told stories of love and life.

"Would you like anything to drink?" asked Louella. "Though, you'll have to get it yourself," she winced.

"No. I'm fine. Would you like anything to drink?" Mason asked in return.

"Scotch neat. Next to the piano," she pointed with her finger.

"No problem," he said as he made his way to the drinks cart.

"How long..." began Louella before coughing.

"What's that?" Mason asked.

"Sorry. How long have you known?"

"Oh," he said while handing Louella her tumbler filled almost to the rim with scotch. "A month. Though, the final piece was found last week."

Louella glanced at her glass, her eyes darting but her head still.

"You think I'll need this much?" she asked in a low gravelly voice.

"Do you think you'll need that much?" Mason smiled.

"Touché," said Louella, lifting the glass to her mouth. "Where do you want to start?"

"Start at the very beginning. It's a very good place to start," Mason laughed.

"Ok, Julie Andrews," joked Louella. "How are you handling this?" she asked.

Mason shrugged.

"I mean…it's not something that sits brilliantly, I'll admit. It also makes one wonder what kind of people Miles and Jean Valentine were to pull this off."

"Don't blame them," whispered Louella.

"If I'm not to, I suggest you start from the beginning, please, Mrs. Stone."

"As I'm sure you now know, I'm American. I was born in Florida in 1930. Despite the war, I had a wonderful childhood and was entirely devoted to my family. My best friend at the time…" Louella paused, struggling to reveal hidden truths she had long since buried in the depths of her subconscious.

"Was a young woman named Caroline Monroe," Mason continued for her.

"It's shocking to hear someone say so after all these years," said Louella, taking another sip of her scotch.

"When I first saw the picture of Caroline and Tank, you referred to her as 'Caroline Monroe,' but her full name wasn't written on the picture or mentioned in any of the boxes you gave me."

"Caught me out," Louella sniffed. "Yes. My best friend at the time was Caroline Monroe. She was several years older than me and was also a babysitter occasionally, but because she was a neighbor and so many of our contemporaries were involved with the war effort, we became extremely close. Sisterly even."

Louella paused to think.

"Around 1943, I would have been thirteen, she would have been twenty—or thereabouts—she met a young pilot from Canada who was in Florida training. She was smitten instantly. His charm captivated her; he was equally besotted. They became engaged a short while later and planned for a wedding in Canada in 1945. I was to be a bridesmaid. I still have the dress somewhere," Louella paused again—processing her memories and images—grappling with telling someone the secret she had worked so hard to hide her entire life.

"At the end of 1944, Caroline was on her way to Toronto to visit Miles and meet his family for the first time. Unfortunately, as she was about to cross the border, she received a telegram from Miles telling her the wedding was off, that he'd met someone else. That someone, as you know, was Lady Jean Fernsby."

Mason nodded.

"Caroline came back to Florida crushed. She was desperately in love with Miles, and the future she had been imagining—that she was planning for—came crashing down. I don't think she left her bed for a month. It was a further blow to her when she learned Miles was already re-engaged and that his wedding would take place at the same date, time, and location as the one she had planned."

"All he did was swap out the bride," Mason said, shaking his head.

"All he did was switch out the bride, that's correct. Caroline became—though I couldn't verbalize this at the time—but she became fixated, unhealthily so, on Miles. When he entered politics, she asked people to send her newspaper clippings and magazine articles so she could follow his career. I think she believed Jean had stolen her life, and Caroline resented them both for it. It was very sad. She let it be the defining moment of her life.

"Anyways, I met Atticus..." she paused again, trying to distinguish the truth from the lies.

"In 1949...not 1944 as you've told me in the past. Your first visit to Highclere was in 1952, not 1948," Mason noted.

"How did you learn that?" Louella asked, taking a gulp from her tumbler.

"We checked Highclere's guest books. Your first entry was in the summer of 1952, and then we found your wedding certificate," Mason smiled.

"You and Cordelia are very good at this," she sighed. "Yes, I met Atticus in 1949. I knew he was the love of my life. Never had a second doubt, and nor did he until I had to go away for a period..."

"...because you were pregnant..."

"I. Well... I had discovered my passion for counseling and psychology and was taking several college courses, with one requirement being a volunteer internship. Not many male psychologists would take on a woman intern, but I found one. I knew on my first day that the doctor was a womanizer. We always know. While I was guilty of participating in the flirtation while working at his practice," Louella took a deep breath, "the events of my last day at his office weren't what we'd call consensual today. Sadly, it wasn't out of the ordinary either. So, you could've knocked me over with a feather when, a few weeks later, I learned I was pregnant."

She stopped to wipe a tear meandering down her right cheek.

"You were stuck between a rock and a hard place. You couldn't tell Atticus, but termination also wasn't an option. So, I assume you called your best friend..."

Louella dipped her head.

"I went round to Caroline's and asked her what I should do. We both agreed Atticus couldn't know. Caroline had an aunt just outside of Hamilton who had gone through a similar experience, and she agreed to take us in. I say 'us' because Caroline was by my side the whole time. We concocted a story that I had to move to Canada for school, and I implored Atticus not to follow me, saying I had to focus on my studies. Caroline told her family she'd always wanted to live in Canada and couldn't pass up the opportunity. So, just after Christmas 1949, we caught a train from Florida to Hamilton. I was three months pregnant, not showing just yet.

"As the months went by, the question of what to do with the baby became increasingly urgent. I didn't want any record of my giving birth, and I certainly couldn't keep it. Caroline offered to adopt it, but I advised her to hold out hope she'd find a husband and have her own children. Caroline's aunt, whom we were staying with, helped to broker a private adoption with a local farmer and his wife. Still, I wanted the child to have the richest, happiest life possible, and I felt guilty leaving it with a struggling farmer, no matter how lovely and caring they would've been..."

"So, Caroline contacted Tank," added Mason.

"It was May 1950. I was due in a month, and we still hadn't decided what to do with the baby. Caroline read in the paper that a young, recently elected member of parliament would speak at a steel factory in Hamilton. The paper didn't mention a name, but Caroline read between the lines and realized it was Miles. She went to the speech without telling me and pulled him aside afterward. He was pretty surprised to see her, but she explained she needed his help, and he owed it to her. You know Miles, he loved being needed. He designed his entire life so the people around him needed him—it allowed him to keep control—a trait of narcissism. Caroline walked through the door of her aunt's home with this tall, handsome man and introduced him as her former fiancé. I'd never met him before. I was twenty years old, and he seemed like an angel from heaven.

"Miles told me that his wife had given birth to a baby girl in February and that since she and my child would be so close in age, he could raise them as twins. He could arrange a birth certificate using his parliamentary authority that matched Drusilla's, and no one would be the wiser. It would be a private birth at home, and then we'd hand the child over to Miles and Jean and continue with our lives without the incident hanging over me. He invited me to be in the child's life, offering to hold a cabin at Highclere Inn & Carriage House open for me to visit every summer and at Christmas. It was an elegant solution to an unfortunate problem. I gave birth on June 9, 1950. Miles collected the child two days later. Caroline and I remained in Canada until the autumn of that year before going home.

"Atticus and I started seeing each other again. We married in 1951 and moved to Canada in 1952—at my urging—where we made a wonderful life for ourselves. We spent our first summer at Highclere a few months later and formed the closest of friendships with Miles and Jean," said Louella.

"How did Gran take having a child thrust upon her?" Mason asked.

"Poorly. He bamboozled her. She didn't have a say, a recurring problem in their marriage. It took some time for Jean to warm up to Stuart, but then their relationship strengthened into a traditional mother and son pattern."

"And you ripped all this out of Tank's diaries before bringing them to my office?" Mason asked.

"I did," she smirked while finishing her scotch.

"Why?"

"Stuart is a part of your family. He is your family. I didn't want that to change. He knows he's not blood-related, but I didn't want him to be treated any differently than he had been these past seventy-three years. He doesn't deserve to become an 'other,' not at this point in his life."

"He's aware that you know about his adoption?" Mason asked.

"He is," Louella agreed.

"Does he know you're his mother?" Mason asked leaning forward, kindness in his eyes, his hand reaching to hold hers.

"No. He...doesn't," she answered, her words caught in her throat, "and he shouldn't. There's no point."

Mason nodded.

"Do you need another drink?" Mason asked.

"I think so," she smiled as Mason took her glass and went back to the drinks cart.

The late afternoon sun streamed through the windows, loose dust floating through the beams of light. The faintest sound of birds returning for spring could be heard in the distance.

Mason returned to his seat across from Louella and handed her another full glass of scotch.

"Thank you. I'm going to need it," Louella said as she took a sip, and Mason nodded.

"So. When did you find out Tank had lied to you about the birth certificate and had used your vulnerability to solve his very big problem?" Mason asked.

"1969."

Chapter Fifty-Nine

"I assume that by 1969, you and my grandparents were thick as thieves?" Mason asked.

"That's correct. We got along instantly that first summer in 1952. We began spending time together socially when they would come down from Ottawa, or we'd stay with them for the weekend or meet at Highclere. We were very, very close," answered Louella Stone.

"When did you start seeing my grandmother as a therapist?"

"Probably around 1967? Miles was campaigning for the Liberal leadership and had been underhanded in his efforts to do so. She resented that he didn't involve her in his decision to run for the leadership. Jean felt they should be a team with equal decision-making, but twenty-plus years into their marriage, she was reaching her wits end with his constant pushing, belittling, and bamboozling of her. The press had given Miles 'The Tank' as a nickname a few years earlier. She felt that if he was going to bull her over all the time, she, too, could play that game. She had a lawyer deliver divorce papers to him while he was sitting in Parliament," Louella laughed.

"I read that in his diary. He was pretty pissed!" shared Mason.

"Oh, was he ever! It was a warning shot from Jean to get his attention. She left him briefly in the early 1980s but didn't have the emotional strength to go at life alone and start fresh at sixty years old. She knew she was stuck with him. He could be a pill, but she loved him."

"So, in 1967, you and Gran have your first session?"

"I wouldn't call it a session. It was one friend counseling another," Louella clarified.

"Got it. So, in 1969..."

"It was the summer of 1969..." Louella began.

Mason laughed.

"I kind of love that! '*The summer of '69,*'" he sang.

Louella snorted her amusement.

"It's accurate in this case. Anyhow, Atticus and I were at Highclere with our children—so it was August—Miles and Jean were coming from Ottawa with their family to celebrate Miles's birthday at the resort. I'd just gotten out from my swim when Jean walked down from the inn to the beach, white as a ghost. She had tears in her eyes and was trembling. I wasn't the only person at the beach, so Jean being seen in public looking so distraught signaled that something horrible had happened. She asked if we could speak, which I, of course, agreed to. The inn was full, so she came to my cabin, and I kicked everyone out. She sat down and warned me that what she was about to say would shock me. I didn't believe her. I thought I knew her deep, dark secret, and little surprised me anymore.

"She told me that one of the neighbors' dogs had been digging around the area that would become the burial plot—and had gone home with a bone in its mouth. The dog's owner thought little of it until a house guest pointed out that it was a human bone, not animal…"

"Jesus," Mason sighed.

"The police and county were called to investigate, and Jean was in a right panic because she believed she knew who the human bone belonged to," Louella paused again to take another sip of her scotch.

"…her son," said Mason.

"Her son," agreed Louella, "that sent me into a right panic because I immediately thought of Stuart, but that didn't make any sense as I had seen him and Lawrence the week before. She was right—I was shocked."

"But the bone was indeed Stuart's? The *original* Stuart?" asked Mason.

"No, it wasn't. It was an adult bone," Louella shook her head.

"Just for the sake of clarity, this was the first time you were ever told, or that it was ever implied that Drusilla did, in fact, have a legitimate twin brother who had died?" asked Mason.

"Correct. Never, in my wildest imagination, would I have guessed such a scenario could be real, yet there was Jean, my best friend, sitting across from me, releasing her anguish at the loss and replacement of her infant child," Louella's eyes filled with tears once more. "She never told me how the original Stuart died, just that it was a horrific accident at home that was avoidable and could never be disclosed publicly, or Miles's career and ambitions would be ruined. He doesn't detail how the death happened in the diaries either. She was distraught when Stuart died, and her own will to live dissipated. She thought Miles should've been truthful that the secret of losing a child and hiding it was so corrosive that she didn't know how to live with herself. The child was buried in a small oak casket made by Emmerich Dawn—Ahren's father—just outside of the burial plot. Jean panicked. She thought the casket had broken open and the dog had gotten inside…"

"…but it hadn't."

"No. It turns out some farm laborers who died on the job half a century earlier were buried in the same area, and as I said, it was identified as an adult bone that was dug up."

"How did you feel when you learned Tank saw you as the answer to his problem instead of being altruistic?" Mason asked.

"I was angry. Hurt. I felt used for political purposes. I wondered what type of person I handed my flesh and blood to. Any human who can casually hide the tragic death of their infant son and then replace him with someone else's child because of political ambition was despicable to me. I found it revolting. I chose not to confront Miles—and we left Highclere the next day and didn't return for four years."

"What made you come back?"

"Time and space, plus I missed seeing Stuart. Miles never had an appropriate amount of grief or self-doubt about what he'd done. It was very transactional. Jean did, though—it ate her up. She judged herself for the rest of her life for being weak in the face of her loss. I felt she was too hard on herself. They gave my Stuart the world's best life. Miles wasn't much of a father, but Stuart had everything he wanted or needed. He was a bright, well-rounded person with a big heart, goals, and ambition. He was loved by his brother and sisters and his mother. I also concede that Miles and Jean were much better about Stuart's homosexuality than I was or would've been if I were in their shoes. It took me time to process that, and he's my son. That experience taught me to judge Miles less. The love of a child is absolute, though complicated. No matter how hard we try not to, we project hopes and dreams onto them that aren't theirs and become their unasked burden to carry."

"My grandmother never knew you were Stuart's biological mother?" wondered Mason.

"No."

"You never wanted to tell her?"

"It wasn't my confession to make. It was Miles's."

"Did you tell anyone about the original Stuart's death?" asked Mason.

"Not a soul. Not even Atticus."

"Since Emmerich Dawn made the casket and buried him, is it safe to assume Ahren knows about the original Stuart?"

"I'd say so. However, that man is a bastion of loyalty. He'd never reveal the truth if it weren't his business. I wish there were more honorable people like him in the world."

"Atticus never knew Stuart was your child?" questioned Mason.

"No. The only person who knew, other than Miles, was Caroline. We didn't tell her aunt either."

"What happened to Caroline?" Mason asked.

"She and I drifted apart when I moved to Canada. Oh, we exchanged Christmas cards, but I think she felt it difficult to watch me be so close to the Valentines and a life that she felt should've been hers. She never married but adopted eight children, the crazy woman," Louella half laughed, and half cried. "She was a very unhappy person and thought children would help make her whole. She died by suicide in 1987. When I learned she died, I was devastated but happy that she and I had reconnected a few years earlier. I went to visit her and met her family. There's a group picture on the piano from that trip."

"How did Laverna find out Stuart was adopted?"

"Twelve or thirteen years ago, the 1969 disposal violation popped up when Muskoka Lakes refused Miles his casket. I guess he told her when she asked what the violation was about," Louella shrugged.

"And Stuart? When did he find out he was adopted?" asked Mason.

"About a week later, Laverna told him. The hell that brought on. I thought Miles was going to die during that period. Stuart...reacted justifiably poorly. That woman is a bit of a bitch," Louella snorted.

"Clinical term?" Mason smiled.

"Of course!"

"So, Tank told Laverna about the death of the original Stuart?" asked Mason.

"Yes, and then she told Stuart."

"From what Cici and I can guess, it was failing to report Stuart's death and Tank's callus reaction of replacing his child that formed the basis of the blackmail material in 2011 and 2012—not long after the tiny pool of people who knew the truth had ballooned. Based on what you're telling me, only Tank, Granny V, you, Emmerich, Ahren, and Caroline knew the truth for sixty years. Suddenly, that number nearly doubles to include Laverna, Stuart, Gil, and I'd assume Aida—more lips to sink the ship. Did someone blab? Or did they use the information for their own means?" Mason asked, scratching his head. "Did Tank write about it in the diaries? All the grizzly detail?"

"He did. I found passages in 1950, 1969, and 1993—the year I flew from overseas to give blood to Stuart after his accident—2010, 2012, and 2013. As I said, Miles didn't say how Stuart died, just that he did. I suppose someone could've read the diaries and learned the truth. Perhaps the pool has never been as small as we thought," Louella guessed.

"Only the immediate family would've had access to the diaries until Tank married Aida. Since then, the Cliftons would've had every opportunity to read them before they were stored with you," noted Mason.

"Not true. People came in and out of Miles's house constantly. Norah Tripplehorn worked out of there for decades, and other employees did, too. Their housekeeper Geneviève Talbot, drivers, security, assistants, coordinators, cooks—it was never-ending. Anyone prone to snooping could've found them. I'm not sure I've helped narrow the field for you," said Louella with a weak smile.

Mason could tell that the old woman in front of him was tired. Her voice had become weaker even if her memory was still sharp. He had all he'd come for and could see Louella's nurse parking out of the corner of his eye.

"I can't thank you enough for reliving this with me. I know it was exhausting, but I appreciate it," Mason said, standing up to put his coat on.

"It was cathartic," Louella responded.

"Did you know before Thanksgiving that Tank had left Highclere to Aida?"

"No. I was as surprised as you lot were. I didn't see it referenced in the diaries—of course, I wasn't looking for details about Highclere. Only Stuart and me."

"You don't have the pages from the diaries anymore, do you?" Mason asked.

"Stuart burned them," Louella replied.

Mason's eyes widened.

"Did he read them?"

"No. He just dumped them out of a box into the fire. I told him they were all the pages I could find that referenced his adoption and the original Stuart, plus the blackmail, and I took them to protect him. He didn't learn from them that I'm his mother."

"I'm sure he appreciated you covering for him—even if he didn't know you were sparing him one last twist," Mason added.

"I was covering for all of us," Louella replied. "And it wouldn't have been a twist. It would've been a twist of a knife. However, if you want copies of those pages, they're in the gold box on the piano."

Mason laughed.

"You made copies?"

"You never know when Mason Valentine or Cordelia Bradshaw will show up demanding the truth. I assumed that if I was dead and you needed to piece Stuart's story together, you should have access to all the facts."

The front door clicked open.

"Good evening, Mrs. Stone," shouted the nurse as she removed her shoes.

"Hello. I'm just finishing with a friend. Come get me in ten minutes," Louella responded.

Mason approached the black grand piano and slid the lock of the gold box to lift the lid. There they were. Photocopies of 474 pages of Tank's diaries, which made Mason wonder...

"Which photograph is of Caroline Monroe and her family?" Mason asked.

"Black frame. About ten of us are on a lawn. She had curly hair," described Louella.

Mason scanned the dense collection of designer frames, settling on the picture in question. He walked it over to Mrs. Stone.

"This one?" he asked.

"That's the one," she nodded, looking at it through her eyelashes.

"Do you mind if I take a picture of it?"

"Not at all," she agreed.

Mason looked at the picture before taking out his phone. Everyone looked happy, but Mason knew all too well that mental illness hijacked smiles for invisibility cloaks. He snapped three pics and put the frame back.

Mason headed toward the door.

"Thank you again," he said, collecting his car keys from his pocket and pushing the automatic door button.

"Think nothing of it," Louella replied, following him to the hall.

Mason was about to exit but turned around to Louella once more.

"It's unnatural for a parent to outlive their child. It goes against the laws of nature, and over the years, I've seen many elderly parents die after losing a child. In your case, your two children have passed, as well as your husband. I always wondered where you mustered the strength to keep going after your insurmountable losses. I've always admired you for it and assumed that your godson Stephen gave your life vigor, but it just occurred to me that you still have one child left to live for."

"Live and die for. Like any mother," Louella nodded.

Mason smiled and waved to Louella as he slid into his car. She watched him for as long as she could until the grand white doors closed before her.

Louella Stone's lifelong secret was now free to live on the other side of the door.

Chapter Sixty

To: Stuart Valentine; Jocelyn Valentine-Campbell; Guillaume Regan; Drusilla Valentine-Brisbane
CC: Mason Valentine; Oliver Valentine
From: Lawrence Valentine
Re: Easter at Highclere

Gang—
Bad news. We're experiencing a 2005 redux.

Ahren just called (and Makayla sent pictures, which are attached). Due to the surprise warm weather in Northern Ontario, all of Lake Belvedere's feeder lakes and rivers have flooded, and the excess water has now migrated toward Highclere.

As of today, the water level is already past the beach and just about to overtake the bridges. Ahren expects it to get as high as the entry roundabout, meaning the old inn, the carriage house, and the lion's share of the cabins and cottages will also be surrounded by water. Athabasca and Gay Acres are on high enough ground that they should be ok, so I'm meeting Oliver, Mason, and Gil to sandbag where necessary, get the boats locked down (so they don't float away again), and move any excess gasoline from the buildings.

The point is—Easter plans have to be scratched.

Please do NOT travel to Highclere. It is NOT safe.

I'll keep you updated.
Lawrence

Chapter Sixty-One

"I tell you, Cordelia, no word of an absolute lie—he was the greatest lover of my entire life. He was. The. *Greatest*. Lover. But when Arnold came to me and said, 'Trish, will you make me the happiest man on earth?' I had to decide whether I wanted to be sexually satisfied or the richest woman in the city. It took me several days, but it was my esthetician, Ling, who decided for me," paused Trish Morris, Cici's oldest and most high-maintenance and shallow friend.

Trish took a sip of her cosmopolitan and fluttered her eyes in such a way that Cici thought she was in for a profound comment.

"What did Ling say?" asked Cici, faking interest.

"Ling said," paused Trish. "She said, 'Miss Trish...my ring...it comes from donation pile,' and Cordelia, it was like Christ himself spoke to me. It was profound. I have never wanted to believe that the Lord would speak to me so directly, but Ling clearly mouthed the Father's words, and to be honest, Cordelia, my greatest fear..." Trish choked up, "is that I'd have to use a donation pile."

"Isn't your esthetician's name Carol?" asked Trish's fiancé, Arnold, who was cozied up to his emaciated, much younger bride-to-be in a green leather booth at one of Ottawa's hot spots.

"Is it?" asked Trish. "Isn't Carol the Gardner?"

"No, that's Jake. He's a man," replied Arnold, nuzzling his nose against Trish's neck.

"Then who is Pedro?" she asked puzzled. "Pool boy?"

"Financial manager," replied Arnold.

Cici couldn't take it anymore. She could feel her brain cells seizing up and dying, but not before she got one jab in.

"Arnold, how do you feel about not being the best lover Trish has ever had?" Cici asked, finishing her glass of wine.

Arnold, who wasn't a day younger than eighty, flinched.

"Who needs to be the best lover when you can be the best man?"

"Uh huh," replied Cici, pivoting in her chair, desperate to track down her server and get the hell out of there. "Check, please," she whispered across the room once she spotted him.

"Ohhhh," Trish growled at Cordelia. "You just have to hear this. It's the most romantic thing ever."

"Do I?" asked a puzzled Cici Bradshaw squinting. "No biggie if not."

"No. You must. You just MUST. It's just so romantic. So, the top lover," Trish then lowered her voice, "Sammy," she whispered with a wink, "he came over to my house to seduce me after we broke up and I had accepted Arnold's proposal. It was adorable. There he was, this little muscle man soaked through his shirt with sweat, rain, or a sprinkler, maybe? Anyways, he's at my door, and I say, 'No, Sammy. No means no,'" Trish said like she was teaching a teen about consent. "So Sammy left, but what I did NOT know was that wee Arnold here had installed security cameras at my home to make sure I was always safe..."

Uh-huh—sure—'security,' thought Cici. *It's more likely he's a perverted predator.*

"...so Arnold sees Sammy on the cameras, and my Arnie calls his friends at the police and pays for all the stoplight camera footage in the area. He followed Sammy's route home and had him beaten to keep me safe," Trish cooed with romantic tears rising in her eyes as she leaned over and kissed her elderly love.

"Harold," said Arnold.

"What darling?" asked Trish.

"His name isn't Sammy. It's Harold."

"Are you sure?" she asked, her heavily made-up eyes wide and her blond ponytail bouncing around her head.

"Yes. That's the name he used when he filed suit against us," replied Arnold.

I'm going to vomit, thought Cici, who picked her phone out of her bag and said, "Oh. This is my husband on the phone. I'm so sorry I have to go," Cici lied as she stood up. "Truly lovely to catch up. We'll have to do this again in another twenty years," she added, throwing cash on the table.

"Oh. Arnie, you'll be dead then!" whined Trish.

"Here's hoping!" waved Cici as she bounced out of the restaurant as fast as her Manolo Blahniks could take her. "Oh, and Happy Easter!" she shouted behind her.

"Why am I friends with her?" Cici said to herself once outside.

The unseasonably warm weather made for comfortable walking conditions, so Cordelia decided to hoof it back to her mom's.

Arnold was the type of character Cici would've loved to hunt down and expose when she was a working journalist. He was obviously rich by unethical means, was predatory and possessive over beautiful younger women, and had no problem paying off police to access camera footage to track down and intimidate his enemies. All around, a real winner.

Poor Harold Mendoza, thought Cici as she crossed the street from the Château Laurier Hotel to the old Ottawa train station, which was housing the temporary offices and chamber of the Canadian Senate.

Mendoza? Cici thought to herself, confused about where the name came from. Trish said the man's name was Sammy, but Arnold called him Harold.

Oops. Harold Mendoza was Maxwell Farnsworth's husband, Cici realized, smiling at herself. She wished Arnold had collected Mr. Mendoza's traffic light footage instead and could tell her who his harasser pretending to be Drusilla Brisbane was.

"Wait," Cici said to herself, stepping off the sidewalk to sit on a bench along the Rideau Canal. She had an idea and took out her phone to suggest it to Mason.

Less than five minutes later, Mason replied.

Brilliant! It's the weekend, but I'll ask Margot to 'encourage' Stellan to put a rush on it! –M

* * *

"Where's Gene Kelley and Debbie Reynolds when we need them?" laughed Mason as he passed his brother Oliver another sandbag.

"Dunno. Should I get the Ouija Board, and we can find out?"

"I wouldn't be against it," said Mason, passing sandbag number one hundred and seven as he hummed "Singin' in the Rain."

Less than seventy-two hours had passed since the water level of Lake Belvedere rose. It started slowly, with the waves growing incrementally larger, reaching further inland. First, the docks and beach were submerged, followed by the flower beds and expansive lawn. The water then climbed uphill, lapping against the foundations of the original inn and carriage house, eventually surrounding them. Finally, the water drowned the four bridges and devoured the roadway.

By the time Mason, Lawrence, Oliver, and Gil arrived to help Ahren and Makayla secure the property, the lake had expanded so much that they had no choice but to park their cars at Valentine Chapel on Highclere Hill. From there, Ahren ferried them to Athabasca Cottage and Gay Acres in a rowboat.

The rise in water levels was aided by the tail end of a tropical storm, which was dumping and fanning additional feet of rain onto the already waterlogged shore. The family agreed this was worse than the flood of 2005.

The open water was traversed by barges and pontoon boats carrying flood supplies, moving turtle-like to avoid unseen dangers hidden within the depths. Local authorities had already reported three deaths by drowning, and advisories were issued to warn those with an interest in cottage country to stay home—or if you were already in a lake district—to leave until the lakes could be drained. At which point, the receding water would cause a new set of problems because of the lake's gravitational force pulling anything it touched off land and into the middle of the bay.

The first floor of the carriage house was already brimming with two feet of water after the lake surged through a broken window. Family photos, trinkets, and books floated in the tea-colored drink, with some already having escaped the carriage house and headed toward a new home. Oliver used an old piece of wood with the word "ZOOWIE" painted in bold technicolor on both sides to replace the shattered window. It was one of a set of boards displaying the "POW," "ZAP," and "BAM" of the *Batman* classic TV series' fight scenes, which the cousins used while making their mini-action videos as children.

Thankfully, the burial plot was far enough uphill that water was unlikely to damage those in their final resting place. If the water level reached the back 39 acres—which it looked like it might—the toxic soil could join the runoff, causing a domino of problems for the locals.

"I think that's everything," announced Lawrence as he kicked off his water-filled wellies in the back hall of Athabasca. "I suppose the cleanup is unlikely to be our problem," he admitted.

Mason felt a pang in his chest.

While many questions had been answered, he and Cici still hadn't identified Person X. Until they could do so and prove that they deliberately harmed Tank and caused the rest of the mayhem—the Valentine's eviction date stood.

"Ollie and I are going to change and head back to the city. Ahren will row over to pick us up. Are you sure you want to stay overnight? You might not be able to get out tomorrow," Lawrence said to Mason.

"Yes, I'm sure. It's 2:30 pm on Good Friday, traffic is going to be miserable, and since we're doing Easter dinner at Ollie's on Sunday, I'm not in any rush to head out," lied Mason who decided to stick around when he overheard Gil say he was staying at Highclere until Sunday. Mason wanted to know why and wondered if it had anything to do with Person X.

"Ok. I'll ask Makayla to tie up a canoe at the back door, so you're not trapped," offered Lawrence as he marched up the stairs.

* * *

Freshly showered, Mason sat at the dining room table and again reviewed the evidence he and Cici had collected to date. Mason hoped that if he stared long enough, something new would appear to him, ideally a confetti canon with a big neon arrow saying, "This is Person X."

Before he was settled, he noticed a new message from Margot Ambrosia.

Darling Mason,

Yes, indeedy, we will get on it immediately (oh, I love an accidental rhyme!). Stellan will make the call now and have it reviewed overnight. Oh, how I do hope this will provide you with some answers!

Also, I am in receipt of the package sent by your office, and we are on standby.

Happy Easter. More anon.

Love Margot

Good. This was good news! Mason smiled, then stood and walked to the front window to look across the larger-than-usual patch of water between Athabasca and Gil and Stuart's cottage.

Their lights were off.

Odd, thought Mason. There wasn't anywhere Gil could reasonably go that would be worth risking his safety to return after dark. The water was still rising, and surprises lurked under the surface everywhere.

"I wonder where he went?" Mason said to himself.

* * *

Cordelia hung her coat by the front door and walked into her mother's kitchen, where Tobias was making dinner.

"What's cooking good-looking," she asked, pinching his ass as she went to the fridge to take out a bottle of white wine.

"It's Good Friday! So, of course, we're having…pesto chicken," laughed Tobias.

"Did the apostles eat pesto chicken? Are we finally historically accurate?" teased Cici, uncorking the Pinot.

"I was planning pancakes but was reminded by our son that's Shrove Tuesday. Not Good Friday. Speaking of which, when did that kid get smart?"

"He's always been a smart-*ass*, so maybe he's always been an intellectual but hid it behind bitchiness?"

"He takes after his mother," winked Tobias.

"Har, har," Cici replied, placing the wine bottle back in the fridge.

"Your phone just beeped," said Tobias.

"Are you sure?" asked Cici, who hadn't heard it.

"Yup. It's your specific beep for Mason-related things."

"Oh!" responded Cici, putting her wine glass down and trotting to her coat.

Cici took her phone out of the coat pocket and wiped the smudges, mucking up the screen against her sweater, before unlocking it.

"Holy shit," said Cici. "Shit, shit, shit," she said again.

"What?" called Tobias, walking from the kitchen to the foyer. "Is it Mason?"

"No. The tracker I attached to the marble container in the woods pinged a location seven minutes ago," Cici said, screen-grabbing the location data before she copied and pasted it into Google Maps.

"Where is it?" Tobias asked, looking over Cordelia's shoulder.

"The location is on Lake Belvedere and not far from Highclere by boat, but I guess you'd classify it as on 'the other side of the lake.' I don't know what's there, though."

"You better send it to Mason," advised Tobias.

"You're right," Cici agreed before doing so and putting her phone into her pocket.

Tobias looked at the worry in his wife's eyes.

"It doesn't mean Person X is there. The power could've flickered, and the cell jammer went offline briefly," Tobias reasoned.

"I know."

"He is most likely very safe," he said.

Cici's phone soon beeped Mason's specific tone. She pulled it out of her pocket and read the message. Her hand covered her mouth, and she gasped.

"What?" asked Tobias, coming around to look at the message. "Oh no," he whispered.

The tracker pinged at Norah Tripplehorn's cottage.

Chapter Sixty-Two

"I'm going over there!" Mason shouted to Cordelia and Tobias on speaker phone while he zipped up his boots.

"Mason, no. You don't know what you'll find!" Cici pleaded. "Wait until daylight. Wait until I can get there."

"I'd take her advice, Mason. It might not be safe," added Tobias.

"It's Norah Tripplehorn, how unsafe could it be?" Mason reasoned, wrapping his scarf around his neck.

"It might not be, though. Mason, listen to me. It could be a plant, and you're walking into a trap. I love you, but when faced with danger, you scream like a girl and run," explained Cici. "You are self-described as a lover, not a fighter!"

"Or maybe I am a fighter, and I'm about to crack this bitch wide open because Gil is also out somewhere. What if he's there? It's the perfect confluence of events!"

"Mason!" called Cici from the phone.

"Gotta go. I'll tell you what I find," said Mason, ending the call before sense and reason could be talked into him.

* * *

"Fuck!" shouted Cici, slapping her hand against the wall.

"Go!" instructed Tobias.

"I'm not close enough. I'm six hours away." Cici started pacing the kitchen, taking gulps of her white wine.

"What about that girl from Winnipeg?" suggested Diane Bradshaw, Cici's mother, before taking the receiver off the landline and leaving the kitchen.

"Skye!"

Cici took out her phone and pressed dial.

"It's ringing," she explained while still pacing. "Come on, Skye. Pick up, pick up."

"Well?" asked Tobias.

"No answ...Skye! It's Cici. Can you call me when you get this message? Or just text me to let me know your location. I might need your help," Cici hung up.

"Call Lawrence and Piper. Or Oliver?"

"Have you met them? They'd have 50 choppers and the entire National Guard out looking for him!"

"Isn't that what you want?"

"No! I want backup, not a rescue team. We're not at that point yet."

"Makayla?" suggested Tobias.

"Brilliant!" screeched Cici, high-fiving her husband. "No answer...Mack, it's Cici. Can you call me as soon as you get this? Thanks," Cordelia threw her phone on the counter. "Fuck, fuck, fuck!"

"Ok. Gorgeous, calm down," instructed Tobias, grabbing his wife by the shoulders and looking her in the eyes. "He's ok. You're ok."

"Am I? Is he?" trembled Cici.

Tobias rarely saw his wife's vulnerability appear. Cordelia was a master at hiding her anxiety, keeping her cool, and knowing who to trust and what to do. When cracks in her veneer of poise appeared, he knew she was doubting the only person she could completely count on. The person who always rescued her when no one else was coming—herself.

"Mason is going of his own volition, and I assume you've got a tracker on him somewhere," said Tobias.

Cici smiled and looked up at her husband.

"Yea. I do," she admitted. "A few for safety."

"Good. Keep an eye on where he is, and if he's not gone from Norah's place after an hour, then panic."

Cordelia nodded and stepped away from her husband.

"You're right."

"I just spoke to your Uncle David," announced Diane Bradshaw, placing the receiver back on the landline. "He's going to lower his seaplane into the Ottawa River and fuel it within the hour. He can have you to Lake Belvedere within 90 minutes of take-off and will be ready to go—all weekend long."

"Really?" asked Cordelia.

"Really. Now..." said Diane, "who wants Pesto chicken?"

Cici scooped her mother into her arms and gave her a tight squeeze.

"Thank you," she whispered as her phone rang.

* * *

Mason parked his car half a kilometer from Norah Tripplehorn's cottage and made his way through the unfamiliar woods until he reached the edge of Norah's expansive lawn. Her cottage was a small but beautiful two-story, very traditional Scandinavian Scribe log cottage built on a rock cliff. It had a stunning view overlooking the main waterway of Lake Belvedere, with a charming deck wrapped around the entire house and a comfortable fire pit built into the rocks with red

Muskoka chairs circling it. Norah's property was high above the natural waterline of the lake, keeping it safe from extreme flooding.

It was quiet.

Mason couldn't see any cars or recent car tracks in the mud, and the lights in the house were off with the blinds closed.

While still hidden behind a large maple tree, Mason slid on his infrared goggles to scan for security cameras and hidden camera lenses. He felt very James Bond—just a bit more fabulous.

He started from the left side of the property and turned his body a full 360 degrees, including the woods behind him.

Nothing.

It was clear.

Mason removed the goggles and returned them to his messenger bag, pulling out a flashlight before leaving the safety of tree cover. His heart rate rose once he was in the open air of Norah's lawn. He was nervous but still safe. His confidence and instincts had grown since Labor Day.

While moving closer to the house, Mason kept looking at his phone signal to determine when the cell jammer would be close enough to cut off his ability to call for help.

Twenty feet away, he still had a signal. He shone the light under the roof's eaves before turning behind him once more to ensure he wasn't being followed.

Still quiet.

Ten feet away, and five bars were still flashing. Mason took the first step of the wrap-around deck but didn't hold the railing to avoid leaving proof he'd been there. Up he went until he was outside the door to the cottage. He had only lost one bar of service.

Mason pushed his face close to the glass window at the top of the deck's steps. The blinds were down but not all the way—an inch above the bottom frame was open, so Mason crouched and beamed the flashlight inside.

He couldn't see anything. He stood back up and followed the deck to the lakeside, where there were two sets of sliding doors without curtains and blinds. Mason flashed the light inside and saw a cozy living room with large plush blue couches, a television, a fireplace, a long dining table, and an open-concept kitchen in the distance. He tried the doors, but they were locked.

Mason hesitated, his heart pounding in the silent darkness. Just then, a gloved hand shot over his shoulder, clamping his mouth and wrenching him back. His flashlight tumbled away as he stumbled off the deck.

* * *

The figure who emerged onto the lawn of Norah Tripplehorn's cottage was at first a formless shadow until—certain he was alone—he switched on his penlight.

Trent Callahan's outline took shape in the thin beam. Though diminutive, his presence was unmistakable as he carefully searched Norah's property.

Unknowingly following Mason's stealthy path, Trent edged toward the cottage and mounted the few steps to the deck. With an effort to mute his presence, he shone his light through the windows, his beam skittering across the furniture Mason had scrutinized just moments earlier. After several minutes, Trent withdrew into the shadows from whence he came, his task apparently fulfilled.

* * *

Mason Valentine and Makayla Dawn huddled in the small dark hatch beneath the deck, their presence swallowed by shadows. They watched in tense silence as Trent meandered around Norah's property. They decided to breathe and speak only when they were sure he had vanished into the woods.

"Mack," Mason whispered as they crawled back into the night air, wiping dirt and grime from their knees. "What the hell are you doing here? Why the hell was Trent here?"

"Cordelia called me. Said you'd gone to break into Norah Tripplehorn's house, and I responded, 'Why break in? I have a key.' But just as I got here, I noticed Mr. Callahan getting out of his car and heading in this direction. So, I went off-road, drove up the snowmobile path, parked, ran, and pulled you down so he didn't see you," she smiled. "You're welcome," she added when Mason said nothing.

Mason seemed bewildered.

"No, of course. Thank you," he said, his hand on his heart. "But what the fuck was he doing here? Is he following me?"

Mack shrugged.

"I don't know. But if we're gonna snoop, let's do it quickly in case he returns," she advised while waving a key beside her face.

"Wait, why do you have a key?" Mason asked, still trying to regulate his heart and breathing.

"Pa and I look after this place too. Senator Valentine used to pay us as a gift for Ms. Tripplehorn. Even though he's gone, we felt a duty to keep looking after her."

"Won't she be upset if you go in without her permission?"

"Probably, but I called her on my way here. Said I wanted to make sure the flood and rainfall weren't affecting her place," answered Makayla as she ushered Mason to the main door.

She pushed the key into the lock, swiveled it left, turned the knob and they were in.

"That was much more elegant than I was planning," admitted Mason, nodding his thanks to Mack.

"What? Were you going to take a rock to the window?" she asked, flicking on the lights before lowering the control to its dimmest setting.

"No, Mack," Mason groaned playfully. "I wasn't actually going to break in. I might have allowed myself entry if a door happened to be unlocked, but that's as far as I was going to go. What do you take me for? A common criminal?" he responded while absorbing the charm of the space.

"This is lovely."

"Yea, eh? I'd love to be in a place like this. Three bedrooms upstairs with one bathroom. A half bath is down here, and a view that can't be replicated."

"Basement?" asked Mason, wandering between the living room and the kitchen.

"No basement. She's on a rock," Mack laughed, "that's why there was a hatch for us to hide in."

"I know of cottages built on rocks with a little crawl space of a basement. It wasn't a stupid 'city folk' question," smiled Mason.

"What you lookin' for, anyway?" wondered Makayla.

Mason turned to look at her.

"Are you sure you want to know?"

She frowned.

"Will I find myself back in an ankle monitor?" she asked, jetting out her leg in an amusing "Hokey Pokey" move. "The last one just came off."

"No," replied Mason, who was now going through the drawers in the kitchen.

"Well then, lay it on me."

"Cici and I found a marble cargo box…well, more of a container really…buried in the back 39 acres. It was heavy, which prevented us from moving it. Somehow, someone else took it in the middle of the night, but not before Cici could attach a GPS tracker to it. We couldn't get a read on the tracker for days, but it pinged today from this location."

"Would it fit in the closet?" asked Mack.

"No, it would take up a fair chunk of space. It's not down here. Can we go up?"

"Yup. Just wipe your boots," she instructed.

Mason and Makayla climbed the narrow wooden stairs to a tiny landing surrounded by four doors. They checked each bedroom and the bathroom. Nothing.

"I'm not sure the floors could hold the weight of the marble," sighed Mason, "I guess it's not here."

"Maybe it was in a truck that stopped here for a few minutes, which is why this is the location you were sent?" suggested Makayla, turning off the lights and closing the doors behind them.

"Could be," agreed Mason, biting his lower lip. "But the signal coming from Norah Tripplehorn's cottage, of all places, feels intentional," he added, descending the stairs back to the main floor.

* * *

"Any news?" asked Tobias as he placed the pesto-lined dirty dishes into the kitchen sink.

"Phone says he's still at Norah's. The signal hasn't gone down, so I guess there isn't a cell jammer there after all," replied Cordelia before placing her phone—screen up—on the counter.

"I assume you don't believe that. That there isn't a cell jammer?" suggested Tobias.

"No. I don't. Otherwise, getting just a few seconds of location data from the tracker would be impossible. Where's the jammer and the marble box is the question?"

* * *

"Well, thanks for coming to my rescue, Mack. I appreciate it," Mason said to Makayla once they had exited Norah's cottage and locked the door.

"Not a problem. I'm happy to help. I hope I didn't hurt you too badly when I pulled you down," she smiled.

"Even if you had, I'm just grateful that you got to me before Trent. His arriving here so quickly after me is fishy."

"I agree. Also, I'll follow you back to Highclere and row you to Athabasca so you don't have to wrestle with the canoe," she laughed and nudged Mason with her shoulder.

"That bloody canoe is my worst enemy! I watch people all summer long glide above the water like it's an extension of them, and then I get in, and the bastard tips right over!" Mason scoffed, bouncing down the steps onto the grass.

"Center of gravity is key," smiled Mack.

"Not my strong suit," Mason winced.

The two walked a few feet along the lawn when Mason paused. Mack continued a few more steps before she realized her companion wasn't with her.

"Something wrong?" Mack asked Mason.

He stood still for a moment. Thinking. Trying to remember what Norah had said to him at Christmas.

"Does she have a second structure somewhere? A shed? Guest house?" asked Mason, looking around him.

"She does!" remembered Mack. "She told me it was going to be an art studio and guest cottage for her daughter but decided to rent it out for revenue. Help to pay the bills."

"Where is it?" Mason wondered.

"Just on the other side of those trees," Mack said, pointing to a small patch of forest on the opposite side of the lawn.

"Do you have a key?" asked Mason, already walking in the direction Mack had indicated.

"I do, but I've never been inside," she replied, running to catch up to Mason. "I'm not sure we should go in. Isn't the renter protected from an unannounced intrusion?"

"Yeah, but didn't you hear we got hit with the tail end of a tropical storm? Who knows what damage it caused? We should check it," he winked, walking into the cluster of trees and overgrown grass that separated Norah's home from its sister structure.

The closeness of the healthy evergreen trees provided a dense natural privacy screen between the two buildings.

"Does the art studio use the same driveway as the main house?" asked Mason, his hand in front of his face to shield from the low-hanging branches.

"No, it has a separate entrance off Highway 9-14."

It didn't take long for Mason and Mack to make their way to the other side of the tree barrier, almost running into the quaint single-room shack.

The studio sat claustrophobically amongst the trees, with only a skinny dark roadway covered with significant overhang providing an entrance.

The lights were off, but an opaque fabric from the inside covered the windows. A car had been there—both Mason and Makayla noticed fresh tire marks in the roadway and the smell of maple logs still emanating from the steel chimney.

"Maybe we shouldn't do this?" suggested Makayla, hanging back while Mason walked to the door.

"Why? We won't be long."

"Someone could be in there or coming back. What if Mr. Callahan checks this building, too?"

"I don't think anyone is here, and someone might indeed come back, so we'd better get in and out before they do," Mason urged.

Taking the keys from Makayla, Mason unlocked and pushed open the hefty blue door. He stepped inside and ran his hand along the inside wall, feeling for a light switch.

"Ouch," Mason whispered, recoiling his hand.

"What?" asked Makayla, feeling heightened and on edge.

"Cut my finger," he replied, sticking it in his mouth.

"On what?"

"I think loose wallpaper," Mason answered, looking at his finger to see how badly it was bleeding. It looked ok. "We better put on gloves."

Mason once more felt around the inside, stretching his arm as far along the wall as he could without stepping in. His fingers found a round disk with a button in the middle, which he pushed while holding his breath.

Ceiling lights, desk lamps, and multiple yellow flood lights lit up, the brightness at first catching Mason and Makayla off guard, causing white stars to appear in their vision.

Mason's hands clenched as his eyes adjusted from the outdoor darkness to the inside luminance. His heart was beating out of his chest. Beads of sweat wandered down his forehead and under his arms. He turned to look at Makayla, whose already white skin had become practically translucent—drained of blood.

"I can't speak," mouthed Mason.

"I can't breathe," replied Mack.

* * *

"Your phone beeped," called Tobias from the kitchen.

Cici ran down the stairs, through the foyer, and to her phone, which was charging at the kitchen counter.

"Crap," Cici muttered after reading the alert.

"What now?" asked Tobias, his anxiety growing.

"I've lost Mason's signal."

Chapter Sixty-Three

Mason was dumbfounded.

Unable to speak.

Incapable of expressing the feelings and thoughts racing through his head.

Each time he tried to say something, nothing but air came out.

Makayla remained outside the door while Mason walked toward the center of the room. He turned in a circle twice, trying to adjust his eyes and mind to the straitjacket-level insanity he was looking at.

Every wall, surface, and ceiling was plastered with photographs of Miles "The Tank" Valentine. Pictures printed from the internet, taken from magazine articles and newspaper clippings. Lawn signs from Tank's political campaigns tiled most of the ceiling while *"Go the Distance with Miles Valentine,"* cartoons that were distributed to constituents in the 1960s, carpeted the floor.

Mason moved to get a closer look at one wall where he saw signed book jackets, political postcards, headshots from every decade, "Vote Valentine" hats, foam fingers, Miles Valentine flags, buttons, large photo prints from conspiracy conferences, alien stickers, and Canadian currency with satanic symbols.

He couldn't believe it. The obsession, the collection, the disorder, and chaos. He put his hands on his head, subconsciously stopping his brain from exploding as he moved to another wall.

"Oh fuck," whispered Mason when he saw photos of his late grandmother Lady Jean Valentine with her eyes and heart cut out, framed by other disembodied limbs he recognized from famous photographs of her, which were now cut to shreds. She wasn't the only dismembered relation tacked to the wall. There were dozens of pictures of Mason himself with his eyes and heart removed and one delightful exhibit where his crotch had been cut out and stabbed into the wall. Talk about carving off a piece of the fruitcake.

Further down the wall was a collage of long-lens pictures taken of Mason and his entire family, including his nieces and nephews, going about their daily routine at Highclere.

When he stepped back, he recognized that copied pages of Tank's diaries were also stapled to the wall. Pages detailing Louella Stone's pregnancy and the tragic death of Drusilla's infant brother. Addresses, passwords, and disturbing notes about family members had been crossed over with red exes.

Satellite views of Fernsby House, Highclere, Louella Stone's house, and Tank's home in Toronto had been printed poster-sized and hung with handwritten notes about access locations, security, and staff routines.

"Mason?" said Makayla, who had color back in her cheeks and was looking at the wall opposite him.

Mason turned to see Mack looking at shelves of pill bottles, the same sent to her for distribution. A security drive was streaming live footage from hidden cameras at Highclere. Pages of printed texts between Mason, Cordelia, Skye, Baroness Ambrosia, Mack, and family members were stacked on a desk. Their movements had been monitored in real time by hacked fitness and sleep-tracking devices. The pieces Mack had stolen from the carriage house were displayed over several cabinets, while the three missing gold spheres sat on tissue boxes alongside equipment that looked like a pressure sensor. On the floor, in front of it all, were the twelve mini "Doors to Nowhere," each with a safe containing the ashes of one of Lady Valentine's Golden Retrievers.

"Is this a shrine? Or lair?" asked Makayla, her voice hoarse.

"It's the manifestation of an obsessed sicko, is what it is," said Mason, his wonder and shock beginning to dissipate as next steps formed. "Mack, I need you to take pictures of every inch of this place. Don't miss a thing. Get as close and detailed as possible. I'm going to see if there are any clues as to who this nutbar is."

"It's not Ms. Tripplehorn?"

"Could be, but I'm not sure."

* * *

The opening riffs of *Jesus Christ Superstar* sounded from the tiny speaker at the back of Diane Bradshaw's old television.

"You know, they make these bigger, brighter, and easier to use these days?" Tobias pointed out to his mother-in-law while waving his hand around the TV.

"I like what I have, thank you very much. It works for me," Diane responded.

"That's all that matters," he smiled.

"Has Mason's signal reappeared?" she asked.

"Not yet. Cici is checking something on her computer. She'll be down in a minute," Tobias replied just as Cici's phone beeped.

He leaned from the couch to the coffee table to look at the screen.

"Anything?" wondered Diane.

"Yes, he's back online," Tobias announced, unable to hide his relief. "Cordelia! Your phone dinged. Mason is back online and on the move!" he yelled to his wife.

"Thank God!" sighed Cici as she came downstairs. "I knew I had nothing to worry about. I'm sure he'll text me if he found anything of note," she added before plopping between Tobias and her mother. "In the meantime, let's enjoy the movie," she nodded with a smile as she took her wine glass from the accent table behind her.

After feeling tense for a few hours, Diane, Cici, and Tobias breathed in a relaxed rhythm as the overused VHS squealed a few bars of the movie's soundtrack.

"What does GS1 mean?" Tobias asked, still looking at the television.

"What's the context?" asked Cordelia.

"Your name for Mason's tracker. Why is it called GS1?"

"It's not. He's saved as MMV."

"Can't be. Your alert said GS1 was moving."

Cordelia snapped her head toward Tobias.

"What?" she said, standing up. "Where did you put it?" she asked, searching for her phone.

"Right here," said Diane, handing it to Cici.

"Oh fuck!"

"Language, Cordelia!" scolded her mother.

"GS1 is the tracker I attached to the gold sphere! It's moving...How? It's not possible anyone could've found it!" she said breathily, running her hand through her hair. "There was no way," she repeated, looking at the tracker's location. "Mason is still offline, and the sphere seems to be traveling by boat across the lake!"

"Going where?" asked Tobias, looking at the screen with Cici.

"Toward Norah's..."

* * *

"Whose dresses are these?" asked Makayla, photographing under an old coffee table. Mason walked over and unraveled one.

"My grandmother's," he answered.

"There's a bunch of them. Where did they come from?" asked Mack.

"They were in storage at Tank's house. They must have been taken from there, which isn't surprising considering the diary pages on the walls. Who is this person?" wondered Mason, rolling the dress up and replacing it under the table. "How's it coming?"

"I've taken over 200 photos. Any sign of the marble box?"

"No."

"Could it be outside?" suggested Makayla.

* * *

"How close is the sphere now?" Cici called from the kitchen while frantically calling Mason and Makayla's cell phones from the landline.

"I'm not an expert, but it's moving quickly. I'd say five minutes. Mason still isn't online," replied Tobias.

"Fuck, fuck!" said Cordelia.

"Fuck indeed, dear," agreed Diane nodding while clutching her pearls with her withered well-lived hands.

"It's picking up speed!" Tobias warned, watching the tiny red dot make its way closer to Mason.

* * *

Mack turned off the lights and shut the door behind her while Mason searched the perimeter. He felt the ground with his foot and hands, deciding not to use light in case Person X returned and saw them from a distance.

"Well?" Makayla called in a hushed voice.

"Nothing," replied Mason, "I think we'd better...fuuuuccccckkk!" he called out before being drowned by snapping twigs and the crunch of dead leaves.

"Excuse me!?" asked Mack, confused and hustling to where she heard Mason's cry.

"Changing teams, are we?" she quipped, approaching him around the far side.

"No, no. Sorry. I tripped over an extension cord," he said, rubbing his knee and nodding toward a thick black cable, its orange-encased prongs now dangling limp from its outlet.

* * *

"Mason's back online!" shouted Tobias.

"Really?" ran Cordelia, yanking the phone from her husband's hand.

"He's still at Norah's or thereabouts," advised Tobias.

Cici handed her phone back and returned to the landline to call Mason once more.

"Wait!" called Tobias.

"What? What what?" asked an anxious Cici, the receiver still to her ear.

"The sphere stopped moving."

Cici held her breath. "They've been spotted."

* * *

"I pushed it back in," confirmed Makayla, ensuring the plug was in place.

"The cord is snaking toward this bush," said Mason, following it.

* * *

"He's offline again!" noted Tobias.

"FUCK!"

* * *

"Found it!" confirmed Mason as he stepped through the twigs of the bushes. The black marble box with its repeating text and frog décor was there and still in one piece.

"Mason!" called Makayla from behind.

"Hold on."

"No! Mason—we have to go! A message from Cici just came through, we've been caught!"

"What?" he replied, snapping a few pictures as he backed out of the bush.

"We've been caught—we have to go!"

Mason pivoted, his eyes locking with Makayla's determined gaze as they plunged into the dense trees, racing toward Norah's house. The haunting remnants of a deranged fanatic's shrine of obsession and vengeance were abandoned in their wake.

Chapter Sixty-Four

"Oh my God," mouthed Cordelia as she flipped through the photos Mason and Makayla had taken at Norah's just twelve hours earlier.

"The building...it...well, it felt thick with anger, an almost dark obsession, and I guess revenge," recounted Mason to Cici over FaceTime. "It didn't feel like the work of an obsessed fan or a delightfully unhinged stalker. It felt violent. It felt vicious and obviously calculated despite the chaos."

"Yeah, and considering the amount and diversity of the Tank paraphernalia, we were right in assuming that this person has been planning and preparing for years," Cordelia said slowly. "The telescope photos go back almost twenty years, even earlier than the assumed beginning of the ground poisoning," she added, eyeing herself in several of them.

"I noticed because I have thicker hair in them," Mason smiled, taking a sip of tea and a bite of chocolate muffin.

"Say what we will about Laverna—she's given no indication that she hated Uncle Tank. If anything, it was the opposite—I suspect she learned to love him. Greed is her main failing; greed leads people to moral lapses and underhanded decision-making. What we're dealing with now is a festering hatred of Tank and everything he did, was, related to, and stood for," said Cici, throwing her reading glasses onto the bed behind her.

She was still in her white terry-cloth robe despite it being after 11 in the morning.

"The only person who best fits the bill is Trent Callahan. Not only did he seemingly follow you to Norah's, but he has the history, motive, and means to pull this off," she sighed. "I still think he's too convenient—yet sometimes we overthink motive when it's really quite simple."

"Where's the sphere now?" Mason asked, peering out his front windows, wondering what Uncle Gil was up to.

"Norah's. Then it went offline," replied Cici, looking tense and frustrated.

"The other three spheres were there, so I suppose the box has since been opened," said Mason, leaning his head back and looking at the vaulted ceilings.

"Mason," said Cici through the screen, "you need to pack and go home."

"Why?" Mason shot back.

"You're protected at home. You have security and your family. This person is watching Highclere on camera and likely has keys to every building—there are detailed maps on their wall with access points and blind spots. Their lair is just across the lake, and having opened the marble box, the incentive to remain hidden is gone. They have accomplished everything they planned. Auntie V said the family's ultimate protection was in that box. It's now in the hands of someone who is willing to be violent and has form for it. In my experience, when a con is done, and an investigator still hasn't identified the bad guy, they often reveal themselves for fun. When they do, they have no further motive to play nice," Cici explained calmly though her face said, *I'm not fucking around.*

"How do you know this person isn't freaking out because we found their shrine? We know where it is, and they know we were there. All the evidence of what they've done is twenty minutes away, and if it's been moved out, we have the pictures. Norah will identify who the renter is. I don't think it behooves this person to come after me. We know too much!" Mason argued.

"Mason, Norah could very well be Person X!" Cici pointed out, becoming aggressive.

"If it's Norah, then I think we're fine," Mason scoffed.

"Did you not comprehend what you saw last night?" Cici asked, anger rising in her voice. "You just said to me you felt darkness, anger, and revenge. When those three feelings are sewn together, they combust. Mason..." she said, staring into the screen, "this isn't up for discussion. You are to pack your bags and go back to Toronto. If you don't, I will call your mother, who will send in special forces, a handful of helicopters, and armored vehicles to get you the hell out of there."

Mason nodded; he knew she was right. He also knew that when it came to Piper Valentine, Cici was not exaggerating. It was best to leave while it was still his choice.

"Ok," he nodded. "I'll go."

"Thank you," she smiled. "Once you get back to the city, send me your notes and observations from last night, and then I'm going to reach out to my contact at the police services. It's time to bring in the authorities. The level of danger is too high, and after last night, we have more than enough evidence and new investigative paths to put a name to Person X once and for all. We'll need the police to finish this by bringing in Norah, Laverna, Trent, and Gil. I'll wait for your notes before I make the call," finished Cici while standing from her childhood desk and walking to the chest of drawers beside her bed. She opened her bag and lifted out her keys before returning to her computer.

"I'll have this on me all day," she said, shaking her keys in the air, "if there's any trouble..." Cordelia didn't need to finish her sentence. Mason was the one who was insistent on backup measures.

Mason nodded.

"I'm sorry we couldn't carry this over the finish line together, but you're right. I'll let you know if I hear from Margot about her assignment. Otherwise, I'll get out of here stat," he smiled, lifting his empty plate and mug.

"Ok. Talk when you get home!" waved Cici before logging off and closing her computer.

Mason did the same, placed his dishes in the sink, and ran up the stairs of Athabasca two at a time to pack his bag and drive home.

* * *

Guillaume Regan stood at his living room window, watching as Mason closed the curtains of Athabasca Cottage and turned on the outside flood lights. The universal signal at Highclere Inn & Carriage House that a family member was heading home.

Gil was relieved. He didn't like that Mason had stuck around another night. His being at Highclere complicated things, and risked harm to his nephew. While Gil and Mason weren't what anyone would refer to as close, Mason was family, and it was time for his family to stop getting hurt.

The end, Gil hoped, was now.

Gil turned and walked to the kitchen to see if Stuart had messaged him.

Still nothing.

It was unlike Stuart, even if they were fighting, to go over twenty-four hours without sending, at the very least, a heart or wave emoji. On Thursday morning, when Gil left for Highclere, Stuart dashed off to the market before paying a visit to Louella, whose declining health prevented her from accepting his Easter invitation. Stuart hated the idea of anyone being alone on a holiday and insisted on bringing Louella flowers, a pie, and some goodies.

It was thoughtful gestures such as these that made Gil wonder if Stuart had a sense that his biological mother was Louella. Was his attention and affection toward her altruistic, or was there an underlying invisible, indescribable blood bond that compelled him to care for her? Knowing Stuart and his penchant for secret-keeping, Gil wouldn't rule out that Stuart learned some time ago the name of his birth mother and said nothing.

Gil looked at the clock; it was almost noon, and Stuart hadn't called or texted in nearly two days. His anxiety was rising, but Gil decided that he'd wait a few more hours before panicking.

In the meantime, there were other matters to freak out about.

* * *

Mason was midway up the hill to Valentine Chapel when his phone rang out a few bars of "Rule Britannia"—Baroness Margaret Ambrosia's ring tone.

Darling Mason—Isn't technology stunning? Thanks to the magic of facial recognition and AI our task was much easier than I for one thought it would be. Cordelia was brilliant. We could indeed follow the traffic cameras in and around Harold Mendoza's home the day he met with the imposter of your Aunt Drusilla. We confidently isolated the café where they discussed the jewelry box and while following the late Mr. Mendoza's activity was relatively simple, the tricky bit was identifying the imposter of Mrs. Brisbane. The selection is deemed accurate as she was also seen on camera at Heathrow.

Hundreds of screen grabs are attached.

Happy Easter!

Love, Margot

Butterflies filled Mason's stomach. Was he about to learn the identity of Person X at last?

His finger hovered over the compressed file. He hesitated. Why didn't he want to press it? Was he worried it would be someone unexpected? Someone that hadn't crossed their minds at all?

Screw it, Mason thought to himself and tapped the file to download the photos.

He finished his climb up the hill while enjoying the unexpected sunshine. The weather was predicted with near certainty to be further torrential rain; however, the wind was stronger than expected and pushed the storm off sooner than estimated. Mason couldn't help but be amused at all the cars parked next to the chapel. Despite the warning by Muskoka Lakes to stay away until the water had receded, very few took the advice and were using the small parish parkette as a ferry point to their properties.

Opening the trunk, Mason tossed his bags inside before checking the download's progress. As he walked to the driver's seat of his car, he beamed when he saw it was complete and the file had exported the screen grabs to his Photos app.

There they were.

Hundreds of screen grabs waiting for him to identify the woman pretending to be his Aunt Drusilla. He started at the first picture, which was unclear and fuzzy. He could see dark hair pulled back and a lovely dress, but her face was difficult to discern. Sliding to the next picture, it too was cloudy and low resolution—though he could identify Harold Mendoza in the foreground. Gliding his finger across the screen, Mason went from one picture to the next before finally landing on a clear black-and-white photo taken from a bank ATM across from a Pret A Manger location. A slender woman, in a becoming—though relatively short—dress with dark hair in a messy bun, exited, holding her sunglasses in one hand and a coffee in the other.

"No. Way," Mason whispered as he pinched the screen to zoom in before checking the next few photos in the sequence to ensure he wasn't seeing things.

He wasn't. There she was—clear as can be.

A familiar face, after all.

"Good afternoon," called a lovely-looking woman with a very upper-class British accent.

Her gray hair, with streaks of blond, was held in place by a pink headband with pearl and gold decorations. She was well equipped with rain boots, a utility jacket, and an umbrella, which she was using as a makeshift walking stick to support her on the mild incline of the hill leading to the chapel's parking lot.

"Hi there. Afternoon!" Mason called back as he selected a handful of screen grabs to send to Cordelia.

"Would you mind me terribly asking if you're from the area?" asked the British woman.

"No. I'm from Toronto," Mason replied.

"Sorry, I should be more specific. Do you have a home in the area?" she wondered.

"Of course, that's what you were asking!" Mason laughed at his idiocy, forgetting to send his message to Cici. "Yes, I have a family place down the hill. Are you lost?" he asked, putting his phone in his pocket.

"I'm not sure, to be truthful. I've been looking for Senator Miles Valentine's resort—yet it seems to have been washed away," she said, removing her pearl headband to tame her flyaway hair.

"Unfortunately, Senator Valentine died in August," Mason told her. "Did you know him?"

"Yes, I knew he'd passed. Though, I'm not sure if I knew him. I might have met him, and if I did, it indeed would have been some years ago, but my family was friends of his wife," she said, placing the headband back on her head.

"Aida?" Mason asked, removing his sunglasses.

"No, Lady Jean Fernsby. Do you know if Drusilla Brisbane is here?" she asked.

Mason, exhausted from the night before, wasn't following the conversation. Who was this woman, why did she want to see Drusilla, and how did she know Lady Valentine?

"I'm sorry," said Mason with a smile. "I had a late night and am a bit out of sorts. I should introduce myself; I'm Mason Valentine. Senator and Lady Valentine were my grandparents," he said, extending his sweaty hand.

"Oh, of course. Mason, so good to meet you, and I am deeply sorry for the loss of your grandfather. My condolences," she offered while shaking Mason's hand.

"I'm sorry, I didn't catch your name?" Mason asked, tilting his head.

"Oh, my apologies! My name is Joy Sauveterre."

Joy laughed.

"Don't worry, I do it all the time. So, to answer your question, no, Drusilla is not in the country right now. I think she's in New Zealand, but don't quote me on that. As you astutely observed, we have been hit with an unusual flood, and Highclere Inn & Carriage House is a bit difficult to get to at the moment. Otherwise, I'd have welcomed you and given you a tour," Mason said.

"That's very charming of you, thank you. Not to worry. I was in Canada and decided—quite last minute, I admit—that I'd venture to the famed cottage region and stalk the Valentines to quell my curiosity. I trusted all would be here for the holiday, but I understand why you're not, considering the condition of the area. I won't keep you any longer, but thank you, Mason, for humoring me," said Joy, extending her hand once more.

"My pleasure. Think nothing of it. I'll tell Drusilla you came to call," Mason said, releasing his hand and walking toward the driver's side of his car.

Joy stepped a few feet backward before turning and continuing toward her rented car but then stopped.

"I know it's none of my business," she said, having reversed course and followed Mason as he opened his car door, "but I am dying to know if the keys were needed and worked."

Mason turned to face Joy.

"The which worked?"

"The keys. The gold spheres. Curiosity killed the cat, I know, but after all these years, I'm ever so curious about what they were holding safe," she said with warm eyes and a gentle smile.

"I'm sorry," Mason said, shaking his head. "Who did you say you were?"

"Joy Sauveterre—oh gosh—I do apologize. Sauveterre is my second husband's name. You'd know me as Joyce Redstone."

* * *

"Darling, we can just order takeaway. It wouldn't be the end of the world," offered Stellan McManus after looking at his wife's mangled exploded turkey.

"No, Stellan! I am determined to successfully cook a turkey this year, and I shall. This is why I'm doing something of a dry run," explained Margot in a Barbie-pink apron, opera gloves, shower cap over her hair, and a three-string pearl necklace.

"But dearest, we aren't entertaining this year. We can keep it simple. The children will be fine with it," he explained to his wife.

"No, no. Our not entertaining is the very reason I'm able to problem-solve cooking a turkey. I read twelve hours was the appropriate amount of time, but as you can see from the dust this silly bird is coughing up, that was clearly wrong. I have two more birds in the deep freeze. I will get this right!" Margot said absolutely while picking pieces of dry brittle turkey off her apron. "Also, dear, I wouldn't put it past you to have planted an explosive in the cavity just to prove some wayward point," she scoffed.

"To that end, did you remove the insides?" Stellan asked, backing his way out of the kitchen.

Margot looked at him.

"The dressing? I hadn't put it in yet," she replied.

"No, the heart and lungs," he chuckled, echoing from the front hall.

"Say again, darling? Stellan?" called Margot, following him to the sitting room. "Are you telling me that the organs haven't been removed prior to purchase?" Margot asked with earnest surprise.

"Oh Margaret," Stellan further laughed, picking up his iPad and taking a seat on the long white sofa.

"Why should the chef have to remove such things? Do I need to snip arteries, too?" asked Margot, readjusting her shower cap as their front doorbell rang.

"To borrow an American turn of phrase," Stellan began while standing to answer the door, "saved by the bell!"

"Only just, dear. I will require an answer to my query," Margot noted while walking to the drinks cart in the sitting room to pour a brandy.

Stellan checked the security camera before opening the front door.

"Good evening, sir," greeted a young, handsome Metropolitan Police Agent, sporting an awkward beard while decked out in pedestrian clothing.

"Inspector Davis. Happy Easter," welcomed Commissioner McManus. "Shouldn't you be with your family in Suffolk?" he asked.

"Indeed, sir, and I do plan on making my way there shortly. However, I was forwarded this missing person's report from my counterpart in Canada. As you requested, we've been quietly monitoring activity related to the individuals you've expressed an interest in, and this report was flagged," Inspector Davis explained, handing Stellan a three-page printed document with the words "Highly Confidential," written in bold along the top.

Margot approached Stellan from behind and handed him his reading glasses while greeting Inspector Davis.

"Happy Easter, Inspector," she beamed at the young man.

"Thank you, your ladyship, and to you as well," he returned.

Stellan read every word on the first page before proceeding to the second. After consuming all the information on the second page, he flipped to the third and final page. With Inspector Davis in front of him, Stellan handed back the package and took off his glasses.

"Any orders, sir?" Davis asked while placing the report into a black disposal bag.

"This has remained off the books?" Stellan wished to confirm.

"Absolutely, sir," Davis replied.

"Contact the Commissioner's office of the Royal Canadian Mounted Police and request an encrypted, offline video call for this evening," Stellan checked his watch. "I'll make myself available whenever the Commissioner is available. I'm unsure of the Canadian Government's protocol, so I suggest we speak to the Cabinet Secretary as soon as possible. In the meantime, station a vehicle and outriders out front and await further instructions," ordered Stellan.

"Yes, sir. Immediately, sir," replied Inspector Davis before turning on his heel and departing his boss's classically British white front stoop.

Stellan closed the door and turned to Margot, who was holding brandy, her face etched with anticipation.

"My chest is tightening," confessed Lady Ambrosia, analyzing the expression on her husband's face.

"Where's the parcel from Mason Valentine?"

Chapter Sixty-Five

"It's so shocking," sighed the real Joyce "Joy" Redstone once Mason had finished sharing select details from events since Labor Day.

Joy sipped her prosecco while continuing to process Mason's story.

"It sounds like something out of a book or a film. I robustly apologize for the role I've played in it," she said, defeat in her voice and expression.

"You are the last person who needs to apologize," Mason replied warmly. His hands were wrapped around a mug of peppermint tea.

They sat in the farthest corner of the Belvedere Brewery's wood-paneled library, which was empty because of the holiday and flood.

"What would be helpful is if you could tell me how you came into contact with Drusilla's imposter," he said.

"Why yes, of course," Joy nodded as she moved her prosecco aside.

"When my grandmother Rosamond was alive, she instilled upon me the importance of delivering the gold box and the four spheres with haste to the Valentine family upon the death of the Senator. Of course, we hoped it would be my mother who would be the one to see out Lady Valentine's wishes, but as you correctly noted earlier, they both died in the same plane crash several years ago.

"The responsibility was thus left with me, and I took it very seriously. As the years collapsed into one another—which happens at my age—I grew concerned that I'd somehow missed news of the Senator's death, which, of course, I hadn't. He simply had longevity on his side!" she laughed. "So, to ensure the moment didn't pass me by, I asked my grandson to arrange one of those alerts the internet sends when a news story is published with certain keywords. You understand what I'm referring to...I hope."

Joy smiled awkwardly, self-conscious about her limited understanding of a Google Alert.

Mason nodded.

"Speed forward a few years, and the day finally came. My inbox beeped with a notice of Senator Valentine's death, and I immediately went to work trying to contact the family, but that proved to be an unexpected challenge. I couldn't find a phone number online for any of the Senator's four children, nor was there one for the Senator himself. I emailed a generalized inbox I found on the Senator's website, but I didn't receive a response. I assumed—with some prayer for good measure—that he and his second wife lived at the same address as when Lady Valentine was alive. I wrote a letter and sent it by courier to his home," she paused to take a mouthful of prosecco.

"Is there any chance you have the delivery confirmation stored somewhere? I'm curious who signed for it," Mason wondered.

"I'm not sure, but I will search my inbox when I'm able."

"Thank you. I'd appreciate that. You were saying that you sent a letter by courier," Mason prompted, eager to hear the rest of the story.

"Indeed...two days later, I received an email from Aida Valentine thanking me for my condolences and informing me that Drusilla Valentine-Brisbane would give me a ring at the number I provided in my letter. I replied graciously and waited. I think it was the next day when the call came through. Drusilla and I—or I suppose the individual whom I believed to be Drusilla—had a charming chat. She mentioned that she had flown to Britain from her home in Italy and would be flying on to Canada the next day. She offered to accept the box and transport it to Canada on my behalf to save me a trip, which I felt was quite considerate, except that I don't live in England. I live in France..."

Mason nodded, realizing why he and Cordelia's search for Joyce in the UK had been fruitless.

"...and I wouldn't have been able to travel to London until the following day when she was to fly to Canada. She graciously offered to move her flight one day to accommodate me since it was important to her mother. I took the Eurostar from Paris the next morning. I met Drusilla at St. Pancras and had a cup of tea. I turned over the box and returned home." Joy finished with a shrug.

"Did you have any inkling that something was amiss with Drusilla? Did anything not quite make sense to you?" Mason asked before eating a handful of peanuts.

"Nothing. She was perfectly amiable. Knowledgeable about the family and the circumstances of the Senator's death. I suppose I noticed she was younger than I'd have thought, but cosmetics nowadays are so advanced it didn't seem too out of the ordinary."

Joy took her final gulp of prosecco while Mason pulled his phone out of his pocket. He opened the screen and swiped to the black and white ATM photograph of faux Drusilla.

"Is this the woman who claimed to be Drusilla?" Mason asked, handing his phone to Joy, who pinched the screen to zoom in.

After scrutinizing the image for a moment, Joy handed Mason's device back to him and nodded.

"Yes, indeed. That is who I gave the box to."

Mason nodded while biting his lower lip and scrolling back to photos taken at Tank's funeral.

"You will probably find this a bit unsettling. The woman you met with is one hell of a dedicated imposter because she indeed flew to Canada with the box. When she arrived, she pretended to be you," said Mason, showing a picture of the fake Joyce Redstone holding the sumptuous gold box containing the four spheres.

Joy shook her head. Her hand was over her mouth, and a glassy film appeared in her eyes.

"My word. This is…shocking," she said through her fingers, "and frightening."

Mason put his phone face down on the table.

"Have you had any contact with Aida Valentine or her family since that first email?" he asked.

"No," she said quickly.

"So, they don't know you're in the country?" Mason wondered, hoping he wasn't frightening the kind woman before him.

"No. No, I can't see how they would unless they're watching me," she replied, her eyes opening wide at the thought.

"Joy, I doubt they're watching you," he reassured the older woman, who released a deep sigh of relief. "You're safe. I promise," he nodded, his eyes sincere. "What would be helpful is if you could find the delivery confirmation for the letter you sent to Aida. That will help me zero in on who plotted the imposter and the sphere swap before the burial," Mason urged while signaling their server for the check.

"It gives a rather new meaning to the term 'burial plot,' doesn't it?" Joy laughed.

"Someone fancies themselves cute with the puns. I give them that," Mason agreed, tapping his credit card on the machine.

Joy stood and looked Mason up and down before placing her hands on his shoulders.

"The Fernsby family did a great deal to keep my family and others in Sussex safe during the war. They were vilified for it, and our inability to return their safety in kind was a matter of considerable regret for my grandmother. So, on my grandmother's behalf, I ask you, Mason—are you safe from danger? If you are not, I'd like to stay with you," she said, her lower lip trembling. The emotion of personal loss and remorse over past wrongs swelled in her soul. Mason leaned in and hugged the woman he'd met a few hours earlier.

"I'm safe," he whispered.

A statement he didn't believe to be true but couldn't in good conscience pass any additional burden onto Joy—she'd done her job. Their hug lingered until Joy's arms went limp, and she pulled back. Tears meandered down her cheeks.

"I'm sorry," she said embarrassed. "I just met you. I suppose it's a mother's prerogative to worry," she conceded.

The two dressed in their coats and walked out of the Belvedere Brewery. With a second, shorter hug, Joy slid into her rented car and, with a wave, drove off.

Mason wasn't sure what to do or where to go. He promised Cordelia that he would drive back to Toronto, yet events had been unfolding at speed since their video call. If Joyce found the delivery receipt before the end of the day, Mason could learn Person X's identity that night or the next morning—Easter Sunday.

Person X likely remained at Norah Tripplehorn's house overnight and knew that Mason found their shrine of Tank. They'd, without a doubt, assume he took photographs for evidence. The walls could feel like they were closing in on Person X, and Mason guessed they were actively dismantling the house of horrors or preparing to destroy it. Mason couldn't ignore that Person X had been several steps ahead of them for months, partly because of the surveillance of their phones and smart devices. It was reasonable to assume that Person X knew about Cici's plan to brief the authorities. The convergence of these factors could cause Person X to make a quick escape unless Cordelia was correct in predicting that they'd reveal themselves in a campy flourish before exiting.

Either way, Mason believed staying close to Highclere for another night was wise—but where to go?

* * *

Mason decided to stay within forty-five minutes to an hour of Highclere and rented a hotel room at the Muskoka Wharf in Gravenhurst. As he closed the door of his modest, though comfortable, room, he drew back the sheer blinds to inspect the lovely vistas of Lake Muskoka, including its famous steamship, the Segwun, which was still docked for winter. The flooding hadn't yet gone further south than Lake Belvedere; however, in due course, this lake would face the same barrage of rising water beds as the northern lakes drained into each other.

Having stopped to eat in the neighboring community of Bala, Mason was set for the night and eager to inspect the images Lady Ambrosia had sent him of Drusilla's and Joyce Redstone's imposter. When Mason first saw faux-Joyce at Tank's funeral, he sensed a familiarity, as if she'd walked out of a warm memory that had been repressed since childhood. What memory that was, Mason wasn't sure, yet he was confident that FauxJo (as he now referred to the mystery woman) was someone he'd met before and spent time with.

For Christmas, Mason digitized his mother's photo albums—all fifty of them—to preserve and keep safe the thousands of photos she'd taken over their lives (nine thousand, eight hundred and forty-one photos, to be exact). During the drive from Highclere, Mason wondered if Apple's facial recognition could identify a young Faux Jo if she appeared in any of Piper's vintage photographs. The technology wasn't perfect, but Mason had limited options without Cici's high-end software at his disposal. He believed so wholly that Faux Jo was part of Highclere's history that she must have been photographed at some point.

Mason opened the Photos app on his laptop and went to the people icon in the center of the search bar. Using Faux Jo's face from the ATM picture, Mason labeled her and asked the program to review additional photos of the person he'd chosen. After confirming that the app had correctly identified her in other pictures provided by Margot, the software went to work, scanning thousands of images, hoping the imposter lurked in the background of a moment from decades earlier.

* * *

"Mason just texted. He's having car trouble and is staying at a hotel on Lake Muskoka," Cordelia shared with Tobias and her mother, Diane, after the children had gone to bed.

"Do you believe him?" asked Tobias.

"I believe he is at a hotel in Muskoka. The tracker says he's there," Cici agreed, opening the fridge, hoping to find an open bottle of white wine.

She knew her anxiety was warranted and rooted in love, but she had to trust that Mason was taking precautions to keep safe. Cici told him to leave Highclere, and he did. She knew no one would look for him at a random hotel on a different lake. Plus, as far as she could tell, no one was tracking him other than her.

Still, it didn't bring Cordelia as much comfort as she'd have liked.

Something felt off.

* * *

Mason sat on the quilted cover of the room's double bed, watching reruns of *The Mary Tyler Moore Show* on Television Classics. He realized he needed a few minutes to separate himself from the facial recognition search to breathe and feel normal again. Mary Richards, Lou Grant, Ted Baxter, and Sue Ann Nivens were the perfect antidote, providing Mason's mind a much-needed respite and distraction for the first time in what seemed like years.

When visiting a bedridden and inconsolable Sue Ann, Ted Baxter accidentally activated her vibrating mattress as Mason's computer chimed the arrival of a new email. Standing and performing the biggest stretch he'd ever remembered, Mason pulled out the desk chair and felt his stomach flip when he saw in the top right corner of his screen that the new message was from Joy Sauveterre.

He moved the cursor toward his mailbox when he noticed another message flashing on the screen. Facial recognition asked Mason to confirm the identity of a close-up, grainy shot of someone sitting in profile.

The quality of the photograph made it difficult to discern facial features, and to Mason's eye, the person was likely nothing more thrilling than a random face in the background of an old photo.

However, curious if the app was suggesting the person might be someone Mason knew—someone already labeled from years' worth of unencumbered iPhone photo snapping—Mason clicked outside of the dialogue box and scrolled to the top toolbar, where he was once again asked if he'd like to confirm additional faces.

He clicked 'yes.'

Instantly, the same grainy picture appeared in a circle, this time with the program assigning it a name.

Mason tilted his head.

Confused.

On the surface, the identification was unremarkable. Yet, it occurred to Mason that he shouldn't have many—if any—new photographs of the individual from the past several days to trigger a confirmation of their identity.

Wondering the origin of the new photograph, Mason double-clicked on the grainy face, which displayed the whole picture for review.

The picture filled the screen.

Mason jumped up in shock.

He held his chest and gasped; the desk chair fell behind him, causing a loud thud.

"No!" Mason said at full volume, grabbing his head. "No," he repeated, lifting the chair off the ground and tucking it under the desk.

His heart raced, and sweat pooled under his armpits. Unable to sit, Mason stood at the desk. He clicked to confirm the identity of the person in question, which led to a second window being populated in real-time with dozens of new photographs—all of them from CCTV cameras in the UK, all of them sent by Margot Ambrosia that afternoon, all of them with Faux Jo in the same frame.

If they were together in London, they were working together, which Mason knew meant one thing.

He'd found Person X, who, along with Faux Jo, flew to collect the gold box and spheres.

Which reminded him that Joyce had just emailed. Mason returned to his computer. His leg was restless, jumping up and down. His mouth was dry, and he was having trouble swallowing.

Holding his breath, he opened the email from Joyce. Attached to it was a PDF delivery confirmation. He felt faint, but Mason knew he had to look.

He tapped to open the file.

There it was.

"Fuck," whispered Mason.

Person X had signed for the letter from Joyce.

They must have flown with Faux Jo to London, stole the spheres, replaced them with silver junk, and built upon a long-time plan to bring down Tank Valentine and his family. A plan built by obsession or vengeance?

Why though? Mason wondered.

Mason picked up his phone to call Cici with one hand while switching windows on his computer with the other. He was about to capture a screenshot of the mosaic of photographs featuring Person X with Faux Jo in London. But before he could, the app asked him to confirm Person X's identity in one last picture.

One Mason himself had taken a week earlier.

He clicked to review it.

There they were again. Mason hadn't realized it at first, but the person in the photo was undoubtedly Person X.

Everything made sense.

Chapter Sixty-Six

Mason hadn't slept. His mind raced, his heart thumped, and a slight headache had formed behind his right eye. As he pieced the timeline together overnight, he realized that Person X had spent decades planning, plotting, integrating, and executing the ultimate act of retribution.

They had all been duped.

Mason pressed send on the email he'd started typing in the wee hours of the morning. It was now 8:20 am on Easter Sunday, and he decided he had to go back to Highclere and destroy the tablecloth with the access codes for the twelve mini "Doors to Nowhere" embroidered into it. He and Cici had been puzzled by how Person X had found the fourth sphere, the only missing key to accessing the vital information Lady Valentine had placed inside the marble box. Before Thanksgiving, they'd hid it in a weighted waterproof toolbox and floated it down to the lake floor with a bungee cord connecting it to a buoy. It should have been impossible to find. Only Mason and Cici knew where it was—except, he realized, that wasn't true.

Mason was packing his bag when his phone dinged with a WhatsApp message from Joyce Redstone.

Mason—I spoke with the family members who assisted my grandmother in fulfilling Lady Valentine's 2002 order. The miniature "Doors to Nowhere" (including the dog vaults they unlock) are reinforced with hardened high-carbon steel. Which means they are almost impossible to drill into with most commercially available tools. The same steel also protects the wiring that runs through the door. My best guess (between the marble shell and reinforced interiors) is that it would take over 500 hours to break into each one without the codes. Good luck! Stay Safe! -Joy

Excellent, thought Mason. When he and Makayla invited themselves into Norah's art studio, the mini doors didn't appear to be damaged, meaning there hadn't been an attempt to open them by force. If there was one thing Mason was now sure of, Person X was so obsessed with their plot to take from the Valentines that they wouldn't go on the run without first learning how to gain access to the vaults. Person X's mission wouldn't be accomplished until doing so, and Mason had to stave off the discovery for as long as possible. If Person X knew how to access the marble box and where the fourth sphere was, they'd know—or would soon learn—about the tablecloth, and Mason needed to get to it first.

He slid his thumb to his contacts and dialed Cordelia, who hadn't returned his texts, emails, or calls in almost twenty-four hours.

"We're sorry, the person you are trying to reach is unavailable. Please try again later," said the automated voice on the other end of the phone.

Where is she? Mason wondered. He didn't have time to think about it. He shoved his phone into his pocket, scanned the room to ensure he had left nothing behind, and departed Muskoka Wharf in Gravenhurst for Highclere Inn & Carriage House.

* * *

"Is there a service outage?" called Cordelia before entering her mother's kitchen. "I keep checking for text messages—but I haven't received anything since around 2:00 am."

"Looks like it," agreed Tobias, standing at the counter. "My phone is in SOS mode only. No Wi-Fi either."

"A network outage? Today?" Cici said with mild disbelief.

Something wasn't right.

Taking a breath, she walked to the landline, picked up the receiver, and tapped Mason's phone number before placing the phone to her ear.

"Weird," she said, moving the phone in front of her and inspecting the number she'd typed. She turned the receiver off and dialed again.

"Nothing. No dial tone," she noted, hanging up the phone.

"It's voice over internet protocol. If the network is down, then your mom's landline would be too," advised Tobias before adding, "but to be safe, I'll reset the modem and see what happens."

"I'll talk to the neighbors in case it's just us," Cici offered before leaving the kitchen. In her experience, genuine coincidences were rare anomalies, and even then, she seldom believed they occurred without some form of human manipulation.

* * *

Mason parked his car at Valentine Chapel and descended Highclere Hill on foot before jumping into the canoe he'd left near the entrance gate the night he ventured to Norah Tripplehorn's house.

With surprising speed and stability, Mason oared his way to Athabasca Cottage. The water level had dropped about an inch since the day before. However, parts of Highclere were still under three or four feet of water.

He emerged from his yellow chariot and ascended the rear steps, frantically hunting for his key. When he attempted to unlock the door, fear coursed through him. A slender beam of light seeped through a minuscule gap between the door and its frame—someone had been or was inside.

Determined, Mason adjusted the keys in his palm, his grip tight on the fob he had activated at Christmas. With bated breath, he nudged the door open using his foot.

A low croak from the door hinges sounded as Mason slid into the house, closing the door behind him. He walked on his tiptoes through the mudroom, and before entering the adjacent living room, he crouched down against the wall and used the camera on his phone to check for uninvited visitors in the front rooms.

No one.

Keeping his shoes on, Mason walked into the living area before checking the dining room, den, and kitchen. All empty.

Sighing in relief, Mason placed his phone on the dining table and climbed the stairs toward the linen closet. He slid the double doors of the walk-in closet open and stood on his tiptoes, reaching to the top shelf to pull down his various seasonal tablecloths.

Mason felt tears in his eyes as he pulled the Twelve Days of Christmas tablecloth from the pile, complete with patterned snowflakes behind each scene. Person X hadn't gotten to it yet.

Placing it under his arm, he closed the doors and returned downstairs just as his phone vibrated. Without picking it up, he looked down to read the message.

I saw you're here. Stay at Athabasca. I have something to show you -Mack

Mason checked the time—he'd have to hit the road within the hour to make it back to Toronto for Easter dinner. Weighing the pros and cons, he decided he could spare a few minutes for a fire and a quick chat with Makayla. Mason wrote back:

Ok. Come now. Have to get to Toronto.

Mason dialed Cordelia's number and placed the phone to his ear.

"We're sorry. The number you have dialed is unavailable. Please try again later," said the automated voice yet again.

"Shit," Mason said to himself as a shudder ran down his spine.

He wanted to jump to conclusions but didn't have enough time to worry. He sent a text message to Tobias and put his phone back on the table.

Mason marched to the double-floor fireplace, opened the glass doors, and tossed the tablecloth inside. He spritzed a few drops of lighter fluid onto the fabric, then reached to the mantle, pulled down a barbeque lighter, and touched the blue flame to the edge of the fibers. The silver embellished threading caught fire, jettisoning flames across the replica tablecloth, jumping from embroidered image to embroidered image. The partridge and her pear tree were aflame while the five golden rings melted into each other. The growing fire ran around a layer of lace before bursting upward through the center of the silk, burning the Christmas tree and its coded bulbs. Tears ran down Mason's cheeks as he watched his grandmother's act of defiance crumble to ash.

Closing the glass doors, Mason returned to the dining table and checked his phone for a reply from Makayla.

Nothing.

Mason was running out of time. He sent Mack a question mark to speed her along and went to the cupboard to take out a drinking glass, which he filled using the water cooler. Nobody trusted the tap since learning of the property's toxic soil. He drank the entire glass in one gulp and sat at the table, waiting for Makayla's reply.

Where is she? Did she find something new at Norah's? Wondered Mason.

Overwhelmed with unease, Mason stood and went to the front windows. He opened the curtains just enough to peek at Stuart and Gil's cottage. The blinds were closed, and the lights were on outside. It seemed Gil had returned to Toronto for Easter dinner.

Mason chewed on his lip as he paced back and forth in the living room. Lost in his thoughts about the tumultuous journey since Tank's death and wondering about Cici's whereabouts, Mason's left foot gave out from under him, causing him to fall to his knees.

"Fuck," he exclaimed with frustration.

Once he regained his composure, Mason resumed pacing, only to have his left foot give out again. This time, he yelped in pain and rubbed his knees before plopping down on the floor, resting his back against the couch.

Feeling lightheaded, Mason touched his chest, noticing his breathing becoming labored. His hands tightened with tension.

"What's happening to me?" Mason asked himself.

His vision blurred, and he felt a heaviness in his limbs.

Mason fought to keep his eyes open, but they kept closing involuntarily.

"No! No, no," he muttered, his focus turning toward the drug-laced water cooler.

"Oh God," he muttered, slowly sliding down the back of the couch until he was sprawled on the floor.

Unable to stand, Mason summoned his remaining strength to roll onto his stomach and drag himself across the wooden floor. Each breath felt like an elephant was sitting on his chest. Desperate to reach the dining table, his energy waned, leaving him unable to move further.

"Come on, come on," he growled, slamming his hand down to push himself onward.

But he had reached his limit.

Mason took a deep breath and rolled over to slide under the table. He tried to push it with his right foot against the underside, but it refused to move. Exhausted, his leg dropped back down.

"Please," he murmured, eyes drooping, feeling his arms go numb.

Mustering his remaining strength, he raised his leg again, this time using the table's edge to kick upwards. With tension in his lower back and pelvis, he managed to tip the table over. Mason's phone and keychain tumbled to the floor and slid into the kitchen.

Still on his back, Mason used his one-functioning leg to push himself toward the kitchen. When he felt his keychain brush against his head, he rolled onto his stomach and grabbed it. With trembling hands, he pressed the silver button on his blue fob.

Straining to keep his eyes open, Mason squinted at the tiny blinking red light on the keychain with his left eye. He closed his eyes, his breaths shallow and erratic. Despite fighting the effects of the poison, unconsciousness was inevitable. Just before he lost consciousness, two hands grabbed his left arm and turned him onto his back.

Mason's eyes fluttered open, his vision blurred. He could just make out the outline of a familiar bald head.

"Gil?" Mason whispered before succumbing to unconsciousness.

* * *

Cici tried to relax on her mother's old couch, but her restless leg wouldn't stop bouncing. The entire subdivision was without Wi-Fi or cell service. She had gone door to door—often catching the irresistible aroma of turkey seasoned with spices and cloves—and every house she visited confirmed the outage.

Every hour that went by, Cici felt more and more restless.

To avoid complete mutiny by their tech-dependent kids, Tobias loaded them in the car for a drive, leaving Cici to stew in her anxiety.

Trying to calm herself, Cici remembered an old meditation technique Drusilla had taught her. She sat in a yoga pose and took a deep, cleansing breath. Just as she began to imagine calming waves, the doorbell rang, breaking her brief moment of peace. She got up to answer the door, finding two sturdy police officers on her mother's porch.

"Is this your home?" they asked.

Cici explained who she was, noticing four more police cars on the street, their lights flashing brightly.

"We received a report from your neighbor. They're out of town for the holiday but were alerted about the internet outage by their security system. After reviewing footage from their door camera, they saw suspicious activity at this house just before the disruption. A woman was seen connecting a device to an outdoor outlet."

"A signal jammer?" Cici interrupted, quickly piecing together the reason for the lack of cell service and internet. Her instincts had been correct.

"We're not sure yet. We want to search the area to ensure it's not an explosive device," said the older officer, who had a salt-and-pepper beard and a scar above his eye. "However, we shot down five drones circling the community, each equipped with wide-reaching cell scrambling capabilities. I suspect you might be right."

"How long will it take?" Cici asked, her worry increasing.

"Not long, ma'am. One more thing—this neighborhood's ingress fiber optic line is about ten blocks away—it was dug up and cut overnight. The line was restored about thirty minutes ago, which allowed us to gather more footage. Do you recognize this person?" he asked, handing her his tablet.

Cici nodded.

Chapter Sixty-Seven

When the police officers disconnected the cell jammer, Cici's phone exploded with urgent messages. Panic-stricken, she turned to her mother, who stood nearby at the kitchen counter. Without a word, Cici read Mason's email sent earlier that morning, outlining his shocking discovery. The last line left her speechless.

"I have to go," Cici announced, sprinting from the kitchen and rushing upstairs to gather her belongings. "Mom, call Uncle David and tell him it's 'go time,'" she instructed before packing a bag.

Within moments, Cordelia darted down the stairs, decked out in black and sporting a backpack. As she tied her boots, Diane's anxiety was palpable.

"What happened?" she asked.

"The person we believed was Joyce Redstone was an imposter. She was outside your house last night cutting communication lines and installing a signal jammer," Cici replied, tucking excess shoelace into her boot. "Mason has uncovered the truth, and now 'they' know. He's in danger."

Before Diane could respond, her cell phone rang. She answered it.

"It's Tobias," Diane said, passing the phone to Cici.

"Tob?"

"Cord, thank God! The blue fob on the keychain is blinking red…"

Without a second thought, Cici threw the phone back to her mother and dashed away.

* * *

Mason shivered as an icy chill swept over him. Sensation slowly returned to his limbs.

"Fuck!" Mason burst out, forcing his eyes open and kicking water into the air.

His hands were bound behind his back with zip ties, tethered to the electric garden fence between the carriage house and the original inn.

Sitting chest-deep in water, Mason surveyed his surroundings and spotted the familiar pressure sensor he had seen at Norah Tripplehorn's. It was rigged to the fence, accompanied by wires leading to a small generator resting on a crate a few yards away. The cruel irony of potentially meeting the same fate as Tank, his namesake and predecessor in death, was not lost on him. However, Mason also had the distinct disadvantage of a water-filled basin to accelerate his demise.

Throbbing pain pulsed through Mason's head as the sun dipped below the horizon and the full moon began its ascent.

"Oh, yay, Mason! Yay," came a voice from behind one of the evergreens. "I'm glad you're finally awake," the voice clapped.

"If this is a meeting of my fan club, I would've happily signed books without the drugging and tying me up bit," Mason joked, attempting to keep calm and take control of the situation as best he could.

"Aww. You're just the sweetest. I have always been a big fan, but I admit," the voice continued, now pretending to talk through one side of her mouth, "I find your writing a bit dullsville," she laughed.

"Really!?" replied Mason with mock horror. "More dullsville than Tank's?"

"I wouldn't know. I didn't read his. I just use the dust jackets for darts practice," she laughed again.

Mason stared in her direction as she left her shield of green pines and walked into the light.

At first, Mason could only see a figure emerging from the shadows—a voluptuous silhouette blurred by the setting sun behind her. But as she drew nearer, his eyes widened in astonishment at seeing a long purple braid cascading over her shoulder.

* * *

"Ninety minutes…an hour forty-five at most!" Cici shouted into her cell phone as she slammed on the brakes, bringing her mother's car to a screeching halt outside Uncle David's house on the Ottawa River.

"She's on her way, and I'll be taking off by boat from her place once we touch down at Belvedere," she added, focusing on the voice on the other end of the phone. "Alright. Stay safe!" she concluded, hanging up and grabbing her rucksack before stepping out of the car.

With a burst of energy, Cordelia darted around the perimeter of Uncle David's majestic home at Rocky Point on Crystal Beach. Appearing from the bushes by the water's edge, she bound down the grassy slope to the beach.

"Uncle David!" Cici exclaimed, waving as she raced toward him, the plane's propellers spinning, ready for take-off.

Cici waded into the ankle-deep water where her uncle stood waiting. He helped her into the cockpit and shut the door behind her. David moved to the pilot's seat, climbed in, and backed the plane away from the shore. The hills of Quebec behind them were bathed in a vibrant pink hue from the setting sun. The engine roared as the plane's nose turned east, propelling the seaplane forward and causing the water's surface to ripple beneath it.

Upon reaching a safe altitude, with the Parliament buildings visible in the distance, David and Cici veered the plane westward, setting their sights on Lake Belvedere and Highclere Inn & Carriage House.

* * *

"Are you surprised?" she asked.

"Oh, come on. The purple wig is a bit much, don't you think?" Mason sighed, shaking his head.

"Sad. I wanted you to think I was your friend, Skye," she said, pulling off the wig and throwing it into the water.

"Valiant effort, I give you credit for that," Mason said, smiling and nodding. "The trouble is I already knew it was you. So, sadly, the wig deflection was wasted on me. Top marks for effort, though!"

"Oh poop," said Bianca Anders as she crouched next to Mason from outside of the electric fence. "Have you known long?" she asked, resting her head adorably on her hand.

"No. Not at all. You did great work there. I realized it was you only yesterday," Mason said apologetically. "I'm sorry if I ruined your fun."

"Never mind that! I marvel at your deduction skills, Mason. What gave me away? If you don't mind me asking. There's always room for improvement with these things," Bianca asked, flicking water against the fence.

"Well, for starters, next time, I'd suggest you wear a disguise in foreign countries. You were caught on CCTV in the UK with the fake Joyce Redstone," Mason explained.

"*THAT* is how you found out?" laughed Bianca.

Mason had to admit she appeared to be enjoying herself.

"It's just so stupid!" she cackled again.

"I suppose I should've figured it out a titch sooner. Probably after you magically appeared at Aida's house the day I was trying to hack into Tank's emails. You were obviously monitoring the place—otherwise, as I said earlier, solid effort," Mason smiled. "I assume his SMS verification code went to your phone via a burner number?"

"Yuppers! Genius, right? It's easy to get fake phone numbers with the last four digits of your choosing," she smiled.

"Clever! Well, if you hadn't tied my hands behind my back, I'd have clapped for you," he admitted.

"Can you whistle?" Bianca asked.

"Sorry, no."

"Smack your lips together?"

"Is that now a form of congratulations?" Mason asked.

"It could be! Oh well," she said, standing up and walking around to the other side of the enclosure. "I have always had faith in your abilities Mason, but even I'm impressed with your deductive skills. I knew Cordelia would be a challenge for me. I even went a bit more hands-on with her, and still, she worked her way around it. I guess I expected that, but you..." Bianca said, placing her hands on the electric fence, causing Mason to wince, "...have been a pleasant surprise."

"You've broadened my horizons," Mason complimented, still looking uncomfortable with the placement of Bianca's hands.

Bianca followed Mason's stare and laughed as she danced her fingers atop the fence.

"Oh! You think this is on?" she giggled while her index and middle fingers did the can-can.

"Can you blame me?" Mason replied.

"I suppose not, but I'm disappointed you think I'd zap you before having our wee chat. Credit where credit is due, Mr. Valentine, and credit I give to you," she said, clapping her hands again.

"So, what's the shizzle then?" Mason asked. "What happens next?"

"Well, thanks to you and Cordelia, I have more loose ends than I'd have liked, so I'm just going to 'tie them up,'" she said in air quotes. "Then we're off!"

"Am I considered one of your loose ends?" Mason asked.

"Well, yeah," she laughed.

"That's kinda rude, Bianca," Mason chastised.

"Oh, is it?" Bianca replied with mock remorse. "I guess one can indeed appear rude in these circumstances," she shrugged.

"Well, bygones and some such," Mason nodded.

Bianca stared at Mason, a smile on her face.

"We've done three canisters around the inn and two around the carriage house," came a voice behind Mason. "We shouldn't need more than that."

Mason knew the voice. He twisted his head and saw Gil walk toward the fence.

"Mason, do you know Gil?" asked Bianca, jokingly introducing the two.

"Yeah, we've met," Mason replied.

"Mace," Gil greeted. "You've lost weight. You were easy to carry," he said.

"Flattered," Mason groaned before looking back to Bianca. "And where is the third one?" he asked.

"The third what, darling?" Bianca questioned, tapping her finger on her chin.

"Oh, please. The skinny one. Acne. Yadda, yadda," answered Mason.

Bianca and Gil looked at each other and smiled.

"I'm right here," called Marko, waving from a second-floor window of the inn.

"Ah!" smiled Bianca. "I forgot, you know our son," she said, moving toward Gil and grabbing his hand.

Mason felt as though that plot twist had punched him in the gut!

"Alight," he mumbled. "I'm big enough to admit I didn't know he was your son. I just knew he was part of your shenanigans," confessed Mason.

"Really?" Marko wondered, still hanging out the window like a Muppet.

"Yeah, sorry, kid! You made a bunch of rookie errors. When you found the Highclere listing from 2013, you claimed to look up family names from Tank's obituary, but Gil's last name wasn't noted in any publications. Also, it's impossible to find the Highclere listing online because it was never distributed digitally—we checked with the development company who put in the offer. Hand-delivered or faxed only. You'd only find it if you had it or made it. They confirmed it looked like the genuine posting, but there were some inconsistencies, and the website where you claimed to have found it doesn't exist. The checkbook you gave Cici, which led us to discover that Louella Stone is Stuart's birth mother, had a copyright date of 2022 on the back flap, and the ink still smelled fresh. She knew instantly it was a forgery—but delighted it was all correct information!

"In fact, she'd assumed since Christmas when you effortlessly found the disposal violation from 1969 that you were working with our Person X. We decided that as long as you were feeding us information, we were pleased to accept it. Obviously, your mother here wanted you to point the finger at Trent. Pushing the report about the Manitoba land dispute was meant to set our sights on Norah, Trent, or both. It was almost clever! But you made it too obvious. Too convenient.

"The only way you'd know about Louella was if you'd read the diaries or knew someone who did before they'd been censored. You also lied about there not being financial transaction records in Tank's emails from the 2012 blackmail. Cici found a handful over Christmas, yet they were magically gone from the hard drive after we gave it to you. Also, Cici found the real Marko, the one who was paid a nice sum to sit out the year so an imposter could take his place, which, by the by," Mason laughed, "you all rely WAY too much on imposters."

"Feedback acknowledged," Bianca said coolly.

"Of course, 'Marko' was also the only person who could have known where we hid the sphere. You'd have seen it on Cici's screen. We tried to tail you a few times, hoping you'd lead us directly to Person X, but no luck," Mason noted, looking up at faux Marko. "What's your real name?" he asked.

"Miles," laughed faux Marko.

Mason guffawed.

"That can't be true," he said, looking to Bianca and Gil, who were unmoved. "Oh, for fucks sake. You named the kid after your mortal enemy?"

Mason rolled his eyes.

"It was Miles who brought us all together; it seemed like appropriate homage," said Gil.

"Well, I'm bored now," announced Bianca. "Gil, honey, turn on the genny. Miles," she turned to look up to her son, "finish up. Then spray the interior of the office."

Gil walked toward the fence-connected generator, and despite the chilly air and freezing water, Mason felt a bead of sweat drip down his forehead.

Think. Think.

"Wait!" Mason called out.

"What?" shouted Bianca, irritated.

"I'm just curious. What exactly are the rules of my captivity?" he asked. "Do I get toilet breaks? Water? I don't want to bug you if I don't have to," he said, dripping with charm.

"Good question," replied Bianca. "I hadn't thought about it," she said, looking down at her boots. "Ugh, I do apologize, Mason—these have been my first real kidnappings. It's an unexpected consequence of your snooping, so this part of the plan isn't as well thought out as everything else I've done," Bianca confessed.

"Oh, think nothing of it. I wasn't criticizing, just curious. Come back to me when you've thought it through," responded Mason.

"Very gracious of you, Mason," smiled Bianca.

"Pleasure, treasure," Mason replied.

Bianca sighed.

"Mason, I've always liked you," she admitted.

"Oh, the feeling was mutual, I promise!" said Mason.

"Was?" Bianca questioned.

"Well, a few points deducted for a decades long con, wouldn't you agree?" Mason squirmed.

"Fair," Bianca nodded. "I think less of you for being so nosey," she admitted.

"We're even then?" Mason suggested.

"We will be."

Bianca clapped.

"Gil. Turn it on."

Gil leaned down and pulled the rip cord of the generator, igniting the engine and powering the fence Mason was tied to.

"Mason," said Gil as he walked toward him. "You know what happens when a toaster falls into a bath, right?" he asked.

"Yes..." Mason said.

"Keep imagining that every time you want to get up," Gil said, smiling, before lifting a branch out of the water and throwing it at the fence, causing sparks to fly.

Mason closed his eyes to shield them from flying embers, and when he opened them again, Bianca, Gil, and Miles Jr. had vanished.

Chapter Sixty-Eight

As the sun disappeared, Mason grew colder. His teeth chattered, his limbs went numb, and the frigid lake water threatened to freeze him.

Mason's memory of the events leading up to his collapse at Athabasca was blurry. He faintly recalled trying to activate the emergency SOS button on his keychain but couldn't remember if he succeeded.

If he had sent the signal, help would arrive soon. But if he hadn't, he was alone. Regardless, he knew he had to keep Bianca talking to buy himself more time.

"Bianca!" Mason's voice rang out through the trees and water.

No response.

Determined, he called out again. This time, he heard splashing in the water.

"Yes, Mason, what can I help you with?" Bianca asked.

Realizing time was running out for him, Mason appealed to Bianca's ego.

"I know it's not the best timing, but since I'll be dead soon, I'd so appreciate it if you could fill in some narrative and timeline gaps for me. Just out of sheer curiosity."

Bianca looked at him, her face impassive.

"Alright," she agreed, a small smile spreading. "It's so hard to stay mad at you. What do you need help with?" she asked while turning off the generator to better hear her captive.

Mason wasted no time.

"When did you first plot your revenge against Tank? Was it around 1987?"

Bianca crouched next to the fence, reflecting on the question.

"Good question," she replied. "I had always fantasized about bringing justice to Miles Valentine, even from a young age. It took me years, but in 1987, destroying him became my life's purpose," she smiled.

"But if I'm not mistaken, you didn't meet him until twenty years later?"

Bianca chuckled.

"Oh, I had met him in various ways long before that. I even rented a room here for a week just to study him. I knew he would forget about me if I didn't flatter him during those encounters. It was my way of getting close, assessing his circle, and finding my way in."

"Did you seek out Laverna?"

Bianca shook her head.

"No, it was a fortunate accident. A twist of fate! I was already working in the brain injury wing before her husband transferred there. Phil had been on my floor for about two weeks when I saw Laverna greeting Miles and the soon-to-be late Jean Valentine at the elevator. They brought flowers and visited her and Phil. It was a stroke of luck for me," Bianca explained in a sing-song voice, a glimmer of satisfaction in her eyes.

"You found your route in," Mason nodded.

"I had," Bianca smiled. "And in truth, it wasn't hard. Laverna told me Miles Valentine would be her ticket to getting Phil home. While marriage wasn't originally her plan, she realized it was the best outcome for him and her mother. Aida would be comfortable, and Phil could be cared for at home. They needed Tank's money, and he was oh so willing to hand it over."

"They conned him?"

"In a manner of speaking, but I take the view that they firmly believed he needed them as much as they needed him. You see, Mason, he didn't like his children; they didn't adore him as he thought they should. True, he tried to force affection and reverence but couldn't make it stick. The Cliftons, however, were prepared to fill the void. Take care of him, give him the family he always dreamed of, and in doing so, they'd be rewarded mightily. If anything, I'd call it a 'low grade' con," Bianca acknowledged. "And it was much easier for me to slip into the mix and do what I had to with two buffoons already playing the man. Who was going to think I wanted anything from him? I was just a 'friend' of his stepdaughter. If anyone were going to look suspicious, it would be Laverna and Aida. So, yay me!"

Bianca grinned while pretending to shake pom-poms.

"Why did you need to kill him? He was one hundred years old. He didn't have many years left," asked Mason.

"Ugh," Bianca grunted, "It wasn't in my original plan. Then I discovered he was going to change his will to leave Highclere to charity, and that was unacceptable to me. He couldn't be permitted to sign it, now, could he? He'd have looked like a hero to the orphans... elephants...or immigrants—whoever he was leaving it to. I wasn't going to let him die a savior. Louise Harris couriered a copy to his house, which I pocketed, hoping he'd forget. He didn't. After he fell, Laverna worried the new will was at Louella Stone's and that if found, it could incriminate them."

Mason blinked four times.

"Incriminate them in what? They didn't plan his fall."

"It was anxiety stemming from a guilty conscience," Bianca sneered.

Mason sighed.

"Do you think your mother would've wanted you to avenge her like this? To hurt innocent people, to cast suspicion on innocent people..."

"They're not innocent!" Bianca interrupted with anger, her pleasant manner gone.

"She wouldn't have wanted you to do this, Bianca," Mason shouted.

Bianca's face reddened as rage gave rise within her. Mason worried he'd gone too far.

He just needed more time.

* * *

"Cici!" called Uncle David through the plane's headset, "We can't land on the water."

"Why?" Cordelia asked, panic rising further.

"There's too much debris in the lake because of the flood. We might land on a barrel and tip the plane. We need a runway," David advised.

"The closest private airport is a thirty-minute drive from Highclere. We don't have that kind of time!" she replied.

"What about a field? Empty stretch of highway or road?" David wondered.

"Actually, I know where one is. It's make-shift, but close to where we need to be."

* * *

Bianca opened the gate of the enclosure and walked toward Mason. She crouched down and took his face in her hand, digging her fingernails into his skin.

"You know nothing about my mother," she seethed.

"I know her name was Caroline Monroe," Mason began, wiggling his head to release the pressure from Bianca's hand gripping his jaw. "I know she was engaged to Tank," he spat out. "I know Tank acted like a callus asshole by dumping her via telegram..." he paused in pain, "...while she was on her way to meet his family and get married. I also know that he kept the wedding plans and date and just changed the bride," he finished as Bianca shoved his head into the fence before releasing him from her grip.

"Can you imagine what that does to someone?" Bianca asked anger in her eyes, veins throbbing from her forehead. "To have been promised a life by someone only to be discarded like a piece of shit because 'he found someone better?' My mother didn't deserve that. What she deserved was the life Jean Valentine had. I deserve the life your father and you led. No Valentine is worthy of what they have because it was supposed to belong to my mother," she said, grabbing Mason's head again and pushing it into the fence once more for good measure.

Bianca towered over Mason.

"She never recovered, Mason. Can you imagine? To be so unwanted by someone? To be viewed as a disposable object by some shithead who didn't deserve her love to begin with? He broke her soul, he broke her life, and she never got over it. You think you can tell me what my mother would've wanted? If you found her bloody body after she'd blown her brains out, I bet you'd feel the same way I do," Bianca hissed, leaving the enclosure.

"Bianca, listen," Mason said, stretching his jaw between words. "He could be an asshole. I'm the first to agree with that. I even called him that to his face when he was alive..."

Bianca smirked.

"...he was a narcissist, and he lacked empathy. It's why he had a piss poor relationship with his family, but you're giving the man too much credit for how your mother's life turned out. Was he that important to her? Was his betrayal really the major inciting incident of her life that sent her off the rails? Of course not. She had free will, Bianca, and from what I'm hearing, a preexisting mental health condition that she couldn't outrun. I saw the picture of you and your family taken during a visit with Louella and Atticus Stone. She wouldn't want you to seek vengeance against us. She'd want you to seek happiness for her, for you, and everyone else in that photograph," Mason pleaded.

"No," Bianca whispered. "She'd want me to do exactly what I've done. None of you deserve the life you lead," she said before adding, "and neither does he," using her chin to point toward the Callahan cottage.

Mason at first stared at Bianca.

But then, it made sense.

"Oh my God," Mason said as a surge of understanding raced through him. "You said Aida and Laverna were two buffoons to hide behind...but there's a third buffoon," Mason said slowly. "That's why you were so insistent on pointing us toward Trent Callahan," Mason scoffed, shocked.

Bianca grinned.

"Oh? Do tell darling," she hissed.

"Your whole motive has been to punish Tank and his family because you believe his actions denied your mother a fruitful, wealthy, happy life—and by extension denied you a fruitful, wealthy, happy life. But, in the process, you found someone who hated Tank just as much as you did, and you tried to be damn sure the blame for the mysteries surrounding the Valentines could point at him because—especially in the moonlight, I see it now—Trent is your biological brother."

Bianca's grin remained as she raised her hands to clap at Mason and nodded.

"As I said, your deductive skills have been a real surprise," she cooed menacingly while clapping.

"According to our research, Trent was an only child. That's why he was so protective of his cousin, Scott Owens, during the Tripplehorn farm debacle—they grew up as brothers—and why he inherited his father's fortune alone. I assume you're the product of an affair by his father?" Mason guessed aloud. "Which is how Caroline came to adopt you. You've been killing two birds with one stone this whole time. Taking from and destroying Tank and the Valentines while pinning it on the brother whose wealth you believe should be half yours."

"Pretty fun, isn't it?" Bianca replied with a scowl. "I'm not even sure Tank was the political figure who pressured the Crown Attorney to send Scott to trial, but it made a great reason to ignite, stoke, and stir up Trent's hate for the Senator. Trent was easy to get worked up. I slid into his life in the late 80s under a fake name and disguise, whipped him into a hateful frenzy, and then vanished. The next time we met, I was Bianca Anders—he had no idea we'd met before. It turns out our penchant for vengeance comes from our father's side," she laughed.

"Well then, haven't you gotten what you came for? You have Tank's money. You stole that through blackmail," said Mason.

"Those diaries were a helpful read," she admitted. "Lots of damaging material. Easy to play on his ego there."

"You've ensured his family knows that he was responsible for his infant son's death and that he ridiculously replaced him with another baby to avoid a scandal. A detail that will now change our entire family structure and our views of both my grandparents. You poisoned our land and drove the value of our most prized possession to almost nothing. You got the marble box, the twelve dogs, and everything else you came for, and you've planted the evidence to point to Trent Callahan. So why not just walk away now? You, Gil, and Miles Jr? Go live your lives."

"We will, but first, we gotta toast the evidence and the witnesses. It's all gotten messier than I hoped," said Bianca, walking toward the generator.

Mason whipped his head to look at her.

"Witnesses?" Mason asked. "More than just me?"

"Come on, Mason. You know you're not the only person who could squeal on us," she replied with smug satisfaction.

Mason thought.

Who?

Oh no!

"No!" he called out. "Leave them. They're not up on what we know. Bianca, I'm fair game. I'm Tank's flesh and blood, but they aren't. They are victims of his narcissism as much as you are. As much as I am. Let them go. I beg you," Mason said, fear and tears in his eyes.

Bianca stared at him. Motionless. Unnerving Mason.

"No," said Bianca, inserting the rip cord into the generator before pulling it back out, igniting the machine again. "It'll be a hot time in the old town tonight!" she sang at Mason before looking at the inn's second floor. "Miles?" she shouted.

"I'm down here," Miles Jr. replied from around the corner of the inn. "I've sprayed the hallway and the room door where we put Mrs. Stone and Stuart. I also dumped four more canisters."

"Where's your father?" she asked, looking at the sky as a plane flew overhead.

"He took the empty canisters next door, then was going building to building to collect pieces for kindling," Miles Jr. replied.

"What are you spraying?" Mason asked, his heart sinking.

Mother and son looked at each other, then to Mason.

"You'll know soon," said Bianca, walking toward Miles Jr. "Oh, and Mason," she said, turning around. "I'll make sure a choir sings that Spice Girls song you like so much at your funeral. 'Viva Forever,' is it?" She laughed before singing the lyrics and walking away.

* * *

Guillaume Regan was searching for a hammer, chain, and nail gun when he stumbled upon a striking long feather in the kitchen of Athabasca Cottage.

Gil approached the feather, stooped down, and picked it up. Its exquisite beauty and flawless texture captivated him, relishing the softness as it graced his fingertips.

Tucking the feather into his pocket, Gil made his way toward the door when a shovel smacked him in the face, causing him to crash to the ground. Before he could comprehend what had happened, a second blow landed squarely on his head.

* * *

Louella Stone's eyes fluttered open, filled with confusion and uncertainty. She found herself lying on a yellow carpet, her gaze fixed on a ceiling fan. The sound of movement caught her attention, alerting her to the presence of another person in the room.

Despite her immobility without her wheelchair, the elderly woman summoned every ounce of strength to lift her torso and survey her surroundings. As her eyes swept from wall to wall, she realized she was inside Highclere, specifically the sprawling "groom's room" on the inn's second floor.

With sheer determination, Louella used her arms to shift her body and turned just enough to lay eyes on Stuart, lifeless and unmoving on the floor across from her.

* * *

Cici sprinted toward Norah's cottage, weaving through clusters of trees and overgrown grass.

"Cordelia!" Norah shouted from the deck.

"Norah!" Cici called back, racing toward the older woman.

"They're coming!" Norah confirmed, taking Cici's hand and hurrying to the art studio on the other side of the property.

For a moment, they let go of each other as they maneuvered through the dark pathway of pines that separated the buildings.

Once they reached the other side, Norah grabbed Cici's hand again and led her into the building. The windows and doors were wide open, and all the lights were on. Cici stopped in the center of the room, turning in a circle to absorb the madness of Bianca's shrine to Tank. Her hand covered her mouth as she muttered her horror.

"It's sickening," Norah said, helping Cici find the right words. "It's a manifestation of obsession fueled by vengeance against a man and his family."

Cici's mind raced. Mason was right. It all made sense.

Out of the corner of her eye, Cici saw the twelve "Doors to Nowhere." As she walked toward them, an air horn emanated from the lake.

"She's here!" Norah informed, pulling Cici's arm and sprinting back to the main building.

"The police are on their way?" Cici confirmed again, evading branches in their path.

"Yes, they are."

The two dashed across the lawn toward a grassy slope with stairs leading down to the dock. Cici spotted Makayla waiting for her in a small steel boat with the outboard motor running.

Norah stayed at the top of the stairs, cheering them on.

"Good luck to both of you!" she hollered as she watched Cici leap over the last few steps and land in the waiting boat.

Makayla pushed them away from the dock, and the two waved back at Norah as they set off toward Highclere.

* * *

Mason gingerly wriggled his hands and wrists, trying to free himself from the zip ties without putting pressure on the fence and activating the sensor. He felt a tear in his skin and watched as blood swirled in the water around him.

"Fuck," Mason said.

His bravado and mock humor from earlier had well left him. Mason supposed that this was the end of the road. For a boy who used to let fear dictate his actions, he was undoubtedly going out a changed man. Sooner than he had hoped, but he couldn't deny that he had lived a life he was proud of. He made a difference to others and worked to better himself, his family, and the community. What more could he hope for?

He bowed his head, prepared to resign to his suspected fate, when he heard "Mason" whispered from behind him. "Do not move," the voice advised.

"Skye?" Mason asked, unconvinced it was his friend.

"Shh," she urged. "I'm going to cut the ties. Take a second to catch your breath, and when you're ready, give me a sign, and I'll power down the generator, and we'll bolt," she instructed.

Mason nodded, and seconds later, he heard the snap of the ties breaking in two as he removed his hands from their prison and rubbed warmth and blood back into them.

"I'm aroused by your granny badassery," Mason whispered to Skye as he repositioned himself into a low crouch, looking at the windows of the inn and peering around the side of the building to make sure Bianca, Miles Jr., or Gil weren't coming. He turned and saw that Skye, with her bright smile and purple hair, had stealthily hustled to the generator.

Mason gave one more cursory look before turning to Skye and giving her the thumbs up. Skye flicked the generator off. Mason opened the fence, ran to Skye, grabbed her by the hand, and the two ran through the water to the far side of the carriage house.

Chapter Sixty-Nine

"Mack, veer around Thomson Island—we need to approach Highclere from the west. We'll dock directly on the lawn," instructed Cordelia to Makayla, who skillfully navigated the boat, avoiding floating obstacles.

"Not a problem!" Makayla shouted in response.

"What's our estimated time of arrival?"

"Ten minutes."

* * *

Mason and Skye dashed into the narrow strip of forest that separated the carriage house from the Callahan's, trying to catch their breath. The high water levels had left them panting for air as they came to a stop.

"Skye, I can't thank you enough," Mason gasped, trying to regain his composure.

"Yea, yea. Save it for later," she interrupted, pulling a hidden duffle bag from the trees.

"I've got dry clothes and your lace-up black boots."

She handed the bag to Mason.

"They've got Stuart and Louella trapped on the inn's second floor," Mason whispered, getting undressed behind a large balsam tree.

"What are they planning to do?" Skye whispered back.

"I don't know! They said something about kindling and have spread some substance around the inn and carriage house. They've been spraying the inside walls and doors too," Mason replied, now down to his black skivvies. "Oh, Skye. You brought Spanx!"

"We can't afford to have any extra flab bouncing around right now," Skye replied, glancing down at her stomach.

* * *

"Did the generator turn off?" Bianca asked Miles Jr. as they stood at the roundabout.

"It is quiet," he confirmed.

"Shit," said Bianca, seizing Miles Jr.'s arm before stomping through the water toward their captive.

They passed the office windows, trudged across the sodden lawn, and made their way to the electrified enclosure between the inn and the carriage house. As Bianca's pace eased, her jaw clenched in disbelief and fury. The generator was dead, the gate wide open, and Mason had vanished.

"Fuck!" Bianca angrily exploded as she stormed to the generator, violently tossing it into the water. The splash echoed amongst the stillness of the night air.

"He must be nearby. He'd have passed us otherwise," said Miles Jr., trying to soothe his raging mother.

"Mason Valentine is intimately familiar with these woods, you useless shit," Bianca snapped, her voice dripping with venom. "Let's smoke him out."

* * *

"Did you hear that?" Skye asked, her eyes fixed on the forest's edge after an unintelligible shout and splash.

"I think she's onto me," Mason suggested, now appearing in dry all-black attire, including a utility vest and leather gloves.

"Mace," Skye said, approaching him, "from what you told me, I think they're planning to torch the place."

"What? She wouldn't!" Mason whispered. "It's not gasoline they're spreading. It doesn't smell."

"They might be using bioethanol fuel, which doesn't smell like gas. Think about it. Highclere is the evidence. The poisoned pipes, the investigation corkboards, the toxic ground. Burning the inn could ignite the forest—a forest with petroleum in its soil—which would be the perfect way to get rid..."

Bang!

Skye stopped abruptly when an explosion occurred in the water nearby.

"Oh shit! Gun!" Skye stammered as another shot rang out, knocking off a branch from an old pine.

Mason grabbed Skye's arm and pulled her behind a tree.

"Skye, you have to go. Head northeast a few meters deeper into the forest. You'll find an old treehouse belonging to the Callahan's. Go there and stay safe!"

"No, I need to stay with you," Skye protested.

"Once it's clear, come back and make sure Stuart and Louella get out of the inn," Mason instructed, pushing Skye in the right direction. "Go!" he whispered.

Skye then ran through the muddy water to find safety.

Mason looked up and knew his next move. Clinging to a sturdy branch, he anchored his foot against a knot in the tree bark and used his limited muscles to pull himself up to the lowest hanging branches of the ancient maple tree. Bit by bit, he climbed higher until he could transfer to a nearby evergreen—at which point he knew he was hidden from view.

* * *

Bianca armed herself with Hollis Valentine's old shotgun and ventured into the creepy, flooded forest. With her weapon ready, she scoured the shadows for her target, Mason Valentine.

No sign of him.

Undeterred, she pressed deeper into the woods. With each step, the meager light from the inn grew dimmer, swallowed by towering trees.

Bianca searched left and right but found no trace of anyone.

In frustration, she cocked the shotgun and unleashed a wayward bullet into the unknown. She pivoted and fired another shot into the dense brush before reloading and shooting two more rounds into the barren branches above.

Satisfied, Bianca retraced her steps back to the carriage house.

* * *

Louella crawled along the worn carpet with waning strength until she reached Stuart's motionless body.

With a trembling voice, she whispered, "Please, be alive," as she touched his face with the back of her hand. Pressing her ear against his chest, she exhaled a sigh of relief when she heard his faint breaths. Exhausted and chilled, Louella rested her forehead on her son's arm. She had to ensure Stuart's safety.

Gently tapping his cheek, she pleaded, "Stuart. It's Louella. Wake up."

* * *

Makayla silenced the boat engine just fifty feet from Highclere, allowing silence to cloak their arrival. Makayla and Cordelia gripped paddles and propelled themselves toward the expansive drowned lawn surrounding the carriage house.

With one powerful stroke of their paddles, the steel boat glided to a halt and grounded itself on the shore.

"I'll track down Mason and Skye. You find your grandfather," Cici instructed Makayla, her tone urgent. "And once you have him, go!"

Makayla nodded in agreement and stepped out of the boat before heading toward the property's forest border. From there, she would circle to the far side of Highclere through the back 39 acres.

* * *

Mason watched Makayla journey beneath his hideaway, using the dense terrain to camouflage her movements.

"Cici must have arrived," Mason said to himself as he descended from the tree and moved toward the edge of the lawn. Crouching behind a bush, he watched Bianca and Miles Jr., thinking through his next move.

* * *

"Here you go," Miles Jr. said to Bianca outside the inn, handing her a baseball bat with bioethanol-soaked fabric around the top.

"Thank you, darling," said Bianca before clearing her throat. "Attention, Mason Valentine!" she shouted, her voice echoing through the stillness of night.

"Truly, I must admit this has been a thrilling delight for me, as I'm sure it has been for you. You are cleverer than I gave you credit for, and I'm sure you're delighted to hear that. What with your robust ego, something you inherited from your grandfather yadda yadda. Now, I have a proposition for you," she shouted as she pulled a lighter out of her pocket. "As you can well imagine, I need to skedaddle, yet I suspect you won't allow me to do so, which is a bit of a bummer. So, here's the deal—if you show yourself and willingly wait in the inn, you, Louella, Stuart, and your beloved inn will live to see tomorrow. If you don't, well then," she continued as she flipped the lid of the silver lighter open, emitting a flame from within. "Then you'll have at least two deaths on your conscience. You have thirty seconds," she concluded, igniting the bioethanol-soaked fabric, engulfing the bat's tip with a large, untamed flame.

* * *

Mason remained in place; his eyes narrowed on Bianca. He felt his heart race. His palms had become sweaty in their gloves. He felt frozen in place. Fear pulsed through him. He knew it was a trap. No one was going to win, regardless of what he did. At least, if he could get closer to Bianca, he might have a chance of gaining control of the situation or providing cover while Cici worked to release Stuart and Louella.

Mason took a breath, steeled himself, stood to his full height, and stepped out of the trees' darkness into the lawn's light.

"Ok!" Mason shouted to Bianca as he walked toward her with his hands up.

"I didn't say you had to have your hands up, Mason."

Bianca rolled her eyes.

"A dramatic queen, aren't you?" she laughed as he moved toward her.

"Oh, pish," Mason scoffed. "You're calling me a drama queen? This from the lady who decided she needed to get back at the man who hurt her mommy's feelings?" he mocked. "That's right. Your mother was dumped nearly *eighty* years ago, and you're such a snowflake that you *just* had to seek revenge on the man's family. Give me a fucking break," Mason spat out, rolling his eyes.

"This is almost a sexy side of you, Mason," replied Bianca, her face visible in the light from her makeshift torch. "It's a stupid side. But sexy," she added.

"Oh, thank God!" Mason mocked. "I've always wanted to be fawned over by a nutjob like you," he said. "Ribbit ribbit," Mason spat at her, followed by a single clap, taunting Bianca before repeating it. "Ribbit, ribbit," he croaked again slowly, menacingly at Bianca with disgust. "Tell me, oh queen of the frogs, what bit are you the proudest of?" he asked just feet away from Bianca.

She grinned.

"My favorite part," she paused, "has been watching all of you scramble to prove that Miles Valentine loved you."

Mason stopped—surprised.

"What?" he whispered.

"That shithead takes your precious Highclere from you in an underhanded way, yet you don't take him at his word. 'He *must* have been manipulated,' you all think. By whom? The Cliftons? Me? 'He *can't* have hated us *that* much,' you all beg God to be so. Yet you search for his posthumous acceptance, failing to believe his actions were his own. Your grandmother knew he didn't love you. She knew your fate and who her husband was. Yet, you all still didn't want to believe it. 'He was blackmailed out of his money? So wretched!' you all whine, but why did he give in? To hide his abhorrent behavior at watching his tiny baby die, then just replace him with the next available child that comes his way. Sure, that's an act of a loving father—NOT!" she taunted.

"So, he pays me off to save himself and then blames it on the very son he virtually stole to solve a problem of his own making. Did he tell you that the back 39 acres had become a biohazard years ago? No. Why? Because he wanted to leave you with the stinking mess. I might have done the poisoning, but he's the one who signed nature's death warrant and allowed Highclere to become worthless. He could've dealt with it years ago—though I admit I would've just kept going—but he made it easy for me. He came up with an asinine theory about where the chemicals were coming from, and that was that," Bianca smiled. "His money is mine, his house is Aida's, his resort is poison, his son is a bastard he bought after killing the first one. Your grandmother's things, I'm sure, will also soon belong to me because I'm far more intelligent than you.

"All. He. Loved. Was. Him. Self. And his family wants to blame his failings on everyone else rather than accepting him for what he was. So, my favorite part, Mason, has been watching you and your undeserving family march around for the last six months, desperately looking for alternate facts and proof he loved you. It's pathetic," Bianca finished, spitting out her last line just inches away from Mason before adding, "My second favorite was watching his skull smoke after he fell," she smiled.

"You're a cunt, you know that?" Mason said, reaching for Bianca's arm to grab the fiery bat.

"Feeling's mutual," Bianca replied, throwing the torch next to the inn before Mason could stop her. The flame catapulted across the streams of fuel floating on top of the flood water.

"No!" Mason shouted, running to the stack of old wooden boards he and Oliver had placed next to a tree days earlier.

He picked up a large square one and walked toward Bianca.

"Hey, B!" Mason called.

Bianca turned to face him, and with one swing of the board, he slammed it into Bianca's face, knocking her into the water.

"Viva forever that, you bitch!" he seethed.

As he threw the board aside, he noticed the word "ZAPPO" painted on one side.

"Mason!" Cici shouted, running from the front of the inn.

She stood next to her cousin as they watched the fire loop around and attached to the 150-year-old building's wood siding before the uncontrolled flames split course and propelled toward the carriage house. The fire affixed itself to the outside of Tank's old living space and rapidly climbed upward.

"Oh my God," Mason shouted, holding his hands to his head. "We have to get Louella and Stuart out," he cried as the fire caught hold of aged wires and shot to the inn's roof.

"Are they..." Cici asked, panicked.

"In the groom's room!" Mason replied. "You try going from inside. I'll try from the outside," he instructed.

Cici sprinted toward the inn's door, and Mason went to the old steel trellis running alongside the west side of the building.

* * *

Smoke billowed into the groom's room. Louella lay low, trying not to inhale. She could feel heat radiating through the walls and the floor.

"Oh, dear," she cried, shaking Stuart. "Wake up, boy! I can't lose you too!" she shouted as someone started banging against the door.

"Hello?" Louella called to the banging. "We're in here!" she shouted in her hoarse voice,

"This is Louella Stone. I'm here with Stuart Valentine!"

The banging stopped. After a moment, the head of an axe chipped through the wood.

* * *

Cici smashed through the inn's door. The fire had already engulfed the office and destroyed the boards of evidence she and Mason had collected.

Covering her mouth, she pushed through ash and falling debris between the foyer and the dining room when she tripped forward, landing on her hand. Cici cried out in pain as she flipped over to see Miles Jr. standing above her, holding the shotgun.

"Professor," Miles Jr. greeted Cordelia, smoke and flame rising behind him.

"Marko," Cici said while standing up. "We both need to get out of here alive," she urged, holding out her hand, signaling for him to give her the gun.

"No. We don't," he replied cocking the gun.

Chapter Seventy

Mason climbed the trellis to the second floor. Looking through the window, he saw Louella and Stuart on the ground.

"Oh God," Mason muttered as he clung to the third-floor window ledge, determined to reach the groom's room. The flames had engulfed the ground beneath him. He glanced up, noticing the roof ablaze, its fiery tendrils piercing the night sky.

Mason kicked in the groom's room window as a shot echoed from below.

"Cici!?" he called into the fiery night.

The flames closed in, forcing him to jump into the room.

"Mason!" Louella coughed.

"Save your energy, Mrs. Stone. I'll get you out of here," Mason huffed as the axe at the door broke through the top half, revealing Skye on the other side.

"Skye!" Mason shouted, sprinting across the room to pull the door as Skye kicked.

"Harder Mason," Skye called as she kicked the bottom of the door.

"You're going to have to use the axe on the bottom, too," Mason urged as he pulled.

* * *

"You always were a pussy," Cordelia said to an unconscious Miles Jr., having knocked him out with the heel of the gun after he fired.

"Cordelia!" called a voice from outside.

The fire blocked the door she'd come in from.

Cici's voice trembled, "Hello?"

Through the flickering inferno, she caught sight of Gil's battered face. Steely determination filled her as she raised the gun, aiming it at him. Her words cut through the tense air.

"Piss off, Gil."

"Wait, Cordelia," Gil urged. "I have to get you out! I have to get Stuart and Louella out."

"Don't try, Gil. I will shoot you. I know you're in this with Bianca and Marko," she shouted, her eyes intense and precise.

"No. Cordelia—it was an act," Gil pleaded. "I convinced Bianca to let me in so I could stop her and protect everyone. He's not my son. I faked DNA results so Bianca would trust me," he shouted.

The ceiling of the office caved in.

"I don't believe you!" Cici replied. "Wait, what? Your son?" she asked, perplexed.

"You must have missed that," he grimaced. "Cordelia, listen. When this is done, look at the enclosure's fence where Tank fell! I disconnected three sides from the generator. Mason was always safe. He wasn't going to trigger a surge. His side was cold. I prom...Cici behind you!"

Miles Jr. grabbed Cici's throat from behind and dragged her backward.

Cordelia snapped her head back, knocking out Miles Jr. with her skull, before turning and kicking him square in the chest. She dove to the ground as the floors above the stairwell collapsed into the basement.

Ahren covered Gil with a tarp before rushing into the fire to rescue Cici and Miles Jr.

* * *

Skye turned to see a section of the third floor falling away, taking the stairs with it.

"Mason!" Skye called. "We're trapped."

Mason did a 360, taking in the room. Fire poked through the wood floor in the hallway, and smoke emanated from the yellow shag carpet beneath him.

"We'll have to go out the window," Mason yelled at Skye, who had pushed the door open.

"Mason, take Stuart!" Louella called, feeling the heat on her fingers.

"We'll get you both out," Mason promised as he went to the window.

"Mason!" called Makayla from below, carrying a fire extinguisher.

She ran with Cici as Gil followed.

"Mack! We've got to get Louella and Stuart out of here. Skye is with me," he yelled before looking at the carriage house, which was entirely in flames. Out of the corner of his eye, Mason saw swirling lights on the water slowly heading their way.

Police helicopters flew toward the property from the north.

"Cici, flames are poking through—we have to get them out," he advised, turning to look at Stuart, Louella, and Skye. "Skye...I don't...I don't know what..." his voice faded before cracking.

He was exasperated, unsure what to do, and verging on tears as he looked to his friend for inspiration.

Skye assessed the room.

"Hand me the sheets," she said, and Mason did so.

"We're going to use sheets as a sling," Skye instructed as she pulled one sheet under Stuart. "We're going to put each of you in one, then drag you to the window and try to lower you down using tied sheets as a rope," she commanded.

"Stuart first!" begged Louella.

"We're not leaving either of you," Mason argued as he slipped the comforter under Louella.

Flames from below burst through the carpet on the opposite side of the room. The fire ricocheted up the far wall, devouring the wallpaper and ancient carpentry. Mason went back to the window.

"Mack, throw me the fire extinguisher," Mason yelled down to Makayla who did so. Mason unpinned the red canister and fired the white solution against the outside wall, trellis, and part of the eaves, windowsill, and inside wall, extinguishing enough flames to buy more time. He threw the empty cylinder back down.

"Skye, you need to be on the trellis," Mason ordered as he turned from the window to drag Stuart across the floor.

"It won't hold me," Skye protested.

"Skye, it has to be you. If I can't get out, that's okay. I'm not letting you die because of a nut job," he said, pushing her toward the broken glass.

"But Mason..." she turned to face her friend, tears glistening.

"Go."

Skye climbed out the window using the flimsy third-floor ledge for balance. She extended her right leg into a square cavern of the trellis before swinging her body toward it. The upper screws of the trellis had loosened as the wall increasingly burned away.

"Mason—I'm ready!" Skye called.

Mason went to the window.

"Throw this over the top bar of the trellis and pull it like a pulley," he said, throwing the tied sheets to Skye.

Skye threw her end over the metal top and descended a few feet to ensure it wouldn't give out when the rung beneath her foot snapped, causing Skye to fall backward into the water.

"Skye!" shouted Cici as she ran to her friend.

"I'm ok," Skye said, winded. "Cordelia, you have to go up," she coughed.

Cici sprinted to the trellis, jumping over low flames, and pulled her body upward until she could reach the sheets.

"Ready!" Cici called to Mason, who hung his head out of the window.

"What happened?" Mason asked.

"Later!" Cici argued as Mason went to the floor and pulled his uncle to the window ledge.

"Mrs. Stone, remind me to get a trainer," he huffed.

"I'll pay for it," she quipped.

Cici felt the sheets loosen as Mason lifted Stuart off the ground. Cici pulled down, lifting Stuart from Mason's arms and up and over the windowsill.

"Got him!" Cici called as she lowered Stuart into the arms of Gil and Makayla.

"Yes!" shouted Mason as he turned to Louella. "Your turn now," he said, tugging at the sheet beneath her.

"No," Louella said. "You go."

Mason looked at her.

"No, I'm getting you out," he said, pulling her toward the window.

"Mason, this is it for me. It's time. Remember what I said to you at my house?" she asked, embers falling around her.

Mason shook his head and felt tears sting his dried, burning cheeks.

"You have a son to live and *die* for," he said, his lips trembling.

"The key is knowing which you need to do," she coughed. "Mason. Please go."

Mason looked at the old woman, resignation in her face. She had the eyes of someone who knew she was about to be reunited with the people she loved and missed the most. Mason even wondered if he saw a bit of excitement and relief.

Still, he couldn't do it.

"No," Mason replied. "I'm getting you out," he said, pulling Louella to the window. "Cici, the sheets!"

Cici flung them to him. He leaned down and tied them tightly around Louella's sling.

Mason lifted the much lighter Louella to the windowsill. Cici felt slack on the sheet rope and pulled when suddenly the old industrial kitchen and propane tanks beneath them blew. Cici, still holding onto the trellis, flew backward into the water. The trellis fell on top of her as the west wall detached from the inn and fell away toward Skye, Makayla, Gil, and the unconscious Stuart.

Louella's brittle body fell back to the ground. The force of the explosion hurled Mason across the room. Louella moaned in pain as she lay flat on the carpet, fire rising from the floor beneath her. Mason crawled toward her, their tear-streaked faces locking gazes. With a desperate grip, Mason clutched the frail hand of the elderly woman, unwilling to let go. They were in it together until the end.

Their grip tightened as the ground beneath them crumbled, condemning them to the fiery abyss below.

Chapter Seventy-One

Four months, twenty-nine days, and twelve hours later...
* * *

Baroness Margaret "Margot" Ambrosia linked her arm through Piper Valentine's as they tearfully descended the sun-drenched grassy slope from the burial plot toward the footpaths of Highclere Inn & Carriage House.

"Pitch-perfect service, I do believe," Margot suggested with a smile as they made their way to the ruins of the old inn for a second ceremony.

The heat of the late summer day activated the smell of stale char and bonfire from the decimated buildings, which hung thick in the air.

"It was just right, wasn't it?" Piper agreed, wiping her eyes and avoiding eye contact with the eleven moving trucks lined along the road, now filled with the remaining belongings of the Valentine family. "I'm so glad you could be here today," Piper told Margot.

"Of course! Stellan and I wouldn't have wanted to be anywhere else," Margot replied with a heartfelt smile as the parade of family and close friends, including Angel Conner with pet squirrel Lenore, Roland and Viviane Mast, Norah Tripplehorn, Geneviève Talbot, Joy and François Sauveterre, Ahren and Makayla Dawn, the Fishers, and Trent and Kendell Callahan, marched along the pebbled roadway en route to the grassy beach, which had lost most of its loose sand when the flood waters receded during the spring.

"In my humble opinion, no funeral is complete without a bombing of bird shit and a touch of Julie Andrews!" Mason shouted from the water's edge to the approaching mourners descending the lawn's steep section.

"Mason!" his mother shouted back, rolling her eyes.

"What? He'd agree!" Mason laughed, steadying himself using a Mary Poppins parrot head umbrella as a cane while his leg continued to heal from the events of Easter.

"Don't make me have to put you in a timeout," Skye chimed in, dressed in a vibrant rainbow-colored traditional ribbon skirt as she took Mason's left arm to assist him in walking toward the circle of chairs arranged for the guests.

One by one, the mourners took their seats, Drusilla Brisbane next to Cordelia, Tobias, and their children. Oliver and his wife, Angelica, sat with his mother, Piper, and his sister, Jeannie, and her husband, Forrest. Lawrence took his place by his sister Jocelyn and her husband Ezra, while the rest of the attendees scattered amongst the remaining chairs, some of whom stood behind the circle.

The breeze was warm. The lake sparkled like diamonds on the water in the late afternoon sun. Boats slowed to get a better look at the gathered crowd and the eerie decimated remains of the lake's oldest building before moving along and leaving the assembly of people their privacy.

Holding a large seashell filled with buffalo sage and cedar in her right hand, Skye walked into the center of the circle, her smile wide, warm, and welcoming.

"Aanii Boozhoo, and welcome. I'm Skye Cadieux. My spirit name is 'Guardian of Sky Medicine.' I'm a Knowledge Keeper from Treaty One in Manitoba, although I've lived in 'Tkaronto' for ten years. I'm a mother and a grandmother, and I'm honored to be with you today for this special ceremony," she greeted while turning in a circle, beaming her smile to all the attendees to ensure they felt welcome and seen.

"In this shell, I've combined three of our sacred medicines, which we will use to smudge as a group and smudge the environment. A smudge is an act of clearing the air, the mind, the spirit, and the body. Smudging allows us to stop, slow down, and become mindful and centered. It allows us to be grounded and to let go of negative feelings and thoughts. The type of feelings that inhibit a person from being balanced and present," Skye shared.

"The first medicine I have is sage. The smoke from the sage drives away negative spirits and will cleanse us and this place of the darkness that befell it in March. I've also sprinkled in cedar, which will help carry our prayers to Creator and further cleanse our energy. Lastly, tobacco—which is one of the most sacred medicines in my culture—will help to carry our thoughts to the spirit world, to Creator, and to the loved ones and relations who are no longer in our physical world," Skye explained while striking a match and touching the flame against the dried leaves of sage.

Skye gently blew on them as the flames flickered into view, transforming the fire into a comforting haze that wafted from the embers of the shell. Skye fanned the smudge with a feather, intensifying its warmth, and invited Cordelia to join her. Handing Cordelia the shell, Skye smudged her ears, eyes, mouth, and body. Thanking Creator when she'd finished, she invited Cici to do the same, which she did.

"Cici will now go around the circle, and if you'd like to smudge, you're welcome to. There is no right or wrong way to do it as long as it is done with an open mind and heart," said Skye, handing the shell to Cici, who turned and started with Lawrence, who stood to envelop himself with the cleansing smoke.

Skye turned once more to the group.

"We're here for many reasons today," she began. "Of course, we mourn the loss of our family members, the loved ones who died while being selfless. Those who ran into the fire when most would've run away. Their souls were lifted to Creator that very night on the back of the last plumes of smoke released by the inn before she, too, returned to the earth to rest after having provided shelter, love, and community for 150 years to the Valentine family and all who've lived within her. Their spirits will forever be one with this beautiful place. In the soil, in new life and budding trees, the ashes of the past fertilizing the future, leaving traces of personality and soul in every blossom, breath, and birdsong that comes next.

"I watched as Gil Regan ran into the inn that horrible night. My ears were ringing from the kitchen explosion when Gil shouted for Mason and Mrs. Stone, who'd fallen into the basement—buried beneath burning debris," Skye placed her hand on her chest, her eyes glassy with tears. "The fire department and their barges were almost to shore, but Gil knew Mason and Louella didn't have time to wait. He walked resolutely into that fire, and when he resurfaced with Mason sometime later, we cried with relief that a miracle had happened. Mason was alive. We were hopeful Mrs. Stone could be saved, too. But when Gil went back for her, we faced a sad and all too frequent truth; eventually, even miracles must play by the rules of Creator's divine design. In all its fury, the fire made it impossible for Gil to fight his way back out.

"We should all take solace in the knowledge that Gil and Louella were together when they died. They both knew and had experienced love and family and the love of one specific person at that," Skye stopped to compose herself, tears escaping her eyes.

The memory washing back over her was overwhelming. She could almost feel the smoke from that night sitting in her lungs even months later. Looking around the circle, she sought comfort in the misty expressions of those gathered in grief. Primal loss permeated every soul—love due to loss and loss due to love.

"We thank Gil and Louella for what they meant to this family and this place. They now both rest in the burial plot with their other loved ones, reunited in Sky World forever.

"And now we have one more difficult goodbye today, and that is to this place."

Skye opened her arms wide, her palms and face looking toward the heavens.

"Highclere Inn & Carriage House has been the tissue that has connected all of you for generations," she continued, looking around the circle again. "It was never just buildings or land, not for the political family who owned it, not for the guests who visited every year, and not for the staff who came to call it their favorite place on earth. Highclere has been a spirit, a way of life, a way of being. It was a summons to odd, though lovable contrarians, artists, and those with unique family structures and lost souls searching for a safe place. Senator Valentine said, 'Everyone who finds Highclere does so because they have a Highclere-shaped hole in their heart.' For each of you, as you leave here today for the very last time, be thankful for having held open that heart space to embrace this place and know you're leaving here whole and enriched.

"Oliver will pass each of you a yellow tobacco tie. Please hold it in your left hand, and as you prepare to depart, place all your prayers and thanks into the tie, and then return it to the earth before you go. Mason wants to say a few words." Skye finished stepping toward Mason to help him to his feet.

"Don't worry, I won't be long-winded, talk about my Spanx, or moan about the travesty of needing to import this fabulous Mary Poppins umbrella from Turkey since I couldn't find one anywhere else. Fascists," Mason joked, breaking the emotion, and the entire group laughed.

"I want to thank my friend Skye for leading us in today's ceremony. I felt it would be an appropriate and meaningful way to say goodbye to Highclere, Gil, and Louella," Mason said, turning to his friend while squeezing her hand.

"Also, my Uncle Stuart asked me to thank all of you for coming to the remembrance ceremony at the burial plot this afternoon, and he apologizes for not being able to attend. But he decided after Gil and Louella's funerals in May that he would never return to Highclere," Mason shared before he stopped and turned to face what remained of the original inn.

The centuries-old structure had become nothing more than a footprint of black with a few charred beams pointing heavenward. The only item that survived the blaze was the stained-glass window that Lady Valentine had brought from Fernsby House in the 1940s, which was installed in one of the dining rooms. After 5:00 pm each day—all summer—the sun beamed through the multicolor glass fractals, projecting a bright, joyful rainbow blanket over the ruins—a few minutes of beauty covering tragedy.

"I also quickly want to express my gratitude to all of you. You've played an integral part in all our lives, but specifically over the last year. I'm grateful for all the old friends," Mason looked at the Masts, Angel Conner, the Fishers, Norah Tripplehorn, Gen Talbot, and Ahren and Makayla. "As well as the new ones," he added, turning his gaze to Joy and François Sauveterre, as well as Trent and Kendell Callahan. "If there has been one positive outcome from the chaos, we managed a bonus summer at Highclere. I love this place and all of you. It has been an honor and a privilege to spend time together. We really are a family," Mason said, choking on his words.

His eyes were uncharacteristically not hidden behind dark lenses.

Once Mason completed his remarks, the group stood and said their last goodbyes to each other and their common link—the place they loved the most. Skye took the smudge and walked the property to finish cleansing it so it, too, could begin its next chapter.

* * *

"They are all here and officially released back to you," Stellan announced to Mason, Cordelia, and the rest of the Valentine family and close friends as he removed the police evidence tape from the twelve mini "Doors to Nowhere" and the large black marble cargo box.

"Yay!" said Mason, finally able to run his fingers along the carved letters and etched frogs of the flattop marble, which was closed but with the four gold spheres in position.

"Funny, isn't it," said Lawrence while approaching his son. "There's no way to avoid the saying in this instance—Bianca was indeed the craziest box of frogs we've ever had," he laughed.

"Major understatement, frankly," agreed Mason.

Lawrence looked at the marble container.

"What does it mean? The IIIVMCMLIVXMCML?"

"It's your brother's birth and death date. Stuart *Hollis* Valentine was born on March 5, 1950, and died on May 10. His body has been safely buried inside of this box for the last twenty years. Before then, he was in an unmarked plot, but Gran moved him before she died to ensure he wasn't disturbed. She gave Louella's son the middle name Maxwell to differentiate the two boys and to honor her first love," shared Mason.

"What did she want us to find inside, other than Stuart?" asked Lawrence.

Mason shook his head.

"Bianca told the police that there was an envelope with unimportant Highclere paperwork and a letter from Gran, but she burned them after she opened it."

Lawrence sighed.

"I highly doubt it wasn't important. Still, she holds the cards. I guess we'll always wonder what Mom wrote and why she felt it was only safe with Stuart," he said before joining a conversation between Cici, Margot, and Stellan.

"Stellan, I don't think you've formally met my husband Tobias or my mother Diane," introduced Cordelia as they exchanged greetings. "Stellan kindly received special permission to co-lead the RCMP's investigation into Bianca and Highclere's destruction since there was a connection to Harold Mendoza's death at Fernsby House in the UK," Cici reminded them.

"I remain struck at how you knew to travel to Canada so quickly at Easter," Diane commented while thinking about the dire events of that weekend.

Stellan nodded his head with appropriate gravitas.

"Thankfully, it was Mason and Cordelia's forethought. I was working on instinct but within the confines of the law, of course. It was evident from Mr. Mendoza's letter that the location of his death—Fernsby House—was connected to Mason and Cordelia's investigation in Canada. Officially, I couldn't provide resources outside of our inquiry into Mr. Mendoza, the eventual suicide letter, as well as a few special requests for Mason. An old ski companion of mine, however, is top-level at Ontario's Provincial Police, and he agreed to quietly assign an agent to keep watch over incoming reports about certain persons in and around the family.

"At Easter, my DI was forwarded a police report from the Toronto detachment that Louella Stone's nurse had arrived for work to find her house ransacked and Mrs. Stone missing. While I knew through Margot that Mrs. Stone was on the periphery of the various goings on, I didn't fully understand her significance until I reviewed a package Mason couriered to Margot for safekeeping. It had copies of all their evidence, including confirmation that Mrs. Stone was Stuart Maxwell Valentine's biological mother, and that was the secret for which Senator Valentine was blackmailed. It was obvious that Bianca Anders—who hadn't yet been identified—was cleaning up her loose threads and that the Valentine family was in danger. Mason also revealed that he and Cordelia had been bugged and tracked for some time, so Margot and I decided to fly to Canada unannounced in case Person X was listening."

"By the time we landed in Toronto, I had an email from Mason with an addendum to the original package, which outlined Bianca Anders as the person who had blackmailed and attempted to kill Senator Valentine as revenge for her mother, Caroline Monroe," Margot added, shaking her head in disbelief as she looked up at two red cardinals singing in the grand maple providing her shade.

"However, justifiable panic ensued when we couldn't reach Mason or Cordelia on their mobiles."

"Bianca had sent Delia Reid to Mom's neighborhood to block communication signals. I was offline for over twelve hours," added Cici.

"Delia Reid? Wasn't she a server here a million years ago?" asked Roland Mast as he and Viviane joined the discussion.

"She was," confirmed Cordelia.

"Right, right. She was Thatcher Reid's daughter. Both lightweights from what I can remember. His political rise went up like an H bomb when it was learned he'd been tapping his toes under the pee pee stalls in the men's room," laughed Rolly as he took a sip of his martini. "There was a rumor the old bulldozer Tank leaked it."

"She was fired during Germaine LeBlanc's tenure as manager of the inn, so the mid-1980s. I suppose Delia had some pent-up animosity and was happy to play the roles of Drusilla and Joyce Redstone for Bianca...and a hefty payday," said Cici.

"These birds either need more erect worms in their lives or major therapy," suggested Rolland with a wink while Viviane looked horrified.

"Margot finally connected with me once service was restored and the jammer removed. While racing to Uncle David's to fly to Highclere, I spoke to Skye and Norah. Skye was already on the lake for the weekend, and Norah was driving up. She was being lured to Highclere by Bianca to join the body count since Norah could name Bianca as the renter. Thankfully, I reached Norah early enough that she instead went to her place, which was used as a dispatch point," added Cici.

"And for a dried-up granny, I move ninja-like. Except for the dust I leave in my wake," chuckled Skye, walking toward the group. "I spotted Mason tied to the electric fence when I arrived, and my first stop was Athabasca to get him some dry clothes which is where I found Ahren keeping watch. He planned to nab either Gil, Bianca, or Miles Jr. to give me time to free Mason and for Cici to arrive with Mack."

"Once Skye cut me loose, and I knew help was coming," began Mason, limping toward the ever-growing party, "I thought I could hold off whatever destruction Bianca had planned until the police arrived, but I couldn't."

"No one can ever say you didn't try your best," assured Viviane Mast. "Trent, how did you get roped into this?" she asked as Trent joined the group.

The formerly combative neighbor of Highclere had a subtle smile on his face.

"My anger management problem is how I got roped in," he laughed.

"I spoke to Trent just before Easter to ask him why he had requested a copy of Tank's death certificate in the autumn. He was shocked by the accusation and sent me his phone log," began Mason.

Trent then took up the story.

"It became apparent that whoever was masterminding the mysteries around the Valentines had been trying to point the guilt directly at me. While I have said and done some awful things to the family, I agreed to a legitimate truce with Mr. Valentine some years ago and stood by it. In late 2013, Laverna told me that her mother would inherit Highclere and wondered if I wanted to buy it. I said I'd rather wait until Mr. Valentine died, but when she showed me a file of all the dreadful letters I had sent the Senator over the years, I felt my hands were tied. Despite knowing about the earlier bout of toxic soil, I signed an agreement and advanced $250,000 under the condition that she cut my signatures off the letters—which she did.

"When Mr. Valentine died, I kept my word and met with Laverna at her husband's hospital to prepare the sales documents and provide another $250,000 dollars as interim funding until the estate was out of probate. Then, Norah called me after Christmas. She said that while she didn't feel honor bound to alert me, her faith told her she should do the right thing. She revealed that the soil of Highclere was still highly toxic and that Mason and Cordelia had discovered our families' history concerning the Manitoba land dispute. That should've been virtually impossible to find. It's written on a typewriter. Much to Laverna's annoyance, I delayed moving the purchase forward, but I felt paranoid that I was being painted to look guilty by someone. I decided to start keeping watch of Highclere and the Valentine family."

"When I went to Norah's house the night Mack and I found Bianca's lair, Trent had followed me there, worried I was walking into a trap. He was leaving his place when he saw me skedaddle without bags. With it being night, he felt something was amiss."

"I didn't realize it was Norah's house, which is why I was worried. Once everything seemed okay, I left," added Trent.

"I just can't believe Bianca is your sister," Viviane marveled.

"Well, I've always wanted a sister," laughed Trent. "But she's not. We did a DNA test. I suppose she just decided one day that I was her brother, and she'd make me pay for an imagined sin perpetrated by our imagined father. It's all rather unhinged. I do now remember meeting her around 1989, before I left Manitoba. She worked at my office and whipped me into a right frenzy about Mr. Valentine's political overreach and almost brainwashed me into an unnatural level of hatred toward Mr. Valentine. I take full responsibility for my subsequent actions, but I'm shocked at how I let her influence me. I'm just glad the ordeal is over."

"What will you do with Highclere when the sale closes?" asked Diane Bradshaw.

"Nothing. I withdrew from the sale. As far as I know, Highclere hasn't been sold, but my intel might be out of date," admitted Trent.

Mason smiled.

"Ok, Valentine family, if you can congregate around the twelve doors, we'll get 'er done!" Mason instructed.

The friends and former guests of Highclere disassembled while the Valentines took formation.

It was Cordelia who, at Christmas, theorized that Lady Valentine had personally hidden her belongings and heirlooms. Drusilla's picture from Christmas 2003 showed Lady Valentine wearing her jewelry with the Farnsworth-designed jewelry box exhibited in the cabinet behind her. The Easter 2004 photo, however, revealed a perplexing absence—not only was the jewelry box missing, but Lady

Valentine's wedding and engagement rings vanished as well. As Mason noted, Lady Valentine never parted with her rings. The absence of these treasured accessories on her bare fingers led to the striking realization: Lady Jean Fernsby-Valentine herself took steps to hide her belongings—and upon review of Tank's diaries from 2002—they knew why.

* * *

August 4, 2002,
There are days I don't understand my wife. As a good Christian, I always attempt to give her the benefit of her emotions and feelings. I try not to discredit that. However, I must confess that her emotions can be a bit tiring for me and have been our entire married life.

Anyway, I invited Aida Clifton to visit us at Highclere. She's coming tomorrow, but Jean claims I didn't ask her permission.

I'm quite confident I did.

When Jean said I hadn't, she got upset and locked herself in her room. I knocked on the door and asked her if I apologized and agreed that it had slipped my mind, would that calm her down? She told me it didn't matter because I wouldn't believe my apology...which would be true.

Jean was always quite willing to support Aida after Wentworth Clifton died, and of course, the four of us spent a great deal of time together many a moon ago. I'm unsure where the new animosity comes from, but I hope Jean doesn't embarrass me.

I'd like to be on my best form and most charming for Mrs. Clifton.

August 6, 2002,
I seem to have done it again. Jean is again furious with me over Aida Clifton's visit—and I'm baffled as to why. Aida arrived yesterday, and Jean was initially her usual, cordial, well-mannered self. This morning, however, Jean claimed to have overhead Aida, and I talk about "second marriages," and she took umbrage with my hypothetical musings about what I'll do when Jean dies. True, I told Aida about Jean's health issues some weeks ago. A decision I didn't seek permission for from Jean, who is angry with me for divulging something she said was "personal" to her.

I reminded her I am her husband, and anything personal to her is personal to me, and I have every right to tell my friend what my wife is going through.

Jean disagrees.

August 10, 2002,
Aida Clifton left today. After she drove away, Jean sat next to me and asked that I wait until she's dead before pursuing my next wife.

I have no idea where her paranoia is coming from.

August 22, 2002,
We had all the guests from the inn over for cocktails before dinner tonight. Before the doors opened, Jean—out of nowhere—told me I needed to be careful with Aida Clifton. I demanded she explain to me what she was referring to.
She smiled at me and said, "But since you won't be—I'll have to do it for you."
Her paranoia is surprising.

* * *

Lady Jean Valentine knew beyond a doubt that her husband would remarry upon her death. He had, after all, started auditioning his second wife years before Lady V died—and worse, he hadn't even tried to hide it. Unable to trust her husband to distribute her possessions to her family—or the motives of whomever he'd marry—she enlisted her old friends, the Farnsworths, and hatched a plan.

Skye had correctly assumed that the red snowflakes behind each day of the twelve days of Christmas stitched into the tablecloth were codes—they just didn't know for what—until they dug up the marble cargo box in the woods. The twelve codes were clearly connected to the twelve Golden Retrievers. On one of the canceled checks to Farnsworth Marble & Designs, dimensions had been written in the memo. Mason deduced the dimensions for a mini door with a vault underneath it and a marble slipcover for camouflage. Twelve perfect mini "Doors to Nowhere" were buried in the burial plot, each containing one of Lady Valentine's precious goldens—nestled alongside her priceless heirlooms. It was ingenious. Who would think she'd hide anything with the dogs? Mason and Cici hoped that Person X wouldn't think anything other than prize-winning ashes were inside the vaults and kept it that way.

Now, the family stood together, eager to be reunited with Lady Valentine's possessions and family heirlooms. Mason took out his phone and pulled up a picture of the now destroyed tablecloth that his grandmother had given him as Oliver and Cordelia readied themselves to input the codes into the standing portion of the doors.

Mason read the first code to Cici, which unlocked the first vault. He then shouted the second snowflake sequence to Oliver, hearing the pleasing "click" of the locking mechanism of Lady V's second golden after having done so. Cordelia and Oliver went from one door to the next, inputting the code sequence one by one until all twelve vaults had been opened and all the treasures within were revealed.

Each safe was filled with priceless heirlooms, trinkets, and memories belonging to Lady Valentine. Her wedding rings, pearls, and assorted broaches were distributed between the vaults. Yet, as the family looked closer, the fine diamonds and beautiful cut pearls were the least important items stowed away.

Dozens of aged, tea-colored war letters were tied together with twine. Holiday pictures from the 1920s to 2000s were sealed in protective plastic. Diaries and journals from Fernsby ancestors dating back generations were tucked together. Handwritten family trees, school report cards, drawings, letters, and notes Lady V had been given throughout her life by family and friends, including congratulations for her children's births, had all been saved and hidden.

Lord Fernsby's war medals, commendations, and the secret code system used by the "Door to Nowhere" to ensure safe passage for soldiers through England's interior waterways were also preserved for historical purposes.

"I'm overcome," whispered Drusilla as she flipped through never-before-seen childhood photographs of her mother.

Mason and Cordelia stood back and watched as the family made their way through the treasures that had been waiting decades to be found. Mason held the original ancient Christmas tablecloth in his arms, absent of hidden codes and clues. He was ecstatic to have the real thing.

"There were too many deaths, but overall, job well done, I think," said Mason to Cici, who was helping to steady him.

Cici nodded.

"True, but we lost Tank, Gil, Louella, and Highclere all in a year," she pointed out. "I'm not sure there was ever a good outcome to any of this. All the mysteries are solved, though," Cici added.

"Except one," Mason smiled before adding a campy exaggerated wink.

Cici looked perplexed. She thought through the unusual goings on of the last twelve months—and then.

"The cows!" she laughed.

"Still NO idea where they came from or where they went. Bianca told the police it wasn't her," Mason mentioned while laughing.

"Ok, so one mystery left we may never solve. Perhaps the oddest one, though," noted Cici while watching Drusilla walk toward them holding a folded paper.

"You should read this," she advised as Mason took the paper and unfolded it.

My dear family,

I understand you may believe me to be as eccentric as my mother for devising this intricate plan to safeguard and conceal my possessions from Miles. While my husband possesses one or two qualities, he's also controlling and manipulative. When I received my cancer diagnosis, I expressed my desire to distribute my belongings while I was still alive to ensure that each family member received what I intended for them to have. Unfortunately, Miles vehemently opposed this idea. He argued it was appropriate for a husband to inherit his wife's belongings after her passing and then distribute them at a suitable time.

However, this is just Miles's way of saying, "I will use Jean's cherished heirlooms as leverage to manipulate our children and maintain their obedience." I am well aware of his intentions, but I am also ill, dying, and no longer willing to engage in an uphill battle with him. I failed to protect myself and my children during my lifetime, and I am unwilling to repeat the same mistake in death. My dear friend Rosamond Farnsworth-Ford and her family have assisted me in fulfilling my objectives with their exceptional craftsmanship and expertise. If you are reading this letter, you have received the gold box and oval, spherical keys, along with my letter directing you to the dogs' final resting place in the burial plot for further information.

As a gentle reminder, if Miles has committed the ultimate betrayal and attempted to seize Highclere, kindly contact Maxwell Farnsworth via Rosamond or her daughter Claire, and he will provide you with guidance to safeguard it.

Love, Mom, Granny V, Jean

Mason looked up to his aunt and then to Cici.

"Shit! So, Gran stored instructions about how to save Highclere alongside Stuart Hollis Valentine's body in the black marble box? That's why the letter she left in the jewelry box asked us not to think differently of Stuart and referred to one-fifth of her most prized possessions. She knew the information was safest with the original Stuart, but that also meant exposing the truth—the death of her child."

"What could she have done to safeguard Highclere?" asked Drusilla.

Cici shrugged while taking out her phone and scrolling through her contacts.

"I'm not sure, but I know someone who might be able to figure it out," she said.

"Wait," said Mason, causing Cordelia and Drusilla to look at him in surprise. "I know…"

Chapter Seventy-Two

Aida nervously twisted her gold watch as she watched the mid-September hustle outside the large bay windows of Coffee 'N Tea, a boutique coffee shop just outside the gates of Governor Boulevard. Chosen for its proximity to her house, Aida hoped to release some of her anxiety by walking to her meeting. However, the cooling air and emerging red amongst the trees only exacerbated her tension.

Having finished her tea, Aida basked in the sunlight while adjusting her flying nun-style hat before smoothing imaginary wrinkles of her shapeless burlap dress. As she squinted her eyes to check the time on her watch, the light that had been blanketing her in warmth became blocked by a towering figure. His silhouette eclipsed the brightness from the outdoors, putting Aida in shadow. She looked up to see Mary Poppins' umbrella staring at her.

"Hello, Aida," greeted Mason with a warm smile as he sat in the beige suede chair across the table from her.

He removed his sunglasses and propped his umbrella against the wall as he unzipped his light autumn jacket.

"Mason," Aida smiled while awkwardly standing to embrace Mason before sitting back down and patting his hand instead.

"Would you like another...was that coffee or tea?" Mason asked, pointing to the empty cup.

"It was tea. Earl Grey, and yes, I'd love another. Calms the nerves," Aida laughed nervously.

Mason signaled a server and ordered two Earl Grey teas and a basket of baked goods to share.

"Thank you for agreeing to meet with me," Mason nodded while taking a sip of water.

"Not at all," Aida smiled, wiping imaginary saliva from the corners of her mouth. "I'm happy to have the opportunity to ask how you're doing in person," she said sincerely.

"I'm doing much better, thank you. Thank you again for the lovely flowers you sent while I was hospitalized. I was shocked you found peonies in March!" Mason marveled.

"It wasn't easy. However, I knew they were your favorite, and I wanted to make sure you knew that I...we...were all thinking of you," explained Aida—remorse and guilt leaking into her expression.

"It meant a lot," Mason replied, biting his lip as the server placed two teapots and mugs on the table with a wicker basket of goodies.

"I've been trying to sort out what I've wanted to say to you for days now," Aida started while lifting her white teapot and pouring the steaming liquid into her mug, "but of course, now that you're here, I've forgotten it all."

She smiled, replacing the ceramic pot before stirring in sugar.

"Feeling is mutual," Mason replied with sincere warmth. "And to be clear, what happened with Bianca wasn't your fault," he added.

Aida didn't look at him.

"Oh, I'm not sure the Lord will think so at the end," Aida replied.

"What makes you say that?" Mason asked.

"We trusted Bianca. We loved her. We unquestioningly brought her into our lives and, by extension, yours. Yet, all she wanted the entire time was to dismantle Miles and his family," Aida said in wonder before sipping her tea.

"How could you have known all those years ago?" Mason asked, taking a sip of his.

"Hindsight, of course, the signs are obvious. The way she befriended Verna out of nowhere when Phil was first in hospital. Within a week of the meeting, she transferred units full-time to the brain injury ward. She gained Verna's trust—encouraging Verna to reveal my family's deepest secrets during late-night conversations. She quickly became indispensable to us, always there when we needed something. A ride to an appointment, to watch the house, and check the mail when we were on holiday. She helped me move into your grandfather's home—not that I had much that needed moving. She was a saint at our wedding. We didn't have a coordinator, so she took on the job herself. I thought it was because of altruism when it was a means to her end. It was all a lie. We were duped and tricked into loving someone with an agenda," Aida sighed, taking a scone from the basket.

Each took a sip of their tea.

"Funny, isn't it? I've said nearly the same thing multiple times in the last year. Though, not about Bianca," replied Mason without malice nor intent to injure—it was a statement of fact. "It makes you feel a bit crazy, doesn't it? You wonder what was true. Have you been an awful judge of character this entire time? Too trusting? If someone has used you as a means to their end, people you grew to love, then can one trust any relationships to be authentic?" Mason asked while tearing apart a scone and smothering it with clotted cream.

"I can see how that would be frustrating," Aida nodded before changing the subject. "How is your leg?" she asked.

"Much better, thank you. Physiotherapy is going well, and it should be back to normal in a few more months."

"And Stuart?" she asked with a warble.

"Not good," Mason breathed. "When Bianca kidnapped him, she used enough sleeping pills to knock out a herd of elephants. While he was unconscious, he had a minor stroke, and Drusilla has lived with him ever since to monitor his recovery and provide for him. Uncle Stuart was thankfully unaware of what happened between his abduction and waking up in the hospital. We waited a few days before telling him Gil and Louella didn't survive the fire. Auntie Drew gave the news." Mason took a mouthful of scone.

"Did I read correctly that Gil had learned that Bianca was the mastermind?" asked Aida with warmth, curiosity, and concern.

"He had. Gil spent years tracking answers to Highclere's mysteries, including Tank's blackmail. It drove him crazy, and he spent their savings trying to find peace of mind. He left a video on his computer for Stuart that explained everything, including when he discovered Bianca was our Person X and had a mixed-race son named Miles—he faked DNA to convince her he had been the sperm donor to gain her trust. He planned to ingratiate himself to learn what she was up to and stop her or call the police. He discovered it was Bianca shortly after Thanksgiving. She told him everything she'd done, and the capper was her plan to destroy the inn—he didn't want that to happen. So, he stuck with her that weekend, planning to stop her before she could cause any damage.

"Unfortunately, things got chaotic fast, and he couldn't cleanly sabotage her plan as he wanted. Stuart went offline a few days earlier, which Gil believed was because Bianca had abducted him, which she had. I also got in the way. The same day he was going to call her in, I went back to Highclere, where she had poisoned the water cooler and took me hostage as well. At one point, Gil had gone to Athabasca for a chain and to call 911, but before he could do that, Skye lured his attention with a feather while Ahren knocked him out with a shovel," Mason winced. "We didn't think Gil was playing for both sides, just that he was involved and needed to be stopped. Ahren held him captive, during which Skye freed me, and Bianca set fire to the inn."

"How did Gil die if Ahren locked him at your place?" wondered Aida.

"Gil came to and told Ahren everything. Once Ahren was sufficiently convinced, he released him, and they ran to the inn," Mason replied, taking a sip of water.

"Heavens," sighed Aida. "Thank God Gil at least saved you," she added.

Mason nodded, not making eye contact with Aida.

"Yeah," he paused, "I'm going to struggle with that for a while," he said, looking into the distance.

"Mason, it was God's will you were saved," implored Aida.

"If one were to believe that, then was it God's will that Gil died instead?" asked Mason.

"The infinite plan isn't supposed to be fair; it's supposed to be true," replied Aida.

Mason looked down at the paper napkin he had been crumpling in his hand.

"When Louella and I fell through to the basement," Mason began, his voice breaking. "I knew it was over, and that was ok. I was stuck under burning wood beams and could only see Louella's hand from across the room, but it was moving. I hoped she'd get out at least."

He cleared his throat.

"There was a moment when I was losing consciousness, and I thought the center of the flames was opening wide and turning white, almost looking like an angel," Mason laughed. "Wishful thinking. Or I've watched too much *Touched by an Angel*. It seemed real, though. I heard Gil call my name, and that was the last thing I remember before waking up in the hospital," he finished.

The two sat silently while a group of young students entered the store, laughing and smiling without care.

"If any of us had known…" Aida trailed off.

"But…one of you did know," Mason replied. "Laverna knew."

Aida's eyes became wide with indignation.

"She couldn't have," Aida insisted. "She'd have told me," she replied, crossing her arms, bunching the excess fabric from her tunic across her chest.

"I'm sorry," Mason apologized. "But she did and has since admitted it. Gil met with her on Valentine's Day, and he told her almost everything he knew about Bianca—except the identity of her adopted mother because he didn't know—and she did little with his information. He tried so desperately to convince Laverna that he followed her after lunch to meet with an architect about redoing your house to keep pressing her with the facts."

"Well…what would you have expected her to do with the information? She'd be dead, too, if she confronted Bianca. She saved herself," Aida said.

"She talked to Bianca," Mason confirmed.

Aida repositioned herself in her small seat.

"Oh?" she replied.

"Both Bianca and Laverna were questioned by the police the night the inn burned," Mason said, noticing Aida's expression of ignorance. "Laverna lightly questioned Bianca about some of the information Gil had told her, and Bianca admitted to aspects of it. Enough that Laverna was concerned, but she was blinded by their friendship and chose not to push."

Aida sat in shock. Laverna hadn't indicated that Gil approached her with Bianca's betrayal. Most surprising of all for Aida was that Laverna let it go. Aida had thought she raised her children to have a strong and just moral code—yet she had to admit that perhaps Verna's moral code could be adjusted for convenience, not unlike her own.

"Now, the real reason I'm here," Mason said, reaching into his coat pocket and revealing a stapled roll of paper. "One of the pleasant surprises through this ordeal is how organized my late grandmother was before she died. She knew Tank was planning to swiftly remarry upon her death..."

"What?" interrupted Aida. "How could she possibly? I didn't even know," she protested. Mason smirked and arched his eyebrows.

"Lady Valentine knew her husband very well. She knew Tank believed everyone, and everything, was replaceable and suspected that once she died, she would be replaced in a flash," Mason replied.

Aida looked away.

"I'm not here to rehash history—it is what it is," he said with a smile. "Anyway, she knew Tank would remarry, as she was a frequent victim of his habit of breaking promises and knew his pattern of doing what he wanted. To that end, she hid her priceless belongings and fantastic family heirlooms in custom vaults for her dogs, which were buried in the burial plot. When Laverna redesigned the grave site, the dogs and their vaults were never reburied. The vaults were moved to the third floor of the carriage house before Bianca and Marko, er, Miles Jr., moved them the night after Tank's funeral. It was an astute decision on her part because we found correspondences between Tank and Drusilla from five or six years after Gran died, requesting her jewelry be turned over, and Tank refused.

"We also found emails—which you and Laverna were cc'd on—seeking appraisals of Gran's most expensive items so Tank could sell them for cash. A plan that faltered once Tank couldn't find the jewels, so he instead filed an insurance claim," Mason shrugged. "My Gran was a smart lady—but also a very sad one," he said before unrolling the papers in hand and laying them face down on the table.

"See, Gran knew Tank lacked empathy and emotional reasoning. In his skewed brain, he couldn't distinguish nor appreciate the difference between a wife of sixty years who was the mother of his children and a second, late-in-life wife. His emotional connection was to the role and responsibilities, not the person. So, in a sense, he understood—in a clinical way—how to interact with the position of 'wife' rather than the individual. This is why Gran assumed Tank would use her possessions as leverage with their children before ultimately leaving them to you, including her personal and sentimental mementos, which he did. Because you were his wife and bequeathing the entire estate to wives is what husbands do. She also suspected that Tank would try to either give you a piece of Highclere or the whole thing. Which, of course, he did that too."

Aida nodded.

"Except he didn't."

Mason paused, sipping water to allow the news to sink in.

"I don't understand. You've already moved out," Aida noted.

"True. Well, I should be more specific. He did leave you Highclere—but only one acre of it," said Mason, his tone and expression warm as he flipped the papers over and turned them toward Aida.

"My friend Kenny Blackwell had a team at one of his development companies go through Highclere's ownership history with a fine-tooth comb. They turned over details that even a forensic auditor would've missed. Tank could be tricky—we all know that.

"Anyway, in 2003, the county asked if they could buy one acre of Highclere's back 40 acres for municipal purposes. A hydro metering station was already on site, and the county offered to sever the land and take care of all the details to make it happen. Tank said yes, and after a few signatures, the county wired $200,000 to Highclere's trust account and took ownership of one acre.

"However, as I've just learned, that was a ruse. You see, after my great-grandfather Hollis died, Highclere reverted from a trust held between Tank and his sisters to a private, single-ownership structure after he'd bought his sisters' share of the property in 1973. So yes, it belonged to Tank fair and square once his sisters' checks cleared. When Highclere was put back into a trust in 1993—at the urging of his family—there was a reference to a 'settler' or 'original owner,' which was left ambiguous and undefined. While the 1993 trust was an iteration of the original trust, it was legally a new document and not a continuation. If it had been a continuation, then the 'settler' would've been Hollis, but because it had been privately owned for twenty years, the settler was Tank. He had the power to revoke the trust—which he did.

"All that to say, Tank apparently forgot one critical piece of information between 1973 and 1993—that he transferred the ownership of Highclere to Lady Jean Valentine in 1985 to deflate his assets while being considered for the senate. Highclere was a money pit. It cost a fortune to run and never made a penny; he didn't want his name attached as 'owner' as it could be viewed as a liability. It smelled of a reckless, indulgent leader who enjoyed losing money to play king of a resort. Not an appealing look! Therefore, legally, the settler who could revoke the trust was not Miles Valentine. It was Jean Valentine. Jean Valentine revoked the trust in 2003 and sold the entire property—minus one acre—to herself for $200,000. She placed 49 acres into a separate trust, naming her children and grandchildren as trustees and beneficiaries. The one remaining acre of woods was owned by the governing trust from 1993—which was once more updated in 2005—and that is the trust Tank revoked and left to you. So, I've come here today to share this with you and to let you know that we'll be moving back in," Mason finished with no particular joy or emotion.

They were all victims of Tank's antics and narcissism, but Lady Valentine knew as much to be true and used her final years to protect her children from their father.

"I see," said Aida, scanning the papers. "You should probably tell this to Laverna or Louise. I'm hopeless with these things," she half-joked.

Mason smiled.

"No, you're not, Aida. What you are is mad. And when you're mad, you play dumb and use Laverna as your pit bull, so you appear to have clean hands. You know exactly what this means," Mason replied.

Aida pushed the papers back to Mason.

"I'm not mad," she said. "Laverna and Bianca fought for Highclere to be left to us in place of his money after the blackmail. It never felt right to me."

"Then why didn't you reject it?" Mason asked.

"I don't know, Mason," she sighed. "It was never about 'things.' It was about Phil's home care and supporting my grandchildren's education. Volunteering has been my main form of community work, but I also wanted to donate financially to the causes I care about. I wanted to leave an estate behind so future generations wouldn't struggle like I did. I want them to sleep peacefully, knowing they will never be 'without.'

"I'm a third-generation immigrant, and despite my family's hard work, we've never achieved the financial security we hoped for by moving to Canada. I don't think many people would've made a different decision if they were in my shoes. You can't judge me for it."

Mason nodded.

He didn't judge her.

"I get it. You must be thankful that all the surviving money that was blackmailed from Tank will be returned to you," Mason smiled while folding the papers and putting them back in his coat pocket.

Aida grinned.

"You heard that?"

"I did," Mason said, noticing worry encroach on Aida's face. "And on behalf of the family, we stand by what we've always said. We never wanted nor needed his money. Technically, what he left you was Granny V's money, but we rejected it decades ago to be as independent from his clutches as possible," Mason nodded.

"That's very big of you," admitted Aida.

"We appreciate all the items you've boxed up and given us over the last several months despite the will. There are one or two more pieces at the house that belonged to my great-grandparents we'd like back—including their dining table."

"Of course, just send a list," Aida nodded.

"See how civil this could've been had we all just sat down from the get-go to talk out who has what and where it should go rather than leaning into the nastiness of Labor Day, testy letters, and surprise police and lawyer visits?" Mason began while signaling the server for the check. "You fell into the trap of treating us like Tank did despite knowing better. I didn't expect that of you."

"Lingering hurt and frustration from the beginning of the marriage, I suppose," suggested Aida as Mason tapped his credit card against the server's pay terminal.

"I guess to that end, Aida, I want you to understand that we were all victims of Tank's narcissism, ego, and thoughtlessness—and I'm including you and Bianca as well.

"Miles Valentine made decisions in his interest and his interest only his entire life. It drove my grandmother nuts. Once he made a decision, he declared it final, often causing unintended consequences for many others because of his lack of empathy. He showed little concern for how his actions affected people unless there was a direct effect on him. While Tank indeed wrote the nasty letter he left us—it was written in 2010. Bianca changed the date to mess with us. She knew we'd believe it was recent because Tank had a history of pulling a 'bait and switch'—especially when he knew he wouldn't have to face the consequences. After all, he didn't care about the implications Caroline Monroe would face after he discarded her via telegram, and that decision had far-reaching and very recent effects.

"He didn't care about marrying you four months after Gran died or how that choice would reflect on you. Before all the recent madness, I assumed you were just as manipulative and hurtful as Tank was at the beginning of your marriage. However, now that I understand Tank's psychology better, I realize you didn't have many options. What else could you have done? You were struggling, and then came someone who seemed like an answer to your prayers. Of course, you followed his lead and avoided rocking the boat. You couldn't push back, and Aida, that's what he wanted from you."

Aida sniffed while putting on her burnt orange jacket.

"You make Miles sound like an absolute monster. Many would disagree with your characterization of him, especially as being unkind."

"As they should," Mason said, standing up. "Two truths can exist at once, Aida. Miles Valentine wasn't much of a father or grandfather, but his need to be needed and fêted meant he did a lot of genuine good for many people, even if his reasons were confusing for him. I want people to remember his generosity and kindness as altruism and celebrate him for it. I want everyone to remember him however they wish to. Their truth of Tank isn't the antithesis of ours. It's just less nuanced and personal," added Mason as he took his Mary Poppins umbrella to lean on.

Aida walked a few paces ahead to open the glass door as the two emerged into the beautiful autumn light.

"If you say that, then I don't understand why you hated him?" asked Aida as Mason put on his sunglasses before walking toward Governor Boulevard.

"Oh, Aida, let me be clear—we didn't hate him!" Mason laughed. "It would've been much easier if we did, but our trouble was that we loved him very much. That love kept bringing us back to him battle after battle or gave us hope he could change. Tank didn't understand love or family. Much like marriage, he understood its role and principles but not its sentiments because he couldn't feel them. Even though he didn't like us very much, he believed he loved us because he knew he should."

"Do you think he loved me?" asked Aida, catching a falling leaf.

"He thought he did, and probably just as much as he thought he loved my grandmother. It's hard to quantify for a man who lacked feeling," Mason admitted before stopping at a crosswalk. "I'm going to grab an Uber from here. I appreciate you meeting with me," he said, leaning in for a hug, which Aida returned in kind.

"I'm sorry again about Bianca," Aida said, her voice breaking.

"For the record, her real name is Heather Monroe," Mason noted.

"Well...whatever her name, I never thought so much rancor and death could stem from my actions. I have much reflecting to do," she noted while releasing Mason.

Aida gave a small wave once more as she walked toward home.

"Aida..." Mason called when she was a few feet away.

Aida turned and arched her eyebrows.

"The almost nineteen years we were a family," he paused, "were any of the laughter and good times as real for you as they were for us?" he asked.

Aida nodded.

"Oh yes, Mason. Much of it."

Mason smiled, then moved his gaze, catching sight of a bus shelter poster showcasing the latest exhibit at the Royal Ontario Museum. With the rest of his day wide open, Mason decided to strengthen his leg by exploring the uniquely titled, though familiar, display.

As Mason's Uber pulled up to the curb, he grinned when he saw a new message appear on his phone from hunky civil servant at the Privy Council's office, William Marshall. After seeing the headlines of the fire at Highclere and Bianca's arrest, William was one of the first to hop in a car and drive to Toronto to visit Mason in the hospital. They'd stayed in touch ever since.

"Ah, Mr. Mason!" the driver exclaimed, looking at his phone to double-check his passenger's name as Mason settled into the backseat and buckled up.

"That's me," Mason confirmed, sinking back into his seat as the world outside the window started gaining momentum.

"Off to the ROM, correct?" the driver asked.

"Exactly. Thank you," Mason nodded.

Curiosity twinkled in the driver's eyes as he gazed at Mason through the rearview mirror.

"So, anything interesting on exhibit there?" he inquired.

"Well, I'm about to discover the answer to an apparently relentless and age-old question: *What exactly is Apropos of the Anus.*"

* * *

FOR IMMEDIATE RELEASE:
The Valentine family is pleased to announce the rebuilding and reopening of Highclere Inn & Carriage House at Lake Belvedere, Muskoka.
Reservations are now open at
www.highclereinn.com
--END--

Mental Health Support

If you, or someone you know is experiencing a mental health crisis, there is help available.

Crisis Text Lines:

Canada:
Text "CONNECT" to 686868

United States:
Text "HOME" to 741741

United Kingdom:
Text "SHOUT" to 85258

Acknowledgements

Wow! This has been one hell of a journey.

First, I'd like to start by thanking YOU, the reader, for investing your time and imagination into this story.

Huge thank you to Michael Baker, who believed in "A Box of Frogs" (which was originally titled "The Burial Plot"). Valerie Eisenhauer for her endless support through every step of the creative processes and reading, re-reading, and re-re-reading this book. She built my self-esteem on days when I thought my writing was absolute garbage (and there were many of those days!) Thank you to my editors, Allison Lay, Brian Meyer, and Tom McFadden. Also, a big shout out to Bia Shuja for creating the most perfect cover art in the world.

Thank you to my family who supported me and the writing of this book from day one. My parents, Peter and Catherine (Sass) Hellyer. My brother Jordan Hellyer who did a pre-read of the manuscript. His wife Isabel and their children, Evelyn and Augustus. My sister Emily Hellyer-Joseph, her husband Charles, and their children Wyatt and Juliette Joseph. My best friend Elyse Shrubb and her family Corey, Cole, Sullivan, and Zoe Gunn. Kelly Hashemi from Treaty One in Manitoba who lovingly helped Skye Cadieux come to life. Also, thank you to Ahren, Johann, and Robin Sternberg. Special thanks to Krislyn Jagt.

Big thank you to John and Jan MacIntyre, Susanne Boyce and Brendan Mullen, Amanda and John Sherrington, Claire, Clive and Violet Mackintosh, Amy Regan, Amanda Armstrong, Simon Paluck, Taunya Paquette, Krystal DiMarca, Pierre Schuurmans, Donna Jennings, Esperanza Vargas, Gary Hall, Dr. Hazel Ipp, Dr. Kerry Sinkowski, Chris Shaw, Sue Reimer, Dawn Broker and Grace Sheldon. Jacquie Siu-Chong, Bernadette Kennedy and Marisa Cormier. Extra special thanks to Diane and the late Ron Rudan.

This book was written during a period of poor health, and I'd like to thank Bryan Hague, Cole Keddie, Michelle Graham, and Gabi Castillo for getting me back on my feet so I could finish the manuscript.

A beyond-the-grave thank you to my late grandparents Mike & Joan Murray and Paul & Ellen Hellyer all of whom I felt were spiritually beside me while writing. A very special shout out to my late grandmother, Ellen, who died twenty years before the publication of this novel but was the inspiration behind one of the main settings. She referred to her seasonal garden as being her "burial plot." When she passed, we scattered her ashes there per her wishes.

Special thanks to the *St. Ermin's Hotel* in London for always taking such good care of me and *The Crane Resort* and their wonderful staff in Barbados.

Also, the makers of Spanx – my lifesaver.

Thank you reader!
x Josh

Milton Keynes UK
Ingram Content Group UK Ltd.
UKHW040358211024
449759UK00020B/55